My Quest For Computer Cognition

Amy Soldier

iUniverse, Inc.
New York Bloomington

My Quest For Computer Cognition

This story is a work of fiction.
Personal names and character incidents are linked
for drama and the edification of the reader.

All graphics and illustrations inside this book
are claimed by myself and should not be reproduced
without written permission.

iUniverse books may be ordered through booksellers or by contacting:

iUniverse
1663 Liberty Drive
Bloomington, IN 47403
www.iuniverse.com
1-800-Authors (1-800-288-4677)

ISBN: 978-0-595-53167-7 (pbk)
ISBN: 978-0-595-63229-9 (ebk)

Printed in the United States of America

iUniverse rev. date: 1/5/09

Contents

FOREWORD

Imagine..., a nation has been recognized and called for duty.
Challenged to lead.
To construct a foundation for all humanity.
To become the envy of all nations and of all people for all time forward.

Imagine, the intentions of the Creator God
inspire human mind and hand to create systems mimicking biological cognition.

— | —

This story is from the perspective of a Creator.

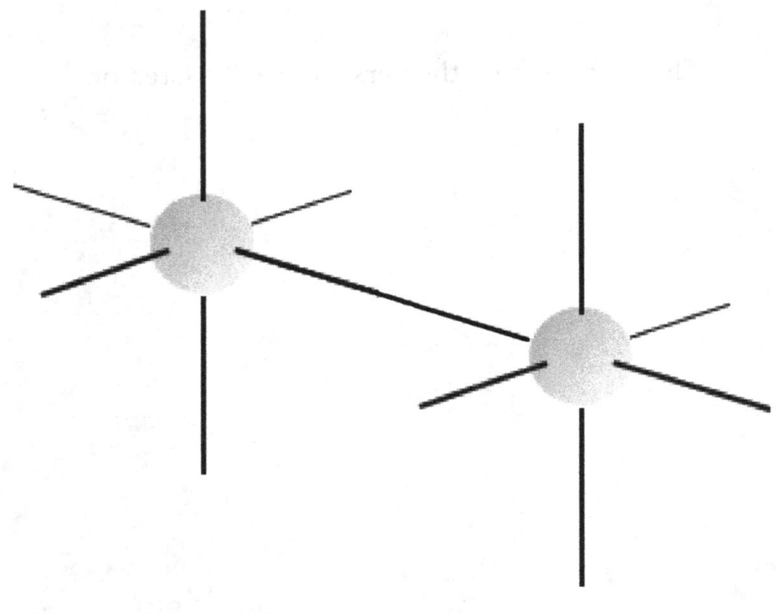

Preface

As the early Americas were being colonized for trade, and the discovery of unknown worlds accelerated, the seeds of traditions of civilizations past came with it. Whether from Hammurabi' code, or Rome's senate, whether from Jesus or Moses, the Americas were being given that indelible stamp of influence from some of the most powerful nations of the time. Cherished ideas of government, economy, science, and law were to weave themselves from one people to another, leaving the fabric of society we have year in, year out, today.

Today, with our wealth and power unequaled in the world, the peoples of this nation are facing what seems the next of the major hurdles in the advance of our American civilization. These challenges seem twofold: to squelch depravity and baseness in our own American condition, and in the world, and at the same time to advance the quality of life issues.

With this introduction in mind, one hope I have for this book is to install a sense of logical rationality in the readers mind towards subjects that were once considered incongruent, and thus impractical or impossible to tackle. Another hope is to cause the challenge within future generations towards realizing the goal of the existence of a cognitive computer mimicking biological life forms.

Within this book is a dissertation entitled *A Treatise on the Nature of Life.* The treatise hypothesizes methods responsible for the core survival instinct mediating and governing all biological life, and by consolidating laws of science to further imply that the foundation for moral Law derives from within the nature of the human physical system.

The moral Law described is a spiritual, metaphysical Law. A Law which on its own speaks to the mature man and woman of the nobler Ideal. Indeed, it is this Law and Ideal all humanity seeks and strives for from within their own being. This Law and Ideal are central themes I had in mind as I wrote the words to *My Quest For Computer Cognition.*

—|—

Do not be surprised that I tell you
you must all be begotten from above.
— Jesus to Nicodemus

Do not be surprised that I tell you
you must all become as little children.
— Jesus to the Disciples

I think, therefore I am.
— René Descartes

I

Civilized Within The First Century

—I—

The boy walks to the puddle of water and stops. One foot steps into the water, and the other foot stomps down to splash a moment away. The trail out from the village has brought him towards the edge and the expanse of the Field now before his eyes. A delightful scene of red anemones and blue iris encourage a burst of energy from the seven year old. Early morning and fresh moments of wonder occupy the mind, pondering to wander and venture to where this morning?

The boy walks through verdant wadis. Stepping past the trees and shrubs growing alongside the path, thoughts of sitting himself near the Road to wait and watch for morning travelers coming out from or going into the village, and a quick foot placed wrong to the ground bring both knees down. Both hands and an arm slide atop the dirt and the loose stones along the path. Quick to stand upright, sensations of stinging pain course up his legs.

Mouthing an unuttered, *oh-aah!* The boy hobbles towards an arrangement of rock and log protruding from a nearby mound of earth, and with one foot the boy jumps and lifts himself up upon the log.

The hurt inside the knees bring tears. Turning to settle himself upright and balanced, feet dangle from the side of the log. The boy feels both his legs move, turning circles round and around. The legs stop turning and both feet turn circles in the opposite direction. Round and around the feet turn. His feet stop moving. Legs rise up and stretch forward. Elbows rest back upon the rock and both legs begin to move with gentle twists and turns. The ankles turn the toes inward and then twist the toes out.

Feeling less pain the boy brings his feet and legs back to himself. Inching forward and then sliding from the log, toes touch the ground, ankles turn the heels down upon the ground and a jolt of pain is brought into his knees. The boy turns to hop back up upon the rock and log.

Sitting forward and anxious, again his legs begin to move. The feet turn slow motions round and around, in time making the hurt inside his knees seem less to be.

A gust of warm air twirls twigs and dust through the niche of earth the boy sits inside of. A smattering of detritus pelts the boy. The wind subsides and the boy opens his eyes to the large spots of soft, green moss growing on top and down the sides of the log. Cool to touch, he wades his hand atop the moss. Fingers turn cold as they slide inside the moist, stubbled clumps of fibers.

The voices of strangers are nearby. The creaks and clirks from a bending wooden wagon. The sound of heavy rolling wheels crushing, cracking pebbles to ground…

Visitors to the village are infrequent. Excited by the sound of passing travelers, the boy turns to look uphill towards the Road and to glance upon a bundle of grapes between the leaves of a nearby vine branch…!

Beyond reach of an outstretched arm, the boy slides from the log and hobbles to the branch. Looking through the leaves, grapes are seen to grow high up alongside a large rock protruding from the steep wall of earth. Vines and clusters of grapes wind through a jagged cut of earth below the rock. Several branches wind through the crevice down to where the boy stands.

Standing on his toes, picking and eating grapes the boy lowers the vine branch. Turning through the leaves to find no other grapes, his attention turns to the branches high above. Grapes growing on these higher branches have burst and bled spots of color upon the rocks along the wall.

Hasty steps along the path, a first step up and then a painful second uphill step and the boy stops climbing. The hill is much too steep to climb, and the boy steps back down to the path.

Trudging footsteps along the path, thoughts turn back to home, to explore some more too, and his knees still hurt.

Dang darn, I wish there were more grapes.

A moment to glance towards the moss covered rock and log, and then up towards the boulder. Halting backward steps and, for a moment to stop and stare at the vine branches growing along the earthen wall.

Quick steps back to the single branch above the path, and lowering the branch to pick a grape. It's delicate and firm, sweet to taste. Picking another grape and to hold the branch to watch a cluster of grapes add new grapes on top of themselves. Eyes wide with wonder. Dim sparkles of light anticipate the appearance of other new grapes.

Branches high above the boy bow and sag. Stiff vine stalks tense with the weight of new grapes. Twisting, turning stems and leaves on the wall break pebbles and dirt into free fall to dust the boy head and shoulders.

Short steps foraging through the leaves and the boy wonders if perhaps to gather some grapes to share with mother and father.

Happy they will be ...

Raising the hem of his smock to form a pouch, several bunches of grapes are snapped from the branch and placed inside.

Trotting along the path and through the field, quick steps bring him inside the village and through the doorway of home.

The boy looks into one room and then into another.

Oy vey!

Hurried steps out through the back doorway and the boy turns, colliding with mother.

"Jesus, slow down."

A cherubic smile. A cursory examination, an inquisitive look, and mother brushes a leaf from his hair.

"What you got in there?"

The cloth is unraveled.

Mother stoops to fondle several bunches of grapes. Mary stands upright, takes a step back and plants an open hand upon her hip.

"Where'd you get all the grapes?"

The Seventeenth Century North American Continent

A crisp, clear air. Cold to smell. A Hunters' moon casts an effervescent shine upon the surroundings.

The watch follows the last cobblestones away from the log cabins, stalls, and shops. Downhill footsteps through open fields towards the path and trestlework crossing the canal. Traversing rocks along the shoreline, stepping up, down, and around the mounds of sand and beds of eelgrass, ... an uphill sandy, rocky trail borders the forest line. Crossing a second dirt bridge and the watch is brought back inside the community of homes and shops, and he climbs the watchtower nestled against a timber-framed bulwark of the colony.

A usual of nights. A stray domestic loosed from its pen. The sound of sea waves and the cries from loon and gull. Shallops and barks sway, lax rope brought taut with restraint. Neither fire nor weather harry the hour.

The watchman stops his climb and turns his face east, gazing up to a starry sky. Hands and face cool against a subtle breeze. The movement of air foretells Dawns light. Standing at the top of the tower and facing east, south, and then west, a slow, strong voice cries three times, "All's well ...!"

... and we envision the first of the earliest American policeman.

—|—

— | •

The Force Is Culpable

"How many in there, Walt?"

"Fifty cages—with fifty-two coming, heading this way, Pa."

Mara and Brenda are walking the path from the chicken coop towards the truck. Each girl carries a wooden cage with two live chickens inside.

"You and your sisters decide who rides along this time?"

"We are," the girls say in unison.

"Wanda says she wants to go somewhere tonight, Pa. So Brenda and I are going."

The girls place their cages at the back of the truck for Walter to stack, and then walk back to the chicken coop.

Neil wants to check on Sean before they travel, and steps towards the tractor shed.

"Plugs were dirty again, Pa. Have to spring for a new coil I think soon."

"Before we pull in those grapes next week. Points and plugs, whatever it needs. We'll bring the bailer back from the fields, too. Try to find out why the twine keeps bunching, clogging up."

Sean lowers the metal panel to the engine compartment. Tools on the bench are collected and placed inside the metal toolbox. The toolbox is brought up and wedged securely between the fender and the seat of the tractor.

Wanda grabs a chicken with both hands. Flapping wings, cackles, and squawks greet Brenda and Mara as they step inside the chicken coop.

"Listen to me!" Wanda says as the girls step to stand beside the last two empty chicken cages. "When you get there just stay inside the truck, all right?"

"Make sure the doors are always locked."

"Don't be fooling around either. Pay attention," Vern implores. "Those soldiers are hungry all the time. Oh, they'd just love to get their no-good hands on one of you two to put in a pot and cook up for dinner."

Vern grabs a chicken by its neck and lifts the bird up from its roost. The fist of her hand turns the neck of the chicken sideways with violent squawks and flapping wings towards Brenda and Mara.

"A lot more meat on both of you two than any of these silly chickens!"

Mara and Brenda crouch down and unlatch the cage doors. Bowed heads hide their giggles and smiles.

Chickens in their roosts sound a constant alarm of warbles and squawks to their intruders. Vern steps beside Mara and turns a fallen lock of hair away from her forehead.

"Wanda, ... they laugh."

Vern stoops to place the chicken through the opening of the cage. Mara presses the door of the chicken cage against her forearms. Vern then releases the bird and removes her hands from the cage. Mara latches the door while Vern rises to clasp Wanda's hand.

"Jesus, Lord, we pray to keep our Brenda and Mara safe from the very bad and evil soldiers that they'll see at the camp today."

"Our two sisters are brave, it's true," Wanda injects. "They're so small..., and easily fitting inside one or two of these chicken cages that those rotten, terrible men—," Vern interrupts, raising her voice, "would stick 'em in to sneak 'em into the camp without anybody noticing!"

"Jesus, we love them both very much, so please keep them safe."

"If it be Your will," Wanda says, lifting the cage up from the floor.

"Come on, let's go. That's all the chickens counted."

Sophie steps down from the porch and walks towards Walter strapping cages to the back of the truck.

"Walter, where's your father?"

"He walked over towards the tractor shed, Ma. He's with Sean."

Neil presses the drain pin on the float bowl at the bottom of the carburetor. Gasoline and water condensate dribble down his two fingers and hand.

Sophie steps inside the tractor shed. Caution tempers the optimism to her words.

"The radio says the Red Army is close to entering Warsaw."

Neil listens and wipes his hands with a rag.

"Said the Germans took heavy losses in a retreat," Sophie furthers, "barely got anything out. In France somewhere. A Falaise Pass or something it was."

Stepping outside and walking towards the truck, *last few months news has been good for the Allies.* Discouraging reports of the war will soon follow, or so it seems to be.

Wanda steps up alongside mother and father.

"Counted out a hundred and fourteen, Pa."

"Jethro's coming over tonight?"

"He said he could take me and Vern into town, this afternoon, to see a movie."

Wanda places her wooden crate upon the back of the truck. The tractor engine thunders loud while Sean drives from the shed. Vern places her cage upon the tailgate of the truck and begins a quick pace of steps towards the tractor.

"I'll get the food," Sophie suggests. "You'll probably want to get going soon."

Wanda pushes her cage towards Walter, kisses her father, and quick steps bring her to stand and ride alongside Vern on the fender tail of the tractor.

Steel wheels slide into the sand as Sean turns the tractor onto the path behind the barn. After some twenty odd years here on the farm any stretch of brown dirt regularly traveled on by tractor or automobile have become these lengths and patches, sunken piles of sand scattered in different places around the farm. To be noticed and mentioned in jest, at times as idle conversation how sand has come to replace portions of the farm land routinely packed down and then broken up by the weight of machines being driven on it.

The green grass in front of the house grows to the gravel and shoulder of Red Arrow Highway, with the grass in the front yard spreading to surround the line of trees along the west side of the property. A variety of hearty, crabby type of grasses the horses enjoy feeding on grows inside this better green grass in the front yard, with more crab grass than good grass to grow and spread itself in clumps and patches towards the east side of the house. Long lengths of this scruffy crab grass grows further on towards the barn. Grass and weeds together inside patches of sandy dirt wind inbetween and then beyond the three large pawpaw trees standing alongside the curve to the driveway. All green grass stops growing at the side of the barn, beyond the trees and the fence along the east side of the property, and along the eroding line of grass marking the large pile of sand at the porch side of the house. A picket fence in the backyard separates the grass in the back of the house from the pasture and hay fields where the animals are supposed to graze, and where a harvest of grapes and rotating crops of corn and soybeans are grown every year.

Two narrow ruts of deep sand evolved over the years from Red Arrow Highway to the porch side of the house. Carved into the grass of the front lawn, the ruts guide the back end of the truck as it swish and sways from side to side. Rear tires spinning through the sand ride up and then slide down the solid hump of dirt and green grass growing in the middle. The truck pushes itself onward, forward, through those two narrow lengths of sand and up to the porch side of the house.

Here at the porch the truck will park, and here at the side of the house the parked truck sits on the edge of a large sunken pile of gray sand that has risen up and spread itself around. Thick in the center, the sand spreads out thin only for as far and as wide as the truck requires for it to do an easy one hundred and eighty degree turn from the porch and then have it facing back towards the road again.

Our hands dig into this pile of sand in front of the porch. Scooping and then pushing handfuls of dry, off-white sand up and over the side of a hole eventually to find someone with half their arm down inside, and the cuff of the hand scrapes on top of the more solid, packed-down brown dirt. A final handful or two of loose dirt and gray sand are pulled up and away, and with our curiosity satisfied we find something else to do.

The wide and sunken pile of sand outside the porch extends towards the entrances of the barn. Two shallow lengths of sand inside the tractor shed join with this extended length of sand drawn close to the barn, with the loose sand inside the ruts spreading out and into the scruff of weeds and vegetation near the silos and the chicken coop in back of the house.

The sand towards the barn narrows as it winds between the barn and the tractor shed, with another mound of brown dirt and scruffy crab grass and weeds rising up from in-between two tractor ruts of sand. The ruts curve to wind behind the barn, pass alongside the cattle troughs before turning again and to begin the long and straight length of tractor trail into one hundred and forty acres of farm land.

There were other shorter, lesser patches of sand that grew to mark places around the farm. A bend in the creek that flows through the north side of the property has sand to step upon as we wade into the water. The cows trampled meandering patches of grass and sand out from the hay field as each day they would make their way to the water troughs behind the barn. Though no place grew and came to compare to the size, the shape and the amount of sand that had placed itself just outside the side porch of the house.

Some of my Moms first memories are to things such as these. Thoughts she would first realize to herself and towards the place she called home.

The cleats of the tractor's steel rear wheels puncture to rip the ground, to paddle and grind the dirt, separating large grit grains of sand from hard, brown dirt. The front steer wheels twist the surface of the ground as they grip for traction and begin to turn the tractor. The sand naturally mixed in with all the soil around these parts of Michigan, to continuously break the ground with a truck tire or steel tractor wheel and then wash the brown soil away with several seasons of rain and melting snow, in time all that remains are the heavy particles of sand.

The tractor engine is loud. Powerful metallic vibrations ripple into every piece and part of the tractor, to not uncomfortably sting wherever supporting hands grip and feet rest upon as you ride.

A distance out and along the tractor trail, Wanda nudges Vern and Sean for their attention. Her hand points towards the field. Two groundhogs scamper together along the cut field, bumping around and about the gently rising mounds of earth and then vanish from sight.

The tractor arrives at an opening of barbed wire. Sean turns from the sandy ruts, steering the tractor between two fence posts and up inside the open field.

A first and then a second automobile accelerates past the truck. Neil maintains a thirty mile an hour top speed.

"How far away is it?" Mara asks.

"When will we get there, Pa?" echoes Brenda.

"Not long. About an hour away."

Walter suggests to his sisters they play a game.

"Find letters of the alphabet on any signs along the road. Look on someone's license plate or at the side of a passing truck. Anywhere. Wherever you see letters of the alphabet as we drive along."

"We'll begin trying to find the letter a. Call it out and point to where you see it so every one else sees it too. Then we'll look to find the letter b, and then c, and by the time we get to the fort the person who found and called out the last letter is the winner."

"We were at the letter k when we got there last time, and I won, so we might not get to the end, to the letter z by the time we get there this time either."

Turning the truck off the main road and driving up to the checkpoint of the fort, Walter will want Brenda's attention.

"Brenda, look. You can see the fort coming up now."

Neil rolls his window down as the truck slows, stopping alongside the guard booth at the entrance to the fort.

"Welcome to Fort Custer," the guard says, pausing to look at and acknowledge everyone inside the truck. "And a good morning to all of you folks."

Neil hands the guard several pieces of paper through the window and after a brief telephone conversation the guard returns to the truck.

"Sir, back up and then follow this road around the perimeter of the fence. Follow it to Custer Lane, then turn right. You'll park near one of the last buildings and houses on the road."

"Give these papers to a Sergeant Stern to sign. He'll have some men with him to get your truck unloaded."

Neil follows the road for a distance and turns the truck at Custer Lane. A handful of men can be seen standing on the loading dock of a building. Several men jump down from the dock. One man in a U.S. Army uniform steps out and away from the group and walks towards the truck with an upraised hand of greeting.

"Mr. Diamond, I'm Sergeant Stern. Glad to see 'ya. We've been looking forward to these chickens."

The sergeant steps back and brings a quick look towards the men near the warehouse.

"I suppose they're ready. Just back the truck to the loading dock there."

Prisoners step near with their hands in motion as they join with the sergeant guiding Neil and the truck towards the platform.

"Whoa, that's good. Right there," the sergeant says, and Neil turns off the engine and steps outside.

Walter steps outside to watch tie-down straps being unfastened. The tarp covering the back of the truck is raised and chicken crates begin moving hand to hand from one prisoner to another.

Leaning against the open door, Walter notices the expansion of the camp grounds from the last visit. A row of half a dozen new buildings are at various stages of completion inside the chain link fence. A shout and Walter's attention is brought to the far side of the fence.

A man rips open a large paper bag and then tips the bag dumping the contents into a wheelbarrow. Another man rakes the powder with a hoe.

Several men on their hands and knees pound their hammers to the floor of a nearby building. Another group of men hoist individual boards of wood up to another floor.

Walter turns to look inside the truck.

"You coming out or you want to stay inside?"

Brenda and Mara bring themselves as if ready to step out from the open door. Glancing towards the men unloading the truck, Brenda looks to Mara and Mara looks to Walter.

"Come on out and walk around some," Walter says. "Stay with me."

The three wander towards the front of the truck, kicking stones around.

"Howard, I'll talk it over with my wife. I'm sure we could find some work."

"Let the Captain know, Neil. We've doubled the capacity of the camp the last six months. Got able bodied men that could do work if needed. I mean a lot too, believe me."

"I will," Neil affirms.

Along with an occasional bark of an order and the jocular chatter among the prisoners unloading chicken crates, nearby instruments of music waft the air. Sounds from a Vivaldi concerto, allegro, Opus VIII, RV 269.

"Against the Cubs at Ebbets Field. Early this month," the sergeant says.

"They lost both games, though he hits a double and drove in a run. Kid's only sixteen."

"What's his name again?"

"Tommy Brown. Brooklyn Dodgers."

The truck is parked inside a group of four buildings. To the right of the warehouse a mess hall and kitchen for the guards. Opposite the warehouse and mess hall are two residential structures built before the military converted the area from training camp to fort. The first structure is the home of the commander of Fort Custer. The second structure is a guest house. A large room in the guest house serves as a meeting room and for celebrations and the occasional itinerant theater or musical group performing for the entertainment of the guards and prisoners. This morning an ensemble of German and Italian soldiers practice inside the guest house, with the sounds of Vivaldi emanating from an open window.

Standing near the truck and the children hear the sound of music. Walter looks through an open window of the guest house to watch the hand of a man moving a bow across the strings of a cello. Realizing the source of the music, Walter steps to stand underneath the window.

"The older boys got thinking about school last year," Neil recalls. "Went into East Lansing, to Michigan State and saw the Wolverines practice. Other than that, don't drive around or into Chicago often. The radio gives us scores to local—"

Neil stops the thought and looks for the source of the melody he's hearing.

"Howard, is that real music?"

Sergeant Stern turns towards the guest house.

"Sure is. Over there, Captain Iommi and crew."

The sound of a lone violin captures the attention of Neil and the sergeant.

"Transferred here a couple months ago," the sergeant says with a perplexed look.

"They're not troublemakers. That's not why they're here. Word has it they travel to different camps, to play music."

With a bemused smile the sergeant adds, "I suppose it gives them something to do."

Several prisoners unloading the truck take notice of Walter, Brenda, and Mara standing near the window of the guest house. One prisoner unloading crates from the truck steps away and walks across the open space between the four buildings. Stepping up the porch steps the man walks through the front door of the residence where the musicians practice.

Soon the prisoner steps back out of the house with a Capitano Iommi and an Oberleutnant Butler. The three men stand along the porch rail and survey the situation for a moment. Sergeant Stern will observe the arm and hand of Butler point and gesture his way. Butler and Iommi nod in agreement, and Butler steps down from the porch.

"Morning, Lieutenant Butler."

"Sergeant Stern, please excuse my interrupting of your conversation. Please, look."

Lieutenant Butler gestures to have Neil and the sergeant taking steps to observe Walter, Brenda, and Mara as they stand several yards away below the open window of the guest house.

"The children show interest in music, yes?"

The lieutenant extends his arm and hand towards the porch.

"My fellow soldiers and I would be very appreciative if you would allow us the audience of your family."

Neil and the sergeant are caught off guard. Surprised and apprehensive, an immediate response to the invitation is not forthcoming.

Sergeant Stern removes the cap from his head and brushes his hair back. Placing the cap back on and the sergeant brings an eye-lifting, head-turning shrug of the shoulders look of why not to everyone.

The sergeant steps in front and then away from Neil. "Just say no if you don't want to."

Several tall stacks of crates remain on the back of the truck. A moment to watch the men handing and tossing crates to one another, Neil turns towards Captain Iommi. Arms forward, both hands grasp the porch rail. The man alongside Iommi folds his arms across his chest. Both men indignant to their own humility, they stare down at Neil and the sergeant.

Neil turns towards Lieutenant Butler and looks into the man's eyes.

Placid eyes motivated by, seeking approval. Swayed by any wind of doctrine.

A squint to his eyes, Lieutenant Butler brings quick though subtle nods of his head to assure and encourage a sense of propriety with Neil. Eventually Neil nods his approval towards Lieutenant Butler and Captain Iommi.

Lieutenant Butler calls for the children.

"Hello, children! Children?"

Walter and the girls are brought to the front of the house and escorted up the steps. The family is brought through a hallway and then into a large room where Iommi and Butler and several prisoners clear the center of the room of chairs, a desk, and table.

Men carry a maroon colored sofa into the room, placing it in front of three men with musical instruments in hand. One prisoner pushes to adjust the sofa farther back from the musicians while another turns one end of the sofa to have it facing towards another fourth man seated at a clavichord. Fluffing the cushions and pillows lying on top. A footstool is brought in front of Brenda and the children settle themselves upon the sofa. The musicians toy with their instruments while they wait for the commotion in the room to settle.

Curtains are separated. Both windows opened to allow more sunlight and fresh air to circulate. Two men step to the sofa and present plates of warm apple strudel and bottles of Coca-Cola to the children.

Neil refuses a plate of strudel. He takes hold of one of the two cold, wet bottles of Coca-Cola offered to him and Sergeant Stern.

Brenda is the first to see the Persian cat wander through the doorway and into the room.

"Mara, look. A kitty."

The cat squats to lick its paws. A prisoner stepping towards the doorway and the cat quickly lifts from its haunches and scampers from the room.

By any standard Neil could have imagined the residence they are inside of is, on first impression, quite a scene. The interior furnished with simple decorations and amenities that bring the place to appear quaint and cozy indeed. A hat rack and coffee table with vase and fresh cut flowers upon first entering. A wood paneled hallway. Tasseled, tied back curtains on windows. A plush rug lay on the floor of one room with mirrors and framed paintings along the walls of another room. A very cozy place indeed.

Neil watches a group of ten, fifteen men enter the room. The men are jovial crowding towards one side of the room, anticipating the musical performance they are about to hear.

Captain Iommi steps to huddle with the four musicians. He warmly embraces a man's shoulder and words are exchanged between all four of the men. Each musician glances towards Neil and the children with smiles of good fortune. Iommi steps to bring a cello upright from its lean against an empty chair, straddling the cello as he settles himself down in the middle of the four men.

The next minute or two are the brief, curt volleys of sound as the musicians began to play through what they know to be their most difficult movements to coordinate together.

One musician begins a soft, flowing sound from his instrument. The man stops playing and brings bow and violin from the shoulder. An unintelligible murmuring in German and Italian is heard between the five musicians. Again the sound of music resonates through the room, and with several instruments playing together in harmony all sound suddenly stops. The men clarify this or that to themselves with a nod or two. A movement of hands to convey something particular.

The family's attention becomes fixed upon the movements of the musicians as they bring their instruments into a particularly furious exchange of sound, and then to have all sound quickly dismantle. The sound from each musical instrument separates to be by itself until silence.

Two men step from behind the sofa to stand in front of Neil and the children. Banjoes in hand both men pluck individual strings and turn to adjust tuning pegs on the necks of their banjoes, eventually to have a quick up and down strumming upon the strings of each banjo as each player nods an acknowledgment towards Captain Iommi.

A moment of silence in the room and Captain Iommi speaks towards his four guests.

"Antonio Vivaldi," and the seven musicians begin the concerto in G major, allegro, RV 532.

It's difficult to describe how one feels and how one reacts to hearing classical music for the first time. Objectively speaking one uses the word sound to describe the phenomena of a specific type of radiation effecting the human auditory organs. When employed the word sound is neutral, implying that the radiated energy affecting the ears is neither good nor bad. Qualifying any sound with the use of the word noise describes the moments of sound as annoying or distracting, and as such the word noise implies a bad sound. On the contrary the use of the word music describes sounds that are pleasing to the ear, and good.

The moments of sound from the musical instruments will bring Neil and his family to these primordial sensibilities. Deliberately created, coordinated sounds such as these have never touched the children's ears. Connecting the sight of the players movements upon their instruments to the sounds that were then being created kept their attention and wonder. However sounds take their passages within the human brain to stoke its capacity for emotive characteristics, this event will create those first connections within the formative minds of the children.

The first composition finishes to have the sounds from a second Vivaldi composition resonates through the room: the sonata in A Minor, allegro poco, RV 44.

Iommi slowly draws the bow to rub across the string of the cello and the sound of this long and final note to be interrupted by the sudden hand claps of applause and the bravos of accomplishment from all the men that have gathered inside the room. Brenda, Mara, and Walter respond in kind, their own enthusiastic hand claps to be noticed by all the men.

Iommi turns to converse with two of his fellow players. These men speak a few words to the other men. Another name is heard brusquely spoken into the receding din of applause.

"Claude Debussy."

Iommi and the men begin the scherzo in G Minor, opus 10, *"assez vif et jeu bien rythmi."*

Neil looks over towards his children. Walter leans forward with his hands under his thighs. The girls sit Indian on the sofa. All three are quite attentive to the scene before them.

Across the room Sergeant Stern stands, leaning against the doorway with another Army officer.

Perhaps an extra five or ten men to the fields and quickly pull in and pack up those grapes this year ...

Extending the barn and adding another row of cattle stalls was a project for the spring, though some helping hands could have these built before the winter weather sets in.

Neil ponders these thoughts while the musicians play into Pachelbel's Canon in D Major.

Strengthen the upper ribs of both silos. A wonder they survived the winds of the last thunder storms, maybe have someone climb up there and take a look.

A sense of impracticality discourages further thoughts.

It's a distance between fort and farm to transport prisoners back and forth every day,

If they were to build something temporary, something on the farm maybe for the men to stay and sleep in...

Neil stands and steps towards Sergeant Stern to discuss the matter further.

The distant rifle shot couldn't be heard above the rumble of idling diesel engine. A moment to scan the field from the top of the wagon, and Wanda will watch Vern hurry to some place in the field and picking something up from the ground.

Sean maintains a steady rhythm of pitching the last of a pile of hay up into the wagon.

"Looks like she got one," she mentions down to him.

Gathering and throwing the last of the pile up to her, Sean jabs the prongs of the pitchfork deep into the ground. Wanda climbs off the wagon and stands alongside Sean. Together they watch Vern walk towards them through the field. Vern raises the dead groundhog up over her head, triumphantly.

Walking up alongside them and her fingers begin to turn the groundhog's fur down flat against its skin, exposing both entrance and exit wounds.

"Went through its neck."

Climbing upon the tractor fender, the groundhog is placed inside a burlap bag near the seat. Vern lifts a canteen of water. "It stopped running, stood still for just a second." A drink of water, she steps down from the tractor and walks back into the field. Lazily dropping to the ground, making herself comfortable, again to scan the rolling mounds of open field for anything that pops its head up or runs along the ground. A couple of hours time and Wanda will lay in the field with the rifle, and Vern will pitch hay into the bailer from on top of the wagon.

Warm and humid air all morning. Large white clouds and their shadows pass into and out of the field, to present a completely blue sky by early afternoon. Not a cloud of any size above or seen moving along the horizon.

Layers of sticky sweat, each dusted with stray bits of hay in the eyes, in the ears, in the shoes done too many times encourages Sean to consider the work in the field to be finished. Being warm and humid made the hours seem slow. A good number of hay bales are on the ground. Pa will see they put in some work while he was gone.

Only recently, half an hour before they'll finish and head back to the house has Sean noticed the mildest of breezes occasionally come and go. Vern climbs down from the wagon and takes hold of the canteen from the tractor. After pouring water into her mouth she walks over and offers Sean the canteen.

"Let's get going?"

"Yeah, sure. I'm getting a bit hungry."

Standing away from the tractor Vern gives a shrill whistle and waves her hand to Wanda.

Wanda waves back, unloads the rifle and walks towards the fence and tractor trail. Sean unhitches the bailer from the tractor, climbs into the seat and steers the tractor along the flat, open field towards the trail.

The groundhogs are a nuisance. They dig tunnels and build underground nests in the fields. The tunnels aren't the problem, the nests are. Large hidden holes in the ground. A nest dug out and to the size of a pumpkin for three or four of the critters can grow to the size of a hollow fifty-five gallon drum that ten or twenty of the varmints live inside of. A tractor can break an axle if a wheel rolls over a nest a certain way, or take a day to dig the tractor out.

Kneeling up upon the fender Vern brings one arm across the back of the seat. Sean turns down into the sandy ruts and the weight of the right front wheel breaks through the dirt, caving in to drop inside a ground hog nest. The tractor pitches, Vern slides off the fender and on to her hands and knees as the tractor wheel rolls on top of her.

Sean hurries down to find his sister up on one arm. Half of her left arm is held underneath the metal of the large steel wheel.

"Oh, get it off of me!" Vern pleads.

"I'll go forward."

Vern knows something — more than one thing broke inside her arm and hand. Unable to free herself, the pain develops into a cold and numbing state of shock.

Sean slowly lifts his foot to engage the clutch. In predictable manner the rear wheel rolls several feet off Vern's arm. Sean jumps back to the ground.

"Let me see," he says, helping her sit up straight.

The steel wheel rolled against the back of her forearm, pushing the arm flat onto the backside of her hand and then into the ground. The wrist broke, and bone has broken through skin.

"Not good, Sis." Sean climbs upon the tractor for the canteen of water.

"This may sting a bit."

Pouring water on the open wound, Sean brushes the lacerated skin with thumb and fingers to remove particles of dirt. He takes his shirt off and wraps the wound.

"I'll go get Betsy and tell Wanda."

Wanda shuffles her feet along the ground, looking up towards the tractor.

Why has the tractor stopped moving? Maybe running out of gas, and they're putting the spare quart in is all.

Sean sprints out from the front of the tractor.

No! Fear brings Wanda to run towards Sean.

"Vern got hurt. I'm getting Betsy," Sean says running past her.

Sophie hears Sean outside the house.

"Ma ...! Ma!!"

Stepping out onto the porch to watch Sean dash across the sand towards the back of the house. Stepping off the porch and around the corner, and Sean is mounting Betsy and prodding her to run.

"Whoa! What happened? Where's—"

"Vern's hurt, Ma. Broke her hand, kinda bad."

"Went into a hole and Vern fell off," he says, almost to cry. "The wheel went over her arm, Ma. Some bone is sticking out of her hand."

"I'll go get her. You go inside and call Dr. Mellencamp."

"They're all the way back there. By the wall."

"Tell Dr. Mellencamp that Vern has a compound fracture," and Sophie brings Betsy to full gallop.

The wound is cleaned and an operation is performed to determine the extent of the injury. It wasn't until late in the evening that Dr. Mellencamp will discuss her condition with Neil, Sophie, and Sean.

"We'll want to keep her here in the hospital for the next several days," Dr. Mellencamp explains. "Get a head start if complications develop."

Looking through the folder of papers in his hands, Dr. Mellencamp reads, '*Penicillin ...*,'

"Kevin," asks Sophie, "what's going to happen? Is she going to be all right?"

"We'll know more twenty-four, thirty-six hours from now. I've seen these new medicines work miracles. She stands a good chance of staving off any problems from an infection. An accident of this sort even four or five years ago, ..." ends with a stern frown and disconcerting turns of the head.

"We'll have to wait though. It's still early. I won't be able to say anything for another twenty-four hours."

There is little else for Dr. Mellencamp to do. He thinks the family may want to be alone for a while.

Before leaving the room he has a word with Sean. He's been quiet, looking out the nights dark window a distance away from their conversation. The doctor imagines how he must be blaming himself somehow for the accident.

"It wasn't your fault, Sean. You couldn't've known."

Sean turns towards his father, still trying to comprehend his responsibility for what happened.

"No more rides on the tractor, ... I know that much."

Dr. Mellencamp puts a hand on his shoulder, "I'll let you people be alone then." He walks out of the room and approaches Sister Janet from Catholic Hospice in the corridor.

Having finished with other obligations around the city, Sister has stopped at the hospital before the end of the day to inquire of new admissions, noticing a patient admitted several hours ago. A farm accident involving a seventeen year old female.

Skimming the chart she reads: 'Open segmental fracture of the left hand with contamination, ... no major hemorrhaging, ... Catholic.'

Sister imagines the next five, ten days may be difficult with this case. She expects someone from family to be with her as she makes her way to her room.

"Evening, Sister."

"Yes, been a long day," she confides with a smile. "Mrs. Walker, and it's a boy."

"Finally," Dr. Mellencamp chuckles.

"A son. A son!" he says with slow, labored syllables.

"A son," Sister repeats with a laugh. "Yes, yes, of course. I've been there the better part of the afternoon. They're very happy."

"Vern Diamond?"

The doctor nods in the direction of their room. "I just left her."

"Tractor wheel crushed the left hand. Second and third metacarpal went through the palm."

Doctor Mellencamp pauses with apprehension.

"Infection? We'll be lucky if nothing shows."

Sister Janet brings a look of concern upon the doctor. Doctor Mellencamp brings his gaze away, and down to her side.

"Administered penicillin within four to six hours. See what happens ... watch her for the next twenty-four, thirty-six hours. You know the routine."

"I'll assign her to you if you want?"

Sister nods in acceptance.

"That's them leaving now. Come, I'll introduce you."

"Neil? Sophie?"

"This is Janet. Sister Janet from Catholic Hospice. Her convent is a few blocks from the hospital here.

"I'll assign her as Vern's nurse. Speak to either one of us if you have any questions about Vern in the future."

The decision was made to have Sophie stay with Vern and have her sleep overnight in an adjacent room. Someone will drive back to the hospital with a suitcase of clothes and things for the two, and then to find Sophie other accommodations until Vern is ready to leave.

Neil and Sean drive the twenty-five miles back to the farm.

Warm, damp air rushing in through the open windows of the truck bothers Sean. Rolling his own window half way up, Sean tells his father to do the same, and for a time a sense of calmness is brought inside the cab of the truck.

"You know how Mr. Styngclok became blind like he is?" Neil asks.

"While he was working at Acme, ... using a new welder they bought. Sometimes he wouldn't bother wearing the eyepieces that protect his eyes. Quick jobs, two or three-seconds to bead a line or to link a chain. Said one day the silver glare didn't go away. Doctor said he burned a spot right in the back of his eyes."

"He told me he can see out of the sides of his eyes like he always did but its like someone stuck a shiny silver quarter in the middle of both his eyes. He can't see a darn thing if he looks straight towards something, right at it, ... he says."

A pause before adding, "That bright spark from the welder burnt a hole—"

A hole in his head?

A short irregular section of the road bounces to shake and rattle the truck for a moment.

"Ahh," Neil raps the steering wheel with the palm of his hand.

Sean turns to his father. "I know. Live and learn."

A moment to recall the hole that stopped the tractor dead in its tracks, and took all day to jack up and roll the tractor out from.

Rolling into and then out of one of those things is the norm.

No more rides on the tractor. Take one of the horses next time, and every time from now on. No rides.

Driving up near the porch of the house and the truck is turned into the sand until it's facing towards the road. An open door and the convenience light illuminates the inside of the truck. Neil looks at his watch. Twelve-Thirty.

Walking to the house Neil and Sean notice the kitchen and porch lights. The porch screen door is open. Light inside the girls' upstairs bedroom.

Wanda and Walter step through the barn doors and watch father and Sean stepping up the porch steps.

"Over here, Pa. We got a new colt."

Walter and Wanda raise their lanterns up, and Neil and Sean turn to walk towards the barn. Footsteps shift and slide on top of thick sand. Through the darkness Wanda asks, "How's Vern doing, Pa?"

"She's fine. Your mother is staying with her for the next few days."

The lantern lights turn away and disappear inside the barn. Stepping to the back of the barn and hanging lanterns light the horse stalls. Betsy is seen standing outside her stall alongside her newborn colt.

Wanda sets her lantern upon a wooden beam of the wall.

"Maybe an hour after you left, Pa. I opened the gate to let them in, came back a while later after fixin' some dinner. That's when I found her lying down, just starting."

"He seems healthy too, Pa," Walter adds. "There doesn't seem to be a problem with either one of 'em. We've been taking turns rubbing him down, talking to him, getting him to know us and all."

"Where's Brenda and Mara?" Sean asks.

"They were here a while ago. They came out here soon after I did."

Walter brings a lantern up above his head to scan around the barn.

"Here they are, over here."

Both girls sleep upon a mound of hay.

"Thought they might've wanted to watch, and help. Don't know how long they've been there."

Neil steps to stand near the two for a moment. He reaches for Brenda and in jocularly desperate fashion says, "Try to make it a handsome name this time."

Raising Mara up from the pile of hay, Sean tells Walter, "I'm gonna come back out."

"I'm kinda hungry. Want a peanut butter and jelly sandwich?" Walter asks.

Nodding affirmatively, "Pa bought a crate of apples and a jar of honey this morning," Sean suggests.

"Yeah, I saw the apples."

Out through the barn and towards the house, Neil gives a short, silent prayer.

Jesus buddy, a bit heavy-duty the last couple days. I'll need some help, to sort it all out, and put it together."

"Mara Mae, is he walking you around or are you walking him?" Wanda asks. "Let him go and come over here."

Mergatroid is getting frisky. The colt has been trotted left and right, forward and back, stop and go, then round and around in circles, and Wanda thinks it's time to give him a break. Mara unfastens the leather strap around Mergatroid's neck, raising the strap up and over his head.

Mergatroid stands still. Ears twitch and turn. Mara brings her hand up and her fingers brush the hair of Mergatroid's ear.

"Go," Mara commands with a push of her hand, swatting his flank with the leather strap. Mergatroid turns and trots towards where Betsy, Betty, and Bob graze in the field.

Mara turns to the fence gate.

"You're getting his confidence," Wanda says to her. "He's getting a little tired of the training part though, I think."

Climbing upon the fence rail, "Maybe she's coming back today," Mara says. "Maybe that's why Pa isn't back yet."

Wanda is up in a tree today, Mara thinks. That's when something happens to someone and they want to go off and be alone for a while.

"Maybe," Wanda says.

Because she doesn't know herself, Wanda can't find other words to say to Mara. Vern's been in the hospital over two weeks. Ma hasn't been home in all that time.

Wanda steps down from the fence. "Listen, I'm going back inside and make something for supper. Find Brenda and I want the both of you back in half an hour and washed up, ok?"

Mara nods, and Wanda turns to walk away.

"Something happened today, didn't it?" Mara asks.

With tears in her eyes Wanda bows her head and turns towards Mara.

"Vern got really sick at the hospital."

"How you know?"

"Walter talked to Ma this morning."

The pain on Wanda's face scares Mara.

"You want to pray again?" Mara asks.

"Sure. Sure do."

Mara and Wanda kneel and take hold of each other's hands.

Mara closes her eyes. "I'll go first."

"Lord, … Jesus, you know I want to see my sister Vern again soon. We have a new horse now. A new colt we named Mergatroid, but Mergatroid won't be his real name unless Vern and all of us agree on it. So we need Vern here so we can all agree on it and then make the name real. Please hurry up and make Vern well, and bring her back home…"

"That's all."

"If it be your will," Wanda says to finish the prayer, and then begins her own.

"Jesus, you know all of us have been worried this last week. You know Vern got really sick because of the accident. Today there was a phone call and Pa had to go into the city … for some reason."

"If you should take Vern from us to be with you I want to thank you for the time I had with her. She was the best sister any one could ever have. Help me to understand your will now, in good times and bad, with life and death, … that's all."

Mara pulls her hands away and stands upright. Looking down at Wanda and her fear grows. Turning to face away from Wanda, eventually to begin walking towards the creek, resigning herself to say, "I'll go get Brenda."

"Mara?" Wanda says. "You'll stay strong for us, ok?"

Brenda has her socks and shoes off. Holding her skirt above her knees, with stick in hand she's attacking water bugs seen scurrying over the surface of the water. Sliding her feet, careful not to create waves and alert the bugs of her presence, Brenda attempts to get close enough to begin hitting them with the stick again.

Mara walks up to stand at the bank of the creek.

"We gotta go back in a few minutes. Wanda's makin' something to eat again."

Brenda brings the stick up above her head. Creeping steps up alongside a bush, several bugs quickly slither underneath the branches.

Mara steps to the patch of sand where Brenda's shoes lie.

Vern is dying? … dying instead of getting better all this time at the hospital?

An absence of thought for several moments.

Maybe, she remembers Wanda saying to her, and with this an answer of sorts.

She may be dying?

When you die you go to be with Jesus.

Searching the mind for more color to embellish this thought with, and an image of a person with white wings comes to mind. Mara recalls Pa saying, *… people don't really have wings in heaven, … a long time ago, people just made that up.*

What's it like to be dying? Just before you die, what's it like to—Brenda slaps the stick into the water.

Slap! Slap! Slap!

A clutch of branches held to her side, Brenda slaps the stick down into the water. A vocal and ferocious slap to the water, and the stick is thrown inside the bush.

Mara turns back towards the slow flowing creek water. Staring into the water and attempting to imagine what it's like to be dying … what happens?

Moments pass. Mara turns to watch Brenda clumsily pulling her wet foot up inside a dry sock, and brings her hands to help. They stand and begin the walk across the field to the tractor trail.

Mara looks at her sister as they step from the field and walk along the tractor trail. A thought to ask her what she thinks.

She's just a kid. She doesn't know.

Still off a distance from the house and Mara sees the truck parked in the driveway.

"Pa's back, come on."

Neil steps down from the porch to look for the two. Mara runs around the tractor shed and across the pile of sand to his arms.

"Hi, Pa. How's Vern? Is she alright?"

Held tight and he places her head on his shoulders.

"Listen to me, your mother..., she's gonna need your help for awhile."

Mara pushes back to look at her father, and the mist in his eyes.

"Because..., because she doesn't have one of her daughters anymore."

Brenda swings around the shed, running until a slow pace of steps brings her in reach of his arm, and they walk up the porch steps and into the kitchen.

"Wanda made us some sandwiches. There's fresh milk in the pitcher, too."

Pouring milk into their glasses, the girls settle themselves into their chairs.

"Vern died at the hospital," Mara whispers to Brenda.

"She died?"

Brenda turns to her father. "Pa, where's Ma?"

"Let her sleep. We'll all talk together in the morning."

Mara steps from the kitchen and into the dining room to find Walter, Sean, and Wanda inside the living room. Walter stands beside a window and looks out into the fields. Sean sees his sister standing at the doorway and asks her if she knows. Mara nods and steps towards the sofa.

"Why?" she asks Wanda. "Why did she die?"

"Something called tetanus."

"Tetanus?" repeats Mara, sounding out the new word.

"An infection."

Mara knows infections..., make you sick.

Why, though? Mara steps from the living room to the back porch steps.

Why did this have to happen?

Couldn't she ...? Couldn't Jesus just have let her live?

Why not? Why did this happen? Why do all of us have to be sad now?

The mind doesn't bring answers. It only wants to make questions.

Betsy, Betty, Bob, and Mergatroid stand together grazing on the crabgrass near the fence at the far side of the field.

Stepping down from the porch, "Mergatroid, it's me."

Climbing through the fence and into the field, "Here boy, come here."

Mara follows the fence hoping not to spook him and have him run away, eventually stepping close enough to pet him.

Brushing the short black hair on top and down the sides of his head, "You're getting to trust me now, huh?"

A soft, short wail suddenly erupts inside Mara, separating the pain and releasing it into an instant fit of crying.

Startled, Mergatroid exhales noisily. Head and shoulders rise up and down, stamping fitful side steps to the ground, and Mergatroid will then stand quiet and still. Mara squats to the ground and buries her face in her arms, crying all the more.

The familiar rumbling roar of an approaching airplane is heard.

Wiping her eyes with the palms of her hands. An airplane flies above the treetops at the far side of the field. Teary eyes blur the airplane as it travels out of sight. The sound of another airplane and Mara brings the cloth of her shirt collar up to dab the eyes. An airplane appears against the blue sky. Growing large and loud, with a roar the airplane passes above the fields alongside the barn and beyond the treetops along Red Arrow Highway. Mara turns to face the fields and waits. Two dots rise above the treetops along the horizon at the end of the field. Both airplanes descend low to the ground and fly directly towards her. The two airplanes grow large as they approach. Deep rumbles of full throttled engines become a thunderous roar as one airplane passes directly overhead. The other airplane passes above the house. Both airplanes fly out of sight behind the trees of Red Arrow Highway.

Airplanes flying alone or in groups of two or three, for several minutes a number of very large and very loud airplanes begin flying above the trees and fields around the house.

Mara hears an airplane in the distance flying farther away from her. The rumbling sound of the airplane's engines slowly recedes. Several minutes pass and no other airplanes approach.

Mara recalls standing on the porch with Sheriff Brown, Pa, and Walter.

"Liberators," the sheriff was saying, "from Willow Run," and, "the pilot 'instruments' are 'calibrated' before they're put on ships across the Atlantic."

Mara looks towards the house. The sun is setting low into the trees. A light turns on inside the kitchen. Walking to the fence, Mara leans against the fence post, eventually to look up and over towards the house again.

The backs and palms of her hands rub her eyes clear, and she turns her head from side to side to stop herself from asking another question she knows she won't be able to answer.

The thought is precocious, determined, measured.

Jesus ...? You are going to tell me why You did this.

—|—

• | —

We Are A Channel

"Listen to this. Basically what it's saying here is all forms of electromagnetic radiation are just the electron of an atom traveling at these different frequencies, in different wavelengths, ... in Hertz."

A lingering moment of silence.

"I knew that."

Another moment crawls along, neither one having yet given the other their undivided attention.

"No, you didn't."

"Yes, I did," is the quick response.

"Yeah, 'cause you already read it."

The best thing Howard's brother Jeff and his friends Jack and Wyatt did to the tree fort, besides build it, was to enable the top three-quarters of one wall of the tree fort to fall forward. Remove the length of wood that holds the platform upright to the wall, an easy push of the hand brings the wall to fall outside. Inspired by the mechanism of a drawbridge falling from a castle wall, the hinged wall of the tree fort falls over with a similar mechanism, effortlessly rolled up or lowered using a system of rope and pulley and weights to balance everything. On any warm sunny day, climbing out on the ledge to read a book or magazine for a few hours was an adventure all by itself.

The clapping chatter of shaking leaves as the wind rustles and rolls to bowl through the tops of nearby trees. Twisting tree branches force nailed boards of wood into moments of stress and creaking staccatos of sound.

The tree situated on an uphill ridge some thirty yards into the woods brought views of the back of the house and the turn of Bykenhulle Road leading towards the Parkway. The fort built half way up into one of the tallest trees in that area of forest also brought a fairly unobstructed view to a large portion of the sky.

Tyler closes his magazine, sits up and inches towards the opening of the tree fort. Dropping his feet to the floor, placing the magazine in chronological order inside the *Popular Mechanics* section of the box, he asks, "Think your father's back from Kalamazoo?"

Howard stops reading.

Is there something better, to do? ... if father is not yet back from town?

Climbing all the way down thirty-five feet of tree and then climbing all the way back up again, such thoughts would always cause Howard to stop and pause whatever he was doing at the moment.

"I'm not coming back up here if he hasn't, so..."

Ballast in submarines competes for Howard's attention. Thoughts that picture his father and the car back in the driveway right now at this very moment are becoming vivid and more compelling than the words inside the magazine conveying compressed air pushing water out of the ballast tanks of a submarine to allow it to rise to the surface.

"You wanna go down?" Howard suggests.

Howard's older brother Jeffery is in the Navy. A letter he'd sent to Mom and Dad had said he will soon arrive at an airfield called Henderson, at some place called Guadalcanal Island in the Pacific Ocean.

Jeff left all the magazines and books inside the tree fort. A whole slew of *Popular Mechanics, Popular Science, Scientific American,* all his magazines arranged more than less by month and year in boxes underneath the two automobile bench seats. A number of hardcover books are up inside the tree fort, too. Some of the hardcover books are Jeff's college textbooks.

Climb down or stay here ...?

Tyler stands beside the shelf and the radio they hoisted up this morning. He squeezes the electrical clamps from the wires of the radio. The wood panel to the top of the radio has been unscrewed and placed upright behind the radio, exposing the arrangement of circuit board wires, vacuum tubes, and electrical components.

Turns of the tuning knob, watching as the thin, black vertical stick traverses short distances behind the rectangle of glass. Anticipation keeps both waiting for the car battery they'll use to power the radio. Tyler looks to the arrangement of antenna wires tacked across the ceiling of the tree fort. The antennae wires point due east towards Detroit.

"You gotta get better reception up here, especially at night."

Howard turns to Tyler and the radio. After they turn the radio on and the hope is that by some stroke of good luck the antenna wires splayed upon the ceiling will have station WXYZ in Detroit come in loud and clear. How great that will be.

Investigating for a better antenna design was the first of Howard's many projects to modify his radio. Because at night his radio would pick up signals from stations with call letters that began with a K, which meant these transmitters were stationed and broadcasting from west of the Mississippi River. Stations from St. Louis, Philadelphia, and Schenectady could also be heard, for a time. Eventually as evening approached distant stations began drifting in and out of reception.

One evening Howard turned to the signal of a distant radio station. The signal began to slowly drift out and then back into reception, and continued to drift the announcer's voice out and then back into reception for several moments until the soft crackle of static through the speaker appeared relentless. Howard brought his hand near the radio and before his hand began to turn the dial, in an instant the crisp clear musical notes of Ray Noble and His Orchestra, with Al Bowlly singing his classic, *"Midnight, the Stars and You"* began to emanate through the speaker. Howard's curiosity was piqued. What could be causing the radio signal to drift in and out of reception? The simple act of his arm and hand brought close to the radio appeared to cause the signal to strengthen.

During daytime hours, radio station WGN from Chicago came in fairly clear. Local radio station WKZO in Kalamazoo could always be tuned in crisp and clear. The one station Howard wanted though was the Detroit station WXYZ where the Lone Ranger was broadcast on. WXYZ's signal could be tuned in after eight or sometimes nine o'clock in the evening. The Lone Ranger show began live at four o'clock in the afternoon and the radio cannot pick up a good receptive signal to station WXYZ during those hours of the day. At times an announcer's voice is heard, but there is too much static interfering with the fidelity of sound.

Already deciding that if a clear reception of station WXYZ cannot be tuned in they'll try pointing the antenna wires from due east to more northern and southeastern directions, tacking and re-tacking the wires in different configurations along the ceiling of the tree fort until the station, hopefully, can be tuned in and heard. If the radio still doesn't bring in a clear signal Howard knows there are other pictures in some of the books at the public library he can look at more carefully.

The idea to arrange the wires in their present configuration came from a single picture of an antenna on the page of a book in the library. The narrative under the picture explained that an antenna boosts the signal of a radio, allowing any radio to become more receptive, more sensitive. The wires strung along the ceiling of the tree fort should allow the radio to be more sensitive to a signal.

Again Howard will take a moment to ponder upon the words *sensitive* and *receptive*, to wonder what those words describe electronically. Sensitive to the noise of the static? Sensitive to the stations' voice or music signal he wants to hear? His thoughts attempt to picture both the noise of the static and the voice or music as two different things combined into the one signal emanating out from a station's broadcast antennae. His thoughts have also brought a picture of the static and the signal as two very different things somehow happening together at the same time. At the time Howard possesses no definitive intellectual tools to label and categorize and to manipulate and animate his interest in radio and antenna design, so his thoughts soon devolve out and into any one of many different kind of moments that capture his attention during the day.

The story he has been reading out on the ledge ends with an illustration at the bottom of the page. A submarine is pushing a white mound of blue water up in front of itself. Waves of water flow along the sides and over the top of the hull of the submarine while it travels through the surface of the water.

He's getting ants in his pants. Fanning through the last pages of the magazine and then inching and rolling himself inside the tree fort, "Let's go."

Herbert lifts the battery from the trunk and places it down inside the metal wagon Howard and Tyler have wheeled up to the back of the car. Herbert fixes a metal strap around the battery. With pliers and wrench an eyebolt is attached to the metal strap.

Pulling the eyebolt and strap up with a tug of the hand, "Let me know if you have problems lifting it up there," Herbert says to the two of them. "And I want you to pour some water on the battery and then dry it off with a rag before you bring it up there."

"You spill any of the battery water on you? Go inside and wash your hands as soon as you can, all right?"

Herbert stops Howard from starting off with the wagon until he acknowledges him.

"Hey you. The stuffs got sulfuric acid in it. It burns 'ya if you spill some on skin, and then leave it there too long."

Howard looks up to his father with quick nods of his head.

After a birthday dinner's dessert of pineapple upside down cake and mint ice cream, Howard was presented with the *Zenith* AM-FM radio kit. Three weeks after opening the box Howard had everything put together and into a working, functional radio. The radio has brought a mild, pleasant odor of burned electrical components into his bedroom. Lying down on his bed and listening to the voice of the broadcaster of local radio station WKZO makes him feel quite proud indeed.

Inviting his mother into his bedroom one afternoon, together they watch the wonder of it all. Three large glass vacuum tubes began to glow orange-blue as electricity heats the small, thin metal filament plates inside. The flow of electrons warm all the components of the radio, each vacuum tube eventually brought to its proper electrical function. Crackles of static electricity resonate from the speaker. Howard turns the dial to have his mother hear the different stations. Reverberations of intelligible voice and a steady stream of musical notes sound out from the speaker.

So many electrical components and systems working together fascinated Howard, begging him for questions to understand how it all is even possible, fundamentally. Both Jeff and Howard had the knack for finding things around the house to take apart. Herbert and Rose saw this somewhat destructive though natural inquisitiveness, and thought it good to spur along and encourage their imagination and curiosity.

Dry-cell batteries for the radio became expensive to replace. Herbert thought of a project which would keep the cost of powering the radio to a minimum.

Before the Rural Electrification Administration brought a source of electricity into large sections of the United States, farms would use propeller driven windmills to perform certain farm tasks such as pumping water out of ground wells, and to turn an electric generator to supply a modest source of electricity for various utilities.

"Show me you know how to step down the twelve volt car battery to have it work with your nine volt radio," Herbert tells Howard one day, "and we'll use the battery from the car to run your radio with. I'll keep the battery instead of taking the discount of a trade-in when I buy a new one. And we'll think about putting a windmill somewhere up there on the roof of the tree fort, to recharge the battery with."

"Think we can do it, Howard?"

Herbert put Jeff to task in a similar way before he spent the money for lumber materials to build the tree fort in the backyard. Herbert had Jeff draw out some rough dimensions for the tree fort, motivating him to collect his thoughts and sketch his ideas to paper. Several evenings brought Jeff out from his bedroom to present his father with still another detailed drawing describing another different design he wants included to the tree fort. Jeff kept all the paper drawings inside a folder.

One page described the single slant to the roof. Another drawing with an arch built into the roof, and the decision was made to build a flat roof for reasons of lower cost and simplicity. There were pages of drawings describing different rope and pulley systems alongside an opening to the wall of the tree fort. Other pages detailing a hinged hatch that was to cover the square holed entranceway cut from the floor of the tree fort. The tree fort itself was sketched being supported onto the three different lengths of tree branches. This initial set of designs became more detailed and simplified as time went on. The paper drawings allowed a rough estimate to be made for the amount of lumber materials required to construct the tree fort.

"It's all mathematics, Jeff," Herbert remembers. "To design something sturdy and strong you have to realize a little mathematics will be involved. It's the language they use when they design the dams, bridges, and the tall buildings of Chicago and New York."

Herbert remembers walking along the path in the woods and Jeff had quizzed him, asking him what he thought was the most stable and strongest geometric solid. Was it the sphere, the cube, or a tetrahedron?

Oftentimes felt the day will come when he'll also hear himself say something similar to Howard. Something along the line of, *Mathematics is the language you'll want to learn.* The notion to relate this bit of advice to Howard impresses itself upon Herbert from time to time. For seemingly little reason the intimation follows Herbert, pronouncing its presence for a few moments during any given day.

When Herbert was in grade school he read a book on the pyramids of Egypt. The book illustrated through graphic pictures and clever words the size, weight, and composition of the large and very heavy square, stone blocks the pyramids were constructed with. With decades of time and through the efforts of tens of thousands of people working nonstop day after day, raw stone was quarried from the ground, meticulously carved to shape, then transported over land and sea eventually to be placed onto the pyramid. The book went on to tell a story of how itinerant people traveling by caravan saw the top triangular tip of a completed pyramid off the horizon. Not knowing what the object is, curiosity brings them closer. The distant triangular object grows large above the sandy horizon, rising high into the sky. Eventually the troupe stands on top of a sand dune to view the entire, gargantuan solid blocks of stone structure a short distance away.

How awestruck, how impressed people traveling new to the land must have been observing a pyramid for the first time, and then to imagine to themselves what type of people live in the land they're now passing through.

What kind of gods do these people know? What type of leader rules a land such a this?

Thoughts of this type must surely have crossed the wayfaring mind. The book left an impression on the young Herbert, so much so that when a school assignment called for him to write a paper, the pyramids of Egypt was the topic. He now reads more into the life and times of the people living in these earliest of recorded histories, and to discover these simple-looking pyramid structures were designed on fairly complex geometric proportions and ratios.

The ruling classes of pharaohs, priests, and sages living in these times believed mathematical thoughts to be a portal into the realm where their gods bring the forces causing all the different types of everyday happenings and odd phenomena to occur on the earth. As these ancient people came to see and understand the world, every event, whether it be the raindrop falling to the ground, the thunderclap and lightning in the clouds, or the waves breaking on the shores of the sea, their gods are using the simple and esoteric mathematical and geometrical properties as the mechanisms and methods which cause these natural events to occur.

The pharaohs, priests, and sages reasoned to themselves that if they were to study and develop a better understanding to all the mathematical and geometrical concepts and principles their gods are using to make things happen all over the earth, and if they were to then employ these mathematical and geometric properties into their own constructions, causing things like pyramids to exist, they themselves would be imitating and thus become more like the gods they revered. Inspired by their religious beliefs and studied by their sages, Herbert came to realize these early Egyptian civilizations had discovered some of the universal geometric and mathematical principles used by people today. The Land of the Pharaohs became an interesting set of facts to write about.

A question asked and left unanswered from this one book Herbert had read was how early Egyptians placed the large and heavy blocks of stone one on top of the other, doing so all the way to the very top of a pyramid? How did they move those heavy blocks up there without modern cranes lifting, and steam or diesel engines to push and pull everything here and there? The book had stated that no one really knew. People only guess how these tasks were accomplished. Herbert conjectured in his report that they possibly constructed sleeves around each large square block of stone, transforming square shape into cylindrical form before it was rolled onto and then off the barges, and eventually rolled up the ever growing sides of a pyramid to be set in place.

Herbert was impressed and came to respect the subject of mathematics more than other courses he took at school. Doing well in all subjects throughout his school years he had no desire to pursue an academic life in later years. After high school he took a job as a deputy sheriff of Van Buren County.

Soon Howard will show his father a hand drawn schematic to a step-down transformer that will link the twelve-volt battery to his radio. Howard's schematic has the word *rheostat* written onto it.

After dumping a bucket of soapy water over the battery, scrub brushing the thing down, Howard dusts the battery with the half a cup of baking soda mother had given him. Howard and Tyler watch the mounds of bubbles form around both terminals of the battery. A few minutes later and another bucket of water is poured over the battery. Howard then pulls and steers as Tyler pushes the wagon around to the side of the house, rolling the wagon into the backyard and through an opening along the stone wall. The wagon rolls over ruts and sticks and rocks that lay along the path of the forest, up the slope and towards the large rock elm tree.

"I'll climb up and let the rope down," Tyler says. Howard maneuvers the wagon directly below the hoist and then waits for Tyler to climb the tree.

A hoist was one of the first things built up into the tree. It raised most of the material used to build the fort. Different brackets to support the hoist against the side of the fort, a two-pulley system and a better rope were added over the course of time, making the hoist stronger and more efficient to use.

After the tree fort was built the hoist is seldom used. Perhaps a jug of Kool-Aid and a package of snacks for when they'll want to spend an overnighter up inside it, or just to hoist books or magazines. Without the hoist the heavy car battery would have been difficult to bring up by themselves.

Tyler allows the circle of rope to fall out from the ledge. Howard lifts the hook at the end of the rope and inserts it through the eyebolt. Tyler pulls the rope through the pulley until all the slack is removed and the rope is taut in his hands. A straight line of rope extends down from the tree fort to the battery.

Tyler attaches three individual ten-pound lead weights onto the rope, and then pulls down on the rope. The battery down below is on the verge of rising though Tyler releases his grip and attaches another ten-pound weight to the rope. Tyler will continue to add weights and pull down on the rope until he thinks he's added enough weight to the rope allowing him to raise the battery up with ease.

"How many did you put on?" Howard yells up to Tyler as the battery lifts off the wagon.

"Six!"

The battery swings arches through the air and *six times ten* is the notion for how heavy the battery is.

"Make sure it doesn't get away from you!" Howard yells up to Tyler.

Both arms pull down on the rope, and there's a bit of effort on Tyler's part. The pulleys outside turn and squeak with each tug on the rope. The battery rises higher, eventually to have the six lead weights clanking down upon the ground and the battery sliding alongside the wall of the tree fort.

Howard grabs hold of the rope and places both feet down upon the pile of weights. Tyler pulls down on the rope, and he's unable to raise and then hold the battery up to place it on the ledge.

"Hey, it's not all the way up! You have to pull down some more!"

Howard raises his arms and grabs the rope above his head. The full weight of his body pulls the rope down, and the battery rises up above the ledge.

"Hold on to it!" Tyler yells down.

"Just hurry up!" Howard yells to Tyler.

Tyler steps out onto the platform. Taking hold of a free hook and chain attached to the beam of the hoist, Tyler inserts the hook inside the eyebolt of the battery, then pulling the chain taut, inserting a single link of the now taut chain through a slot of metal and locking the hook and the chain to the beam. The hoist now holds the battery up in front of the ledge.

"OK, it's on!"

Howard brings himself upright and the rope slips through his hands. He removes three of the six ten pound weights from the rope on the ground. The three weights are brought up and the rope is tossed back down. With the second thirty pounds of weight reattached and on its way up, Howard begins to climb the tree.

Wooden blocks nailed as steps and hand holds at certain heights along the trunk of the tree, climbing the tree has become more a physical exercise and less the personal challenge it once was. He'll take an occasional, really deep breath or two as he stands and looks around for a moment, ... again to realize just how high off the ground he is.

Howard has stopped for the most part believing he'll somehow slip and fall, hitting every branch on the way down. Not scared to climb to the tallest heights in the tree though there are times his body still seems to behave as if it's the first time he's climbing the tree. His body reacts to the perceived danger such heights place him in. Whenever he looks down his palms begin to sweat. The heart beats faster and rougher inside his chest.

Having climbed the tree so many times in the past his senses are sharp. His body is coordinated to all the maneuvers needed at each level of the climb. Without thought reflexively gripping the branch like so and stepping forward, leaning himself over a branch before raising himself up. The knee is upon a branch, reaching for the length of board above his head, he pulls himself up to stand on the branch.

His feet have stepped for balance upon two branches. One hand is placed on a branch above. The other hand grips a branch at the waist. He'll recognize the sense of balance he wants and needs to boost himself while raising his foot up alongside the hand that grips the branch.

A keen sense for every grip of hand upon a familiar length of branch, and the awkward placement of a foot now angled inside that odd crook of branches. It's all familiar. The movements having been thought out and done before. Every position he puts himself into, every effort now lifting him higher are the most efficient regarding time and energy spent. Past practice has made this an almost perfect second climb of the day.

Howard climbs up through the floor of the tree fort and steps to the ledge and the battery suspended near Tyler's feet.

"Maybe bring some of the rope in and lift the battery up a little," Tyler suggests.

Several arm lengths of rope are drawn up inside the fort and after a couple turns around the hand Howard pulls down on the rope. The battery won't rise up off the chain.

"Wait. Let me get into a better position."

Howard leans back against the wall and with the weight of his body he's able to pull the rope around the pulley. Tyler slips the link of the chain up and out from the slot and the battery is brought down upon the ledge. They slide the battery to the edge of the platform and remove the metal strap.

Howard lifts the battery from the platform. Two foot steps allow him to place the battery inside the shallow metal pan lying next to the radio.

A familiar voice calls to them through the walls of the tree fort.

"Howard! Are you up there? Tyler?"

"Aww, no. Not now."

"What's your mother want?"

"Probably supper time."

Howard and Tyler step to the ledge.

"OK, mom! In a minute. Coming down."

Mrs. Soldier stands at the stonewall.

"Tyler Marsh, the two of you come down and wash up. Foods on the table. Ten minutes."

Tyler leans out upon the ledge and looks up to the seven three foot long blades of the wind mill spinning between two large branches of the tree.

"The wind is turning the blades," Tyler suggests. "I'll turn the generator on."

"Yeah, yeah, yeah," Howard says, containing his excitement. He steps to the shelf and clamps the wires from the generator and the radio to the battery terminals.

Tyler flicks a switch on the wall and a modest electrical current is brought to the battery.

The radio is turned on and static interference soon rises up from the speaker. Scanning through the frequency range, the volume of static interference is more pronounced.

Howard mimics an imagined passage in Mary Shelley's book, *Frankenstein*.

"Doctor Tyler, the monster, ... it is alive. Alive!"

Clear reception from three new stations are tuned in and heard before the dial is brought to station WXYZ's 1270 kilohertz frequency. An unintelligible male voice is heard inside the crackling sounds of static. Turning the dial from station WXYZ to the far end of the dial, Howard then quickly scans back through the frequencies to the other end of the dial.

A look through the opening and outside the tree fort to realize the sun is setting low to the horizon.

"Let's go eat and then come back before it gets too dark."

Walking along the path back to the house, "I'm going to have to call my Mom. Ask her if I can stay," Tyler says.

"You boys get that thing working?" Rose asks at the dinner table.

"Yes, Mrs. Soldier. Got the battery hooked up to it. A lot of static though ... now that the sun is going down."

—|—

The electron has been on Howard's mind the last several days. An idea of a very small particle that acts like one of the planets in the solar system. All these small particle-like planets spin really fast round and around the nucleus of the atom. This is how electrons are described.

No books at the library in town delved into the subject of electrons per se. The books that did mention electrons simply repeat a similar paragraph or two of ideas about them before changing the subject. Most all the books simply repeat the same set of basic ideas about electrons as did the beginning paragraph to a chapter in one of Jim's textbooks.

Howard lies on his bed and reads with little comprehension of the subject matter. The symbols for *coulombs of charge* and *Henries of induction* are recognized immediately. Many new and different symbols of notation for electrical properties present themselves upon the pages he turns to.

Some pages have pictures and diagrams that are interesting to look at. His interest remains for a time, though eventually he turns a page and his eyes only scan across the page. Eventually he's skipping through and skimming pages only to look for any pictures.

It's typical of Jim's textbooks to do this. Howard expects any textbooks to have that mathematical language inside it. Math slams the door to his imagination, causing him to stop following along with whatever is being conveyed.

"What you reading?" Herbert asks Howard from the bedroom door.

A resigned shrug of the shoulders and, "Just a book."

Herbert sits down on the bed, to realize the book is one of Jim's college textbooks.

"Just a book? You looking for something in there or just trying to understand it a little?"

Placing the book to his side and propping himself up on one arm, Howard says to his father, "I don't know. How does the electron, ... how does it? How does something so small make something happen so far away so fast?"

Herbert looks confounded. "With the radio you mean?"

"Yeah. It's the oscillator that makes the electrons swerve like, to make a wave, like a wave of water in a puddle, ... from the antennae out into space."

Amusing when it happens: listening to the mental acrobatics of one trying to sort things out.

"It's like that?" Herbert says.

Howard concentrates to articulate the thought as best he can.

"It's like if..., if you throw a stone—" A shake of the head to dismiss the thought.

"Throw an electron is what I meant to say, and no matter how or where you throw it all the other electrons near wherever this electron gets thrown gets effected and thrown around with it too. You don't even have to touch the other electrons and they go flying."

The sweetness of light.

"Sounds kinda wild down there," Herbert remarks. "That book helping any?"

"A little ... sort of," Howard says matter-of-factly, and then resigns with, "Not really."

"Let me look."

The title of the book is, *Introduction to Physics: For the Civil Engineer.* Skimming through a number of pages, eventually turning to the back of the book and referencing inside the index for the word *Electron*. The index cites one page, and Herbert turns to the page.

Electrical phenomena are represented by symbols. The symbols represent the commonly known and understood qualities found in electrical phenomena. These symbols are the words in a mathematical language that can be arranged and manipulated to allow one person to convey concise ideas and thoughts of electrical phenomena to another person.

Perhaps one needs to realize a specific property or condition to include in the design and construction of a specific type of motor, a magnetic switch, a generator, or a type of light system that may be needed, or for any electrical appliance or system someone realizes they may need and require for a particular task. Mathematical equations and symbols pepper almost every descriptive step for constructing all the electrical devices mentioned page after page within the book Howard has been looking through.

"If you really want to understand these things?" Herbert suggests. "If radios and electrical stuff isn't gonna be just some kind of passing hobby with you, you'll have to know and be able to talk mathematically. To someday know mathematics and use it as easily and clearly with others as you're now using words in English to express yourself with."

Herbert flips through the pages of the textbook and takes a moment to gather his thoughts.

Western science has constructed marvelous things. So many new discoveries have been made in the last few centuries, opening the doors to novel though narrower avenues of thought. Herbert knows that before these new discoveries were made public, people used the tools of mathematics to pry them out of…

… out of the gods, he thinks with a grin.

"Of all the sciences like chemistry or physics, mathematics is referred to by some as the queen of the sciences. Without her none of those other scientists could've discovered and explained as much as they did."

Howard listens as his father speaks with enthusiasm.

"Just think if you could understand all these mathematical terms, and then to realize what all these mathematical statements are saying. Imagine the tools you would have to build with then. The tools you'd have to describe to yourself and to others exactly how a transceiver over there in Detroit or Chicago cause the electrons to do something so quickly to the electrons your receiver picks up over here."

He gets up off the bed to leave the room.

"Howard, if you want to understand it," turning to look at his son from the doorway, "you'll have to start taking more math courses at school. It's the language they use, plain and simple."

Not Two Axes But Three

A ring of the telephone and the electric beater is brought out from the metal pot of half-mashed potatoes. Paddles spin to a stop against the countertop.

"I'll get it," Amy intones for anyone who may be thinking to otherwise. Grabbing a hand towel to wipe her hands with, "Gotta check the bread, Mom."

From downstairs I heard the interrupted second ring of the telephone.

"Hello?"

"Yes, hello. I'm Claudia Wittels. Kurt's biology teacher from John Jay Senior High. Is one of his parents there I could speak to for a moment?"

"Uhm? Yes, my mother is here. Hold on, please?"

Muffling the phone against herself, "Mom, Kurt's biology teacher wants to talk to one of his parents?"

"Yes, hello."

"Hello. Mrs. Soldier, I'm Claudia Wittels. Kurt's biology teacher from John Jay. Do you have a free moment? I have to discuss an assignment your son turned in recently. I can call back later if it'd be more convenient?"

Scanning the kitchen, and listing tasks and things to do, "Please, go ahead."

"I'll be as brief as I can. I give each of my students an opportunity to earn extra credit towards their final grade. An easy assignment to pick a topic, any topic in biology and then write about it."

"I mention this to all my freshmen and sophomore students at the beginning of the school year. It can help me to identify early on and then to become more familiar with any of the other, better students I may have in their junior and senior years, for college recommendations."

Ms. Wittels pauses for thought.

" 'K, Kurt turned in a report a couple weeks ago and it's this report of his I'm calling about. He titled the paper a Treatise on the Nature of Life. I have to talk to you and your husband together about something that's happened, or that I think may be happening."

"Talk to us about what?"

"Well, reading his report, this treatise of his, and I allowed others here at the school to look at it too. I wanted some opinion on what he'd written. A little peer review if you will."

"The last several days we've become ...? Oh, how should I say this? Without sounding unprofessional, or strange in some way."

"Some of us are? We're quite taken aback. Personally, I'm stunned."

The notion the person on the other end of the phone may be one of Kurt's friends, and Moms closes her eyes, turning her head with a silent, indignant chuckle.

"Is this some kind of joke?" Moms asks.

"No, not at all," Ms. Wittels explains. "We should probably get together and talk about what he's written."

"Talk about what?" Moms says.

"A number of things. I'll take neither you nor your husband have read what I'm referring to? You haven't read this treatise of his have you?"

"No, I myself haven't. I'm sure neither one of us has."

"If both of you would read it, we'll then be on the same footing, more than less. I really won't be able to discuss things with you until then."

"Spell your last name, please. And a number where can I reach you?"

Writing name and number on a pad of paper by the phone, "All right, Claudia. I have that. We'll both take a look at it with him tonight. We don't usually get as involved with his school work as..., perhaps it's time we did."

" 'K, and after you've read it I think you'll be able to better understand that ...? Kurt there's let a couple of curious cats out of the bag."

The comment adds another peculiarity to the conversation.

"Claudia, would you perhaps tell me what my son's grade average would be right now?"

"Yes, sure. If all his test scores were averaged right at this moment he'd receive a 73 for a final grade. I haven't yet used his report in the average here though."

"Some mischief, then—"

"Oh no, no. What he wrote, and his conclusions inside the treatise. It is a very interesting line of thought."

"Mrs. Soldier, did you and your husband attend university?"

The question is a little too personal for the moment.

"I think—" Moms begins to say, and intending to change the subject. Quick afterthought and the question seems to imply something exemplary about the both of them, and her intention for asking benign.

"Excuse me," Ms. Wittels interrupts. "I'm only curious. What your son wrote could possibly serve as premise to a thesis of some kind. I imagine if properly mentored it could be so. I myself would also like to have a better idea for how much explaining I'll have to do so the both of you can appreciate what he wrote, and help."

"I'll take your asking as a compliment," Moms says.

"My husband is with IBM, an electrical engineer. I was as a nurse for several years at a hospital in Michigan before we married and moved to New York."

"OK," Ms Wittels replies. "I don't think you'll have trouble following the train of thought to what he wrote. After you and your husband have read it over I think it's important that you call back. We'll then be on the same footing when we talk."

"OK," Moms replies. "We'll talk to him and read it after dinner."

"Twenty pages shouldn't take too long. I'll be home all evening if you wish to talk tonight."

"Yes, sometime tonight then. That'll be fine."

With mittened hands Amy slides the rack with the roast outside the oven door. Moms puts a pair of mittens on and they lift the pan from the rack and place it on the counter.

"What'd the teacher want?"

"She wants your father and I to read some thing he wrote for class, and then call her back."

A look of concern, "A teacher calling on a Saturday isn't exactly...," and Amy lets the sentence trail off, hoping Moms will say more.

The bread timer rings.

"She said your brother let some cats, some curious cats out of the bag," and to this Moms and Amy give an eyebrow squinting, head turning glance to one another.

"What does that mean, 'cats out of the bag?"

Moms will think of something analogous.

"If I had some treasure of gold hidden somewhere, and I told you where it was hidden, let's say so you could go and have some? Supposing as I told you where the gold was hidden someone else was also listening to what I told you. This person now knows the secret too, and I didn't want that to be, so the cat is out of the bag as some would say."

Moms sprinkling spoonfuls of flour into the simmering broth in the pan on the stove, circular motions thicken the liquid to gravy. Amy removes the bread pan from the top oven, stepping down from the stool to place it upon the counter.

"During medieval times people would sell little piglets in burlap bags at market stalls. Dishonest vendors sometimes put a stray cat in the bag and have the person take this instead of what they thought would be a little pig. If some buyer happened to be suspicious of the actual contents and looked inside a bag, well, the person now knows and ... the cat was out of the bag."

Amy places the loaf of hot, baked bread upon the countertop.

"I'll go tell them guys to come upstairs in a few minutes."

Festus throws the die across the game board.

"Three to one, come on...!" and Festus explodes to the roll of a one facing up on the die.

"Yahoo! Yes!" he shouts with a laugh and claps of his hands. Festus has broken through a defensive position I'd set up along the road to Bastogne. He picks my two cardboard infantry pieces up off the game board and throws them into the cardboard tray, and it's onto another battle.

Three of my brother's fingertips deliberately grapple themselves as if mechanically upon the die. A steady motion to raise his hand until his wrist, arm, and elbow slant at about a forty-five degree angle with the game board.

"Pink elephants," I say to the dropping die tumbles, hoping it brings me luck to the battle.

A six faces up, which is good for me and my side in that it requires his twice as large attacking forces to retreat from their attacking positions two hexagonal board squares back. My troops on a hill in a forest have at the moment just fought off and repelled a force twice as large as itself, but I'll be pulling these guys back in retreat anyway, in a minute, next turn. Festus obliterated those troops that were stationed alongside these victorious ones. Next turn he'll surround and then destroy these guys if I don't do something with them.

The last of the attacks for his turn is on the other side of the game board in the town of St. Vith, and again my troops are being attacked by an almost overwhelming three to one force. I stay with the pink elephants jinx to the die as it's thrown onto the game board, and luck again with a six facing up, this result requiring my attacked units to pull back two board squares in retreat.

I take a moment to survey the situation within the immediate area around St. Vith, and I decide to take these retreating troops out from the town itself and disperse them into the surrounding countryside. Pushed out of town they are but they are still in full strength, not obliterated like what just happened to those guys down by Bastogne two die rolls ago.

Festus has concluded twenty-four hours of offensive maneuvers. All his battle results have been determined, and it is now my turn for movement of my own game pieces. I take some time to look at and reevaluate a fifty mile line of both his and my own troop positions and strengths situated on a game board map of southwest Belgium.

Festus has brought a number of infantry and armored divisions north in the region near St. Vith, where forests and hills are everywhere and the few roads in this area are all twists and turns. Travel will be slow for him in this terrain. Most of his better armored and infantry divisions are driving west into the forest and hills of the Ardennes as they attempt to recapture and hold the town of Namur. Festus is attempting a different strategy than what the German Army followed during the Ardennes Offensive of December and January, 1944-1945.

If the German Army can drive a force of infantry and tanks through Belgium and to the city of Antwerp within the next four freezing cold weeks of late December and early January they'll have driven a wedge into and through the bulk of Allied forces that are quickly retaking France from them during the Second World War. By the middle of January estimated petrol supplies the Germans carried to drive all their mechanized vehicles will be used up. If they can't refuel those armored vehicles by early January, especially refuel all those tanks they've brought into this conflict, the German offensive is determined to have stalled, and eventually to have failed. One important military objective the German commanders had was to take possession of any Allied fuel supplies they hoped to find stored in areas expected to be overrun.

The game Festus and I are playing attempts to recreate a late period of the Second World War when the German Luftwaffe cannot put and keep airplanes in the air for extended lengths of time. At this late stage in the war any attempted use of aircraft by the Luftwaffe in any one particular area of battle is quickly challenged by a concentrated force of Allied aircraft, and in short order German aircraft are not able to fly into the area of battle with further expectations for completing their objectives.

If weather permits, and for the next and final five, six months of the war the Allies are placing their aircraft for the most part anywhere they chose, and they're able to continue tactical air superiority over any region for as long as necessary to destroy intended targets or to support their ground troop movements.

Historically, this German offensive our game is recreating began on December 16, 1944. On December 23, after seven long days of offensive battle Festus's armor and infantry take the first punches from the air when weather made it possible for Allied aircraft to fly into this area of Belgium. By January 3, The Allies have brought themselves back up to strength and into counterattack mode, and several days after January 3 the German Army is in full retreat with some of their forward units five miles from the Meuse River and the city of Namur.

These are the objectives of this game then: if you're the German player you have a short two, at most three week time to penetrate fifty, sixty miles into Allied controlled territory and then to cross the Meuse River at the city of Namur, which is about seventy miles south of Antwerp. Do this and the game rules say you win the game. If you are the Allied player, sometime during the game you have to stop the German expectations for putting forces across the Meuse River and recapturing the city of Namur, and you win the game.

Up north near St. Vith luck has been with me. Incurring casualties in battle, steadily losing ground and retreating as expected but I have not lost the ability to regroup and maintain a defensive line. I think with a modest amount of luck I'll hold and keep any of his offensive movements in the north to a minimum.

One realizes after playing these type of Avalon Hill war games for a while that there is more luck than tactical skill deciding battle results. The luck that results from the roll of a die that is.

I put my attention to the southern region of the game board. Mindful I am realizing again that if the town of Bastogne falls the one road to the town of Namur is wide open. The fifty miles of open road from Bastogne to Namur has little forest or mountain terrain to place forces inside of and for me to hinder Festus's potentially quick tank movement with. From my point of view if the junction of roads at Bastogne falls in the next couple of days I won't have the time to transport enough equipment and personnel over to and along this one road to Namur to establish effective defensive positions with. Any scattered units in the immediate area I could possibly round up and then put in front of Festus's armored divisions to slow them down somewhat for the next several days won't be alive twenty-four hours afterwards. In actuality I'm waiting for Patton's Third Army just south of here and any of Montgomery's reserves from the north to mobilize up to strength and transport themselves over to this area. It is imperative that I bottle up those tanks from zipping around or through Bastogne until all of these forces arrive a week, ten days from now.

I pull the 101st Airborne and the 10th Armored Divisions back, placing them inside and along the outskirts of Bastogne, like historically, and then bring the nearby pieces from the two-to-one retreat of last turn, along with other units to cover Bastogne's flanks. For the time being this is all the force I can muster up in defense of this critical juncture of roads.

As the Allied player of this game I am a commander who finds himself placed in a situation where my forces are initially caught uncoordinated to hold their defensive positions for any length of time. My divisions and battalions are tactically placed in a defensive manner inside forests, upon higher elevations and in the small towns contained within a fifty mile wide, sixty mile long region of Belgium. For the next ten, twenty days I will assemble these forces of mine and block a very large concentration of enemy infantry and tanks that are suddenly and quite unexpectedly presenting themselves into this area of Belgium. My objective is to hinder and to slow this very large force from wherever it may want to move to as it spreads itself out and along this fifty by sixty mile theater of operations I am responsible for.

Festus is in an offensive frame of mind during the game. Whatever routes he decides this large force of tanks and infantry he is commandeering are to take through the Belgian countryside, eventually and most assuredly he will bring them into contact with some large or small force of mine. This force of mine must now be quickly vanquished. Each day and with each mile he brings himself closer to the Meuse, and before I have time to collect these initially unprepared forces of mine together to present stronger and then ever more stubborn and time consuming resistance to his troops forward movement, Festus has to engage and then quickly destroy these forces of mine. This he has to do if he expects to accomplish his mission's objectives within an envelope of three or at most four weeks time.

From mid-December to the first weeks in January, for the German player the thought should be just to attack, using a brute force strategy to get his forces across the Meuse and securing those bridges in and around Namur.

"How did you get those pieces there?" Festus asks defiantly, pointing directly over the Salm River area north of the town of Gouvy. "Half movement through forest. You have to stop for the river."

He nudges my two infantry pieces back one hexagonal board square. Doing this he reveals that I had in fact stopped for the winding river like he thought I had not, but also bringing to my attention the fact that this forest area he has just pushed my pieces back into has a tiny bit of itself extending back into that board square he has just pushed me off of. I now realize I hadn't taken this little bit of forest terrain and count it as the two squares of movement required to move my troop piece through and then to occupy a forest square. These particular pieces of mine may not now end up situated close enough to prevent his free use of a certain nearby road they were alongside of, this consequently enabling him to use that road to more quickly advance forces into and then out from the town of St. Vith. For the moment this is not a good thing for me and my side.

Sliding the cardboard pieces in my hand along the three squares of the game board I want them to travel through, I move into and through the first square of open field and clear terrain to the edge of the forest square.

"One," I say with consternation, "two, three."

Two and three allow my pieces to move inside that one hexagonal forest square, and because I am now moving troops through a forest any numerical movement of my piece is halved as long as I remain inside forest terrain. I was about to say four, which is the total number of squares these pieces are allowed to move per turn, but the boundary of this forest square that I'm already inside of has that small portion of itself protruding through the borders and into that otherwise clear terrain river square that I want to be situated on. So I do not have the number of moves required to place these pieces into that square.

My mistake.

"You tried to cheat," Festus says to me.

I wanted those guys where I had them before, on the banks of the Salm River and alongside of that road. I saw them where I had them before I'd picked up and moved those pieces to that square ... just a minute ago. Seems like maybe I wanted those pieces over there on that there square a little too much then.

The basement is cool and damp. My brothers and I play any Avalon Hill war game on a picnic table in a windowless corner of the basement, and it's always fairly dark, quiet, and except for short breaks we will sometimes play a game nonstop for ten, fifteen hours straight. Time flies, and it's fun. I feel like I'm inside of a cave but what I think happens, my eyes fix themselves upon the same objects, hour after hour. The same glaring, bright, high-intensity lamp-lit flashes of light that will quickly reflect off the glossy game board as I move to sit or stand, perhaps two or three empty soda cans lie off to the side of the game board, or a half-full glass bowl of cereal sits with the smell of milk and Cap'n Crunch. The cores of apples or the peach pits and orange peels that lay for hours on the table. Any objects lying around the top of the picnic table constantly present themselves bright, so that when I go upstairs for a few minutes to do something or when I simply refocus my eyes off into any of the dark, distant objects that are also down here in the basement, I can feel the strain around my eyes. The muscles of my face are tense. It's stressful to play these games. It is.

There's also another, second type of tax on the brain that sometimes happens while playing these games. Some type of total mental fatigue presents itself and sets in so that I don't even see the obvious scribble of a typographical feature denoting the edge of the border to a forest square on the game board. Because if I did see that little patch of forest terrain inside that there hexagonal square, my mind simply did not register what it was all about.

Across the table Festus has a smug look on his face as he waits for my response.

Crossed eyes and clenched teeth, my words are cued for a theatric response.

"So what is wrong with cheating!?"

Festus smirks and looks down to study the game board.

I am fairly certain of myself, and I am fairly confident neither of my brothers will break the rules to any of these war games we'll play. Rather an imagined sense of realism prevails. Perhaps, for a moment, the smell of an unfamiliar odor is now in the air of the basement. The smell of burning rubber, or corn, a moment where the basement air smells of antique furniture, and the presence of these odors occur as I sit or stand hunched over the game board. With my arm brusquely brushing up inside what I can imagine to be the starched and heavy woolen shirtsleeve I wear, I'm sliding the two stacks of three fingernail-sized cardboard pieces up alongside the northwest borders of a town. I'll stand upright and, while I consider the ramifications for placing these troops where I have, and perhaps I'm satisfied with this decision. I can imagine turning towards a subordinate, saying, "I want the 10th Armored Division there within twenty-four hours, and—"

I now imagine the sound of a door being opened and then hearing it slam shut. The sound of footsteps approaching me. My mind's eye looks towards the silhouette of a person moving inside some shadows of darkness. The silhouette grows large, to stand in front of me, then saluting me. The silhouette extends an arm and hand with a folded piece of paper towards me. I take hold of the paper, unfold it, and it's a message from Headquarters. The message informs me General Patton will have a preliminary force from his Third Army arriving in this regions within the next forty-eight to seventy-two hours, and not within the week to ten days as I've been expecting. Good news, indeed.

The hobby store only stocks the Avalon Hill line of war games. Over the years my brothers and I have collected the games *1914, Afrika Korps, D-Day, Gettysburg, Guadalcanal, Jutland, Midway,* and *Stalingrad.*

All but the game Jutland came with a folding cardboard game board. Game boards of others portray the topographical features of land or ocean during whatever particular time of battle or military conflict a game reenacts. Jutland depicts naval warfare during the First World War, and we use the wide open basement floor and a three foot long yardstick to measure off and scale down the hundreds and the thousands of yards of distance to scale the actual battle situations. The game board for the game 1914 centered on the border between France and Germany from the North Sea to the northern borders of Italy. Afrika Korps' game board drew hexagonal squares all over the coastal roads and cities and mountain ranges a hundred miles inland along the Mediterranean Sea of North Africa. The game board for Guadalcanal depicted the island's jungle, mountain, and coastal terrain. Gettysburg game board depicted approximately twenty-five square miles of land surrounding the Pennsylvanian city.

Perhaps neither Casimir Pulaski during the American Revolutionary War nor Ulysses S. Grant during the American Civil War saw or used objects such as thumbnail-sized cardboard squares depicting theirs and the enemy's positions on a situational map during actual battles. Though I can believe that the eyes of that fox Erwin Rommel had done so, as did those of John "Black Jack" Pulaski and General William C. Westmoreland. Now my eyes stare down upon a similar map and I will observe the changing positions and strengths of military units as they unfold in real time.

The sense of realism, fleeting and only glimpsed in the mind's eye as I look upon a game board, ... of being in the shoes and wearing the cap of someone who was responsible for directing a very significant military campaign in the past. A campaign that, oh? I'm with Alexander the Great, and we're moving through Kashmir, ... I'm standing with my fellow Princes all along the watchtower, ... and when the blitzkrieg raged and the bodies stank, perhaps after months of my own personal military leadership as I was coordinating the moment by moment activities of a large military campaign, it was I who can claim responsibility for causing the results which brought the French and not the English language to have become dominant and spoken within the United States of today. I'm sure it is with these type of thoughts conjured in the back of my own and I suppose my brother's minds, creeping in for a moment or two and allowing us to imagine being there. Yes, this is what brings these war games to be as interesting as they are to play, and so it seems that to deliberately break any rule of a game simply to bring some inconsequential, momentary advantage over an opponent, such thoughts don't even enter my mind anymore.

Amy calls down to us from the top of the stairwell.

"Hey you guys, we're eating in a couple minutes."

Festus picks his face up from stacked clenched fists at the edge of the game board, and then leans back in his chair and intones a German accent through the basement.

"Fraulein, listen. Understand that we don't need food now. We need beer. Bring us beer. Ja."

Her footsteps sound their way creaking through the wooden flooring above us as she winds her way through the hallway and back into the kitchen.

I finish my turn placing the 28th and 106th Divisions within a five, ten mile line of forest terrain near a stretch of road farther out from St. Vith, and I'm thinking over the next couple of days Festus will only be able to use that one single road through this area to transport troops into any offensive positions. All he will be able to muster up using that one road will be a force giving him at best a two-to-one advantage over any one of three separate group of pieces I have situated in this area.

The roll of a die determines who is victorious and who will be vanquished in any one battle. In the particular area around St. Vith, if a battle between an attacking German force twice as large as my defensive force happens to be determined by a die roll of a one or a two, then the rules say Festus won the battle, my men are going to heaven, and his troops get to advance forward.

Though if attacking at two to one odds and the roll of the die brings a six facing up then the rules say Festus has to turn his Panzer and Tiger tanks around a hundred-eighty degrees and start running in retreat because my troops are smacking the bejesus out of his troops over there. I'm being attacked by a force twice as large as I am and for some reason the rules say because of the die roll of a six I should and will win the battle. Perhaps the reason is because I've a handful of really smart captains and lieutenants in these particular battalions, and a number of brave sergeants are giving extraordinary effort to outmaneuver his troops hour after hour, ripping up his tanks with bazookas and tank destroyers and giving the most stubborn kind of battle to anything that wants to travel this particular road leading out of St. Vith that day.

If next turn he determines the outcome of a battle with a roll of a three, four, or a five at two-to-one odds then the rules say I have to remove half of my units he's attacking from the game board and I retreat the remaining units two squares back from wherever they're positioned.

The German player soon realizes the non-decisive type of engagements are the bane for actualizing his military objectives. The consequent loss of precious time and irreplaceable war material inherent with any one single particular engagement is such that if the outcome of any battle did not allow Festus to move closer to the Meuse, than this brings his already tenuous military objective to be seen as even more futile as time goes on.

Festus has to win those battles he puts any of his forces into. He has to maintain forward movement. His turn being twelve hours, my turn being twelve hours, the two together make up one day. Taking a full day or longer to allow movement of additional troops and equipment into an area before initiating a conflict may be the wise thing to do, sometimes, for some engagements. Though if you're the German player and plan to win this game definitely do not develop a tactical habit of waiting and hesitating practically any confrontation, because you'll definitely lose the game.

Time is on my side, not his. Festus doesn't have the luxury of time to always bring forward and maneuver additional troops into ideal flanking positions, and attempting to outmaneuver and or outnumber every confrontation he'll find himself wanting to engage in. Each battle situation is unique with its own set of strengths and weaknesses to make note of but if he does decide to stay in one area and build a concentrated force over a period of time, or to take the time to set himself up and into better positions from which to attack from, well, I can always order my troops to simply stand their ground and have them weather a storm. I may lose these pieces twelve hours from now but I've probably gained something too. Perhaps Festus is not able to surround other nearby units, or he's not allowed to cut off their retreat. Sometimes I have to sacrifice pieces to realize a greater military objective. That means sometimes ordering troops to hold their positions at all costs ... which means I'm probably ordering some guys to their death within the next twenty-four hours.

In past games I've created holes by pulling portions of an Allied defensive line back five or ten miles, doing this to prevent a German player from generating a string of those crippling three-to-one or higher odds in a twelve hour period, thereby saving those pieces for the time being but also losing the entire game in the process. I made a decision and then found out what can happen. Though by standing ground or by calculated, careful retreats, sometimes by counterattack, my objective is to slow Festus's troop movement until reinforcements arrive.

With my defensive objectives clear but unable to mobilize and establish an effective resistance to his blitzing forces, it doesn't take me long to put my pieces into position and to finish my turn. It's going to take Festus awhile to purview my new lines of defense, so I go on upstairs to wash my hands.

The aroma of cooked meat and potatoes inside the hallway makes my mouth water. I'm hungry, too, anticipating filling my stomach full of food as I turn the corner and look inside Max's room, stopping at the door to watch what he's doing. Sitting at his desk, the cardboard-tube fuselage of a new Estes model rocket is in his hand. He's trimming a stabilizing fin with an X-Acto knife as I walk up behind him.

Pictures on the open box and the printing on brochures spread out on the corner of the desk tell me it's a replica of the *Honest John* tactical rocket the U.S. Army built in the 1950s. I watch him slice slivers of balsa wood from a fin, sanding the leading edge smooth, then turning the fuselage to examine another fin.

"You're going to paint that one right?" I ask, thinking if he is he wants to keep it. He probably isn't going to deliberately try to wreck it later on.

Shrugging his shoulders and blowing dust off the rocket, "I don't know yet."

It's a good size rocket to shoot off. It's not a small, ordinary one.

"Time to eat, 'ya know?" I tell him, crossing the hallway to the bathroom.

I lather a bar of soap and water into my hands, and look at myself in the mirror, eventually to bring my eyes to focus upon the reflection of my nose in the mirror. My big nose. The day before yesterday two girls in English class were making fun of it. I couldn't understand what was happening at first.

I thought they were like new students or some other type of odd "things" that wander into class on any given day. They looked a little bit older than students, I'd thought later. The very first day they're in the class and they wanna start talking just to me, and then just like that the two of them start in on how big my nose is. I don't even know their names. Eventually they're singing *Rudolph the Red Nose Reindeer*, and asking me seriously if it was real or not. Telling me that it's not.

"Come on, let me touch it," one of them said, reaching a hand over near my face. They're faking laughter about it all too, like what they're saying and doing is supposed to be so funny or something. I could tell they were like actors on a stage now for some reason. They were almost scaring me the way they were talking to me, like they knew me or something.

"Hey, hear the joke about the two ditzy females," and I'm almost choking on those words for some reason. 'Cause I was scared, and more than a little nervous at them talking so much as they were to me. It was weird, I just blurted it out, and it must've put a monkey wrench into those two giggle machines because they both did simply shut up right after that. They started huddling with themselves, snickering to themselves till the class finally started. After class ended they went up and were talking to Mrs. Mulligan as I left the room. Yesterday and neither one came to class.

Last night I'd been looking at my nose for a good ten, fifteen minutes in the bathroom mirror here, and I came to the conclusion that it is kinda big. It's got this roundish sort of knob like right at the end of it. As far as I'm concerned I don't have to look at it. I'm either going to like it the rest of my life or I'm not going to like it the rest of my life, so I might as well learn to like it and move on. That's it.

"Top of the day, old chaps," I say stepping into the kitchen, walking then to stand in front of the pot roast on the counter.

"Pour the milk?" Moms says to me while uncovering the boiling pot of half a dozen ears of corn-on-the-cob on the stove.

"That's a big ten-four," I acknowledge her with. I get a gallon container of milk out of the refrigerator and start pouring it into the six glasses around the table.

Amy places a bowl of mashed potatoes across the table from me.

"I hope you made them a little lumpy and not totally smooth," I say to her. "Food smells great, Mom."

I hear the sliding glass door open in the TV room, and turn to watch Dad step inside.

Warm spring weather. The snow didn't really all totally melt until just about a week, ten days ago. It's about that time of year we'll see Dad outside all decked out in a knit skull cap, sweater and denim pants, leather boots and gloves, sometimes out there real early on a Saturday morning. With the twelve horsepower *WheelHorse ... of Course!* tractor hitched up to the wagon, it's time for a little physical exertion.

I watch him raking pine needles out of the grass or off the driveway and sidewalk. Trimming dead limbs from the pine trees in front of the house, breaking up any large limbs on the ground with a hatchet or ax. Gathering the leaves and branches and any of the small twigs that may have fallen to the ground during the winter into piles. Dad will leave piles in the front yard, and it's a reason for me and my brothers to hitch the trailer to the tractor anytime we're not doing anything. All these piles are eventually placed in the trailer and then driven anywhere out back by the creek. Let all the collected detritus rot and decay away in a few years. You could go out and do things with Dad anytime if you wanted to, but I don't think he really cares one way or another if anyone does or doesn't.

The change of season puts warmth back into the earth. All the plants and little microscopic bugs in the ground then wake up, revving up their metabolic processes to ingest, digest, and give off that subtle but unmistakable aroma of earth.

Dad bought the two and a half acres of land, one of the two largest tracts out of a cul-de-sac of seven property lots lining Val de Mar Drive. All the lots initially to be sold as undeveloped land. The Fishkill Creek marks the back to four of the seven properties. The Frampton's property lot is one of these other four, and their house is already built with a manicured lawn of green grass growing in front and down along one side of the house to the banks of the creek.

A bulldozer came one day and first thing it did after taking itself off the trailer was to plow down from the curb of Val de Mar Drive into what would become our driveway. Knocking down a couple dozen or more large conifers that were growing up in front, the bulldozer plows further down and out from the ground where the foundation of the house was to be laid. Less than a couple short hours of work are all it takes before the bulldozer crawls back onto its trailer and is driven away. Any more clearing and cleaning of the land is now done by the six of us.

A jungle it was, especially during the following spring and summer months. Long strong stringed vines tangled onto the ground or hanging from trees to pull out and away. Thick green hard to cut and hack through bushes and foliage growing practically everywhere from Val de Mar all the way back to the creek. Fallen logs need chain-sawing, half-dead trees were felled and there were stumps to be dug around then pulled out and burned.

Mosquitoes and large horseflies, swarms of 'em some times, all day long. The horseflies sometimes ferocious enough they'd fly inside my mouth while with both hands I'm straining, pulling on a branch or log. One time I was putting some power into the swing of an axe and just before the metal head hit the tree a horsefly zooms into my mouth and hit the back of my throat. This happened more than a couple of times in fact. I just spit 'em out.

While playing war games we may make flippant remarks to one another that we want and intend to kill something. Jocular moments between solemn, battling minds. Place a bloodsucking horsefly on the back of your neck or on the back of your arm for a third or fourth time in one day and I now realize what it feels like to experience the very real passion for hate, for once in my life, together with thoughts to cause some things bodily functions to cease functioning.

Some people have gone through an entire life never once having to have to put the two together in their mind …, and these events were years ago.

"Get a good workout, dear?" Moms asks from the kitchen.

Untying his boots, Dad looks her way, rolling his eyebrows up and smiling. He brings one of his boots above the waste basket, slapping the boot to dislodge any of the loose dirt or twigs and rocks that may have found there way inside, then doing the same thing to the other boot.

Dad motions with his hand for Moms to come over to where he is. He clasps each of her hands, then cups both hands around hers.

"Kurt's biology teacher called. She wants us to read something he wrote for class."

"Why?"

"Until we've read what he wrote she was a little hesitant to go into any kind of detail."

Dad's looking up towards her while squeezing and rubbing her hands.

"She said after we read it we should call her back."

"She wouldn't say why though."

"She was trying to tell me that until we read his report, his treatise, anything she would say over the phone wouldn't make much sense."

"His treatise? That's what she called it?"

"The name Kurt gave to it. A treatise on the nature of life."

Dad looks beyond Moms now to see Amy and I staring at them from inside the kitchen. We watch Dad stand up, cup Mom's head in his hands and then kiss her forehead. He puts his arms around her and then begins swaying her from side to side.

"You know that was your biology teacher Miss Wittels that called," Amy tells me, placing the individual forks and knives around each of the plates on the table, "She wants to talk with Mom and Dad again later on too."

"Why?"

"You wrote something. She wants them to read it and then call her back."

With melody in her words, *"You did something wrong."*

I look at Amy and I'm not sure what to say though I shake my head no. I can only think of the biology report I'd handed in a couple weeks ago, and she must be referring to that.

"Go call your brothers Kurt," Dad tells me as he moves his chair out from underneath the table.

I step into the hallway and yell, "Come on! We're eating!"

Less than a minute later and we're all seated at the table, with Moms saying grace.

"Bless us O Lord and these Thy gifts which we are about to receive through Thy bounty, through Christ our Lord. Amen."

Grinning towards my twin sister, I whisper, "Thanks are to God."

Moms takes a metal spoon off the table and from behind raps me on the top of my head. To this Amy begrudges a smirking laugh, nodding her head up and down as if I deserved it.

"What?" I say turning to Moms, rubbing my head, calmly pleading my case.

"Mom I really meant it this time."

"Amy, pass the plate of pickles, ... and the jar of mustard, please?"

—|—

Kurt Soldier
Living Environment - Biology
Ms. Wittels
April 1, 1984

A Treatise On The Nature Of Life

The above drawn diagram illustrates the Nature of Life. From the simple, primitive one-celled organisms, to plants, turtles, the praying mantis, and on to the human form, all forms of life operate under the parameters of pain and joy from a homeostatic metabolic state.

The physical processes necessary for primitive life are the ingestion of substances, converting these substances into useable forms of nutrient and chemical energy, and the expelling of waste product. Given a proper medium and habitat the lower forms of life carry out their metabolic processes in a manner that can be termed as homeostatic. The homeostatic state is designated as the area in between the objects above and below the horizontal line.

Archean prokaryotic and early eukaryotic molecular signals [1, 2, 3, 4] initiated genetic systems which monitored and regulated metabolic pathways during homeostatic periods of cellular stress and "indulgence."

Stress and symbiotic relationships are the precursors evolving neurological pain and joy [5, 6, 7, 8]. If all life on earth originated from a single root on the phylogenetic tree of life, further understanding will validate how neural systems of pain and joy evolved from within the earliest forms of life on earth.

The term Pain is to be described as an impairment of genetically governed norm or standard rates of metabolism. Likened to hunger, thirst, sensations of hot or cold as we experience them, a cell or organism can be thought of experiencing pain when there is a deficiency of substances or environmental phenomena necessary to maintain the cell or organism functional at the genetically governed, predetermined rates of metabolism, i.e. homeostasis. Pain is an exigent inefficiency of genetically governed norm or standard rates of metabolism; or a sense of insufficiency, or an excess of substance or phenomena necessary for sustaining or maintaining a genetically induced given rate of metabolism within an organism or cell.

Responses of an organism or cell to the sensation of pain can be growth and or locomotion. Any activity, e.g. particular cellular biochemical feedback mechanisms being idiosyncratic events a cell or organism reacts with as it seeks to maintain or sustain genetically predetermined norm or standard rates of metabolism.

An example of a pain stimulus and a metabolically induced cellular response would be a plant receiving ten hours of sunlight a day and growing strong. Supposing a tree falls now and blocks the path of direct sunlight to the plant. The plant could be thought of as experiencing pain. The homeostatic rate of metabolism of the plant has been impaired, and the response of the plant may be to grow in height or breadth seeking levels of metabolism of the past.

Another example would be to imagine a paramecium subjected to a saline environment. The response of the paramecium to the painful saline stimulus upon its cellular wall may be to cause more energy to be used for locomotion, seeking an environment more compatible. This increased energy response of locomotion in a matured organism is also painful since the organism or cell initially lacks or needs that which it seeks to grow or reestablish. The mature state of an organism or cell is defined as one with fully developed organelles, given a mode average of organelles per life span of a given number of organisms or cells.

The photosynthetic experiments of Theodor Engelmann (1882) [9] brought aggregations of bacteria upon Cladophora chloroplasts absorbing the blue and violet (410, 430, 453 nanometer) and red (642, 662 nanometer) wavelengths of light. The Cladophora chloroplastic organelle evolved out from and maintain cellular homeostasis within an aquatic environment inclusive to the entire range of radiated energy emitted from the sun. The metabolic processes of the Cladophora chloroplastic organelle are inferred by myself to then operate most efficiently, thus have preference for ("enjoy") a medium involving the particular blue, violet, and red wavelengths of light.

A cellular state of Joy is to be defined as an excess of phenomena, substances, or biological activity necessary to keep the genetically governed norm or standard rates of metabolism at the homeostatic level. Joy on a cellular level involves one or many organelles brought to function with more efficiency within the organism or cell. This said stimulus and efficiency of function brought to bear on one or many organelle may or may not be immediately contrary to homeostasis.

Joyful stimuli initiate no recognized metabolically triggered responses within the cell or organism which seek resumption for the previous condition of homeostasis.

The symbiotic relationship of algae and jellyfish are modalities of the joyful stimulus and response. Other examples of joy are best exemplified with artificial descriptions, such as placing a plant in an environment to receive direct sunlight twenty-four hours a day, or placed within an environment where the atmosphere is ninety-seven percent carbon dioxide. Such a joyful stimulus may be to some plants the condition to exploit and thrive without stress. Other plants will begin to reduce cellular activities and metabolic processes necessary for a homeostatic condition to exist so as to be more efficient with the system of cellular activities the plant reacts with while in the presence of an abundance of sunlight or carbon dioxide.

The consequence of a joyful stimulus upon the homeostatic metabolic activities of the cell resolves the cell to adapt, modify, or alter its normal metabolic processes in acceptance of the new metabolic activity a joyful stimulus causes within the cell or organelle. Joy initiates metabolic responses that attempt to incorporate the metabolic activity intrinsic to the joyful stimulus to that with homeostasis. Cellular metabolic responses of joy play to the resiliency of the relationship between organelles that maintain homeostasis.

At the cellular level, the pain—joy spectrum of stimuli introduces two basic modes of cellular responses. With a painful stimulus the cell or organism is active more then less metabolically, and if physically potential, seeking towards previous levels of homeostasis. Moderate stimuli of pain initiates within cells genetically predetermined responses to metabolically reestablish levels of homeostasis within the environment.

If homeostasis should be disrupted within the cell because of moderate joyful stimulus, said organelle's biochemical functions cascade and fluctuate outside of a proper, homeostatic relationship with other organelles. If said joyful stimulus were to remain constant upon the cell, these cascading and fluctuating cellular activities will eventually exhaust the resources and vitality of the organelle(s) as (an) integral member(s) of the cell. Viable homeostasis being given as the norm, maintaining said joyful stimuli sustains organelle / cellular dysfunction.

Two types of environmental stimulus disrupt the homeostatic condition of the single cell. The response of the cell to any homeostatically disrupting stimulus being one of only two courses of metabolic activity which an observer will then use to determine whether a painful or a joyful stimulus to the cell has occurred.

Should stimulus and response of pain or joy within an organism or cell become metabolically intolerable, the destruction of the organism or cell results. These two finite states of cellular endurance are signified by the small, perpendicular vertical segments at the end of the arrows of the horizontal line.

From the observation of cellular activity of any species of life one could not logically conclude that the internal metabolic functions, processes, and systems that maintain homeostasis at the cellular level exist to cause the eventual destruction of said life. That is, for example, the metabolic processes at the cellular level of any species primarily function and exist creating compositions of poisons and toxins to later metabolically trigger and release upon its larger biological structures. There are organelles in some cells with a capacity to enable the cell itself to self-destruct. The capacity to do so is there, yet the cellular homeostatic metabolic process is not logically or truthfully observed to possess and conduct a nature of sabotage, or to possess a self-destructive tendency onto the entire biological system within which it resides. On the contrary, the metabolic process seeks continuum or a preservative quality upon itself. Given homeostasis for the ideal, optimal condition of the cell, the metabolic process can then be said to have placed a value on its self: the value concept called Preservation, or Life. A subjective, normal and internal quality that the metabolic process has placed upon its self.

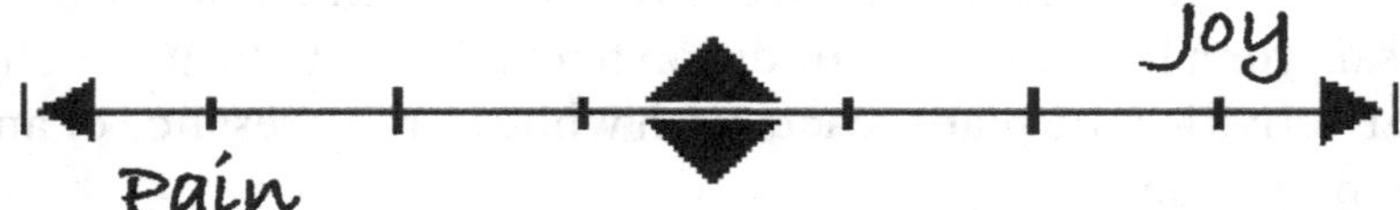

The two parameter pain and joy system allows methods for delineation describing the physical condition a life form acquires or possesses at any given moment.

Also, for completeness, viral properties possess complex chemical structures that interact and manipulate specific outside environments. Their category, at the top of the chemical catalysts and or as the primary forms of life, remains undefined.

Acknowledging natural selection as a valid process for the continuation of species, the breakdown of metabolic processes that eventually cause the cell and the organism to whither and cease to function as a biological system is an imperfection that leads to the next picture illustration.

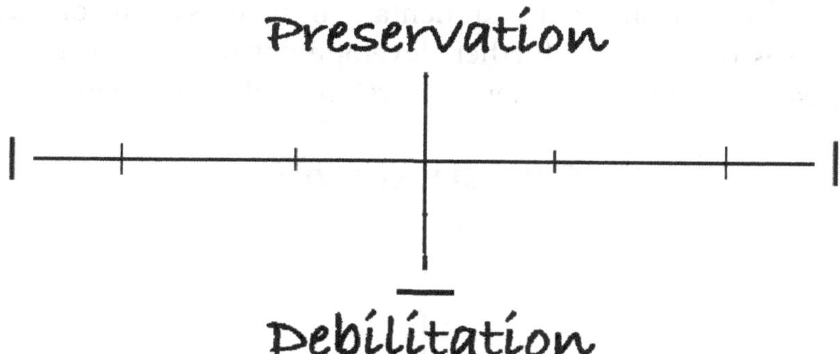

The above illustration represent forms of life possessing a capacity for a rudimentary nervous system. A capacity to integrate different forms of stimuli from the environment. To form interpretations about its self in relation to said stimulus, and then to initiate responses towards the stimulus. This nervous system enables an organism to physically respond to these interpretations with any genetically created physiological structures or apparatus of the animal.

Some examples would be insects and jellyfish: forms of life that possess an elaborate sensory system for the gathering of stimulus from the environment and then to immediately integrate and interpret any stimulus from the outside environment to develop two basic qualities about its self. The two basic, contrary responses that life forms of a picture two class engage to environmental stimulus are Preservative responses and Debilitative responses.

Preservation is defined as an animal's ability to perceive through stimulus to its self in a situation with another animal or object in the environment which cause responses seeking to preserve or nurture itself or both entities in the said situation. Debilitation will be defined as the ability of certain life forms to perceive because of stimulus to its self in a situation with another form of life or object in the environment which can have said life responding to cause harm or injury towards itself and or the other entity.

For examples, an amoeba or a paramecium have marginal capacities to disrupt or encourage upon its self the stimulus it receives from its environment. Though a jellyfish will sting an interpreted threat or take flight, seeking homeostasis with either of these responses. A tadpole will use locomotion to pain stimulus, not possessing a physiological debilitative capacity to respond with. Ants and bees will sting or bite an interpreted threat.

Picture two nervous system capacity is an extension within certain life forms that compliment and magnify the inherent cellular preservative qualities for survival within an environment. Whether the added systems of sensory integration and interpretation, for physical response to the environment are large or miniscule, simple, specialized, or complex in function or purpose is again all dependent on a genetic code which creates the animals nervous system capacity.

To summarize at this point two distinct class of life forms: those that have nervous system capacity for interpretations and responses of and towards the environment, and those that do not. Within this picture two class of life, interpretations of environmental stimulus are perceived within two parameters: as either threatening or benevolent to the system.

With this introduction for a rudimentary nervous system of picture two class of life, the objectives or goals for further development of more intricate processes of integration of sensory stimuli within nervous systems will be introduced.

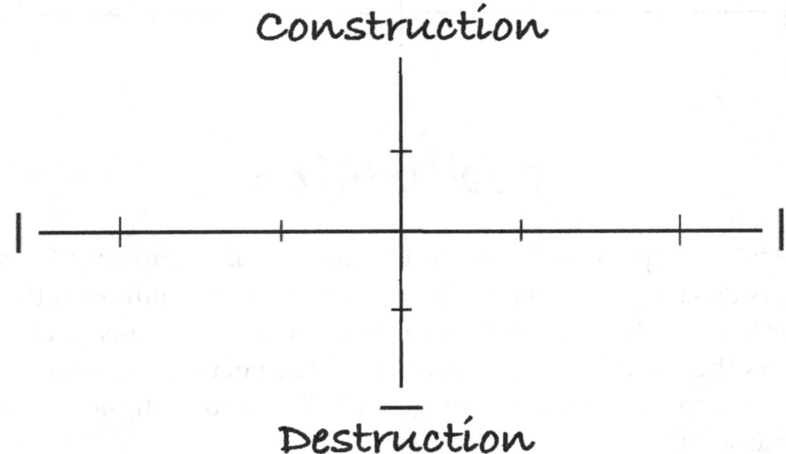

Picture three represent forms of life with the capacity to cognate: to form and retain a distinct state of memory separate from what is brought by instinct. Class three cognitions possess a capacity to involve and apply the element of Time towards objects in the environment, e.g. the chick is ready to fly and feed itself and so food is brought to the nest more infrequently. Capacity to recognize and categorize its self and others as unique objects within the environment, e.g. a canine or feline recognizes verbals and reacts to such. The dog can be trained to recognize and understand the command to fetch the newspaper. Also, in the aquatic environment, while a jellyfish may soon learn a beach ball is not edible and go off in search of other food, octopi and dolphin will completely ignore a beach ball as food. Capacities for emotive states reflecting the pain—joy spectrum exist within a picture three class of life.

From their initial existence in an environment class three cognition require environmental stimulus upon the nervous system to build behaviors from the instinctual, and to give the cognitive structure to what will become the mature adult habits and manners of the particular species of animal. Behaviors from instincts such as beavers building dens, birds their nests; the fight or flight response; in some species, deliberate or neglective behavior of a non-nurturing nature towards offspring is characteristic. This class of nervous system is responsible for the range of behaviors and social activity seen in a wide variety of animals intending their future and furthering their present existence.

To show some variance and interplay between life forms comprising picture classes two and three, on land arachnids, lizards, and insects can be categorized within an upper strata of class two, with primates, canines, and felines comprising an upper class three status, and possessing the more intricate capacities for sensory involvement, integration, and interpretations of their outside environment. Within the aquatic, marine environments, jellyfish and Tardigrada can be categorized within the lower strata's of class two while dolphins, porpoises, and whales are observed with the more intricate nervous systems.

It can be said that of the life forms described to this point none can develop the symbolic conceptualizations or cognitive structures in their minds to know they are going to die as a course of their natural life. Such a cognitive ability would require the capacity within a nervous system to form symbolic conceptualizations pertaining to memories of births and deaths. The animal would have to bring the concept for the element of time to definition upon itself, e.g. ideas such as yesterday and tomorrow are employed in deliberations using an objective state of mind. The capacity to develop linear, symbolic, cognitive structures ultimately leading to the recognition of the ideas of existence and nonexistence, etc., and then to form and appreciate the specialized conceptual constructs of Life and Death, these tasks can only be accomplished with human cognition.

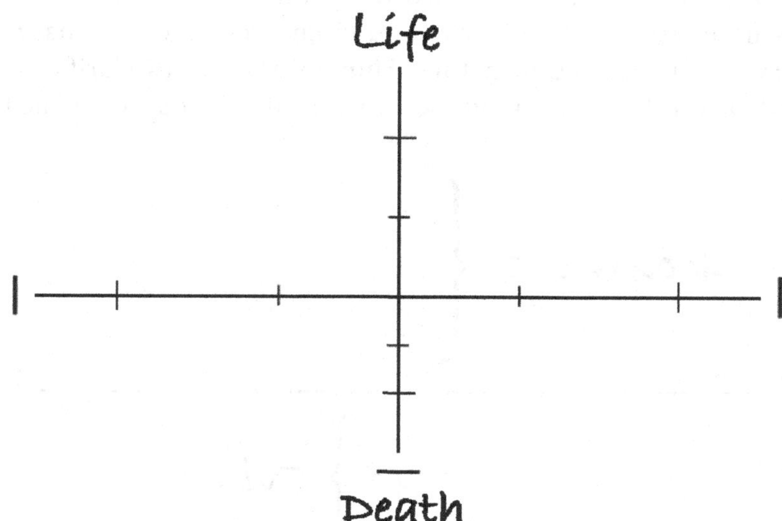

Picture four represents life forms that possess a capacity to realize an ultimate concept of construction|destruction: the life or death of its self and other objects.

The ideal concept of Life is defined as an organization of the mind that can perceive some "thing" alive separate from the animate object. Life in an ideal sense implies a living nature. The cognitive construct labeled Life is as a symbol, or as an idea of something living and then connected to a physical, tangible, or animate object. The definition of the concept of Death is an organization of mind that distinguishes something dead separate from the animate object. Death in an ideal sense implies a nature void of and disconnected from Life.

The cognitive constructs Life or Death can be represented or perceived symbolically within material forms, or conjured as emotive properties, or engaged with endeavors employing ideas of life and death as goals. The concepts of Life or Death can be conceived as separate from the physical, intangible, or animate object.

It is obvious that humans possess the capacity to form the ideal concepts of Life and Death because we commemorate said concepts with rituals of birthdays and funerals. No behavior can be observed in any other animal on the Earth that can be construed as clear recognition and appreciation towards what is defined as the concept of Life and Death.

A dog may forever miss the passing away of its master. Though a dog cannot think the explicit, 'My master is dead,' or express the behavior of such reason. Can this logic be used to attempt an explanation for why, perhaps, a dog may feel no joy or happiness because it cannot smile? To feel no sorrow because it does not ever cry? No. A canine may wonder where that guy who kept giving it food and shelter is and then express behaviors of distress over time if that guy does not come back, but because it cannot bring to itself a definition for an ideal nature of Death it cannot ever acknowledge and appreciate that the guy will or will not ever come back.

The human animal is not only genetically endowed with capacities to preserve and destroy, it has also been endowed with a capacity to conceptualize an idealistic though impractical form of preservation of its self, i.e. the idea of continuous and perpetual life. An ideal concept of Life to form a balance in the mind for the gathering gloom: the inevitable and permanent nature of Death. In our own ways since "Adam & Eve" we humans devise ways and means in an attempt to alleviate and circumvent the eventual nature of Death upon our preservation | destruction nature. Humanity requires clarification of the ideal nature of Life and Death. To do this God the Creator introduced the Judaic Law upon us.

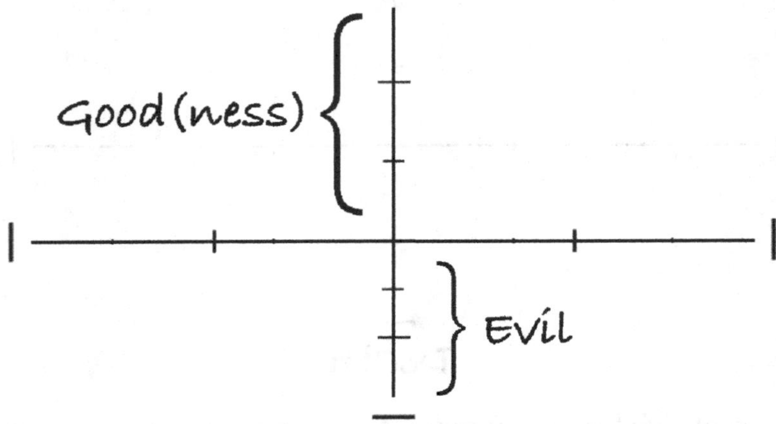

When the Creator God gave the Law to Moses which in turn the Jewish religious authorities expounded upon, human thoughts and actions would become the focal point of and for determinations of good and evil relationships which were then deemed either pleasing or displeasing to the Creator. From the initial Ten Commandments to the Books of the Pentateuch, with acknowledgment for a proper relationship with the Creator God, Jewish law would set the foundations of perceptions within future generations of humanity towards what is, in a basic sense, good or evil. The Law was good, for it gave portions of humanity the directions God said to and not to follow.

Whereas animals and life forms of the previous picture classes were in and of themselves (seen as) the means to preserve themselves, a human perceives the ideal form of life is outside of its self. The Ideal form of Life is realized to be not within our self to preserve our self. What do early humans conjure with new found realizations and perceptions of Life | Death, with attitudes of construction | preservation and debilitation | destruction that first wound their way into cognitive thought a long, long time ago?

The first book in the Bible record one of the first human rationalizations of the world after realizing that, "Death entered the world," c.f. Wisdom 2:24; NAB. The first humans began deliberate thought incorporating these ideals. They began to take on attitudes and ways in search of attaining not Death but the Ideal nature and state of existence with Life for themselves. The human invents pagan religions, builds pyramids, pursues hedonistic lifestyles, and the list is in our histories.

Life and Death in their ultimate idealistic senses are (perceived as) continuous natures and states of existence and being. These ideal senses of Life and Death, with any derivatives of cognition involving these two ideal concepts, will now be qualified within this text by being referred to as 'entities.'

Entities that can be substituted for archaic words like spirits and angels, "Principalities and powers in high places" as Paul aesthetically calls them in his letter to the Ephesians. Life and Death entities that at times are saddled with abstract ideals or nonsense interfering with proper interpretations of the world. They are intangible realities only a human is capable of creating and realizing.

Probably one of the first manifestations or attributes of God for the creation of all was the entity of Truth. God declared and caused the framework for existence of the reality of two plus two to equal four, and that two plus two will not equal three or the square root of negative one. With this hypothetical It established the order and logic of the universe by establishing truth phenomena: the entity of Truth.

After Truth It created the entity of Time and the physical substances of the universe to be governed by other subdivisions of Truth. Truths found in Laws such as the laws of mathematics, the laws of physics, the laws of chemistry, the laws of biology, genetics, etc., so that wherever one is in the universe, in the vastness or in close quarters, two things added to two other things already within a group will always result in a perception of four things in toto within the one group (when using a base ten number system.) Furthering this line of thought one can see a process or movement I will coin the "Chemistry of Entities" develop.

Develop from God the Creator to Its human creation. Love, hate, pain, joy, and all the qualitative subdivisions such as liking more than less, or not liking at all. Trusting more than less, or not trusting at all. Caring more than less, or not caring at all, etc., since from wherever one can imagine the beginnings of space and time, it's all one huge, awesome "Chemistry of Entities." It is building...

God's Love, as I see it in its limited existences found in the world, i.e. the family unit, impels the human towards a mature sense of goodness. Particular acts of affection, care, concern, protection, and intimacy are to be seen as characters of, subdivisions of, or entities of God's love. If these human senses for love can be used as a reflection of the source of love from the Creator, then the absolute ideal sense of Hate will be defined as a quality totally devoid of Love. Hate is not a source or "thing" or a primary entity that functions to emanate hate out as God emanates Its Love. Hate is one's self going further from the mandates of Love (God). Hate pursued to and realized then is ultimately nonexistence.

Picture five represents the Life|Death axis with an applicable qualitative value perspective pertaining to those entities found within the relevant quadrant areas embraced by the laws jurisdiction.

The primary entities of love|hate, pain—joy crystalized, jelled together can then be seen as direction, a way, a path to follow to perceive absolute truth, with eternal life and union with the Creator.

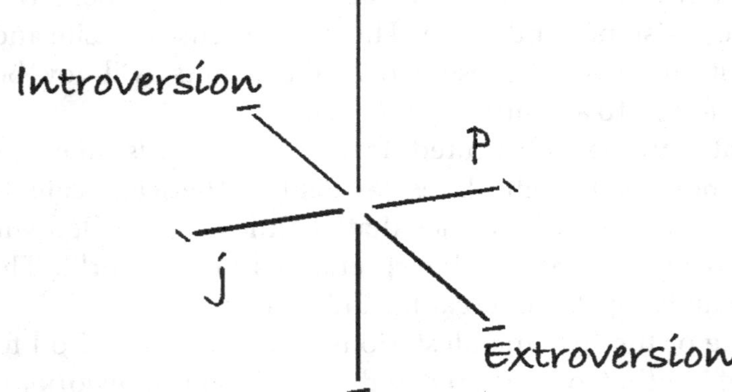

The concept of Introversion involves the realm of the neurological physical self. To define and delineate the realm of Introversion one starts at that place inside the skull directly in back of the eyes. That is, start at that place where you collect your thoughts, and recognize that place in the skull where you objectively realize you are thinking. This is to be the starting point of delineation and the furthest point inward along the axis of Introversion from the center of picture six.

The brain employs neural extensions throughout the body for the gathering of sensory data from the environment. At the end of this network of neural extensions from the brain are the special receptors that respond to environmental stimuli and initiate transmission and realization of a sense to the brain. These receptors are then to be defined as the furthest point opposite from "that place directly in back of your eyes." These receptors are situated closest to center realm opposite from the defining Extroversion axis.

Extroversion is everything outside of Introverted mind' realm. From the closest atoms browsing your epidermis out onto the farthest distances of space and time in the universe, this area is to be the realm of Extroversion.

With these six primary entities placed within a framework involving three axes, the complete metaphysical reality can be described.

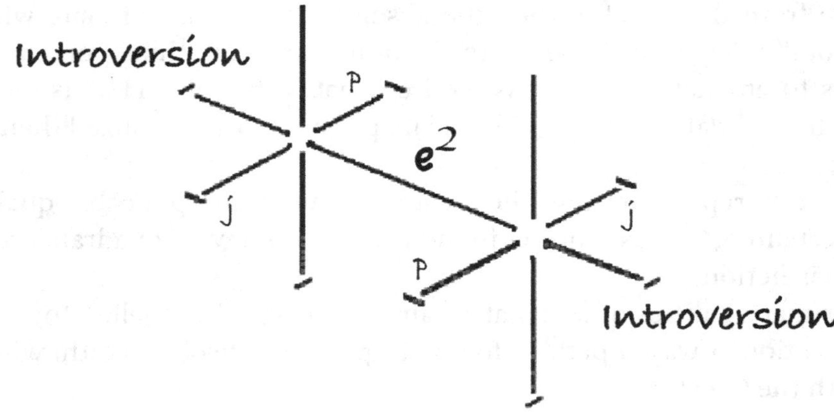

Place two pictures together. Picture seven may represent a group of more than two individuals.

—|—

Dad steps to the television and lowers the volume. He then taps the knob to turn the television off.

A long moment of silence. Mom and Dad settle themselves onto the sofa chair. I'll prop myself up, lean against the arm of the couch and give a quick look their way. Dad looks at Moms and Moms is looking at me, and I pick myself up to sit with my feet on the floor.

Dad's eyes bulge out a little bit. Moms brings her stare away from me and to the pillows at my side. Both self-conscious and only a tad bit uncomfortable with whatever they're thinking.

I strayed off the topic of biology. Brought religion inside the classroom, ... here we are.

"A number of things I was thinking about," sufficed at the dinner table when Dad asked me what the biology report was about. I couldn't think of anything to say to his follow-up question, "Like what?" I just shrug my shoulders and say, " ... stuff."

I didn't break no rules..., I totally dismiss the idea I did something wrong.

Elbows on his knees, clasping the paper clipped pages of my biology report, Dad is staring at me.

Again Moms look up to stare at me. I have to break the silence.

"What!?"

"Who else worked with you on this?" Dad asks.

"No one. I thought it out myself. What did Miss Wittels want?"

Dad raises an open palm, overruling my question.

"So if we had this copyrighted in your name, no one could come along someday and contest you being the only author of it?"

"Definitely not."

Mom and Dad look at each other. Moms then looks at her hands, and her thumb picks at a fingernail as she speaks.

"Seems someone removed the copy of your treatise she had in her files. That's why she called." Moms brings a quick inquisitive look towards me.

"You don't know anything about that though, do you?"

Clowning exasperation at the accusation, I shake my head no, I do not.

"Someone took it," Dad explains. "Perhaps not thinking to make a copy after a reading the first time it circulated around the faculty there."

"Someone who doesn't want her to know," Moms finishes the idea with. "Who is now having second thoughts with it, about it. She thinks someone may try to exploit it on their own somehow, someday, ... maybe."

Circulated? Exploit it? At fifteen years of age, having experienced few of the slings and arrows bred from the plots and devices, good or bad, of the more ambitious type of individual, I do know what the word exploit means. In a minute or two though I'll really know what it means.

"Bolster some political cause, or further some personal social or religious agenda. Who knows? Use your imagination to come up with a few good ones."

I'm a little taken aback, with an incredulous almost mocking scowl towards both of them.

"You know, ... start a religious cult with it," Dad suggests. "With someone else, not you as the leader."

"With this as the way." Dad holds the pages of my treatise with both hands. "The revelation they've claimed to have received from the gods."

"Teachers at school are impressed, for sure," Moms furthers. "They're going to treat it as an academic work

Dad begins to look through separate pages of the treatise, stopping to skim through any part gathered by pinching and flipping pages out and away.

"Miss Wittels calls them an honorable bunch."

Moms halted the pronunciation of the last two words.

"An academic work meaning they wouldn't publicize a work they didn't collaborate on," Dad says. His eyes remain attentive to the papers in his hand. "But inevitably they and others will expound upon later, on their own."

"Exactly what, they're not sure of. A few teachers seem confident you've stumbled onto something noteworthy."

Dad says to me, "You've shown a working relationship, and you've brought together a number of different academic disciplines to present your thoughts with. Without a structured base of facts to base your conclusions, and your reasoning, there's no way to know whether what you say is true or not. Or whether all of it is conjecture, anecdotal."

"My initial thoughts about pain and joy are what matters most, I think. What I've inferred I cite and give reference to. It's not like I made everything up."

Dad looks up at me, and with a resigned chuckle he begins to read.

Moms says, "You've built up your arguments, reached some of your conclusions? By jumping to them instead of leading up to them with facts."

"It's not totally done, either," I say to Moms.

Dad hands the treatise to Moms, and says to me, "We're not evaluating. We want to know what on earth made you write something like this?"

As if expecting to play a Little League or football game within the next hour or so. I remember being as anxious as ever, nervous for something those couple of hours before supper two Friday nights before last.

I came home from school and watched *The Addams Family* and *The Adventures of Superman,* and then after *Batman* and *Speed Racer* were over with I don't want to watch television anymore. I feel like going outside and do something. Supper is less than an hour away and I remember walking down the stairs and through the basement, and at the open basement door I realize I don't want to go outside.

I'm thinking to ask either Festus or Max if they want to play a war game, maybe. Walking up the stairs and into the hallway and looking for either one of my brothers, I imagine actually setting up a game board and taking the time to arrange and sort all the pieces together, and I realize I have no desire to play any kind of game with anyone right now either.

I'm standing with Amy and Moms in the kitchen. They're talking about maybe getting some ducks for the pond. I listen for a while and then leave.

It was too close to suppertime to do anything on the motorcycle. Maybe read a book or a magazine? No. Thoughts of me sitting in one place, this is not at all what I want to do. What I remember is walking around the house and wanting to do something but almost everything I thought of and then imagined myself doing, I then don't want to do it.

These are the moods I recall when later events have left me in wonder whether I'm being set up for some kind of prophetic office.

I'm in a perfectly serious frame of mind after dinner. A full meal sometimes leaves me tired. I'm lying on the bed and began collecting my thoughts for the biology report I want to write. The report is to focus around the single reference point of if, when, and how does something constitute itself being called alive or not, and I suppose I'm as nervous as I've been realizing I haven't exactly thought of anything special or of any particular import to actually begin writing something down to direct my thoughts further along the line of if, when, and how something is alive or not.

Something is alive if it involves respiration. Something is alive if it converts energy for it's own purposes. It has to reproduce itself. Whatever it is it has to have mass that occupies and possibly transits three-dimensional space in some way, shape of form.

These ideas I thought would generate other ideas. They haven't.

The truth is during these last few weeks I've had many a notion of any report I may write turning into a collection of thoughts from other people that I'll read from books in the library, and after thinking thoughts like this it always makes me feel like it's not even worth the time or the effort to bother myself to do. I tell myself redundancies and *blah, blah, blah.* Everything has already been said before. A superfluous academic exercise.

Whenever I give thought to doing so I always like the thought of seeing myself writing something for extra credit, but I also feel once I begin to seriously investigate the subject I'll only find trivial ideas to write about. There are times I imagine not having anything written by the end of the semester and sometimes this thought bothers me and sometimes it doesn't.

I'm lying on my bed and not thinking anything particular, and to realize the word pain in my mind. I begin to think how pain may be used to determine if something is alive. After a bit of thought I realize the use of the word pain when referring to the unicellular organism would sure be a new kind of news to me, and so I want to expound upon and clarify my thoughts for the word pain.

Two categories stood out while I animate what I imagine to be involved to the common sensation of pain. A first category contained any of the initial, preliminary set of factors or conditions that are necessary to bring my central nervous system to begin the actual process causing a sensation of pain to myself. The second category inclusive to the biological systems involved for any single experience and sensation of pain to stay in existence. I brought together two systems I thought were involved as I hurried a definition of pain to myself, and I began to wonder if that preliminary, conditional system could play a role to qualify pain within unicellular things lacking a nervous system.

I get up off the bed and pencil the word pain to some paper on my desk. With a sense of exhilaration I write whatever comes to mind, these first couple of sentences and paragraphs written only to see what I can come up with, and realizing these thoughts of mine are only for the most part basic common sense fact. I reread an initial batch of three, four, five sentences … rewriting some sentences, eventually writing out a paragraph or two of thought and continuing to write and rewrite sentences and paragraphs until I'd felt that sense of importance to have to clearly explain this idea of pain through to myself had lessened. A couple of hours later I've brought out and written ten, maybe fifteen paragraphs of thought.

I'm thinking if I should outline five or ten subtopics of pain from these paragraphs. Any report I write has me first stating to myself exactly what it is I want to say, and then to outline to myself what topics I want to use to accomplish whatever it is I want to say. I knew I was deviating here but I did take notice of a little pattern that was only starting to develop with me this evening; this pattern and manner of putting my thoughts down to paper over the next day or two.

Those particular words being casually presented to me. First pain, the presence of the word comes to mind without an actual premeditative thought to bring it up. The word joy presents itself at different moments like a sign in my mind's eye. In the back of my mind the word joy is there while I think through and write the initial thoughts of and for pain down to paper. I don't know what to do with the word joy though it appeared obvious to include the word when my initial definition of pain began to take shape and eventually made it necessary to do so.

Considering the words preservation and debilitation became more the consequence of my thoughts wanting to compliment the definition I gave to those two previous ideas of pain and joy. I began to write with preservation in mind and to catch the first notion I'm leading into some kind of progression. I've considered only the single-celled organisms and I know there are many other forms of life I'll be referencing. Surely there is more to Life than simple preservation, and I sit at my desk with an invigorating sense of enthusiasm. Apprehension tempers my wonder for whatever this progression of thought I've just now caught a glimpse of may turn into.

Alone and by themselves I definitely would've used these four words and their ideas to order an outline to myself. Instead, these particular words of pain, joy, preservation, and debilitation are encouraging me to reconsider their common definitions in context with the lower forms of life. Sentences I'm in the process of piecing together and writing comprehensible has me also aware and attentive to some other new, inexplicable notion that's beginning to form, and that I'll soon want to turn my attention to.

Sure, I know homeostasis is integral to every cell but where on earth am I getting the idea that the metabolic processes of the cell are causing this state of homeostasis to exist? To listen to myself state the question causes the illogical absurdity to present itself, for of course the metabolic process causes the system where homeostasis is contained, though I can also entertain fleeting, flippant thought for the outside environment playing as vital a role in preserving the cell as the metabolic process seems to be doing.

Because I know I'm not writing from a set of facts to guide me, I'm instead speculating and inferring things. Writing with this frame of mind is uncanny. I shouldn't feel as confident as I do as I write things down. I know I'm writing like silly stuff, so I'm not necessarily surprised to realize that I have no conclusive or leading thought in mind as I pencil a period onto the end of some sentence. Always after a rereading of any set of paragraphs though, things for the most part do seem to be making sense. The things I'm writing down do appear to be developing into something. There is a progression and so I just think to move on.

I finish penciling and clarifying the ideas of debilitation, and something with me seems to be calling for a new set of fresh ideas. That is, if this report is to keep going and not just stop and end right here I'll have to start thinking of new things to...? To think about. I don't know what I should think about next to keep things going though.

Stoic as I sit at my desk, I'm looking inward. Ambivalent I am while dwelling upon this lack of direction. For a time I'm thinking of nothing in particular until these clear notions of construction and then destruction present themselves to mind which further clarify and build upon the preservation and debilitation ideas I just finished writing. The moment is almost epiphanic, and I'm totally confident with the idea I'm into some kind of progression with all this. I am definitely leading up to something.

I write down words I must have known all along but never had the need to use until now. Rereading passages and I'll surprise myself. A sprinkling of big words but with most paragraphs I'm using common, ordinary words to make my points. Clear and concise I am sentence after sentence, paragraph after paragraph. I'm introducing and effortlessly building up one idea and then smoothly leading into another one. How certain paragraphs completely explain an idea, using so few words and so quickly and easily it seems to be. It's as if I'm some kind of poet now, as if I'm carefully and deliberately picking each of these words to create concise ideas using the fewest words possible.

The very act of writing certain words and phrases down to paper, sometimes while rereading any of the last set of sentences and paragraphs I've written cause other notions to spring to mind. These notions come to present themselves and to stay and remain inexplicable only until I've finished writing or reading whatever I was writing or rereading, and then I'll put my conscious attention upon them and...? Most times and I'm listening to myself think nothing. Sometimes I sort of know what I'll have to start deliberating on next and I'll listen to myself jumble my thoughts around. I'll hear myself stumble around with nonsense sounds for words as I ponder the specifics for any train of thought I happen to be on at the moment. Eventually I listen to myself think a clear and concise sentence or a unique word or two or three that furthers along or helps to capture the gist of an idea, and I'll hurry to write the word or to bring an entire sentence or two of thought down to paper.

I'm thinking things through while at the desk or lying on the bed. Thinking of things as I walk through the house or outside for a while. Some of these words and ideas that I write to paper are bookmarks I'll later pick up the train of thought with and attempt to clarify further and deeper into whatever sketchy thoughts I have at the moment.

There are no long periods of deep and perplexing thought. Though I will continue to remind myself into late evening, several times I want to stop what I'm doing and just start writing out some form of an outline for myself. My mind is still sort of fixed on wanting to have a list of things in front of me to organize my thoughts towards articulating how anything is alive or not. I want something to guide my thoughts along with. As the evening wore on I found it easier to dismiss this idea for an outline, thinking it might be better if I just write things down when I first think of them, especially thoughts that will clarify broad ideas such as pain and joy, preservation and debilitation when I first think of them.

I expect to go through an editing process with any report I'll write. Without an outline I'm thinking this one will just be a little bit messier in the beginning than some of the other reports I've written. With scattered sentences in clunky paragraphs extracted and organized together and then to be placed as a new or inside a larger paragraph. Whole paragraphs I'll probably have to lift from one section to insert inside another. *So be it. So it goes. No big deal* is the thought.

It's late evening. I'm not sleepy and there ain't no place I'm going to outside my bedroom. Everyone seems to be in bed and the house is quiet. My thoughts flow with an easy, steady pace of my hand in motion with the pencil to the paper. The feeling of confidence that the report is actually turning into something is with me as I turn off the light to my room and climb into bed.

I'd begun writing late the next morning and found myself thinking and writing, delving into human social and religious things just before lunch. These thoughts I'm writing this morning and early afternoon? Once or twice I have this completely awful feeling come over me that the entire report is turning into a link of baloney.

After lunch I reread the last things I've written. I stop myself from this rereading to bring a fresh sheet of paper in front of myself. A feeling of inspiration welling up at the moment. I've written lyrics to songs, and, I am in the mood for a melody. I'm feeling creative again.

Feeling the urge to write down some rhyming two or three word jingle, maybe a catchy phrase of words…? Instead I draw a horizontal line across a width of the paper, and then I draw a vertical line intersecting the horizontal at midway. I pencil the word pain below and on the left side of the horizontal line. Joy is written above and on the right side of the line. The word love is placed at the top of the vertical line and the word hate is penciled down near the lower length of the vertical line. I stare at the two lines on the paper for a moment. I'm waiting for something else to happen. After a while I haven't thought of anything else and I put the pencil down, pick up the paper and sit back to look at what I drew. Pain is represented opposite joy. Love opposing hate in some way. As a graphical representation it does seem to make a bit of sense at first glance.

Neither by deduction nor induction did I just do this.

The hours of that Saturday afternoon rolled by fast. I notice the sun going down outside the bedroom window, and I'm hungry again. I place the dictionary back up on the shelf and sit back in my chair. Arms folded in front of myself and I'm in thought realizing I'll be using the Jungian terms Introversion and Extroversion too, I guess, in my report now. I'm degrading Carl's original definitions of them enough to perhaps cause another footnote to be included inside future dictionaries definition of these words.

I bring an agonized smile to myself. Rubbing my eyes and my face with the palms of my hands. Amusing myself I am with some preposterous humor to take the edge off what I think Ms. Wittels will think. This is supposed to be a biology report I'm writing. Half a dozen paragraphs back I was thinking about and writing about the Creator God, and I'm now discussing, bringing up psychological and philosophical things.

People use outlines to do reports, I'll remind myself with, attempting to bring some more humor into this uneasy situation I've put myself into. I pick up to reread the rough draft through for the umpteenth time, and I don't even have to read it through in its entirety before I tell myself I like it. I think the report is cool.

Concise sentences and short blocks of paragraphs revolve around the definitions for twelve words, twelve ideas. I weave all these paragraphs and ideas together to have this interpretation of the nature of all forms of life to transpire. The entire train of thought grows from the engine of curiosity I have for what constitutes something being called alive or not, and this premise hitches up to these boxcars filled with precise words and phrases explaining the simple ideas of Pain and Joy, Preservation and Debilitation, Construction and Destruction, Life and Death, Love and Hate, Introversion and Extroversion. Rereading the rough draft through this Saturday evening and I definitely like everything I've written and the way the thing reads. It's totally cool.

By Sunday evening the order to my treatise was set. Over the course of time I've crossed out things. I've done whole paragraph rewrites to clarify a point, and other minor poetic word and sentence structure changes were added here and there. The last two picture representations are heavy-duty material. A magnificent conclusion to the progression.

The basic flow of ideas from one page to the next was set on paper that Sunday evening. I went to bed that night telling myself I'd made practical reference to every form of life in the known universe, from the amoeba and virus all the way to the living Creator God.

"I don't know," I say to Dad, shrugging my shoulders. "I just started writing about things and didn't stop until I thought it was done."

Smiling, placing his hand with a push on my shoulder, "You've definitely got the attention of a few teachers at school with it."

I watch him clasp his hands together and then rest his arms upon his knees. My heart isn't beating fast though every nerve in my body is alive. The sense of awareness is that I am that thing in the back of my eyes.

"One teacher makes him feel like being able to read Darwin's *Origin of Species* before it became public. How as Darwin there had set a wave of intellectual thought through one academic arena after another, this guy feels at the forefront of something similar happening with your paper."

Dad's got a happy smile on saying all this. I just listen. I don't know what to say.

"Whatever becomes of it," Moms adds, "whatever may develop from it, you were the author of the original tome that started the ball rolling. And there are too many who know it's yours for any other person or group in the future to make a legitimate, public claim otherwise."

I remember Dad said that my treatise could start some kind of, *what? A cult?*

"You're another Aquinas, an Augustine," Moms says, leaning over to kiss my forehead.

Argh! Woe is me!

"We're both impressed. Though I think it's going to take some time for me to fully appreciate it."

"Ditto's here," says Dad. "And we're both proud of 'ya too."

Dad stands and they both walk into the kitchen area. A couple quiet moments pass before I hear Dad say, "Summarize your treatise for me, Kurt. Just a couple sentences if you can."

I turn to look at him. I can't see where he is. I hear the soft, sweep sound of air as the vacuum from the refrigerator door being opened is equalized.

"Homeostasis is the biological life force. It seems to propel all life."

I collect my thoughts.

"There are only two types of stimulus that disrupt the homeostatic condition of the cell, what I term pain and joy. Cellular metabolism have only two unique responses to any pain and joy stimulus. The pain and joy terms I use refer to the stimulus and to the course of metabolic activity a cell responds with in response to these two homeostatically disrupting environmental stimuli."

I don't have to say more.

"Keep the volume low if you're staying up."

"I will. Good night, Dad."

I hear the sound of a bite from an apple and then the kitchen door being closed.

I get up and turn the TV back on.

I spent no time doing research, studying nada before I began to write the thing down. It wasn't like I sat in a laboratory for years, starving and cold, so concerned about my box of new Pyrex Erlenmeyer flasks or something, working long hours without sleep analyzing data till I became slightly mad or loony. On the contrary once I began writing things down most of the thoughts came pretty easy, I guess, sometimes faster then I could write them all down, till I just knew it was finished, done.

What was it? Over the course of exactly two days and two and a half evenings, on and off but steady from Friday evening till I went to bed on Sunday, from beginning to end I wrote the thing basically right off the top of my head.

The Paramecium

Mr. Fotals is erasing the black board as I make my way to a desk. Waiting for the bell to ring I watch him reading something on her desk, then shuffling papers between there and the lectern in front of the class. I assumed Ms. Wittels wasn't coming in and that he'll be substituting for her today.

Mr. Fotals also taught sophomore and junior Chemistry courses. He was not especially unique or different from other teachers I had while in what I heard someone say was once the fourth largest school district in New York State. From kindergarten to high school God knows it was to be in the Wappingers Central School District that the spins to my bearings of the world began.

If I showed an interest to learn any subject or topic being discussed during any class in any grade in a school year, for sure any one of my teachers were competent and eager enough to put forth the time and the effort to have me understand something better.

I wanted to know and so I asked. Several minutes with a substitute teacher as she took the time to explain the schwa, long, and short notations for word pronunciation.

"The accent mark is on the second syllable with the word approval," I remember her saying, "so that syllable is stressed."

Second grade, Mrs. James, at the time I could read though glean only superficial comprehension for many of the words inside the dictionary. Though once I knew how to manipulate the notation allowing me to understand proper pronunciation for the words in the dictionary, for years, sometimes for hours I found a sense of enjoyment simply opening a dictionary to any lettered set of words and then to start reading the different words and definitions. It was a cool realization at the time: not one single word or symbol of notation inside a dictionary is superfluous. Every thing inside the dictionary is there for a reason. Dictionaries are packed. They're stuffed with nothing but information.

Certain times, many times in certain classes I just simply do not care what the teacher is saying though. I stop listening and only hear things. A sudden inflection of voice or the teacher's manner of behavior in front of the classroom can have me begin to listen and pay attention again.

Her back is to the class, "Cirrostratus. Altostratus. Nimbostratus," and she's pronouncing each word while spelling it by scratching a stick of chalk upon the blackboard.

If I don't bring attention to myself no one is the worse for wear and tear. Classroom participation is like the old saying, *You can lead a horse to water but you can't make him drink.*

All of my teachers were good teachers. Mr. Fotals did something though that day by provoking me.

Bruce sits at a desk next to mine and I ask him if he's picked a book to report on for Mrs. Edelman's English class. He hasn't.

"I did Jack London's, *To Build a Fire.*

"Good?" he asks.

"Today we finish up respiration and the Krebs Cycle," Mr. Fotals says to start the class.

"Yeah," I say enthusiastically. "It's short and he writes like how your grandfather would tell you a story, around a campfire or something."

Mr. Fotals continues, "You should already know from previous class work that mitochondria are the sites of ATP production. Today we'll explore where all the chemical reactions of tissue respiration take place."

"Glycolysis, the breakdown of glucose to form acetyl coenzyme A, occurs within the cytoplasm outside mitochondria."

Mr. Fotals' finger wanders as it points to areas within a plastic model of a paramecium on the table next to the lectern.

"The Krebs cycle, breaking down acetyl coenzyme A into carbon dioxide and NADPH, takes place in the matrix of the mitochondrion. Some ATP is generated directly during the Krebs cycle, but most of the ATP produced in tissue respiration is generated by the electron transfer chain which takes place across the membranes of the mitochondrion."

Alternating between talking, pointing, and scratching things onto the blackboard, I listen to his monologue but he could just as well be reciting straight out of the textbook, word for word. Some classes it seems there are these times when it's like the teacher is just reading from the textbook for forty-five minutes in front of the class, and in the process not saying anything different or anything more particular than what you got or could get from reading the textbook yourself.

I feel a few molecules of adrenaline jolting me back to the class. Attentive I am with pen in hand and ready to write any interesting words to paper.

I'm not stupid. Those electrochemical bolts I just sensed effecting my central nervous system are, I know, my body's way of alerting my mind to something. Something that isn't good for me. I'm like hurting myself again. I should try to remain attentive to the discussion going on in the class now.

Though what am I supposed to do with the obscure fact that the oxidation of the 2-carbon acetyl group of acetyl coenzyme A occurs in a cyclic sequence called the Krebs cycle? Anything of practical importance, for instance? Supposing I was to remember this and all the other abstruse comments mentioned throughout the day. I'd get better marks on my next test yes, but six months from now I forgot it all too.

I want to do something with all this technical stuff as I learn about it, I think, among all the other distractions I also think to myself.

"Stalked particles on the inner surface of cristae contain the enzymes required to make ATP from ADP and phosphate," Mr. Fotals explains.

It's not that I can't absorb the subject matter as intensely as it's presented. Some times it's just the plain, simple reason of why? Why should I?

"The final hydrogen acceptor is oxygen. NADPH is produced during the Krebs Cycle."

I sit up and watch Mr. Fotals pace in front of the classroom, alternating his gaze from the floor to any one of us sitting at our desks.

"If there aren't any questions?"

Mr. Fotals steps to the blackboard, erases a section of it and then scratches the words prokaryote and eukaryote.

"Tomorrow in class you'll be using the microscopes, so we'll review some of that material for the rest of the class."

He steps away from the blackboard and leans himself over the top of the lectern. I remember these next words he spoke to us as clearly as if they were spoken just the other day.

"Life on earth began with the simple, primitive one-celled animal."

That statement bothers me. I bring a quick series of subconscious, inductive thoughts to myself.

I'm alive, so I'm life on the earth, that's true.

My human body evolved from the simple, primitive one-celled animal? Maybe, maybe not. It's not a "for sure" or an absolute. Probably though it's true.

It was the concluding declaration that caused the speed bumping jar of thought: *simple primitive one-celled animal.*

They're not animals. The microscopic bugs that are found in pond water are not animals. Rabbits and birds, worms if you will are animals. Puddle sludge bugs are, at best, they're like chemical factories. They're not alive, like an animal is alive.

Sorry Mr. Fotals, you're wrong.

I sit back into my chair and fold my arms in front of myself. I pat myself on the back a little bit too now as I get back into the saddle of his monologue.

"Even though they're called simple one-celled animals," Mr. Fotals furthers, "they're not simple in structure at all. They're simple only in relation to the complexity of other forms of life on earth."

I figure his use of the word simple is also being used in the same broad context as the use of the word animal was put forth previously.

Microscopic pond bugs are not animals. Each one of those little microbes is simply a system with many chemical processes happening inside it. Exactly like the chemical things that are happening in pond water that has a chocolate cake with an iron bar in it.

Supposing a small iron bar were placed inside a water filled plastic sandwich bag, this bag is then placed inside a chocolate cake. The chocolate cake is then placed in some pond's water in the sunlight of daytime. Both the chocolate cake that's now in the pond water and these microscopic bugs Mr. Fotals is referring to simply have a large number of chemical things happening inside or around them at any given moment of time. Simply because a whole lot of chemical activity is happening inside or around something doesn't warrant calling it alive; alive in the sense of a person or an animal or even a plant is alive.

It's not really a big deal. Mr. Fotals is just a little cavalier with his words today, and people exaggerate things sometimes. They tell fish stories. It's another opportunity for me to congratulate myself again on how smart I really am, 'cause sometimes things are not what others claim they're all cracked up to be.

" ... with eukaryote having a well defined nucleus regulating metabolism."

The bell rings its three-seconds out in the hallway. This is my last class before lunch and then a study hall right after lunch.

" 'K class, let's not waste time," Ms. Wittels begins the following day. "Class activity is described in the handout. You should each have a box with five slides near your microscope. Don't be too concerned if your drawings are not turning out exact or to scale. The objective of the exercise is to find and correctly identify the organelles of the cell on the slide."

It had recently come to my attention that doing lab activities in biology class and watching a movie are my first and then second favorite things I like to be involved with in a class that isn't going to follow the regular forty minute routine. I don't think anyone entering a classroom and then seeing a movie projector set up and ready to show a movie says something like, "Darn! We're not going to hear so-and-so talk today?" On the contrary. Movies shown in any class have always been a treat of sorts. This being my sophomore year at Jay I'm now at a grade level where certain science courses also include actual lab work as part of the class, and since my first biology lab class I have brought lab class above movies as being the favorite class activity. Biology now being my favorite class subject, then algebra class, then English classes.

One wouldn't know biology and algebra as favorites of mine from my grades. I kept a mid-80's grade average in last semesters English class. The algebra course I'm taking this year is last years freshman algebra course. My counselor said I should repeat algebra again this year because all of my test scores were low enough to make them think I'd have trouble with the calculus. Best to repeat the course before moving on. Acquire a better understanding of the basics of algebra before trying to tackle the higher mathematical subjects.

Biology subjects and topics? I think since those first days in class they've made me attentive. Constantly attentive, no—but they do. They constantly attract and engage my interest and curiosity.

I think it's my attention span in all my courses that keeps my grades the way they are. Something will come to mind during the forty plus minutes of a class to distract me from one hundred percent attention. And while the theory is to have the textbook follow along to complement and expound upon the ideas discussed during class, I seem to derive more information from a textbook alone, or so I like to think.

Dad says the better teacher is the one that can say the same thing in many different ways. If you didn't understand a particular idea the first time it was presented and explained, raise your hand. A better teacher will be able to say the same thing in a different way, and if need be for a third explanation. Dad doesn't understand what's going on.

One bugaboo is the lack of an application towards all the many new things learned in a school year. It would have been a simple matter at this stage in my life to have had someone tell me to just pay attention in class and learn the stuff, and that I have to learn the basics first before I can understand all the stuff that'll be discussed in later classes. Keep a finger on the flow of topics and material presented each day, and don't get too far behind. Because absolutely, the things taught in the past are needed to build a further understanding towards the things that'll be talked about later on. A talking-to along these lines would have helped my grades, sort of.

Maybe..., maybe not.

I've wanted to learn how to make mathematical equations on my own since seventh grade, and I still can't. It became a personal, halfhearted little goal I'd given myself; an impetus to want to pay particular attention in class and learn for. I thought it would be really cool to be able to make an equation for something whenever I felt like it. If I could one day set up an equation to answer a question such as, "Does one become wetter walking or running in the rain?" Everything else being equal.

The two Bernoulli brothers in the late seventeenth century, one of them devised a mathematical statement out of the curved shape a weighted string held in the hands forms. Newton's Second Law of Force = Mass times Acceleration, or $E = mc^2$. How does one do that? To see and realize the factors that will create a working, functioning mathematical statement. To realize you have to square root this factor, or cube this factor, or to not square or cube something.

Einstein didn't write that energy is mass times the speed of light. He wrote that mass accelerating to the speed of light, or mass accelerating at the speed of light becomes or is energy. He used the symbol c^2 as mathematical notation to connote a constant, accelerating speed of light. Why didn't Einstein cube the equation, scratch it out on paper as $E = mc^3$?

What a way to view and to perceive some things of the world sometimes I thought, and I sure would like to know how to do things like this. Perhaps before any one else would do so, I'd do some things too.

Since Junior High, almost every time I went to math class I sort of had this expectation in the back of my mind, this idea that someday I would just know how to turn my thoughts into making an equation for something if for any reason I wanted to put forth the effort to do so. Until my senior year I didn't realize there was a specific branch of mathematics pertaining to what I wanted to do here, so the thought never entered my mind to go off and learn how to do it on my own, especially early on when I had the gumption to do so. I assumed that if I was patient and kept going to math classes, eventually in time I would just learn enough and then wake up one day knowing enough to be able to do so. I thought it would all just somehow come together and fall in my lap. I don't know, if I gave it any real thought at all it was that by wanting it I would just get it … someday.

I remember being mildly disappointed when Mr. Lewis abruptly changed direction and stopped discussing the quadratic equation, after such a short time on it too. He introduced the equation one day and the class played with its algebraic forms for a while: the imaginary roots (not only x and y now but a z axis in complex numbers? One, two, three dimensions …!) If the discriminant is below zero what this defines things to mean. A couple days to do factoring and then poof! Gone. Rarely used the word quadratic again in class. We move on to other topics.

Mr. Lewis began talking about recursive series, Fibonacci numbers, and I want to keep doing things with and through quadratic equations and its x, y, z graphical representation of things. Such a shallow treatment of the quadratic equation and Cartesian coordinates I thought, and of course nothing was learned to have me get on the bus with and go back home to use somehow over the weekends.

I have to drop these attitudes. Drop the losing attitude and stay with Mr. Lewis and the class. Put the thoughts aside and don't start some mood during class. Self-conscious about what I'm doing triggers another one of those, *you're-hurting-yourself-again* jolts of adrenaline to course through me, propping me up and to break in to hear Mr. Lewis say, " … multiplied by the power of negative one has each term represented on a graph alternating between positive and negative."

I know Mr. Lewis, all teachers have to cover a certain amount of material each week. They have to move on. Hey, it doesn't really matter. I'm not the King of Siam or someone special. A haughty type to make a federal case out of how I feel schools should do things to "improve" or whatever. At my age now I use my head to experience life is all. I'm not at any stage yet where I critically judge things as to right or wrong, good or bad, or to take myself too seriously if I do occasionally happen to do so.

Hands on experience, lab class activity is the best way to learn, I think. To be doing something with the hands. I'm watching things as they happen in real time, and I like to think I'm doing things that will have some practical purpose later on in life.

The first weeks of biology class and I knew I was going to like these classes a lot.

"If any one finishes early and wants to use their microscope further," Ms. Wittels informs everyone now, "a beaker of pond water is on the corner table there."

"Use the eyedropper to draw a sample. Place a cover slip on top of the slide or you may not be able to focus in on any thing too well."

"There's less than forty minutes. The sooner you begin the more time you'll have to finish."

Ms. Wittels may be correct about that time limit but I have to take a moment and become a bit more familiar with this thing before I start using it.

The eyepiece at the top of the barrel of the microscope stencils the fact to me that it does a 10x magnification of things. At the bottom of the barrel, there's a three-clicks positional, rotating gizmo that when turned allows for powers of 10x, 40x, and 100x magnification to be used. There's an electric light mounted under the platform. Two metal tension clasps hold the slide on the platform. I remove a prepared slide from the wooden box and read that the bugs I'll be looking at are referred to as *Entamoeba histolytica.*

The amount of light shining up to the platform can be adjusted with a diaphragm mechanism. I turn the plastic knob on the side of the microscope and watch the platform move up and down. The light adjustment is set to midway and magnification power to 10x. I clip the glass slide onto the platform and focus till the views of two amoebas are defined inside the view piece.

I tell myself the picture of my amoeba isn't as clear and detailed as the text book picture of an amoeba. For a moment I'll try to imagine what the quality of the picture views that were probably given to the first eyes ever to peer down the barrel of those first crude microscopes built centuries ago ... and I conclude the views through a microscope back then were probably similar to what I am seeing through the eyepiece right now.

I focus through the different depths and levels of one amoeba's transparent body. Focusing to have any one organelle brought into sharp detail causes all the other organelles not at the same depth to be seen blurry and out of focus.

Curiosity has me rotate the lens to the highest resolution of 100x, and by doing this I put everything out of focus. Turning the focusing knob from one end to the other does nothing. Stacie placing her arms down on the table at the station next to mine causes the view piece to wobble violently.

Forget 100x, I tell myself. Now isn't the time to investigate things too much. I switch down to 10x power and get ready to draw things to paper.

I hear Ms. Wittels say, "David, keep both eyes open and use one eye to look through the eyepiece. It's the preferred way. Try it."

I think they want us to draw these bugs freehand to have us compare the clarity of the textbook touched-up photographs from those observed in a real live laboratory environment. I can't think of a reason why they're having us spend class time drawing these bugs onto paper.

I see the nucleus inside the *Entamoeba,* and I make little doodles of its basic shape on my lined notebook paper.

I try to peer directly inside the nucleus to get a better definition of its structure. Blurred together splotches of bright whites along the edge, and a bright gray color at the center. Ever so carefully I turn the focusing knob. I'm altering that initial bright gray fuzziness at the center to become a dull gray-brown patch of color, and the wall of material surrounding the nucleus becomes clearly defined and distinct from everything else surrounding it.

Turning the focusing knob just a hair more brings the dull gray-brown patch at the center of the nucleus into a blur of dark gray color, and that distinct, sharp boundary wall of the nucleus has blurred out of focus. I wonder if I have focused inside the nucleus or only scanned along the outer surface wall of the nucleus.

From when I know I've just started to focus upon the very top of the nucleus, I'll continue to turn the focusing knob and eventually to bring those crisp and clearly defined sides of the nucleus into view, but to find nothing discernible to have me think I am seeing or saw something inside of the nucleus. All the focused light reflected up from the area inside the perimeter of the nucleus is mostly a mishmash blur of light.

Either the wall of the nucleus is translucent or partially so, and I'm looking maybe a fraction part of the way inside the nucleus, or the walls of the nucleus are opaque and the blurs of light I see are only the irregular outer surface features of the nuclear wall as the different sections fall into and then out of focus.

The next few thoughts I'll remember for a later time, and to check out further.

I'm going to assume that there are no inert chemicals inside the nucleus of an amoeba. Whatever chemicals are inside the nucleus, these chemicals are compartmentalized together into specific groups for a some metabolic purpose. These bundled together "chemical groups for a purpose" are somehow kept separated so that they can perform whatever function they do.

Refining this hypothesis to myself. These chemical compartments, or chemical factories—*realizing, again I don't bother myself to know the Latin language well enough to give a more scientific label to these chemical groups I have in mind*—these chemical factories have walls that either do or do not allow views into the nucleus, and unless the nucleus is conducting only one kind of chemical process that doesn't need any type of compartmentalizing, and I doubt this idea very much, then there must be other organelles, compartments, or factories that would render the nucleus opaque.

Having now made up a hypothesis for the structure inside of a nucleus, I'll set it down as a priority in future lab classes to either prove or disprove. I'll look for the "chemical factories" and or the wall or walls that separate the chemical processes inside the nucleus of any eukaryotes.

I see a dark elliptical shape inside its body. I draw a reasonable facsimile of what this shape looks like, then draw a straight line out from the amoeba to label this elliptically shaped doodle of mine a chromatin. That's about it for this slide. There are not many organelles in this amoeba that are clearly defined.

Paramecium caudatum is the name on the next slide I take out of the box. A few moments to scan things and to again take notice of the nucleus. The nucleus seems to have been in the process of merging with the organelle beside it. I raise my hand and look for Ms. Wittels, waiting for her to notice me.

"What's the nucleus doing?" I ask her. "It's like splitting in half."

Peering down the barrel, she turns the focusing knob back and forth, and then reads the label on the glass slide.

"You won't see that very often," she says. "The larger macronucleus is simply alongside its micronucleus. The moment the slide was prepared and stained brought that angle you see."

"What's a macronucleus?"

"The macronucleus controls metabolism. The micronucleus reproduction."

I nod and look through the eyepiece. A contractile vacuole and a food vacuole are found and I draw their shapes onto the paper. Enough drawing. I'm really not all that enthused doing any of this looking and drawing stuff.

"Riding this weekend?" I ask Larry and then Danny as I walk by their stations.

Probably is implied with nods, confirming a possible Saturday morning rendezvous at The Valley.

I pick up a glass eyedropper lying next to the beaker of pond water and draw a quantity of brown-green vegetable matter inside. I drop a cover slip on top of the bead of water on the slide, and I know I'll definitely be looking at something inside that bead of water once it's set up on the microscope.

The slide is clipped onto the platform and I look through the eyepiece. Things brighten to almost sparkle through the eyepiece. I reduce the amount of light shining up. Debris moves around inside turbulence. Nothing is seen moving on its own accord. I'm waiting an inordinate amount of time for anything to happen before I think to move the glass slide around, and bring more surface area into view sooner.

Something moves along the edge of the circle of light, and I nudge the slide with thumb and fingers to watch a paramecium slither into view. I have to take my eye away from the view piece, to find and swing the lever to restrict more light to the slide. With turns of the focusing knob I bring the moving paramecium to clarity.

Watching the thing for a few moments and the first thing that captures my attention is the movement of cilia along the outside of its body. Short hairs swirl most times together in an orderly, counterclockwise direction round and around its body. Faster than I can blink my eyes the pace of these cilial hairs have accelerated, like the thing is excited for some reason. Within an instance of time the orderly movement of these hairs has changed again, their pace is now at that former slow speed. I watch this paramecium and think it's totally cool.

The nucleus is definitely the most pronounced object inside the body. I notice a continuous movement of liquid flowing inside a type of channel or tube alongside the nucleus. Things are flowing from one part of the paramecium to another. The movement. The flow. The process of transfer. Realizing there is a system impresses me. A sense of vitality. Slow and fast turns of its body. The paramecium veers left and right, darting here and there. The movement of its cilia and the channel of flowing liquid. A fascinating moment of intimacy between the paramecium and I.

My thumbs and fingers nudge the corners of the glass slide to keep the paramecium in view. My attention wanders around inside the paramecium. Most surface features of any of the organelles I care to take the time to look at and focus upon are obvious and distinct from whatever they happen to be surrounded by. The dynamics to everything that is happening at every moment is in such contrast to the previous prepared still slides I was looking at.

All the things happening through the eyepiece now is unexpected. I'm inside another world. Awed and amazed, watching this paramecium is so totally cool!

For sure the most fascinating aspect of this critter is the animated movement of cilia around it's body. I know that many chemical processes are happening all at once to make what I'm seeing possible. Intricate biochemical systems are exchanging and transferring energy causing all those hairs to perform the way they are. Delicate chemical processes occurring each second and every hour onward. I know.

An amusing performance. The paramecium bumped into and then bounced away from a piece of debris in the water. It then went forward and deliberately banged into the thing again, bouncing backwards a second time. It does what looks like a one hundred and eighty degree summersault and moves way from the obstacle.

I determine the paramecium courses through the water at a speed of about two or three times its own length every second or two. It has a steady and predictable manner of movement that sort of makes me think of the bow and hull of a boat. Unlike a boat though there's no turbulence from a wake by the bow as it moves in any direction through the water.

The swirling cilial action of the paramecium doesn't push away any of the little bits of debris as it moves in a forward motion. Instead any particles in the water remain close and seem to slide right alongside those cilial hairs. It seems a little odd and counterintuitive to watch bits of debris remain undisturbed as the paramecium passes by.

Again the paramecium bumps into a piece of debris and bounces backwards. It then travels back up to the piece of debris and slithers itself around it, and to continue on its way.

Molecules of adrenaline jolt me. I take my eye away from the microscope. My attention is inward, and I definitely want to start to think about something. Exactly what it is I want to think about I can't realize yet. I bring my eye back to the microscope. The next few minutes I'm wondering to realize whatever it is on my mind.

This is not a piece of slowly dissolving cake with a rusting iron bar inside it swimming around down there.

I want to explain this entire idea through to myself again. This idea of puddle sludge bugs being alive or not somehow, one way or another, if I can.

"There will be a quiz tomorrow," I hear Ms. Wittels say to the class, "on the organelles of unicellular animals."

Fotals says this thing is alive, like an animal, somehow, ... and I want to hear myself say those words again, and to listen to whatever I may think about it. Ms. Wittels just now referred to these things as an animal again.

Because they're not animals, they can do that. Rhetorically pondering how this arrangement of words slants things. I watch the paramecium for the final fifteen, twenty minutes of class time, unable to articulate to myself whatever it is on my mind.

For the next several weeks I keep toying with this gnawing, absurd notion that perhaps the paramecium had chosen to turn itself and cause the act of sliding its body around the object. It had also made a type of decision with the incident before this. After contact and bouncing back the biochemical machinery of the paramecium brought its body forward to initiate another second contact with the obstacle. So for a time I'm inclined to think that it had attempted to knock the thing down and out of its way. How in God's name did that paramecium choose a different response for a basically similar circumstance?

I know a paramecium cannot make decisions. It just reacts to chemicals in the environment, or to phenomena like hot or cold. It's just chemically reacting to the light from the sun, or chemically reacting to the darkness. It cannot have thoughts as it interacts to the environment. It doesn't have a brain or nervous system to coordinate any stimulus from the environment, and so it cannot have thoughts that allow it to make decisions. In my definition an animal is any thing with a capacity to think in some way, shape, or form. Obviously a plant is not an animal for just this reason.

A book in the library used the word chemotaxis. The random behavior of the paramecium is fascinating, and something is wrong.

Iron always oxidizes and rusts in the presence of water. Liquid water should always start freezing and solid ice melting at a temperature of thirty-two degrees Fahrenheit. Gravity always causes objects to fall downward. Odd that the paramecium strays from a precise, clockwork-like mechanism and behavior I believe they're about. For several weeks I'll ponder what I saw under the microscope, and I'm unable to pin it down into clearer thoughts than this.

Biology is my favorite subject, and as Leonard Nimoy would say to William Shatner, "Fascinating, Captain." Using a microscope in biology class that day certainly was fascinating, for sure.

A month later, a Monday morning and I stand at Ms. Wittels desk flipping through the pages of the treatise, waiting for her attention. I'm a tad bit hesitant realizing some of the things I'm implying within certain paragraphs of the treatise.

It was Mr. Fotals and a paramecium and a reason at that particular time in my life for me to have to write my thoughts down to paper like I did. I don't know. I imagine these three things to be the major instigators that had gotten a hold of me, taking my train of thought onto those sections of track towards a vista and a view of a most fascinating thing in the world: strong circumstantial evidence for the existence of the omniscient, omnipotent Creator.

Bird Shot

"You got it?"

Bang!

That time the kickback from the revolver sort of stung my hands. I'm sitting on Dad's lap, holding the pistol as tight as I can, and even with his hands around mine that last shot really shook the revolver. It sort of scared me a little. In no way could I have kept the recoil of the shot from shaking the pistol out of my hands.

"I did that on purpose. Powerful, huh?" Dad says into my muffled ear.

"Let's try it again. Grip it tight in your hands. Keep your arms stiff."

Dad takes one of his hands away from its hold over my hand. His fingers hold the gun barrel up and pointing level. I adjust the fingers of both my hands all around the wooden handle as best I can, and try to insert my finger up into and around the trigger. My finger isn't long enough to reach inside the trigger guard, much less wrap around the trigger itself.

"I think you better let me pull the trigger. You got a good grip on it?" Dad says to me. I wrap the fingers of both hands around as much of the handle as I can again and squeeze.

"Think you can hold it up by yourself?" Dad says. "Try."

I tense the muscles in my arms and chest. The pistol is too heavy for me to hold up and our arms go down together. The gun butt rests on the table, and I attempt to but cannot pull the pistol up from the table.

"You don't start getting muscle in your arms until you're about twelve or thirteen," Dad says. He brings his hands firmly around mine and raises the gun from the table.

"Ready? Brace your arms. We'll shoot the last three, one two three."

Bang!

Dad's arms and hands hold the gun rigid. The gun barrel points straight out in front of me. I'm holding the pistol grip as tight as I can.

Bang! Bang!

Each explosion punches into my hands and vibrates up into my arms.

"All right, let's put it down on the table."

I bring my arms back and feel both hands and wrists tingle. My hands vibrate inside. We've shot four cylinders worth of bullets so far.

Dad breaks the cylinder mechanism from the stock, spins the cylinder a couple of times before taking a single empty shell casing from the chamber. He takes a live round out of the box of bullets and places the empty shell's brass casing behind the live round's brass casing.

"If I held the bullet like this," Dad says, "and it somehow discharged, you know this brass part—" tapping the two brass casings together to animate ejection of the empty casing, "would fly away at the same speed but in the opposite direction as the lead part?"

I look at the bullet between his fingers and visualize the lead and brass parts flying apart with equal speed and force, and in opposite directions. I turn to look up at him, and he places the bullet back into the box.

"Take the rest of the empties out."

I place the pistol in front of me and begin to pull a warm empty shell casing out as Dad warns me.

"You ever think about wanting to go shooting, before you turn sixteen, you let me know all right? I don't mind having you or your brothers, or even your sister along for some company when I go to the range for practice. You know?"

The cylinder is heavy and requires a firm grasp of my fingers to rotate and place the chambered casing in the exact position I want. I actually have to first use my fingernails to wedge each shell casing out the little bit before I can grip the rim of the shell casing with my fingertips and pull the casing completely out of its chamber.

"Kurt, listen to me. I read in the paper every so often where someone's kid is alone or with one of his friends and he starts playing with a gun they find in the house. Someone winds up shooting himself or someone else with it."

Dad pauses his speech. "They're dangerous. You know?"

"Kurt…?"

I'm listening.

"I've asked your brothers when they were your age the same thing I'll ask you now. I want you to promise me that if you ever want to play with my guns that you ask me first. 'Cause believe me, first chance I get we'll go off somewhere and fire off some rounds together for a while. Just you and me if you want, alright?"

I shake my head, "Yeah, sure."

"Promise? Promise you'll ask me first?"

"For sure. Promise."

"Say you promise you'll ask me first."

"I promise I'll ask you first."

Dad wraps his arms around me, squeezing me with a hug, saying, "I kinda like my guns you know? And I don't want any thing bad to happen with 'em to make me ever say I wish I never had them."

"They're weapons, not toys."

"It's best having two hands, two feet, ten fingers, ten toes, and you're not walking around with a limp in your foot the rest of your life. Just because of an accident that happened one day."

I don't know what to say really, but if he doesn't want me to, well, I won't.

I've taken all the empties out of the cylinder, and I slide off his lap as he begins to stand up. I watch him load the revolver with bullets.

Dad holds the pistol with one hand as he fires it. He makes it look simple. The kickback from each discharge doesn't seem to faze him in the least.

When I get older I'm going to have hands as strong as that, I think.

It was the first Christmas we would celebrate inside the new house. The last several months, evenings and weekends were spent driving over to it and doing whatever was needed to move in before winter's weather set in.

The upper level of the house was ready and draft free, snug as a bug in a log a short six weeks before Christmas. Festus, Max, and I shared one single bedroom. Amy the lucky duck got to have her own bedroom.

The basement was still in need of a bit of work. One door from the upstairs hallway in the middle of the house is the only way down to the basement. Open the door and it's a single step down upon a plywood board at the top of the stairwell. Two electrical switches are on the wall at the top of the stairs. The lower switch turns on the lights at the bottom of the stairs. The emergency shut off switch to the furnace is placed an arm's length higher and directly above the light switch.

A ninety degree turn brings fourteen nailed planks of wood to step down on.

Moist basement air is tinged with the pleasant mustiness of poured, curing concrete. The floor is swept clean. The first months and practically nothing was placed in the basement to take notice of. The wooden stairwell. The wooden and metal window and door frames fixed inside the basement walls, and the four thin, cylindrical iron posts that rise up from the middle of the basement to support the ceiling above, these are the only things down in the basement to look at.

Most times downstairs is the coldest place in the house. The basement is always cooler than the outside air temperature. It seemed to me that soon after moving into the new house the next big thing that happened was that it was Christmas Day.

I was shooting my new BB gun outside the basement door. I'm trying to hit branches, rocks, a patch of snow, anything. Aiming helped to hit or come close to hitting something sometimes, and sometimes aiming didn't help at all. The BB sometimes flew a foot or more up or down, to the left or right of whatever I'd be aiming at.

Standing as I was just outside the door, I saw a wren fly into and then across the backyard, gliding itself out of view behind the side of the house. Knowing there's a hanging chandelier of birdseed tied to a branch on a tree on that side of the house, and that this bird had most likely flown over to it, I went on upstairs and through the house to the TV room. Through the sliding glass doors of the TV room on the far side of the deck I saw the bird hanging off of it.

With its sticky claws dug into the netting surrounding the bundle of seeds, it's fluttering it's wings every so often to right itself into better positions from which to feed from. I slowly crack the sliding glass door open just enough to slide the barrel through and take aim. I'm really not expecting to hit it. One shot and I'll scare it, and then watch it fly away.

The big physics teacher in the sky was sitting in the directors' chair of my life at this moment of time though, so … an uncanny thing. I actually caught sight of the shiny bronze colored BB mere inches the moment it left the end of the barrel. And the BB never left my sight as I watch its trajectory ride up and to the left and then down like a perfectly thrown curve ball that hits the center of the wren's breast.

Wow…!

I saw the BB fall first from where it smacked into it, and then the wren falling. It doesn't even flutter its wings the first five or six feet on the way down, before the railing at the end of the deck blocked my view of watching it fall the rest of the way to the ground. At a distance of eight, nine yards, at that close range I am astonished that I hit something moving, tiny, and bull's-eye.

I put my shoes on and then go on downstairs to have a look. Out the door and stepping towards the tree I see it's lying still. It's staying motionless even as I'm reaching down to pick it up off the snow. Carefully folding an extended wing back inside of itself, in the cup of my hands I look to see if it starts moving in any way. Feathers touch my fingers while I turn it in my hands. Its body lightly rests inside the cup of my hands, and it's odd that the bird and it's feathers already feel cold.

Limp and motionless, I turn it and its neck and head flop to hang over the side of my hand. I paddle the head with a couple of my fingers, bouncing it's head up and down several times thinking maybe it'll start to wake up and move around or something. I stop the bouncing and look to see if its eyes are open or closed. They're open.

There's no puncture of the skin or any visible wound of any kind. Cupping my fingers all around its body to feel if there's a heartbeat, I realize there isn't, and I now look longer and closer into the thing's eyes, to realize that they're not moving around. The eyes don't seem to be moving around at all, and I realize it must already be dead.

Something creeps up through my stomach and into my neck to put a frightening jolt inside me. There are sparkles inside my eyes. My jaw is tense. My heart starts beating slow but hard inside of my chest, and I am suddenly brought to feel so sad!

Oh wow, … what do I do?

I wish I had not done this.

I place the bird back down on the snow and walk up the hill along the side of the house. Stepping along the walls of the garage, looking behind the plywood boards and ladders and the bags of fertilizer for a shovel, and the sadness intensifies like it's coming up through my stomach again. Walking outside and back to the tree, the feeling inside of me is too much. I feel like some heavy thing is on top of my chest and pushing in on it. My hands have a stiff, clammy, sweaty feel. I could almost cry if I really let go.

I start to dig a hole underneath the tree. The first skimming shovels and chunks of half frozen dirt come up but with difficulty. I try balancing myself on the shovel, to wedge the tip deep into the frozen dirt.

"What are you doing? We're getting ready to go to church."

Amy stands beside the open basement door.

I try to think of something to say but I really don't want to start talking about what I'm doing. I look away, step back up on the shovel, wiggling the handle around while poised upright. Quickly hopping off with a jerk of the handle to the ground, and the dirt's too frozen. It's going to take too long to dig this hole and now I have to hurry up about it and then go inside and get dressed.

Amy steps over to see the wren lying on top of the snow.

"You killed that bird? Why'd you do that?"

I place the bird inside the shallow hole, then scrape some of the nearby dirt and snow over it.

"Are you sure it's dead?"

"I didn't mean to kill it. I just wanted to scare it."

—|—

"This is my body. Which will be shed so that sins may be forgiven."

The alter boy shakes the bells, and I watch Father Nicholas raise both hands and the Eucharist above his head. He's turning the bread into Jesus' body now.

Inside the Catholic Encyclopedia they've given a name to what the priest is doing at this part of the service. They call it transubstantiation.

I accidentally shot and killed a bird about an hour ago and now I'm supposed to get into this. Like something is still crushing in on my chest and my fingers and feet can't seem to warm up. The sadness inside me won't go away either, and I can't understand why it's staying so long.

With my hands in a grip upon the back of the church pew in front of me, a memory picture presents itself of the wren's head hanging limp and off the side of my hand, and intensifying the pressure inside my chest. This sad feeling seems to live and be on its own. It's feeding itself by creating thoughts like this with me. I want to really and totally ignore it all.

It's a stupid bird, I tell myself. *They fall out of trees all the time, all over the world. One moment they're alive and perched on a branch. A second later and they're too old for their heart to beat even one more time so off they go, falling from the branch and hitting the ground.*

Tough boogers. That's the way the cookie crumbles.

Probably hundreds of thousands of different birds of prey all over the world at this very moment are smacking up other birds in midair for lunch. Attacking then ripping their little bird bodies into smaller pieces to feed to other baby bald eagles nesting on the steep side of a windy cliff somewhere upon a tall, cold Rocky Mountain ledge.

Thinking like this helps change feelings a little. I smirk at my thoughts.

I feel tired too while I stand. Muscles in my legs and arms are stiff. So strong is its affect on my mind and its effect to my body. It's like I'm starting to get sick with the flu or something. I can't believe something like this feeling is out of my control. Rather, I realize I can't control the way I'm going to react with my feelings to certain situations. I'm just going to ignore it.

"This is my blood," I hear Father saying. "The blood of the new and everlasting covenant. To be shed for all men so that sins may be forgiven. Do this in memory of me."

I am sad, and for what?

If I had my druthers I would have just as soon as had shot the thing to be done with it then too. I mean, that's it, done.

I look at Amy standing next to me and think, if something happened to her, like she broke her arm or something? If I thought it would help I might definitely want to switch on my sadness and be sad like this with her for a while, maybe if I thought it would help her, but I don't care about a bird. Because of a bird I feel like this? I can't believe that I am feeling such a feeling as this, over a bird ... over a dumb bird! My chest aches, parts of my arms and legs ache, and it won't go away. I didn't care about an animal's life before this happened and I don't even care about one right now.

Wow. How in God's name did I get like this? There's no reason.

I'm watching Father Nicholas make the sign of the cross with his hand, and I know he's concluding Mass.

"Go now, the Mass has ended. Go in peace."

The congregation returns with, "Thanks be to God," and I now let my clenched fist slowly fall forward to hit the back of the pew in front of me. I vocally inflect those same exact words with my own Sunday versions manner of them which conveys precisely my feelings that the sheer torture of attending Mass, thanks be to God, is finally over.

Because Amy has already turned away from me, I twist myself to perform more directly in front of her.

"Thanks be to God!" I slowly proclaim to her. This time I draw out the word God for her, and I shake a clenched fist in front of her to emphasize the agony of the situation.

Amy sees something behind me and her eyes open wide. She's startled looking at whatever is in back of me. I quickly turn around and look towards Moms standing in the middle of the pew. Her attention is forward and on the services, though a moment for a side glance our way, and with a tilt of the head that familiar look of attentive eyes is upon us.

She tricked me. I raise the left side of my upper lip and expose the cusp of a fang her way.

People are filing out from the pews and stepping into the aisles.

Mass is finished. Hallelujah!

Moms Is The Best

Moms will always tell us to go and get into our pajamas first is probably why Festus and Max don't like to read the Bible with us any more. They always say they have something else they want to do. It was better this way though, with all of us sitting on the couch now. With Amy on one side of Moms and me on the other, it was perfect.

"Do not let your hearts be troubled," Moms begins tonight. "Have faith in God, and have faith in me."

"In my Father's house there are many dwelling places," she continues. "Otherwise, how could I have told you I was going to prepare a place for you. I am indeed going to prepare a place for you. That where I am you may also be."

"What did Jesus mean when he said, '*otherwise how could I.*' What did he want to say there?"

"That did sound a little clunky there didn't it?" Moms empathizes to us.

I look up to see her in thought. I curl up close to Moms and wait for her to gather her thoughts and entertain this question of ours.

"In Jesus' time people didn't speak the English language like we do today. There are many languages in the world. Some people, using their language correctly, construct sentences differently than ours. They'll put and emphasize a noun before a verb. They'll say a sentence their way that when translated into English would sound like ... oh? *Kurt please, house inside Peanuts put,* and this when translated and spoken our way in English would be, *Kurt, would you please let Peanuts inside the house.*"

"What Jesus was saying, and what he was trying to emphasize to the apostles was his statement that, *in his Father's house there are many dwelling places,* is really true. It's true because why would he say he was preparing a place for them if it were untrue? Why would he say that if there wasn't a house with many dwelling places to begin with?"

I wait for Moms to say more, 'cause I still don't understand what the awkward semantics in that passage want to convey.

"When Jesus said, ... *his Father's house,* he was talking about heaven right?"

Moms agrees with this, nodding her head.

"Why didn't Jesus simply say he's going to get heaven ready for them then?"

Moms is silent for a moment.

"Imagine Jesus walking with the disciples. Mid-afternoon and it's been a warm, sticky, humid day of walking in the hot sun. They still have a few more hours of walking to do before arriving in town. Jesus wants to preach in the synagogue for a time, for a few days, before moving on to another town."

"They want to get to where they're going before nightfall too. But since it's been so uncomfortably warm and they're already kinda tired, they decide to stop and rest for a few minutes along a crop of rocks they see in the distance."

Moms fans through a section of pages to show both Amy and I a single page with the words, *The Gospel According to John.*

"This is John's book, and what he remembers while he was with Jesus."

Moms turns to me and then to Amy. "But he only started to write down all these things about forty, maybe fifty years after they all took place."

"Why'd he wait so long?"

"Oh, I've read some things ... on why. I'll try to explain some of the better ones."

"During those days, ... when after Jesus had brought himself back to life and he was walking and talking with his friends again, he soon began to say to certain people that he'd have to leave them and go away for a while. He told these people to wait for him though, because he'll be coming back."

"Well, one day he did leave. The apostles went on to the mission Jesus had given them. Disciples went about their business, and everyone doing whatever they had to do all the while waiting for Jesus to come back like he said he would."

"The days turn into weeks. The months become years and people become concerned, wondering what could be keeping Jesus occupied for so long. Some people today believe that there was a band of five or six or more apostles who had remained together as a group. This group lived and worked together and are especially concerned for Jesus to return."

"Time passes and still no Jesus. John and Mary, Mark and Luke, Matthew and Paul, at some point in time they came to realize that after all the years of waiting for Jesus to return like he said he would, there now were only a small handful of the original twelve still alive. They're having doubts if Jesus will ever return. Perhaps they had misunderstood him and what he meant when he said he would return back to them so long ago."

"They realize that after they die, no one will be around to tell everyone all the things they heard and saw Jesus saying and doing. So they decide then and there to write down some of the experiences and memories they had while they were with Jesus, and in that way to have his words and deeds written in a book for other people to have and to read."

After a moment of silence I look up.

"That explain things a little bit?" Moms says to Amy.

I suppose it does.

How would anyone know about Jesus if the Apostles didn't write the things down?

Moms continues. "John thinks to try for a quick nap while they rest beside the rocks. He lays himself down upon the sand, closes his eyes and begins to relax. He hears little bits of conversation between Jesus and the others though he's trying not to listen to them too much anymore."

"What the other apostles have been talking to Jesus about all day long, ... in fact for the last couple of days is why can't they have a place all of their own."

Moms mimics an apostle, putting some bass in her voice.

"Come on Jesus, why don't You make us all a palace more splendid than Herod's? Make something way out here, away from everyone. No one will ever know. What's the big deal?"

Interrupting Moms now with, "Because Jesus can if he wants to, right?"

"He can if he wants to," Moms affirms. "But he's on a mission and so he's learned to only use his miracles in away that will make God, his Father, honorable."

"Right now," Moms furthers, "they're probably pestering him, as they occasionally do when they're tired and hungry, they want Jesus to do a miracle to make their life at the moment a little bit easier."

"Imagine being with a guy who makes blind people see, deaf people hear. He makes every type of sick person that's brought before him healthy right in front of your eyes, and all he will do for you—you who are his so called friend, is to maybe miraculously put a patch on your old shoes. He probably didn't even do something as simple as that for them."

"He forged a Roman coin and then put it into the fish's mouth," I say, "for Peter to give the tax man though, remember?"

I sit up on my haunches hoping Moms will start to talk about this again. I don't really believe Jesus would intentionally counterfeit Roman coins to pay taxes, but how did Jesus put that coin into the fish's mouth to have Peter then find it like that? Moms never did come up with a really good reason why he did it like that.

Moms turns to me. "What if there were no laws on the books for counterfeiting back then. Now what d'you got to say?"

Amy sits up and leans over Moms to tell me, "He could have gotten horses for them to ride too, but he made them walk all over the place."

Moms looks to Amy. I watch Amy and Moms stare at each other, and then Moms turns her head down.

"Walk in the hot sun, ... and sleep outside under the stars."

Tears form around Moms eyes. I sit back and look at Amy, and she gets up to put her arms around her.

"Mom, it's ok?"

A second or two to compose herself. Moms shakes her head to throttle the thought away, and then with both arms scrunches us close.

Wiping her eyes, "So perhaps today they're acting really grumpy with Jesus."

"Jesus was walking with John up in front of everyone, leading the group through the trails. Someone was even throwing pebbles at the back of Jesus for a while. Trying to bean him. To get him mad. Playing mean because they're unhappy with him."

"That was probably Judas doing that, Mom."

"Perhaps. All of them know Jesus could help them live better by doing miracles, yet he's making them walk for hours in the hot sun. Leading them out of another town, and he's bringing them into the desert, again! In the minds of many of the apostles it seems Jesus is going nowhere, and to nothing in life."

"Jesus, what are we doing out here!" Philip says, almost hysterical. "Where are we going?"

"For all these months we've been with you, all of us see by the kindness and hospitality of others we will sleep in other peoples homes. We will eat food others have prepared, and wear the clothes others have made and then given to us. Why?!"

Philip then recalls incidents in villages they've been to.

"Total strangers come to you and ask for your help. Your heart is touched immediately for them. And yet our burdens and daily sufferings you will do nothing to ease."

Jesus has been sitting inclined upon a flattened bolder. Looking out towards the hills in the distance, he turns to look thoughtfully towards Philip and, without response he turns away.

Perplexed, Philip steps in front of Jesus, "Why don't you help us some?"

Philip lifts his foot to show Jesus the hole in his shoe.

"Even now as I speak to you, you lay there. Why?"

Jesus tells Philip that he's preparing a place at this very moment, inside his Father's house, where they will all live and dwell together.

Several disciples listen to the conversation of Jesus and Philip a short distance away.

"Judas, hear that?" Bartholomew snaps to those near him. "Jesus says he's making beds for us at his Father's house. That's where we're going now."

Judas nods and closes his eyes to hear moaning and sardonic laughs of frustration and ridicule from those around him.

"Jesus hasn't got a father or his father's house anymore," Judas says. "The horse of the Centurion Longinus killed the Nazorean years ago. Everyone knows that."

"Let's try talking Jesus into going back to Jerusalem," suggests Simon the Zealot. "He should be preaching to the Pharisee's and the Sadducee's. There's no one worth talking to in Samaria. Why are we going there?"

"Peter, listen. You're his friend. Go over there and ask him ...? Ask him if we all get our beds in separate rooms or do we all have to sleep in the same room together."

Peter stands up and throws a clutch of sand to the ground.

"Ask him yourself," he says walking away from their boorish conversation.

"I'm not sleeping in the same room as John," says Thaddaeus. "He snores way too loud. Forget it. I want out, now."

"Hey, where is Big John? Did he also leave us? Where is he?"

"He's lying down over behind those rocks. See his feet sticking out over there?"

"John was not quite asleep, but almost," Moms imagines. "Decades later he remembers the next words of Jesus to Philip."

"Jesus said to them, *Do not let your hearts be troubled. You have faith in God, have faith also in me. In my Fathers house there are many dwelling places. If there were not, would I have told you that I am going to prepare a place for you? And if I go and prepare a place for you, I will come back again and take you to myself, so that where I am you also may be. Where I am going you know the way.*"

"That's cool, Mom."

"John just caught the middle of a conversation."

Moms agrees. "John remembers forty, fifty some odd years later what Jesus had said to settle those guys down from some commotion stirring them up at the moment, it seems."

"Jesus isn't flustered so much by all the things said and done to him. Yes, he finds it necessary to explain himself every now and then, but he stays focused on why he's on this earth in the first place."

Moms continues reading from the fourteenth chapter.

"Thomas now said to him, 'Master, we do not know where You are going. How can we know the way?'"

"Most of the disciples are still in the dark why Jesus brings them all over hill and dale, and simply to preach in synagogues and to do miracles only for the sick and helpless people. It probably puzzles most of them why Jesus won't create his own army, set up their own kingdom on the earth with it, and then just give everything and anything to anyone who asks for it."

"Like Santa Claus."

"Then everyone would like him."

"Do you think Jesus ever thought of doing that, even once Mom?"

Moms pauses for thought.

"Well, the Bible tells us when he was in the desert for forty days his human nature tempted the divine nature inside him."

"This makes some people ask when and how did Jesus know he could do miracles like he did. Did he one day wake up and there was this note on his pillow from an angel, saying, *Jesus, you can do miracles now*? Or as I like to think and believe, that Jesus was born with an ability to do miracles."

"God, the Father of all creation gives time for most if not all forms of life to learn how to use their bodies. Frogs learn how to hop. Snakes learn how to swirl around. Birds from the nest watch other birds and in time understand their wings are there to fly with."

"Jesus was a little over thirty years old when he began doing miracles publicly, in front of others. If I think I know how God does things I would guess that the Father wanted Jesus to also take his time to learn how to use his body, his mind, his power to do miracles."

"So probably at an early age Jesus did something once, sometime, somewhere as a young boy that made him realize to himself that he could do things by wishing, or just by wanting something to be, it then existed for him."

"And God the Father put two pious Jewish people in charge of raising Jesus to learn how to use this miracle power responsibly. While Jesus was growing up he wouldn't've been too human if he didn't make a few mistakes every now and then, ... at first."

Moms furthers. "In a passage Mary is taken and cared for by John after Jesus goes to the cross and dies. Those two then are probably the home base the apostles and disciples will search for when they arrive back at Jerusalem."

"After Jesus left them, a number of the apostles traveled throughout the Mediterranean area, and to different villages and cities in Persia, Asia, preaching the good news of Jesus. Some of these guys went very far away, and some were probably gone a long time."

"When they came back to Jerusalem though, they knew that there would always be a place for them wherever John and Mary happened to be living at the time. Their place is a place for them to wash and rest up, to get something to eat. It was the house of John and Mary they all probably knew to look around for and ask for first upon arriving back in Jerusalem."

"They were like a headquarters," I realize.

"Something like that, sure," Moms replies, indifferent. "Also, since John and Mary were living together they must have shared stories, and together they found the time to reflect on the past. John must have been more than a little curious once or twice in all those years to ask Mary what Jesus was like as a boy. Luke must have been at their house too, and on occasion he will bring up the subject with Mary."

Moms pauses a moment.

"Yet in their collective wisdom they decide not to mention to those whom they thought would read their books how Jesus came to first know or how he learned to temper his power ... for the glory of God. The important things to them were to have a lot of the public words and deeds of Jesus and the meaning of it passed on for others to read about in the future."

"The Book of John is different in so many ways. I always like to think some of the words and memories, the desires of what Mary wanted known to future generations are in this book."

"Mom ...? What d'you think would've happened if Jesus didn't die? If somehow he wasn't put on the cross to die? Do you think he'd've lived on earth forever?"

Moms thinks upon this for a second or two, and then with deliberate, thoughtful motion she turns pages towards the front of the book. Shaking her head she closes the book face down, opens it and leafs through pages at the back of the book. Single pages are turned before she finds what she wants.

"In the tenth chapter of John, verses seventeen and eighteen, Jesus says, *This is why the Father loves me, because I lay down my life in order to take it up again. No one takes it from me, but I lay it down on my own. I have power to lay it down, and the power to take it up again. This command I have received from my Father.*"

Moms is staring down into the page, and she's thinking about something.

"There are no cross-references here. He surely didn't read that command out of somewhere in the Old Testament then, while he was growing up," Moms reasons. "I wonder how and where he did receive this command from his Father."

"To answer your question, I'd venture he wouldn't've had the love and intentions of the Father following him, so we wouldn't've had the Jesus we read about here, either? I don't know."

"Wouldn't it've been better if Jesus stayed here? If he didn't die?"

"Why did he have to die?"

"All right. We'll explore this a little. See where it leads to."

The clock on the wall has just begun a series of soft, bass chimes. It's eight o'clock, and we'll wait for the clock to be quiet before we begin again.

"Keep in mind that the Father has put Jesus on this earth for a reason. To accomplish a goal. The Father didn't plant Jesus on the earth and then just sit back to watch and see what happens."

"Also, Jesus went through thirty years of life before he began to minister and perform miracles in front of people. During the last ten, twenty years of his life he must have given a lot of prayerful thought towards the best way to bring honor and glory to his Father."

Come on, Jesus tells himself. *Forget work and working for a living. It takes too long to earn and save enough money to buy the things you want. Earning money through hard work is for the ordinary people.*

Just turn the stones at your feet into bread, and eat whenever you want.

"As Jesus was growing up and maturing, many similar thoughts probably came up as temptations in his life. And through his own readings of the Scriptures, with Mary and Joseph coaching and counseling him, eventually he comes to realize the mission the Father has in store for him."

Moms stops talking and thinks for a long moment.

"Imagine Jesus working in the carpentry shop with Joseph one day. He's using a hammer to pound some pieces to a wooden wagon wheel together. His attention wanders for a moment and bang! He hits his fingers with the hammer. Oh, the pain. Jesus throws the hammer down to the ground and, blaming the hammer for the pain, he looks at it, wanting it to go away."

Burn, turn to fire, Jesus thinks.

"Poof! The hammer bursts into flames. Joseph smells smoke and as he wanders around the shop in search of a fire he finds Jesus holding the fingers of his hand, and nearby are the hammer's iron head next to the smoldering ashes of the handle."

"Especially during his childhood," Moms explains, "how many times did Jesus think along these lines whenever he saw something he wanted or needed, or that he didn't like or want? That is, until he experienced enough of life to know and then to realize how his actions can effect others and the world around him."

"The tremendous responsibility that the Father had bestowed on Mary and Joseph to raise Jesus to the person he became, and that we know of now in the Bible, is awesome. As an adult we read him cursing a fig tree once because it didn't have any figs on it, and he only flips the tables over, he decides to use his hands to flip the tables in the Temple."

"For the most part, from what we read we can conclude that Mary and Joseph did their part and did a pretty good job of raising Jesus from a boy to a man."

"If Jesus didn't die on the cross? I guess he would've just grown old and died. I don't know of any place in the Bible that says he would've stayed alive forever and not grown old and died," Moms says, and finishing the idea.

Our want for a more realistic answer to the question is unrelenting and we're not letting up on Mom's in pursuit for one.

"But what if he did. What if he became King of the world. Why would that be so wrong?"

A moment or two of time passes before the hammers of Amy and Kurt come around again to hit this nail square on its head, completely driving home the point.

"What if Jesus gave himself the miracle that he was never to grow old, and also never to die?"

For some reason I have to turn and look up towards Moms, to see what she's thinking.

"I guess that's possible," Moms says to us.

"Jesus would become King of the Earth? And do miracles to help everyone on the earth, in those days and all the way up to our times?"

I sit up. Amy is smirking. Her eyes stare down, entranced. I know we definitely got Moms going on a really good question this time.

A squint to her eyes, Moms rubs the page of the Bible with a thumb and the palm of her hand. Eventually to bring an unfortunate look upon her face.

"Jesus would say a miracle and fill all the wooden boats with food," Moms says, "to then sail all over the world and feed everyone. If any boat happens to become lost because of bad weather or some mishap, and with Jesus to realize some people wouldn't be able to eat for awhile, well, he would miraculously make another wooden boat, fill it with food and have it sail away."

"He'd probably make the second boat better too Mom, so it wouldn't sink like the first one."

"Hmm? I don't know about that," Moms replies. "With Jesus as a king doing miracles all the time, everyone's gotten sort of lazy after a while. Two thousand years with Jesus as King of the World and no one really wants to think to do work anymore."

"Complicated things like diesel engines are never, ever thought of and built on the earth, for any reason at all. There's no reason to cause anyone to think to make a radio or a TV, electric lights, telephones, or toasters. No cars, motorcycles, or airplanes exist then, of course."

"Maybe in some places around the world a wooden bicycle or two is built, but certainly everyone who wants a bicycle doesn't have one. Two thousand years with Jesus as king and today people like you and me are still using beasts of burden to get anything and everything important done."

Moms continues, "No pizza's were thought of. No hamburgers or pistachio ice cream or Snicker's bars exist either."

Moms just gave us some food for thought, and something to stew on for a moment.

"Mom, what did they eat back then?"

Again I have to readjust myself on the couch. I try to think of the things they may have eaten, only to hear Moms say, "Oh? One delicacy they had and liked back then…, was chicken soup."

I turn to look at Amy, and she's smirking, too.

"Mom, chicken soup isn't a delicacy."

—1—

Rockets And Mary Christiane

It was the laughing machine and the coffee. The combination of both of them together just made the thought of watching television right now a complete waste of time. I want to do something else. Maybe I'll go downstairs and see if anyone is doing anything in a minute or two.

I had only begun to drink coffee and tea. Getting to know whether I liked them with or without milk and cream, with one or two scoops, or no sugar. Do I like coffee more than tea? Will a regular expression in my life be, "Nothing with caffeine, please"? I'm finding out.

I don't know what the problem is with the TV.

"Oh! ha-ha!"

"Ha! Oh..., ha-ha-ha."

"Ha-ha!"

Every second or third sentence no matter what anyone said they turned that laughing machine on.

"Ha-ha-ha ... Oh! Ha-ha!"

"Ha-ha! Ha-ha-ha!"

"Drink too much and it'll make you feel jittery," was the warning.

I don't think every other spoken sentence said by these television characters is actually so funny it warrants hearing another outburst of laughter from the laughing machine, and I feel like I want to jump out of my skin.

I hear Max yelling outside, and I get up off the couch.

"Kurt! Come on, we're gonna shoot off the rockets."

A spark to my steps as I sprint out the sliding glass door and down the deck stairs. Festus is kneeling on the grass and readying a rocket for launch on the wooden platform. Four other rockets lie on the grass near the platform. Silver igniter wire extend from each rocket's motor nozzle.

The tackle box is open. Packages of igniters. Tubes of individual rocket motors. Tissue paper for wading the igniters tight inside the rocket nozzles, all the stuff is bunched together alongside the blue plastic nine-volt battery that takes up half the space at the bottom of the tackle box. Needle-nose pliers, small jewelers screwdrivers, and other things lie inside the folding tray above the battery.

A moment's recollection and I ask either one of them, "What'd you put in the nose cones?"

"Just baby powder," Max says.

I watched Festus and Max build two of the rockets in the basement a couple days ago. They began talking about hollowing the nose cones and filling them with what they hadn't decided at the time. I assume all the rockets are ready for launch and there's no sense to think of getting myself involved.

I walk away from the launch platform and into the shade of some trees, laying down on the grass to watch them go through the initial pre-countdown sequence of events before liftoff.

Model rocketry seems to be going the way of the dinosaurs, at least with me. It's fun to build model rockets and shoot 'em off, but the rocket motors are expensive and I don't want to spend my allowance money on rockets anymore. The last couple of times at the hobby store I didn't buy anything. I walked around the store and the thought of putting another model rocket together, then shooting it up into the air to watch it float back down by parachute, and the thought doesn't thrill me any more. There's nothing else to do with these things besides shoot 'em off and watch 'em float back down again. The newness has worn off, though Festus and Max seem to have found a way to keep their interest going a little longer.

A rocket is poised upright on the launch platform. Festus connects the two alligator clips from battery to igniter wire, and when his hands move to the battery I do a quick scan of the backyard to see Amy with Mary Christiane Dietrich near the rock garden. They're waiting for the action to start.

I hear the rocket engine ignite and turn to watch the bright red rocket already up past the platform guide bar. A soft screech of sound as the rocket catapults up and begins arching midair somersaults and cartwheels until it spins itself down to the ground prone and motionless. The rocket motor continues thrusting a plume of smoke and bits of earth against clumps of grass until the sudden sound of silence returns to the backyard.

Wow. What happened that time?

I turn and watch Festus already stepping towards the rocket. Max kneels at the staging platform. He's tamping the wadding tight inside the motor of the next rocket. That first rocket didn't travel up into the air more than fifteen feet at it's apogee, and flying maybe ten, twenty yards of distance before hitting the ground.

What Festus and Max want to do now is fire the rocket not straight up and then have it parachute straight down. That's old hat. They're tilting the launching guide bar to an angle anywhere between ten and forty-five degrees and making the rocket fly through the backyard and then into the tops of the trees. Hollowing the nose cones and the powder payloads? Interesting.

I watch Festus and Max set things up for launch of the next rocket, and I think a bit about what may have happened to make the rocket do the loop-de-do the way it did. It's either because the payload weight from the baby powder in the nose cone caused the rocket to become top heavy, this causing the nose to tilt and drop soon after it left the launch guide bar, resulting in the head under tail spin of the rocket to develop, or … the thrust of the motor was too much for the size of that rocket.

Thinking things through a bit more, what happened may have been a combination of both of those two things. Somewhere, somehow the rocket became unbalanced. Once the rocket became unstable to continue in a straight line of flight the surface area of the stabilizing fins didn't create enough of a countering force necessary to bring it to a straight line of flight. Even if it wasn't a balanced rocket if it had larger stabilizing fins there would be no such thing as "too much thrust" then.

I'm just thinking and guessing about it all now. I don't know.

All five rockets are identical in construction. Each approximately a foot and a half in length, a little thicker in diameter than two fingers side by side, with four stabilizing fins. Each rocket has been sprayed with a bright, fluorescent red color. They looked neat lying side by side on top of the green of the lawn grass.

Max readjusts the angle of the guide bar. From where I'm watching from I can see the angle of the launch bar is still less than forty-five degrees. These lower angles of rocket flight are more dramatic in that they don't fly up and then past the tops of one or two trees, zipping out of the backyard maybe never to be seen again. Ideally and for show purposes, between fifteen and twenty-five degrees are the best trajectories to produce that hugging and skimming-just-above-the-ground type of flight. Sixty degrees makes the wonderful power arches, the rocket competing between lift and falling as it traces a path through open sky. At these angles, less than two full seconds of flight time and the rocket is above the treetops and out of sight. Skimmers are the better trajectories to shoot and then watch for. I think they're the best anyway.

The second rocket fires and flies straight off the guide bar and it's on its way to the trees. Thrilling to watch every time: a stationary rocket instantly swish sounding a trajectory through the backyard.

For some reason a rocket will start swerving left or right, or suddenly veering sharply up or down before crashing into something. One rocket once zigzaggedly maneuvered itself all the way through the backyard before hitting a tree. The sights and sounds and the smell of rockets coursing through the backyard is so cool. I'd like to spend an hour and watch fifty rockets go flying off at different times.

The motors Festus and Max are using on these rockets are burning and producing thrust for just under a second of time. You can buy motors that burn thrust for a quarter-second, half-second, incrementing all the way to a full three-seconds of total burn-thrust time. For what we're doing though a longer burning motor is unnecessary, and longer burning motors are expensive. The motors we've been using the last few times seem to have the thrust kicking out as the rocket approaches the end of the backyard. At least that's when it appears the sound of thrust will seem to end.

I've tried to think of things to make model rocketry more interesting. To think of something practical to do with rockets now that I know a little bit about them. I'm putting forth the time and the effort to build something and I want to make it seem like the activity is important in some way. One thing I thought was to create something competitive.

The thought was to employ scale model replicas of historic sea vessels, or model submarines and aircraft, remote controlled model tanks inside combat situations. Perhaps from opposite inlets of a pond of water two fleets of scale model seventeenth, eighteenth, nineteenth century wooden frigates enter and sail towards each other. I imagine the spectators standing on the banks and surrounding this area of open water and chatting up conversation before the action starts. Some spectators sit under their umbrella café tables and with binoculars in hand they watch the pre-battle maneuverings. Commandeered by radio control, uneventful moments pass as each of the vessels sail into proximity to each other. Careful and cautious, thinking and acting as a team the commander of each vessel will seek positions for putting cannon to another, or to maneuver themselves out from harms way.

A bright sunny day it is. Birds chirp in the trees. Babies play, sleep in their strollers ...

A modest gust of wind has brought a first and then a second frigate with billowing sails, and a sudden brisk clip of speed is put to their hulls. As if watching a game of chess several spectators familiar with the sport of model ship battle realize the wind as an opportunity, and a number of vessels are observed turning in an attempt to travel forward bow of other model frigates. A threat to one vessel has been recognized only to have the hapless operator turn the vessel into the wind and the vessel becomes motionless. Seconds of time pass as three operators commandeer their vessels into offensive positions. Perceiving battle imminent spectators rise from their chairs, binoculars brought up to focus upon the four vessels. A first frigate travels directly forward bow and a full sixteen cannon, firecracker-sized broadside hurtles projectiles towards the one ill-fated vessel. I have to imagine the sound from the first crackles of battle have brought all spectators turning from conversation and towards the pond.

Another vessel sails towards the stricken frigate and unleashes a fusillade of cannon fire. Cloth sails are pierced and ripped. Pinewood masts splinter, crack and topple, entangling rigging. Projectiles shatter the pinewood hull. Shards, pieces and bits of plastic and metal splish splashing across the water's surface. The crippled vessel lists port side. Smoke and flames erupt from the hull and this event brings cheers and the clapping of hands. The stern is levered out to rise above the water line. The bow fills with water and with the hull sinking fast a puff of smoke appears, the wisp of smoke rising as the last and final inches of the frigate's stern is brought down and below the water.

I give a hearty and gung-ho yes if this were to be what one of many typical pond water battles are like. I myself would pay a few dollars for an afternoon ticket to watch a number of these mock battles take place. All the while perhaps munching on a hamburger, hotdogs, French fries, and soda too? I definitely could imagine myself becoming a fan of events like this.

After buying an admission ticket I imagine people stand within an open field and watch professional remote controlled operators fly their scale model planes in dogfights a couple hundred feet in the sky. Two enthusiastic model builders of World War vintage aircraft mix a Sopwith Camel with a Fokker DII, and it'd be cool watching one of the model planes exploding parts and pieces of itself into the sky before the rest of the plane swirls down to crack up on the ground. Air battles like this would definitely be cool to watch. I imagine people would enjoy watching and engaging in competitive events such as this if given enough sponsors to reward prize money. Perhaps with some of the better contenders being sponsored, and the event itself is a platform for manufacturers to advertise their products with.

The tank battle scenario I thought through a little bit more vividly than the others, realizing the projectiles fired during a model tank battle will have to be powerful enough to do damage to another tank, and concluding these thoughts with the fact that I'm not going to be a spectator in proximity to where some thing is actually exploding bits of shrapnel all around.

Spectators situated close to a mock battle as it was occurring was the incentive to attend these type of events. Though the vivid, explicit nature of my imagined elements to an actual tank battle made the reality of the situation a bit clearer to myself. Watching land, sea, and air models operating in mock battle in open space may be too hazardous as a spectator sport, but the basic idea of what I'm trying to do isn't that far fetched.

There are millions of people involved in building different scale models of one kind or another but there's a lack of any real practical purpose to further the interest along. After building a model it eventually ends up hanging from the ceiling or collecting dust on the shelf of a room. I'd like to bring a more practical purpose for these models, something no one else is thinking of doing. Maybe I could start making money promoting events, with live coverage rights I'll negotiate to the highest bidder. I'll get myself some big bucks and some real money rolling in.

Over the weeks and months these type of thoughts evolved into a competition where some thing is retrieved.

I thought to have a model rocket shot into the sky to fifteen, twenty-thousand feet and with a homing beacon as payload wherever this payload will drift to and land by parachute the goal will be to find and then return the homing beacon to some other predetermined location. This winning objective is being pursued in competition with two or more teams of model aircraft, ships, and or vehicles.

I imagine the beacon to land upon a water surface and then perhaps to float for a time, with the homing beacon eventually submerging to drift inside some underwater currents before becoming stationary on the floor of the body of water. This scenario didn't appear difficult, and seemed to make the beacon too easy to find and then recover. I want the challenge to be more difficult. Difficult in the range of where this new sport I'm thinking of someday turns into an Olympic event and participants are awarded gold, bronze, and silver medals for their accomplishments. The terrain the beacon lands upon and which the models will have to traverse across should be hazardous to navigate through. Hills to climb, streams to ford, cliffs to rappel, contact with wild animals, and of course any type of contact with other competing models is a threat. Any and all potential obstacles determine the degree of difficulty for the goal of retrieving and returning the homing beacon.

I imagine a situation where two or more of the better models are converging into the immediate area where the beacon is located. All these models in close proximity to each other will attempt to debilitate each other, with the victorious model then able to take possession of the beacon.

So each model has to be equipped to cause debilitating acts to other models or to somehow scare off an animal if this were the situation. These models should not be designed to be passive towards the outside world. They have to be constructed possessing both defensive and offensive capacities so as to function within an environment enabling it to accomplish any of the premeditated acts a designer of a model believes necessary to accomplish the objectives.

After the one triumphant model attaches the beacon to itself, the model now has to bring itself and the beacon to some other predetermined destination as the final leg of the competition. Returning itself and the beacon by the same ways and means it brought itself to wherever it is, or maybe it finds an open space which it now launches itself up and out of by it's own self-contained helicopter apparatus, flying all the way back to the destination.

Waiting for Max to ignite the next rocket, I imagine these mechanical models ...? *Model robots I guess they are. These model robots are ...? Mergatroids.* If I ever do make something of this idea *I'm going to call them Murgatroyds. I think that's a nifty name for these babies to be called.*

Max has his hands placed on top of the battery. The rocket is as quick as an arrow and flies a straight thirty, forty degree angle a good fifty yards before whipping itself into an intersection of branches at the end of a large limb of a tree. The rocket ricocheted inside the clump of branches before the motor went silent. It didn't look like any pieces of the rocket fell down to the ground, and I didn't see anything that would make me believe it crashed into anything as it went inside those branches. I guess it's just hung up there, somehow, and it might be fixable for another flight later on.

The length of burn to these motors is just right. It's not good to have them burning, still thrusting once out of sight. Dad came out once and watched when we were doing this. He told us not to do anything that's going to have to make him have to tell us to stop. OK.

The motors burn fairly clean too, leaving little if any hot sparks we thought at first would trail out of the back of the exhaust and that could start a fire way out in the woods somewhere later on. We're careful with these things. You have to think ahead sometimes about what you're doing, and then just cross your fingers and hope for the best.

Meurgutroyds are going to have to have a number of capacities to collect data about the environment I realize too, and then to relay this information back to an operator to respond with in real time.

The next rocket fired flies through the backyard with a soft swish of sound, flying out of sight and silent inside a mass of extended branches from a couple of trees. After it flew inside the batch of branches the engine went quiet. I'm going to check this one out when they're done, and see what happened. I think that rocket might've smashed and smooshed itself into the tree trunk.

I want to pursue ways to get battles between model robots to work as a spectator sport. Where to start? How do you get people to want to do stuff like this? Watching Festus and Max readying the next and last rocket for launch, I wait for something to come to mind...

The motor fires the rocket past the launch bar and immediately begins summersaults and cartwheels until it's about twenty, thirty yards up in the air. Thrusting pinwheels round and around but slowly falling back to the ground, the motor cuts out and thrust stops. The rocket now goes into silent free fall, centrifugal force keeps it spinning all the way down until it finally hits the ground.

That was a really fine show, as Ed Sullivan would say. A round of applause is in order so I clap my hands as I stand and then start walking towards Festus and Max. They're both walking in the direction of where rocket number four ended up, so I get myself into a little trot to catch up to them. I know all the rockets had baby powder in them so I'm a little more curious about the first and last ones that flubbed up.

Walking fast and I'm soon strolling alongside Max.

"What happened?"

He doesn't answer right away and I assume he's thinking about the first and last rockets too.

"Why'd they spiral around like that?"

He shrugs his shoulders. He doesn't seem to care about why.

"Those one's that spun out were the last of the E engines," he says. "There's just one left. The others were B's."

E's are the most powerful engines Estes makes.

"Probably definitely might've been too much umphf in back. Out of balance with the baby powder up top," I say.

Festus and Max look over towards me and chuckle. Festus nods and says, "Yeah, probably that too."

Festus and Max don't sound all that enthused about why those rockets did what they did. I'm not really interested either. It's just fun to watch them fly through the backyard is all. A little afternoon delight.

Stepping off the weeds and grass of the backyard to the packed down dirt of the trail around the pond, the air is tinged with gunpowder. I bring that aroma of gunpowder to taste sweet inside my mouth.

We walk close and see where high up in the tree the rocket rests. The view directly underneath the tree makes it clear that the thing is intact. Nothing appears broken up. It's lying flat, parallel to the ground on the fork of a branch. I can't see to tell what it is that has it snagged up there, but I imagine it falling off that branch if gusts of wind sway the top of the tree enough times. The tree is not one that's easy to climb, and there's not that much wind around at the moment so it might be up there for awhile.

All the other rockets are found and all have broken fins that need fixing. I walk back to the house and get some milk out of the refrigerator. Pouring the milk into a glass, drinking it down I figure I'll probably be walking around to who knows where for the next few hours so I make myself a sandwich.

Not much of each ingredient but enough raisins sprinkled on top of a modest spread of peanut butter upon each of the two slices of rye bread. A half dozen circular slices of banana are pushed into the peanut butter of one slice of bread. Three separated slices of bologna are placed on top of and off to one side of this pile on the bread. A button of honey is poured on the bologna, and then the top slice of bread is placed and pressed down to insure nothing falls out. It's not heavy but there is some weight to it as I bring it up for a first bite. It's a good sandwich.

For some reason I'm more thirsty than hungry after that rocket show they put on. Another bite of the sandwich and I pour and then force another glass of milk down. This gives my stomach that full, bloated feeling I want. I'll be gone for a while so all this food should tide me over till dinner time, I think. I take the sandwich outside with me, walking up the blacktop of the driveway and onto the asphalt of Val de Mar.

Mary Christiane and Amy are sitting and talking on their bikes at the foot of the driveway.

"If anyone asks, I went into Hopewell," I say to Amy as I walk past them.

I hear both of them ride up behind me.

"What's in Hopewell?" Amy asks.

"Nothing. I just want to see what's in the area around here. From here to Hopewell."

At the intersection of asphalt and blacktop I start hoofing it onto Carpenter Road. A few moments later I hear Amy asking, "Can we go?"

I turn around to see them sitting on their bikes at the intersection of Val de Mar, and I take myself back to where they are. I just pushed the last of the sandwich into my mouth so I have to stand in front of them for a second or two and wait till I've finished chewing and swallowing before answering them.

"I'm not staying on roads very much so if you want to you can't use your bikes."

"Wait here, all right? We'll be right back," Amy says, turning her bike around. They pedal back to the house and once they're out of sight I walk over to sit down against a telephone pole.

I see a ladybug down near my feet. I take hold of the twig the ladybug is crawling on and allow the ladybug to crawl from the stick onto my thumb, and I watch the ladybug on my thumb as I begin peeling strips of bark off the twig.

I think how none of those rockets broke up, splattering the baby powder around inside the trees like we wanted...

I watch a car go by on Carpenter, and then another car passes by. I think I may have drank all that milk too fast. Sitting now the way I am my stomach is bent and it's sort of starting to hurt.

I think, *Oh, wow!* How absolutely terrifically lucky I am to have found an empty, hollow military grenade shell in a steamer trunk, along with some other war stuff someone threw out last week. Heavy cast iron with square knobs all around. I found it in the town dump last Sunday. The weekend before last we saw the entrance to the dump, and then rode into it with our bikes but it was late afternoon and getting dark around supper time so we didn't stay very long. This last time we went though we spent practically the entire afternoon there.

Bill, Paul, Steve, and I rode over there after church. Wasn't long before each of us were rummaging through different sections and piles of the dump, finding and pulling interesting things out and about. There were boxes of clothes, typewriters, furniture, bicycle frames, old telephones, electrical kitchen appliances of every kind, car and truck parts and tires and wheels. Porcelain toilets and sinks and unbroken mirrors and any glass at all I immediately smashed. All the while breathing in that mild but unforgettably pungent air.

Recalling that smell of the dump back to myself and sitting the way I am against the telephone pole, not the sandwich so much but the stomach full of milk is making me feel sort of nauseous. I stand up and feel a small cramp in my stomach. I walk a few steps to maybe relax and work it out…, and to remember some more of the things we did at the dump that day.

We took the gas cap off the fuel tank, rolled up all the windows to a partially stripped automobile before igniting the interior fabric inside. Watching the insides of these six clear panes of window glass all around the car slowly turn black with soot and then each pane of glass, taking its own turn, in time we would hear a crispy ping as the glass of each window heats up and cracks. Each window cracking a number of times in fact, in different places because of all the intense heat I imagine was being built up as the thing was burning inside.

I couldn't see any flames though. I'm watching this car for as long as it seemed to be in a state of combustion and I soon realized how airtight the car was. Noticing how little smoke, almost no smoke at all was being brought outside for the amount of burning, especially the burning of plastics I knew was taking place inside there. I saw how any natural openings in the car, like foot-level passenger and driver side air vents or openings being caused from the fire and heat melting away carpets and plastic trim, pieces of weather stripping snugged up against the doors and trunk lid are burning and melting away and creating new air passages. Up in front alongside the firewall of the engine compartment I saw how any of these newly created air openings and the cracked glass openings were being used to draw and suck air outside the car into the shell of the car itself, and this is what kept feeding all the combustion.

For the entire time the car was on fire all the smoke and all the flames stayed inside where all the burning was going on. Practically no smoke, very little of it ever came out. It was sort of baffling me there for awhile as to why there wasn't any smoke rolling up and out of the thing as it kept on burning like it was.

The fire guys say to close doors in a fire. I really saw why to do so there. Not only were the flames of the fire itself contained, which was sort of expected, but the smoke was as well. All the smoke remained inside the shell of the car.

Eventually I find the steamer trunk. Pulling it up and out from all the other garbage and stuff it was under I realize it isn't heavy with any of the things I can tell are sliding around inside it. Two tension clasps keep the lid down and closed shut so of course I opened it and of course I didn't just toss it aside. Unsnapping the clasps and then lifting the top to find almost all empty space inside except for a couple of white dress shirts, a couple pairs of dark slacks, and what began to look like someone's personal collection of military paraphernalia all slid into one corner.

Colored ribbons and pins are all bunched together, and I have to separate each pin or ribbon out from all the other stuff it's tangled together with before looking at each article a little more attentively. Cloth patches to what were probably this guys former military units. There are a number of discolored pamphlet books of fifty, sixty pages published by the Army in 1951. Perhaps a dozen empty brass high-powered rifle shell casings. I push some cloth away, pick up another one of the booklets and underneath it lay the iron-gray grenade shell. I don't see the metal igniter trigger mechanism though my heart skipped a beat seeing it, and I'm thrilled after picking it up and getting a feel for how heavy it was, realizing that it was hollow but authentic. Absolutely, totally cool.

I look at the grenade for a few moments and then place it inside my jacket pocket. Pulling this guy's trunk further out and a distance away from this immediate area where the dump truck would have obviously dumped all this guys stuff that day, I began looking around for anything else. Nothing turned up though. Nothing like this.

"Why would anyone throw this stuff out?" Steve asks me just before we get ready to ride back home. I don't have an answer.

"I know the guy who owned it sure didn't. Look."

Paul opens the booklet wide to show us a page with an illustration of two hands in the process of wrapping a wire around someone's neck. Above this cartoon-like sketch is another hand drawn illustration depicting a length of piano wire with thick, hand-sized wooden dowels at each end of the wire.

"It tells you how to make it to choke people. To slice the windpipe as you pull it tighter."

"Maybe he was Green Beret," Steve says to Paul, "or wished he was a Green Beret."

I think how if someone was at one time within an elite unit such as that, and then after returning to civilian life he kept books like this around, he did so either to show off or the guy was a little touched.

"Maybe he's dead and she threw all the stuff out after he died," Bill imagines.

"Yeah, she probably hated this kind of stuff then when he was around."

Paul, Bill, and Steve each borrow one of the booklets to take home and read, and I place the three other booklets inside my jacket, zipping the jacket halfway up so they can't fall out as we ride.

Whatever did cause this guy's stuff to be brought to the dump I'm glad I found it. Back home that evening after dinner I soaked the grenade shell with gasoline and then used a paint brush and gasoline to clean it inside and out. An electric drill wire brushed the outside to a dull-gray metallic glow. It's the first thing you'll see on the shelf when you walk into my room now, alongside the ominous predators Coelophysis, Tyrannosaurus, and the armor plated herbivore Stegosaurus.

I hear Mary Christiane and Amy talking as they walk out from the turn of Val de Mar. I stand and wait till we're together and then start walking on the shoulder and blacktop of Carpenter Road. Just a short hundred yards or so from here and we'll be stepping off of Carpenter and towards a trail inside the woods.

"Me and Festus found a truck trail a couple days ago," I say, pointing up and to my left, "that follows the length of this hill."

"They probably made it and used it to get the trucks through the trees to build the tower for those power lines in back of us."

A steep, natural wall of earth rises upwards along the shoulder of Carpenter Road. The hill rises up from the shoulder of the road with a slope that varies from between forty-five to maybe seventy, eighty degrees in some places. Portions of solid rock the size of a car or small truck protrude from the leaves covering the sloping forest floor. These protruding rock faces are hidden within all the many upright trees growing slanted along this steep side of the hill, and only if you know where these rock faces are and specifically look for them at the right time as you walk along the road will you see them.

We've walked to where we're able to go in through the tree line and towards the truck ruts I want to follow. I step into the tall weeds off the shoulder of the road, stepping down and then up from a shallow gully and a few more yards I've stepped through the first line of trees. Stepping further into the woods itself, turning myself around to have both of them practically bumping into and right behind me.

You can't be seen from the road where we are now but you can see the road through all the branches and leaves of the trees.

This is the second time I've been inside this particular forest area and again it strikes me odd that there is less light shining down to the forest floor at the moment. I look up towards the canopy of tree leaves, and, I'm still unable to explain it to myself. It's not exactly dark where I am but there is a lot less light than I would normally expect there to be.

Walking uphill and I find the two parallel ruts marking the path the truck tires a long time ago carved into the ground. Festus and I found that the two truck ruts continue beyond the power lines, and this is where I want to walk to now.

I step over and around a large branch and log that have fallen across the truck ruts. Mary Christiane and Amy trot up next to me.

"Think we'll see any animals around here?" Amy asks.

"Definitely," I say. "Try to watch a little bit where you step so you don't make noise. Anything hears us coming and it'll run away before you can get a good chance to look at it. Could get real close to something before it sees us, if you're not making a lot of noise."

A small green camping trailer, probably used as an office for the power line construction guys is a little further up the trail from where we are now. We can't see it yet but I know it'll soon come into view.

"Every so often look real deep, as far into the woods as you can," I say to them. "Keep your eyes peeled up there in the trees. You might see something for a second before it sees us."

I give myself a little snicker. *Eyes peeled? Where'd I pick that up from?*

If they want to stop and look around inside the trailer that's coming up I won't care, but Festus and I have already been through it and there's nothing in it. There are just two rooms to the whole thing. A kitchen area that you couldn't take more than two steps in any one direction without bumping into the floor cabinet, the stove or sink..., it's an aluminum or thin steel sink with faucets recessed into the longest part of the L-shaped countertop. A white Formica-like countertop that has two metal forks and one single spoon lying on top of it. All three utensils have been washed clean. A single, double door wooden cupboard is above the sink; two clean plastic, tan colored coffee cups are inside it. A pull down stove door is below and to the right of the sink. Two doors open in opposite directions for a pantry cabinet on the right side of the stove. Two similar cabinet doors to the left of the stove open up to allow access to the plumbing underneath the sink.

Thin pine wood slats make for the two shelves inside the right floor cabinet; nothing is on either shelf. Lowering the stove door to find only empty space inside. Three horizontal convex indents placed at different heights along each of the two side walls of the stove are for what I imagine to be where a baking rack slides in and out from, and rests upon. I don't see and never find any metal racks lying around that could be placed inside this stove, though ..., and it's too dark to see much of anything underneath the sink; only the three plastic pipes for the drain and for the two faucet spigots, these pipes run vertically below the sink until they're brought out of sight underneath the flooring of the trailer.

A thin layer of dust is over the countertop but everything else in the kitchen area is clean, literally spotless.

Turning one hundred and eighty degrees from the front of the sink, three steps and my foot is brought to the wall of the other room. I turn to place my back to the adjacent wall and two regular steps bring me to the opposite wall. Two sliding glass windows and screens to the trailer are intact. Curtainless curtain rods above each window. A noticeable absence of dust, and, I didn't specifically look though I'm sure I would have noticed a dead insect or two had I seen one lying or crawling around. I did not. The entire trailer is dormant, empty, and completely neat and clean inside, not like five or ten years of four seasons have been through it.

"Look," Mary Christiane says as the front and a side of the trailer begins to present itself. "Wow, does any one live in there?"

"No. They probably used it for an office. The construction guys. Maybe to hang out in as they built the power lines."

"They just left it?" Amy asks.

"There's nothing in it. Me and Festus already went through it."

"Really?" Amy opens the door and steps inside with Mary Christiane.

A number of tall trees and thick-branched bushes grow to crowd and surround three sides of the trailer. Several tree branches stretch across the top of the roof of the trailer. I notice a round propane tank at the back of the trailer, and I didn't check it out last time. I wonder if there is any gas in it.

Walking along the side of the trailer and the sun has just broke past a cloud. The forest brightens and I watch several long bright shafts of light beam down through the trees. Tree-length long vertical beams of bright light are now appearing and then disappearing. Bright spots of light move along the forest floor. I watch several light beams moving in concert with each another.

Some shafts of light grow shorter, to suddenly thin out and fade. Shafts grow longer and brighten as they move across the forest floor. Intense, narrow beams of light angle down through the different levels of branches. I'll look but sometimes don't find any one bright place of the forest floor that a sunbeam should be connected to. For a few moments I'm thinking of nothing particular, just a sense of wonder is upon me.

A beam of light appears not more than a foot or two away, and I look down to see that the beam spotlights a large, shaggy, overgrown mound of very green lawn grass. Thick bundles of foot long blades of grass bring contrast to the bits of dust particles I can see floating in and out of this very bright shaft of light next to me. I watch dust particles turning in midair, sometimes sparkling as they travel through the light. I extend my hand and place it inside the light beam, turning my arm to feel the heat of the light upon my skin.

I turn away and place my hand in a grip around the handle of the propane tank. My hand slips over the knurls of the handle as I attempt to twist the handle round. I step up and lean against the propane tank, and with a firm clasp of both hands I put another twisting force upon the handle, and then put another strong impulse of twisting force in the opposite direction. I decide to stop, realizing the handle of the propane tank is not able to be brought into any kind of movement at all.

I place my hands on the top and bottom of the propane tank and try to move it around. The tank if fixed solid to the brackets that hold it to the trailer. The idea comes to me that the entire spherical green propane tank has solidified and attached itself onto the back of this trailer. I give myself a little snicker to this thought.

I notice the rubber gusseted hole in the wall of the trailer behind the propane tank. The intake hose to the propane tank has been removed. Again the thought is that the entire propane tank has nothing on it that moves. Not a thing. Nothing on it can be brought into any kind of movement at all. All its pieces have fused and like turned into this one single, solid thing at the back of the trailer, and again I chuckle to this thought.

Painted green bolts and metal straps hold the propane tank upright upon the trailer. Paint flakes peel up and away in certain places. I guesstimate at least ten, maybe twenty years this trailer has been out here. At least ten years I would tend to think. I walk back to the truck ruts and wait for those two to come outside. It won't be long because there's really not that much to see in there.

"Not that much in there," I say to them when they step outside. They're both peering into the forest.

Stepping in front of them towards the power line tower, I suppose they'll follow, and I'm a leader now. I've got the feeling that wherever I'll go they'll simply follow along. Again, and after only several yards of walking away from the trailer I notice the forest turning dark. The intensity of light inside the forest has decreased.

Zigzagging lengths of gray metal soon appear and then disappear behind the leaves of tree branches crisscrossing in and out of sight. I step forward and large fragments of the tower and her six cables of high voltage electricity begin to appear and then disappear behind the trees. Bright sunlit views of golden brown grasses and green shrubs of the field appear through a dwindling array of branches. Single trees and their branches recede. Half the lower tower appears and then completely disappears behind one large branch of leaves. I'm passing through the last row of trees and the view of the base of the tower expands upwards to quickly bring the entire power line tower into view.

Walking into bright sunlight and I look down, squinting my eyes to watch both truck ruts rise up level with the ground and then disappear under the cover of vegetation. Stepping into knee high grass for ten, fifteen yards until I'm standing alongside one of the four large metal legs of the tower. I look up to where this long leg of the tower joins with a latticework of interconnected metal bars and braces giving support to all four legs at this one particular height inside the tower.

I doubt very much Mary Christiane or Amy have ever seen one of these towers up close. It's something to look at for sure, for a while, which both of them do but not up close or for very long. Neither went up and touched the metal. It doesn't seem to impress either one of them as much as I thought it would, as much as it did when I first saw it up close.

Because when I first saw the tower up close it simply did not appear to be as sturdy and strong a structure as I thought a power line tower should look like. I stood looking at the tower for a while and thought, ... *it has to be strong enough to do the job, otherwise those guys wouldn't even have built it.* With this thought in mind I look at the thin steel supporting posts and brackets. Its hollow, naked innards doing seemingly little to hold things together. Looking at the tower up close a second time and this fragile, flimsy appearance stays with me. It simply does not give me the impression of being built as steady and sturdy and strong as I think it should be.

Mary Christiane has wandered to a far side of the clearing, standing near where I know the truck ruts resume back inside the forest. She's inside waist high brush, stepping towards a large rock the size of a small car. The rock seems buried part way and poking itself out from the sloping ground. I watch her stamping down the dry brush and sticks that grow alongside the rock. She's clearing a path around it.

Before erecting of the tower the construction guys clear-cut an approximate fifty yard wide swath from Carpenter Road to the top of the hill and then back around to the base on the opposite side of the hill. No bushes or shrubs stand taller than six, seven feet in height where I'm standing. I step away from the tower until I'm able to look a hundred yards downhill and see a twenty, thirty yard stretch of Carpenter Road blacktop. Stepping and scanning through the open space of bushes and grass I begin to realize the tower is positioned up on a summit of the hill.

I bring to mind the fact that from the truck ruts at Carpenter Road I've had an uphill incline with most all my steps. I look at all the ground extending away from the base of the tower, and it does appear to slope downhill in every direction, sloping downward if only slightly and until the forest growth of trees and shrubs halts any further perspective of ground slope.

The power line tower is on a top of this hill. I'm thinking if the tower may be situated on the summit of this long length of hill we're walking on. I imagine what the contour lines of a topographic map of this hill would look like.

I recall the ground inside the forest we were walking through, and if I recollect correctly the ruts did keep to a crest of the hill. Not always but the ground did seem to have a distinct and mostly downward slope whenever I looked into the forest in either direction left or right.

I notice a herd of deer at the bottom of the hill. I count five of them.

"You guys wanna see some deer?"

Mary Christiane and Amy step over to where I am, and I point to where the deer are.

The forest floor is totally covered with sticks and large, brown leaves. I feel the rubber cleats of my boots sink down and grip the dirt as I step inside the ruts. The ground is good ground for walking on. I remember only a couple large branches and dead trees that fell across our path, obstructive only to the extent of an extra step or two up, over, and around.

"You know this trail so far could have been ridden on with bikes?"

"Think so?" I hear Amy say.

"I know so," I say back to her.

I watch Amy fold her hands and fingers into the shape of a sphere. She blows into her hands, brings her hands down and carefully readjusts her fingers into the shape of a sphere again. She blows into the cup of her hands and the sound of a cooing owl is loud and clear. I'm impressed. Amy is able to bring a strong Indian whistle to sound out any time she wants. She knows how to flutter the sound and all that too.

"How do you do that?" Mary Christiane asks.

I step over to where Amy and Mary Christiane stand together.

"There's two basic ways to position your hands."

Amy's thumbs remain together, side by side, and she folds and refolds her hands into the two different elliptical and spherical shapes in front of Mary Christiane.

"When your hands are cupped round it's probably easier to learn with."

I have to make a few adjustments of my thumbs and hands before I bring a first whistle out, and once I do I turn my hands so Mary Christiane is able to see the way my thumbs are positioned.

Mary Christiane brings her fingers to curve round and tight against each other. She's taking time to align her thumbs together. She blows into her hands and for a moment a weak whistle sound almost begins resonating from inside the cup of her hands.

Amy blows into her hands again. A staccato of half-dozen low bass-toned toots sound out.

"See how her cheeks puff out?" I say to Mary Christiane.

Amy brings her shoulder up and leans against Mary Christiane.

"You have to keep practicing and trying all the ways you think you have to until you can do it any time you want."

"Knowing how to do it anytime you bring your hands together takes awhile."

I watch Mary Christiane blow into her hands a couple times, and then turn to start walking the truck ruts.

Always with a slight downhill to most of our steps now. The forest growth around us has thickened. More bushes and trees are scattered about at any given moment. Not much open space to see distances into the forest as it was only a short time ago. I wonder if the ruts might just stop and end somewhere in the middle of the forest.

I look through the trees and bushes of the forest as it slopes down one side of the hill. With the slope of the ground tangent to my line of sight I keep a focus to the most distant canopy of tree leaves. Walking and staring at the tree leaves twenty, thirty yards in the distance and I'm soon to realize I'm unable to peer out beyond the leaves of the trees to see whatever may be hundreds or thousands of yards away, and then to give me a better idea what land features may be near to where we are at the moment.

Disconcerting to think we might have to turn around and walk through someplace a second time. The thought of traipsing through uncharted forest terrain isn't something I feel like putting myself through the task of doing right about now, though I suppose after walking for an hour in any direction eventually the forest will present something familiar, whether a road or a stream or another trail, something must show up.

I watch Mary Christiane veer from the truck ruts. Shuffling through the leaves towards another large rock, Amy and I step away from the ruts and follow her.

These large rocks she's been attracted to remind me of icebergs, and I imagine large portions of rock that must be underground. Stepping closer and I watch Mary Christiane brushing piles of wet leaves and twigs off the rock. Her foot shovels a collection of leaves from the bottom and sides of the rock.

"You know what my father said?" she says as we step up to her.

"He says the Adirondack Mountains and these particular hills right around here are the oldest mountains on the earth. That they were molded into their form by glaciers."

Mary Christiane's father works at Texaco. She's told us before that sometimes he's away from home a long time, two or three weeks at a time. Mr. Dietrich flies to different places with a team of guys looking at new places they maybe want to explore for drilling oil. These guys aren't with his regular job at Texaco though. They're from some other company.

I place my boot up upon the rock. My sock has bunched up around the toes. I should straighten it out, or I'll get a blister.

"Must be some good fossils around here then?"

"In this part right here, the Taconic Hills? Probably not. Not from dinosaurs if that's what you're thinking."

That is exactly what I was thinking, as a matter of fact. I pull the sock up around my foot and look over towards Amy, self-consciously tying the boot lace. Amy is attentive only to the rock. Her hand goes through motions of picking and sweeping things off of the top and sides of the rock but each motion of her hand picks up or brushes nothing particular off the rock. Mary Christiane steps to stand near Amy.

"There used to be dinosaurs around here, you know?" I say to the two of them.

Mary Christiane stoops to chip at the base of the rock with a stick, then looks up at me.

"Probably. I don't really know, though."

Mary Christiane changes the subject. "He has a book that explains how they think this area of New York and North America got like this."

"A couple weeks ago my father and I were on Route 55, right? Way over near Route 22. It was cool. He showed me this one large rock jutting out of the ground that had all this other rock stuff folded up inside it. Layers of different types of rock are all pushed and sandwiched together inside the larger rock, and you can see the layers above ground for twenty or thirty feet. We got out of the car and looked at it for awhile, up close."

"It was really cool. He said that that particular rock got all squished up like that when all the continents on the earth came together and crashed down by the South Pole. Then all the continents drifted apart to where they are today. You can't tell exactly when but their best guess is those rocks by Route 22 got bunched up like that, and have stayed that way ever since about five hundred million years ago. The Earth did that to those rocks there a long time before there were even any dinosaurs around."

"The Earth is a lot older than that," I say.

"Over four and a half billion, isn't it?" Amy asks.

"Yeah, about that," Mary Christiane tells us. "The oldest rocks they find anywhere that are that old are in places up in Canada."

"He talked about maybe taking a vacation up there. I don't know if it was to see rocks though. I don't know."

"What you just said though, that these are the oldest mountains here? They don't have the oldest rocks in them then?"

Mary Christiane is pensive for a moment.

"All of New York State is under this huge rock [10], The Grenville Plateau."

"The rock first hit this other plate of rock that had a chain of volcanoes running through it about six hundred million years ago, and over the course of a hundred million years or so these two colliding plates of rock pushed up the mountains, these here Taconic Mountains. Supposedly they were a lot higher in the past than they are today."

"The mountains are gone though," I say. "There aren't any real mountains in this area. Maybe one or two large hills, but that's it."

"Like Mount Storm," Amy says to me.

...or, Storm Hill, and I don't care what they say. I don't consider the hills around this part of the New York State to be mountains.

"Kurt, once a mountain always a mountain," Mary Christiane says. "The bases of any former mountains even if they don't have all of their tallest peaks on them anymore are still mountains. No?"

I have to think about that for a moment, and I see what she's trying to say but the words don't change my mind. There are no literal mountains in this area. They're just hills, some hills could be referred to as big hills. I've never seen a cumulus cloud scrape itself over the top of any one of these hills around here.

"Anyway," Mary Christiane says, explaining her thought, "the range of the Taconic Mountains are from places up in Vermont down to Putnam County. And there's a couple of mountains still standing today about half a mile to three quarters of a mile high in this area."

Both Amy and I have found places on the rock for a foot or a knee to wedge itself into. Mary Christiane steps in front of us with arms and open palms turned towards us, as if to plead the idea.

"They think when this mountain range was first pushed up and formed those five, six hundred million years ago, the mountains came to be as tall or taller than the Himalayan Mountains."

"Yikes," I proffer. "Difficult to imagine what happens in the course of a hundred thousand years, much less millions."

"Try hundreds of millions," Amy says. "Lordy, you could probably just fit everything into a good, thick book, if you left out every other rain drop between then and now."

Continuing her thought, "Probably many things in combination could've happened to bring these mountains lower between then and now, given all that time. Simple erosion from rain—"

Mary Christiane is quick to draw her hand up towards us.

"Glaciers and plate tectonics mostly."

I watch her stand silent, and then begin to explain her thoughts.

"The last things to happen around here were a number of different glaciers that came down from the north and carved up all the ground around here. These glaciers came down here slowly, they stayed in one place for hundreds of thousands of years or more, and then they took a long time to melt and retreat back up. Not only did the different glaciers that came down do things but all that melting glacial water running around did a lot of things, too."

With a sweep of her arm Mary Christiane turns to face away from us.

"This hill we're on, I'm no geologist but just from what I do know this hill looks like what those guys call a rock drumlin, maybe an esker or moraine, obviously from the last glacier that came through here."

"Right here, above us," she furthers, "there was a slowly advancing or receding, but always melting glacier."

She folds her arms in front of herself and turns to face the downward slope of the hill.

"A sheet of almost solid ice rises a mile in height. From east to west a huge block of tall ice for as far as the eyes can see, ... with large streams, large rivers of the always melting ice water flows along the ground underneath the glacier. Rivers of melt water are flowing through tunnels of ice the glacier makes inside of itself, ... even on top the water is running around in places, breaking over the tops and along the edges at the ends of the glacier."

"Waterfalls rush over tall ice cliffs ... creating streams and rivers or even lakes on the ground in front of the glacier. For hundreds of thousands maybe for millions of years with some of these glaciers, ice carves down and scoops up the ground as the glacier moves forward, and then..., flowing out with all the always melting water is this dirt and rocks that were scooped up and carried trapped inside the ice of the glacier. Spilling, dropping it all and making a line of rocks and dirt as the glacier melts back, eventually the glacier makes a hill like as long and as wide as the one we're on now."

Mary Christiane turns to look at me. I don't say anything right away, 'cause she might not be finished, and she's making me think. I picture the melting water and the immensity of these rivers and waterfalls, and the amount of dirt and rock being dropped down along any particular area over a span of time to form a long line of a hill like the one we're walking on.

"Some tunnels probably got awfully big after a while," Amy suggests. "Like a Niagara Falls in some places, around certain edges of some of these glaciers?"

Mary Christiane agrees. "Oh, absolutely. Some waterfalls were probably huge, ten times larger than Niagara Falls."

"Glaciers a mile high?" I ask. "Thousands of miles round. That's a pretty big piece of ice, for sure."

"Higher then a mile. They find glacial scrapes on rock almost two miles high on a mountain in the Appalachians."

With the shuffle of leaves, Mary Christiane steps to stand beside me.

"Definitely a little scary, huh? And to think there were people around during some of these times, too."

"Though, no fossils? No mammoths? None at all?" I ask.

I scan into the forest and pick one specific spot to focus on. I focus beyond the one tree and then beyond another tree and a bush, and then focusing past another tree and then still another. I focus beyond one more tree and then farther beyond is an elevation of ground. I'm trying to find and tell myself what it is that will be the last and the farthest thing that can be seen as I look deep into the forest.

"Probably not," I hear Mary Christiane say. "The base of these mountains here are rocks made from volcanoes and these bottom lava rocks then have the dirt from the tops of these stripped down mountains on top of them, and then all the rocks and dirt that have been brought here from all the glaciers over hundreds of millions of years is then on top of all of this."

I'm trying to focus upon a point between two trees beyond that elevation of ground. The two trees and the rise of ground are distorting my ability to focus a clear image upon anything farther. I'm listening.

"Maybe a rock picked up by a glacier from somewhere hundreds of miles away and then carried over here could've had fossils in it. Though even that's not—"

I turn away from the deep view of the forest and look at Mary Christiane. Her eyes turn from me and down to the ground.

"Fossils are found in soft, mud-like rocks on the bottoms of lakes or oceans that once existed around here … then hardened. Fossil rocks are kind of fragile and don't take too kindly to abusive environments like glaciers."

Mary Christiane picks her head up, and looks at me.

"You know, all of Long Island is because of a glacier. As it traveled down it plowed all that dirt and rock up inside itself. The glacier stopped moving forward and then began to melt. As it melted it dropped all the dirt back to the ground. Because of Long Island we know how far the last glacier came down, and where it halted its advance."

"That is an interesting fun fact," I say to her with genuine enthusiasm, and I know in an instant that I'll never forget this little gem of information. The face that said it to me and exactly where I was when I heard it. It's definitely a fun fact about Long Island I'll remember for the rest of my life.

Amy steps off the rock.

"What about this rock. What kind is it?"

Halting steps alongside the boulder and Mary Christiane will stand with Amy, and to turn her head dismissively.

"I have no idea. I'm not too good at all on the rock types."

"Your father probably has topographical maps of the area around here," I suggest. "Looking at a relief map showing elevation gradients of this hill, maybe you could see how a glacier moved down through this area by looking at how the ground is carved."

Mary Christiane lifts her eyes in thought, and nods.

"I suppose, ... could, maybe?"

I step away from the rock and through the fluff of loose leaves and sticks. The sound of a chainsaw in the distance. The thing is being thrown into working bursts of two-cycle engined, full-throttled wails of sound. The engine is repeatedly torquing down a number of times as the blade slogs its way into and through a series of cuts through the wood.

Stepping near the ruts I sense the air inside the forest is moist, earthy, and cool again. I feel invigorated.

If there are no ten, twenty yard long mounds of earth rolling along and obstructing the view of the forest near where we're walking, if the nearby forest floor around me is flat I'm able to look along the ground for a good thirty or forty yards of distance before the proliferation of tree trunks, branches, and fallen leaves totally block any farther and deeper views. It's cool. Everywhere I look, in any direction I could walk onto the ruffled layer of light brown leaves and the small branches that completely and totally cover the entire forest floor.

I pick up one of the brown leaves. It's as large as my open hand. One edge of the leaf is brought to the opposite edge and then squeezed to compress the bow in the middle of the leaf. Eventually the leaf cracks through the middle and into separate flakes. My line of sight follows the truck ruts descending with the slope of the hill, and I see brown leaf covering every rise and descent of ground. The blanket of leaves are inside every ridge and gully. Every piece and part of ground is covered with brown leaves. It's cool to look at.

Half a dozen skinny trees are nearby. Some of the trees are pencil-thin and rise up inches above the leaves. Some are as thick as a broom handle and rise up to waist height, with a couple trees rising several feet above my head. All are immature trees that lack the normal number of green leaf on the few branches they have. There are many of these struggling immature trees in this area of the forest.

Stepping down inside the right truck rut and the soft dirt and pebbles underneath my boots momentarily shift to slide each of my foot steps. Farther ahead and I'll be doing more of these awkward footsteps so I step up to walk along the side of the ruts.

A crow caw and I look up into the trees. Flapping its wings attempting to remain upright upon a branch, I turn to see Mary Christiane and Amy looking up at the crow too. The bird sways with the branch while it folds and curls its wings back into itself. A moment to watch the crow bouncing, perched upon the branch, and the crow unfurls its wings, lifts up to fly between the branches and out of sight.

A gust of wind travels through a section of tree tops. The branches turn and bend and roll with the chatter of clapping leaves. Not one single shard of direct sunlight penetrated through the canopy of branches and leaves up there.

I look inside the forest. Trees and the slope of the ground, the brown leaves under my boots. The forest is not exactly dark but it is a little bit dim in the light department.

A single step forward, looking back up at the treetops. The branches extend perpendicular to the ground for most of their entire lengths, and all the longest branches grow outward at the same height on every tree. Branches of different trees sometimes crisscross each other, with the leaves of one tree branch mingling with the leaves of another tree's branch. It seems every long branch I look at is practically devoid of leaf until the end of the branch where there is a proliferation of green leaves growing.

The arrangement of crisscrossing branches and large leaves are why little direct sunlight is brought down to the forest floor...

Mary Christiane steps to stand beside me.

"What are you looking at?"

I turn to look at her, and then look towards Amy. Both of them stare at me.

"Just wondering."

Stepping forward, I'm following the ruts but looking up towards the different leaves of the trees eclipsing the sun. All I see is a moving circle of bright, scattered light that is reflecting off the leaves that I pass by as I step forward. Every step and at any moment I expect a sliver of direct sunlight to slip through those leaves up there. A good number of steps along the ruts and I'm surprised not a shard of direct sunlight has slipped through to boink my eyeballs. It's an interesting arrangement of branches and leaves up in the treetops and why it appears a tad bit too dark down here on the ground sometimes.

"Wondering about what? What are ya' looking at?" I hear Amy ask.

"It's just the way the trees are growing on down the slope of this hill," I say with a chuckle. "Probably the way the leaves are spread out up there, why it sometimes appears darker than it should be walking around."

For the first five, ten feet of any tall tree I look at there are the short, thin branches growing out from the trunk. Some of these tiny branches have leaves on them and some do not. Half way up a tree and if I see a branch it's a dead broken stub of one. Most all leaf and branch growth happens at the highest section of any tree I look at.

I step over to a tree to have a look at a couple of those tiny, puny branches.

The branch stalk is thinner than a pencil and less than a half foot in length. The branch is dry and brittle, and it cracks off the trunk with an easy turn of my fingers. I break the branch in the middle and the pulp is white so the branch is alive. Another short branch has two thinner branches forking out from the main stalk. Round greenish-white nubs at the ends of both branches, and bundled up inside one of the nubs are a ravel of small white leaves that just don't seem to want to come out and unfurl like a regular leaf on a branch for some reason.

Not enough energy from the tree getting into the nub itself, maybe.

Not enough energy coming from the nub to then put some energy back into the tree and to then finish creating the branch it started to make.

The leaves can't put energy into the tree if they don't unfurl, and even if they do unfurl down here, there wouldn't be much in the way of direct sunlight for them to do anything efficient.

These nubs growing from the branches along the lower trunk of the tree relay some kind of information into the tree. The tree has then determined not to continue creating and extending the branch out and...? To cause the leaves to come out and unfurl?

It's as if the tree has gotten clues and selected a course of action, deciding it wouldn't be worth the effort to unfurl the nubs or to extend the length of any of these lower branches out even one more inch.

I think it through for a moment before I bring the sentence to sound the way I want to hear it said: *A coordination and conservation in the bio-electrochemical energy of a living system*, is why these immature branches are the way they are.

I look back towards the ruts. Mary Christiane and Amy stand maybe thirty, forty yards away and where it appears the forest ends and an area of open space begins. I figure they're probably waiting for me.

"The trail goes off into someone's back yard," Amy says as I step up to where they are.

The ruts have risen up to the flat ground of twigs and leaves underfoot. Knee high, verdant forest growth ends and a swath of manicured, bright green lawn grass extends in front of us. Scanning the foundation of the house to see if I can find anything moving or walking around inside, and no one is to be seen. I turn around and look back into the forest.

...truck ruts, ...south to southeast? I'm only guessing what direction north and south is. I don't know.

A second or two of thought to realize the truck ruts must've connected to a road that must be on the other side of that house. A moment to think and imagine myself walking through the forest without the truck ruts to guide us, and I'm simply not in the mood to be walking through totally virgin forest area right about now, so hopefully there won't be anyone inside that house who might care if they see three people walking across their property to the road.

"Listen, start walking along the side of the property to the driveway, and then to the road. No one will probably care."

I step through the last of the twigs and dry leaves of the forest floor. Up upon the soft, green grass of this guy's backyard and the pace of my steps quicken.

"I hope they don't have a dog," I hear Amy say.

It's not a very large section of open space to travel across. We do a diagonal from the middle to the one side of the property, stepping near the foundation of the house until we're able to drop down from a ledge of earth to the blacktop of the guy's driveway. Each of my steps are quick and awkward. The heel of each boot touching pavement first.

Stepping onto asphalt and the first thing I notice is the thick, tall forest growth of trees and the bushes that grow right up along the sides of the road. Both directions only allow ten, twenty yard lengths of asphalt to be viewed. Odd. The forest we were inside of on the other side of the house didn't have all this congestion of shrubs and bushes around.

"We should just walk and not walk so fast like we're running from something next time," I say to them.

"There wasn't anyone home," I hear Amy say. She's looking at the house, and so I look at the house too.

How does she know if there are or aren't?

I shake my head to throttle the thought away. Right at this moment I don't care, and I'm not asking how or why she knows...

"It doesn't make any difference anymore, if there is or isn't."

Some places the branches of trees and bushes extend out a good foot or more into the road. There is so much greenery extending out along both sides of the road. Undeveloped land and I'm totally unfamiliar with any of the roads into or out of this area.

I look towards the guys house. It's the only thing different to see besides all the dense foliage brought up to the road and practically surrounding us. A second time I look down the road in both directions, and it doesn't help me decide which way may be a better direction to walk with, so I just start walking uphill.

The first fifteen, twenty steps and I immediately sense something peculiar about the road. The asphalt appears flat. Very little if any horizontal bank or slant as the roadway elevates and turns itself towards the right. I'm stepping uphill and there is no lateral left to right pitch being put upon each of my foot steps. Every foot step is placed down flat as if I were stepping straight up the incline of a ramp. After thirty, forty yards of uphill steps I realize the road continues to bear right for an unusually long distance. This road is unusual.

The green of the tree leaves and the branches of tall shrubs poke out along the sides of the road. Branches and leaves brush up against me, and I begin to stare at the farthest distance directly in front of me. I watch as both left and right sides of the road always appear to originate and then split from this farthest point in the road that's always in front of me, with the branches and their leaves to sweep around and then off to my left and right and eventually out of sight. I'm anticipating the road to stop rising and veering right at any moment.

Minutes of footsteps pass by and the incline of the road is brought level. A corner of bright green lawn grass appears on the left. Passing by a row of hedges and the corner of bright green lawn grass becomes a large swath of lawn grass. The road straightens and each step forward pushes brush on the right side of the road farther away, and we walk with rows of houses and their lawns of green grass on both our sides.

The houses in this neighborhood are not exactly old. None appear to be brand new and recently built homes. I look through the grounds and the properties on my left, and then scan through the properties on my right, and I realize I've seen no one single person outside the ten, fifteen front yards I've passed by so far.

Not a single person is outside doing yard work or taking out the garbage. No one is sitting outside sleeping or reading a book. No one is just sitting or standing outside and simply doing nothing at all. There are no people to be seen anywhere.

I look towards the house on my immediate right. Its largest picture window has its curtains drawn. I look to the other side of the road and that house has glare streaking across the glass of all the windows. The rooms inside the house appear dark, and I'm unable to see inside.

I speak loud enough so I know those two walking behind me can hear me.

"Is it just me or do you think it's a little odd that no one is outside doing anything around their house on a Saturday morning?"

Obviously few people live within this neighborhood and we're just passing through, but the fact that not even one single person has been seen outside their house or in their yard doing something, anything, ... I don't know. No one has yet been seen, and it's strange.

The end of the development approaches. Two property lots further ahead and then the forest growth of branches and trees and bushes crowd up and above the road again. Trees tower above the road.

I hear them walking behind me, yet I've heard no responses. I keep my pace of steps and turn to walk backwards.

Mary Christiane is looking from the middle and off to the side of the road. Amy is beside her and looking ahead of me. Each of them glance at me. Amy eventually gives me the weird look, *what are you talking about?*

"It's Saturday morning. You're supposed to be doing something," I say and turn to walk forward.

I hear the fire whistle in Hopewell Junction slowly start winding up. It's twelve o'clock noon. Walking out from the development of houses and I see that the road ahead is going to turn into a dead end.

Approaching at the far end of a circle of asphalt is a single white and black striped metal traffic guard rail being held up by two round painted white wooden posts anchored into and rising a couple feet up from the ground. In back of the guard rail a three, four foot rise of ground. A narrow corridor of open space behind the guard rail appears to be a path leading into the forest. Further inside the forest an open area of sunlight with not so many trees and bushes growing inside it.

I look up at the tree tops towering above me. Circling the edge of the asphalt are the tall tree trunks and a thick wall of bushes, branches, and all the green leaves extending out over the circle of asphalt we stand in.

"Maybe wait here and I'll check it out to see if we want to go in there," I say to them.

I take steps up the rise of ground behind the guard rail. Stepping into the first small clearing I see beyond the next line of trees a slope of open ground. Walking closer I see the sloping ground becomes a steep hill. Several steps down the hill the first cuts of exposed rock present themselves ten, twenty yards away, and as I step further down the hill I eventually have to stop. I'm standing at the edge of a cliff and fifteen, twenty yards straight down below me are a set of railroad tracks. I'm wondering if and how we can get down there without too much difficulty.

"Hey you guys, come on." I want them to see the railroad tracks. I definitely don't want to walk on the road anymore.

Perfectly obvious it's not possible to climb from the top of this cliff to the tracks. The rock face below the cliff is sheer, smooth, having been cracked down by dynamite. With open ground where I stand, a tangle of brush thickens as the hill descends.

Amy steps to cliff's edge and looks down.

"There's another path back there, you know?" she says. "It might bring us to those tracks down there."

I didn't see a path.

"Check it out," I say.

Mary Christiane and I follow Amy up the embankment until she stops near the path. I take the lead. A downhill slope. Several bushes have branches stripped off, sheared with sharp hatchet or saw. The path levels and then rises uphill. I'm stepping inside shallow ravines. The small rocks and pebbles I step upon make me think of valleys that serve as channels during heavy rains. I'm confident the path is on a course towards the tracks, and eventually I see the mound of dark gray rocks and brown, wooden railroad ties in front of me.

I step alongside the steel rails.

"Wait a minute you guys." I hear Mary Christiane say. I turn to watch her untie one of her sneakers and tapping stuff out of it.

Amy is walking towards me with a blue glass bottle in her hand.

"Where do you think this came from?"

The palm and thumbs of my hands break off bits of dried dirt caked onto the glass.

"Who do you think made it?" she asks me again.

There are no commercial markings or insignias. No letters or any numbers on the side or the bottom of the bottle. I rub my thumb and then a fingernail through the thin crusts of dirt held inside the rows of bumpy knurls protruding up and circling the bottom section of the bottle. I still find no information of any kind.

I shrug my shoulders, shake my head and hand the bottle back to her.

Walking away from me, Amy makes an effort to throw the bottle so that it twirls, flying out of her hand like a Frisbee.

"You don't see many blue glass bottles anymore."

Mary Christiane stands and curls the locks of her hair behind her ears, and then rubs her hair back, rubber-banding it to a ponytail. I turn to walk the tracks towards Hopewell.

Stepping along, I hear Mary Christiane blowing into her hands. She's sometimes blowing these short, forced lungfuls of air into that hollow cavity of her hands. Each time not even a hint of a whistle seems to want to start to sound out, ... and I don't know. She knows how to fold the hands together and to play with that space between her thumbs. There's not much information that needs to keep being told. If she keeps trying eventually a whistle will happen, and it's something she simply has to learn how to do by herself.

Right now I really don't know what else to say to her other than what we've already said.

Wow. Not ten minutes have passed and a yikes to all these large loose rocks I'm stepping on. Large rocks lying loose and with almost every step the rocks shift my boot. Each stepping stride places an unnatural angle into my ankles, stretching the muscles of my legs in a way I'm not accustomed to. I step over to walk on the wooden railroad ties.

We follow the railroad tracks into a shallow cut of rising ground. Exposed rock face twenty, thirty feet tall appear on our sides, and I expect Mary Christiane to stop and look at some of this rock. I know this rock was underground before the railroad tracks cut into the hill.

Bushes and trees recede away and encircle the shores of a marsh, and the pile of rocks we walk on rises five, ten feet above the marsh water. Spots of tall reeds and cottontails appear along the banks.

The tracks turn and the rocks buttress up against an approaching pool of clear water. I pick up a rock and throw it with force, projectile straight into the water. The splash brings two ducks rising up from inside the sawgrass.

The rocks aren't uncomfortable to be walking on now for some reason. My legs and feet don't feel so stiff.

"Those are pretty," I hear Amy say. I turn to watch the both of them walk down the slope of rocks and onto a narrow peninsula of land jutting into the marsh water.

I walk down upon spongy, wet grass, following the banks of the marsh and three frogs jump to plop and splash themselves into the water, and then a large, dark green bullfrog jumps into the water. Stepping along water's edge and the bullfrog's hind legs perform several frantic scissor kicks as it squirms to push itself underneath a layer of sunken tree leaves.

If any colorful plant is to be seen in any wooded area I've been inside of I think the orange colored lilies and purple pitcher plants are most frequent. The two violet plants we're walking towards are a dark blue, almost purple color, and growing all by themselves inside a hump of brown grass.

Mary Christiane and Amy crouch down, fondling and turning the stems and petals of the flower. Amy puts her face close to each flower, then breaks one flower off at the stem. She had her hand on the second one when I let her know she might not want to do that.

"Maybe it'll grow more of them like that next year too," I say, watching her then pick the second flower. She stands up, steps towards me, spinning one of the flower stems between her fingers.

"You don't see purple ones around that much," I say. She takes the flower and places it under Mary Christiane's nose, and then under mine.

Mary Christiane is looking out over the water.

"Look at the rabbits."

Across the marsh, I find one rabbit hopping along waters edge. A second rabbit close to the water is taking a drink, or something. We turn and walk back to the tracks.

A dragonfly has been hovering and zipping around us, monitoring us since we've been on this peninsula.

I look to Mary Christiane and say, "You know dragonflies were around before the dinosaurs were around?"

"Really?"

"Yep. Before the crocodiles and alligators even. I think I read something somewhere once saying dragonflies are one of the oldest still living species from those times. They had two to three foot wing spans back then, too."

"Here comes the sun," I hear Amy say. I look up and watch several sunbeams breaking through clouds. Large, puffy cumulus clouds cover a good portion of the blue sky. In contrast to the darker green leaves of tree tops directly in front of us, the sky above looks really cool. It's a beautiful day.

Stepping up the mound of rocks I watch the sunbeams move across the sky.

"Little darling," I say smiling to Mary Christiane and Amy.

I hear her repeating those forced puffs of air and long winded exhales. I can tell she's constricting and dilating that space between her thumbs while blowing into her hands. Futile attempts and I think she may need a little bit of confidence right about now otherwise she may simply give up.

"Let me see how you're doing it." She lowers the cup of her hands in front of me, extending some of her fingers out and then wrapping her fingers spherical again. Concentrating she is to adjust her fingers together and tight. A moment to readjust her thumbs again and her hands go up and she blows into them. Then she blows into them again.

"Let me see your hands. How your thumbs are."

She turns her hands to show me her thumbs.

"Totally air tight?" Amy asks.

"I think so."

I fold my hands together, put a few puffs into them till I get a long whistle going. So she can see what I'm doing I bring my hands down and arch my thumbs to buckle up in front of her, and then bring my hands up and to bring a different kind of whistle's pitch to sound out. I want her to realize that there is more than one way to whistle like this. That there is not just one exact position but several different ways to fold the fingers together and position the thumbs. I put my hands folded as they are in front of her again.

I know that what I'm about to tell her may not be of much help but I think she's making her thumbs too flat. She's not putting enough of an arch into those two knuckles to her thumbs. I myself can make a whistle with the thumbs placed both ways, flat or with an arch. Though it is easier to whistle with a little bit of an arch to the thumbs.

"You don't have to blow so hard with the thumbs arched up. Just keep a little more of an arch to the thumbs." I make the buckle in my knuckles rise up and down several times so she can see what I'm talking about. I bring my hands up and while blowing into the cup of my hands I arch my thumbs flat and then put a buckle into them. While doing this a whistle starts and then stops, starts up again and then stops.

"Try starting out with the thumbs not so flat, and then start to put a little more of a buckle into them sometimes."

Snugging all of her fingers close together and round, she raises her hands to her mouth and starts blowing. A whistle sometimes almost wants to begin sounding out. I hear the turbulence, that venturi sound inside the cup of her hands. She's almost getting it.

"Try moving the position of the thumbs in different ways as you're blowing," Amy suggests. "Just first try to find that spot where a whistle is."

Mary Christiane brings her hands down, looks at them and then brings her hands up again. The very next puff brings a strong sounding, low bass tone whistle out from her hands. Great.

She pulls her hands away with a smile from ear to ear. She's looking intently at her hands, picturing the position and space between her thumbs and the buckle to her knuckles. She's memorizing it all.

Chuckling, Mary Christiane looks at us and making whistles as we walk. They're all at that low pitch almost every time she puffs into her hands. I turn to look at her, and she's quite happy with herself.

I didn't know what it was at first. I thought it was something wacky going on with my legs. I stop walking and plant both my feet down flat upon the rocks.

"Wait a minute, stop," I say.

During the last few minutes, every so often I felt something had been like electrically tingling up the calves of my legs. I thought it was because I was standing and resting my legs from walking along the tracks, but I just now felt my legs tingle again while stepping forward. I'm standing still and I want to feel my legs tingle like that again…

I turn to look at Amy say, "I think a train is coming."

The sound is barely perceptible. A steady high pitched mechanical whine echoes away from the face of rock wall a hundred yards ahead of us. The muffled, vibrating sound becomes more pronounced as it reflects off the wall of rock. There is no mistaking what's going to happen in a few short moments.

I walk down the mound of rocks to stand close to water's edge, and then look towards the entrance of the canyon. The sound of the locomotive engine reverberating. The pitch intensifies from a low bass hum to a treble whine. The whirr of the engine suddenly resonates loud as the front of the locomotive engine emerges from between the walls of the canyon. The engine pulls out one boxcar from between the rocks and trees. A second boxcar then follows behind the first boxcar. I focus my eyes towards the front of the approaching engine as it grows louder and larger in size.

Vibrations in the ground travel up inside my feet. Inside my chest something tickles. The air makes the skin of my face tingle. Vibrations inside me grow stronger and intense watching the heavy metal wheels turning that big locomotive engine closer to me.

I'm getting the sense that the engine is accelerating as it pulls the cars through Hopewell Junction. Traveling out of the hamlet and the engine is at full power and pulling whatever load of cargo it has up to a faster speed.

I step up the slope of rocks to face more in front of the train. Clenching my fist above my head I make up and down motions with my arm. A few more seconds and the guy won't see us anymore.

I turn to Mary Christiane and Amy. "Come on. Do this to make him see us and blow his horn!"

I turn to face the train and raise my fist up in the air and then down to my shoulder. My fist goes up and down. I hope the guy wants to blow his horn 'cause many truckers on the Interstate will see us but won't bother to sometimes.

The engine wails out loud, sounding frantic as it draws close. I turn to see Mary Christiane and Amy standing next to me and waving hello up to the conductor with their other hand. The engine rolls up alongside us and I hear a loud blast from the air horn. A second longer blast of air sounds out as I watch the final length of the engine roll past. Nice!

The first boxcar rolls by. I stand and watch the second and then the third car roll past. The length of each boxcar presents itself in front of me for a shorter amount of time then the boxcar before. Every boxcar that rolls past me is accelerating. In quicktime the entire train of boxcars is moving faster then when I first saw it at the rock wall.

A slow steady breeze slips around me. The mass and the tonnage in motion. I watch everything moving so close to me and calling up flags of caution and danger. There is also the obvious sense for the train being under control. A controlled purpose. I watch each boxcar pass and there's the sense that I'll soon be listening to something I want to say to myself…, and I probably will listen in a moment if I'm so inclined to do so.

The last car passes with a gust of wind that draws all the noise away, and I watch the train roll farther away. A freight train continues to accelerate its load of cargo up to speed. Thinking without really trying to, without words it's pictured in my mind's eye.

The force is as a line. A line with a locomotive engine at the beginning. Gears turning wheels. One heavy metal hitch with wheels is seen to grip another heavy metal hitch, and this hitch with wheels grips another, then another … these are segments defining the line, the force. Imagined to be elastic and taut at the same time, two impressions of force oppose each other, straining, imparting a sense of vitality as Elastic and Taut graft themselves to the vector arrowed line I got from algebra class. Quickly presented images and fleeting thoughts portrayed in my mind meld into a straining, a very vibrant, taut black arrow.

Appreciating them properly and one can approach the forces with their due respect.

There's little if any directing or producing on my part when it goes on. As objectively as I'm able to I just watch and listen to it going on in my head, for however long it takes, and if I want to. It's as if by thinking like this I'm trying to figure something out on my own, as if I'm thinking like this on purpose.

I step up and start to walk along the railroad ties. Mary Christiane is smiling at me, and a modest surprise to her voice as I listen to her say, "You know that train didn't have a caboose."

"I know," Amy says. "I wonder why."

A moment later and I hear Amy ask, "Why do trains have cabooses anyway?"

I give a quick moment of thought to the question, to have nothing come to mind. The question seems like the kind of question that's asked just to have something to talk about. For a moment or two I don't hear anyone say anything.

I'm trying to keep the better part of each footstep landing upon the railroad tie. Sometimes I have to step farther than my normal stepping stride to place more of my foot on the tie, and sometimes for several steps I have to use short foot steps to place most of the boot on the tie. It seems every sixth or seventh step is either a ridiculously short or an uncomfortably long distance to have to bring the boot forward and then down upon a railroad tie.

I tighten the muscles of my left ankle as the heel of the boot is brought down upon the rocks. My ankle is braced with the sole of my foot as it turns over the rocks and to have the toe of my foot pushing off from the beam. The muscles in my ankles feel tired.

"Kurt, you don't know?"

I look over to Amy. She's deliberately crossing her eyes. A mocking, jocular smile on her face, and I give more thought to the question of what cabooses do.

A moments thought and I realize I haven't a clue what function cabooses perform and what they're used for. With a shrug, "I haven't the foggiest notion what cabooses are supposed to do."

The three of us together and neither one of us can say what the caboose on a train is supposed to do. It should be obvious what the car at the back of a train is supposed to do. I think on it some more, ... and still to remain unable to even venture a guess for why people put them there, and what they're supposed to do by being the last car of the train.

"Can you put that in answer form, please?" Amy inquires.

Oh, very good Amy, I think, turning myself around, *sure.*

I look at her with quick affirmative nods of the head, and get myself serious now. She steps up to walk alongside me and without really thinking I just blurt out the first things I think of.

"An idea or thought, ... that lacks relevance, ... or lacks information towards another situation or thought, ..." and I stop talking to think upon what I've just said.

"Nah," Amy says down to the rocks and railroad ties. I look at her and attempt another sentence. This time I take some time to sort out and concentrate on the bits and pieces of the words and phrases I'm using.

"A thought or an idea that ... allows doubt and unfamiliar expressions to function without relevance to ... another's thought?"

My voice trails off of those last two words, and I know I didn't do it that time either.

The last couple weeks Amy and I have been reenacting a scene of the television game show *Jeopardy!* We want to find one way to word the answer to then have the contestant correctly respond in question form with, "What is, 'I don't know.'?"

Bringing this little riddle to our attention at any opportune time, and we think if we simply pose the question differently or attempt an answer at different times, maybe just say anything can be a way for pieces of the sentence structures we want to be realized.

"What are you guys talking about?" Mary Christiane asks.

We explain our conundrum to Mary Christiane, and she mulls it over for a moment.

"All the answers on *Jeopardy!*" she offers, "use objective and commonly known truths for answers. Any answer like, 'I don't know—'"

"What is, 'I don't know,'" Amy interrupts her with, stressing the word 'is.'

"I know, I know, I get it," Mary Christiane continues. "But any answer in that form is just conveying the truth on a subjective, personal plane."

"So what does that mean?"

"It means it can't be done."

I turn to look at Amy.

"Fifty lashes with a wet noodle to this one," I say pointing my thumb at Mary Christiane.

"Miss Mary Christiane Dietrich, please do not ever say never—" I invoke a despairing, mocking tone to my voice now, "'I can't do it...,' around us again. Comprende?"

"You can't know what anyone else knows, or doesn't know," she quickly says back to me. "How can you know what is in someone else's mind?"

I'm just about to say, 'So you're saying again it's impossible?' when she came close to hitting the nail smack dab square on its head, or so I thought.

" ... to know whether when someone says that they don't know, that they're telling the truth."

She stumbled around on that sentence there a little bit. Amy and I stop our pacing, turn up our heads and look at each other.

A squint to her eyes, "To know whether ..." Amy says, her voice trailing off into thought.

Hearing how the structure to the order of the words within a sentence sound out, and thinking how a set of words may progress along different contexts, inflections and tenses ... it does seem to move our thoughts around a little. After comprehending the initial four or five words of any spoken sentence we're soon able to realize if something just is not sounding right.

"When knowing whether..." Amy says, now emphasizing the word 'when.'

"No, no, 'Know..., or knowing whether when...,'" I say, stopping and drifting back in thought after the last word.

The sense for wanting to utter an imperative, and to command the thought into existence, jarbles my thoughts. Forming a declarative seems like the obvious way to go about this. I cannot seem to make words combine and then have the words progress to form a complete comprehensible thought though.

"Listen," Amy says, looking down towards the tracks. "Knowing whether when someone says that they don't know..."

That's as far as those words can go. She realized she can't just start repeating certain words that are part of the initial question and then have these words become part of the answer too. Maybe it can be done that way, though...

"The whether when part messes it up," Amy tells me.

I don't know how she's doing it but I'm mentally picturing the words and seeing them as if on the show, on the TV screen. I think it helps.

"You guys have a few loose screws in your canoes," Mary Christiane says with a short, nervous chuckle. "You know that right?"

I turn and look at her.

"No, come on. Seriously, what would those guys write down and then having the correct answer being in question form is, 'What is, I don't know."?

She laughs at what I said.

"Come on!" I insist, "What's the matter? Imagine you're playing on the show now, for real, for money. Think! ... about it."

"What would they have to write in back of one of those category boards to have made you say then, 'What is, I don't know?' Geez, just try it for a second ... and see if you can do it."

Mary Christiane gives me a queer smile. An incredulous look in her eyes as she turns her head from side to side. Glancing towards Amy, she turns her head down and with a quick pace of steps she's walking several yards up in front of us.

It doesn't happen often. Only recently have I discovered that a double negative in a sentence can really throw me for a loop. Throw me as far as immediately comprehending the sentence concerned. I always have to repeat those kinds of sentences.

'I could not see myself not go to the store,' or, 'He didn't understand that it's not all right to take off his shoes before coming into the house.'

Double negatives are a bit incomprehensible the first time heard, even though no one regularly talks like this. Though on occasion I do read or hear sentences sometimes put across this way.

I will always have to repeat each group of words with the negative in it together slowly to interpret sentences like that. First I have to find both negative words or the prefix or suffix of the two words within a sentence, reversing or canceling the negative senses and then rephrasing and sounding out each of these new group of words to myself as I reassemble the sentence together into a somewhat different but basically the same sentence. Only after doing all this am I comprehending any double-negative sentence.

It baffles me why my mind can't just breeze through double negatives like a regular sentence. Especially baffling when, even after I know how perplexing double negatives are with me, if I'm reading through a sentence and find I didn't understand what I've just read, and then going back and rereading the sentence I find that there are two double negatives inside, I always have to go through this tedious mental process of canceling those two negatives I found, rearrange the words and then repeat the entire sentence to myself a second time. Only now do I comprehend the sentence. If I heard another double negative sentence spoken right at this very moment it'd still be as perplexing for me to comprehend as the first time I heard and knew I couldn't understand these type of sentences.

Farther up the tracks I watch Mary Christiane stop and turn herself around. Folding her arms up in front of herself, I'm stepping towards her and looking up into her face, to maybe see whatever may be the matter with her now.

Contorted lips, her mouth is puckered, and ever so slightly nodding her head. I look away and put a turn to my step.

It's a strained, scratchy voice I've never heard her use before. Her voice is speaking directly towards me as I step up alongside her. I stop, look up and listen to her.

"What is a verbal exclamation from one individual to another..., purporting lack of knowledge ... or comprehension...," Mary Christiane blows a fairly large strand of hair off her face, "...pertaining to any given specific question ... spoken of or from thought."

I watch Mary Christiane clip the dangling strand of hair securely behind her ear, and I look at her while repeating the words she spoke.

What is ... a verbal exclamation from one individual to another purporting lack of knowledge or comprehension pertaining to any given specific question spoken of or from thought.

Wrong. She used the two-word interrogative, '*What is*' to begin her answer with. I really don't care about that. I like how the rest of the sentence makes sense.

Amy pensively toes a rock around. I'm certain she's repeating what Mary Christiane just said. I look down at my feet and see the placard marked $1000 quickly lifting up and out of sight. I hear myself reading the printed words I see on the TV screen, *A verbal exclamation from one individual to another purporting lack of knowledge or comprehension pertaining to any given specific question spoken of or from thought.*

I allow a little time delay to be, imagining that the other contestants are now also pondering upon a question like I am. I then bring an inner voice of mine to utter the sentence, *"What is, 'I don't know.'?"*

I hear the ting of the bell. Art Fleming's voice is saying, *Correct.*

Those words appear to answer the question and the dialog makes sense. I look towards Mary Christiane with a giddy smile. I think she done did it.

Amy looks up, pursing one side of her face into a reluctant smile. We shake our heads up and down and acknowledge the fact together.

"She did it," we say triumphantly to each other.

I'm thinking wow, how difficult this was. The answer probably should be included as one of the bonus questions. Better still, this answer is the final *Jeopardy!* question, where at the end of the show the contestants can wager all or part of their tallied up winnings.

I'm starting to feel awfully lousy right about now too. In my stomach it feels..., it sort of hurts.

"You guys were...," Mary Christiane says. "Uhm? You were just thinking about it as if it's like a big deal."

"Oh man, oh man," I say. "We lost. We're not coming back tomorrow. Mary Christiane Dietrich is."

"Yep," Amy says. "Looks that way."

Amy and I stare at each other for a moment. I give a quiet little chuckle to myself, shaking my head as a loser.

Wow.

I don't know exactly how I feel right about now, but I don't like it. I don't like it at all. Mary Christiane didn't really even have to try. She just concentrated with a few moments of thought and the words just came together for her.

"How'd you do that?" Amy asks. "Wow. D'you know how long...?"

I'm wondering too. What were Amy and I thinking about? How did we stay on..., for so long, looking at the question like—

Mary Christiane has lost a lot of her smile, asking me, "You're not mad are you?"

The hint of a smile is trying to maintain some posture across her face. I don't know what to say to her but I shake my head no.

"No, of course not," Amy says over to her. "Come on, let's keep going."

I look at Mary Christiane as we start to walk again, and I think it was just a game like between us, between Amy and me. Whether either of us ever did come up with a solution really didn't matter, I don't think. Right now though I feel like as if someone slapped me on the back too hard, and with a stinging sensation on my back I have to continue to look and listen to this someone congratulate and talk to me.

I feel ...? Ridiculous. God I really wanted to be the one to find the way to say it. I was trying...! I'm astonished too, and impressed I guess.

I've got to think about what happened, and step to smack a rock with the toe of my boot.

I've heard the phrase, *'There are many ways to skin a cat.'* I suppose this to be one of those times when looking at a problem from a different angle allows one to see another way to approach and then understand how to solve it. After all this time Amy and I have been trying though, what Mary Christiane just did was short of, almost preposterous but definitely spectacular.

I look over to Mary Christiane. She's stepping and facing forward. She says something to Amy.

My hands are cold. I'm sweating a little. I can't imagine what Amy and I were doing wrong trying to figure it out.

Eventually one of us probably would've said something similar..., maybe. Probably for sure if we kept at it.

Oh, wow. I am so...? Mad.

I feel weak, sort of exhausted, too. I'm tired of walking. I don't want to just sit down though. I want to think about this...!

Mary Christiane saw the answer as what, how...?

She probably first saw the answer, 'I don't know' as a simple verbal, spoken sentence ..., whatever that means. After she saw it in that form, in that manner, as a plain old ordinary sentence, I suppose everything else sort of just fell into place. It was easy for her to just describe when someone would actually use the phrase 'I don't know,' and what it means when someone does use it.

I try to determine what exactly I have just thought out, and to realize that the thoughts I just thought out about how she brought that answer together make absolutely no sense at all. I still have no idea how Mary Christiane did that.

Aww, who knows...

Those two are walking together a little too far up in front of me so I step over the steel rail, into the middle of the tracks and then double step my way up to where they are. We walk for a while without saying anything. Pensive eyes of mine stare down upon the ground directly in front of me.

I'm looking at the one boot and then my other boot. My boots become the cogs of a machine that drives a conveyor belt that's carrying all those gray fist-sized rocks and each of those horizontal lengths of brown, wooden railroad ties I see moving down below. With a steady gait to my steps I stare at and become mesmerized to all the movement below me.

One of my two boots is always seen in a repetitive motion of like…? Kicking into or stepping out from the arrangement of gray rocks and railroad ties that enter from the top part of my eyes. The rocks and railroad ties appear to move down from the top of my eyes and into this center area of the ground I've fixed my eyes upon. Two or three feet always in front of me my line of sight watches as the steady flow of rocks and railroad ties from above seem to move under my boots and ultimately out of sight below my eyes. A steady and constant flow of things … with the rhythm of one boot always seen to be kicking itself into view as the other boot is seen to be taking itself out of view…, actually, the amount and size of any one of my legs and boots that I have in view is always in an inverse proportion to the size and the length of the opposite leg and boot taking itself in or out of view. I soon bring a steady, even pace to my steps, and this brings my boots to appear synchronized as they step themselves into and out of view above the flow of rocks and railroad ties.

Focused directly into the center of all this movement below me and not only does it appear that each left and right boot is alternating going in and out in rhythm to the other boot, my boots seem to move as if they are above an almost fluid, continuous motion of rocks and railroad ties. I try to imagine everything I have in view down there presented as if in some kind of single system of things, and as if all the types of movement I see below are somehow synchronized together as a single constancy of things. Eventually I do have all the movement I'm looking upon down below synchronized. My boots, the flow of the railroad ties and the rocks together, everything becomes one fairly steady and continuous flow of things …,

Moments pass, and I stay focused on all the movement below. I get a sense for how the constant in and out rhythm of my boots are, in some way, out of synch with the more fluid like motion of rocks and railroad ties that are moving around down there. My alternating boot steps are in a different kind of predictable order of movement than the rocks and railroad ties that are moving and appearing in a more random type of way, and I can't keep that random but fluid motion of rock and railroad tie meshed together with the alternating in and out pattern of movement I have with my two boots. I want to try to list and label things as parameters, as factors, and then somehow map and organize the various types of movements I'm watching down there.

The heel of my right boot steps down and begins arching forward on top of a railroad tie. My left boot enters into the picture and I'm starting to bring my right boot back out, and to see the black and white sneaker and the blue denim bell-bottomed pant leg of Mary Christiane enter way over on the right side. Her sneaker and my boot take themselves out of view, everything is still in synch with the stride of my left boot stepping down and arching forward. My left boot going out now brings my right boot synchronized with Mary Ann's pant leg and sneaker swinging over a lot closer to my boot, and both my boot and her sneaker are stepping side by side upon a single railroad tie.

I look up from the rocks and railroad ties. Mary Christiane is looking forward and down upon the railroad tracks, looking down at anything that happens to be just a few feet in front of us. I look straight ahead and keep on walking. I can't think of anything to say.

I cannot believe how fast she got that sentence together. I simply and absolutely cannot believe it!

"Hey," I say, and I put a halt to my steps. I do and I don't want to now tell Mary Christiane that she started the answer in question form. I feel silly.

They both look towards me.

"Hay's for horses," Amy says, and I watch both of them turn and step farther away.

"Wait until we get to Hopewell you want something to eat," I hear Amy say to the set of railroad tracks up ahead.

I should say something, if only for the fun of it, though, I saw Mary Christiane with this kind of weird look on her face before she turned around. She did ask and wondered, she thinks I'm mad at her. Oh, wow...,

I put a quick pace to my steps and bring myself up to where they are. I extend my hand towards her and just said what I said and did what I did without really thinking about it.

"Astonished and impressed..., I am."

I don't want her to think I'm mad at her. I want to portray a seriousness of attitude. She looks up at me and an elated chuckle immediately bubbles up and out of her. I stop walking. She stops walking. She curls a lock of hair behind her ear and then extends her hand to me.

I turn the palm of my hand to wrap all of my fingers around her thumb, and then to bring my other hand up to cover her hand with both of mine.

Her wrist, her entire hand is soft and limp as I turn and shake it from side to side.

I bring up a reluctant smile ... of defeat. Tears almost start to well up in my eyes.

I'm shaking hands with a girl.

Chuckling as I let go of her hand, my laugh is a laugh at her rather than with her.

I turn and look to walk down the length of rocks and railroad track in front of me. And God Almighty I don't know what to think right now...!

I take a deep breath, and then a second deep breath. I'm not mad, not really. It was just a game between me and Amy. It was fun to go back to it and play around with it, but that's it. It's done, over..., and I lost or something.

I am impressed, if I'm feeling anything worth feeling.

Scouting For Boys, And Charlie

Amy's bedroom door opens as I knock on it. She's knitting on her bed.

"Wanna lift some weights? Spot me, maybe?"

"All right, five minutes."

Whatever she's knitting, the pattern is not run of the mill. I step over to the foot of her bed.

"What is it?"

"A skirt." Amy flattens and stretches the pink, blue, and white colored design before raising it up for inspection.

"A cross skirt. Jodi designed the pattern." I look at the rectangle of knitted material. Lines of pink crosses against a background swirl of blue and white.

"You like it?"

"Sure, why not?"

"Look at this one." She reaches down alongside the bed to bring another knitted skirt up from the floor.

"Horses on the run. Caoimhe, Marina, Natalie, and I are making different skirts to sell in Jodi's store."

"I'll be downstairs," and I take myself through the hallway, turn the corner and through the door, and then down the stairs. Tonight I'm in the mood to attempt a bench press of at least one set, and maybe do a couple of sets of three to five reps at one hundred seventy pounds. Day before yesterday I pushed three sets of five reps at one hundred sixty. One sixty-five is my actual body weight so I'll be pushing above that from now on, which is cool in itself. Today being a second full day of rest from the previous days' lift, and I think I'm strong enough to handle more weight.

I turn the stereo on and tune the FM dial to the 103.7 MHz frequency ... and picking up a good clean, distortion and static free signal. The station announcer at WQXR says Mozart's *Eine kleine Nachtmusik, 'A little night music'* will be the next melody, ... and the clear sounds of Mozart resonates through the speakers. Individual notes of musical sound accompany my footsteps towards the barbell bench.

I want one hundred-fifty pounds on the barbell to use for a quick set of warm-up reps. I remove two twenty-five pound weights from each end of the bar and then lie down on the carpet to do sit-ups.

I'm thinking because of today's fresh snow on the ground, and that it's night time, all this probably helps boost the reception for the clarity of the radio signal. Unusually crisp and clean sound from the speakers. I'll stop at fifty sit-ups, then do some pull-ups, push-ups, and maybe a number of leg lifts till Amy comes down.

A snowstorm began early last night and ended a couple hours after sunrise, blanketing the entire southern part of the State with a foot and a half of snow. They closed schools and the Scout troop meeting scheduled for Thursday nights, phone calls said the Lodge doors will be open though there will not be regular activities for anyone who does show up. During supper it was decided that with road conditions the way they are, the distance to the lodge is too far. There is not a necessity of some kind to be out on the roads, so Festus, Max, and I will not be there.

Counting up to the last of the pushups I hear Amy walking down the stairs, watching her step towards me, her hands hold a peach and a tangerine out towards me. I reach for the tangerine.

She pulls the tangerine away, placing the peach in my hand. "Eat a peach."

I watch her step over and turn the stereo from FM to phonograph mode, and the next thing I'm hearing is, *I Feel the Earth / move / under my feet*, from Carole King's *Tapestry* album. I take a couple bites out of the peach, wrapping the napkin around and placing it underneath the barbell bench. Amy hooks her feet underneath the barbell bench and begins doing sit-ups. I pick myself up off the floor and walk under the doorjamb leading to the furnace room. Both hands reach up and grab hold of the horizontal bar and I pull myself up.

The first few repetitions I'm lowering myself down to fully extend my arms, and I hold my calves up so my feet won't touch the floor. With all the resistance as I'm able to muster up I lower myself down and raise myself up as slow as possible, so as to make the effort required for each repetition as strenuous as I can.

My arms become tired and I drop to the floor. Amy is still doing sit-ups. I step over to her, squat down and crack the knuckles of my fingers, waiting for her to maybe say something.

With bent knees Amy has a steady rhythm of up and down sit-ups going. Cracking the last of the knuckles and with no comments from her, I get up on the bench press.

Curling my fingers snug around the metal bar, I press my palms up against the barbell and raise it off the rack. Elbows locked, I hold the bar up for a moment before lowering it down to my chest. Exhaling, I push the bar up again.

At the last rep to a third set of four reps I hold the barbell up and balanced inches above my chest. Amy steps to stand and look down on me, placing both her hands underneath the length of the barbell.

"Poor boy tired?" she scowls.

Amy and I can bend and raise the left side of our upper lip, and when we do so our faces seem to be reacting in repugnance or disdain to something. These faces both of us make are nowhere to be seen on any character of a television show. Someday we may be the first ones to do so, ... and I look up to Amy and slowly raise my lip up to her. Quivering this scowling bent lip of mine up towards her before I have to break up the moment and chuckle. I lift the bar up hard and fast with the two of us placing the barbell to rest upon the rack.

No one else in the family can raise their upper lips the way Amy and I are able to do. It's cool.

"I'm still warming up ... not ready yet," I explain to Amy. "I'm gonna go for a hundred seventy though, so I need someone here."

Amy turns away and steps to the free weights along the basement wall. I reach down underneath the bench and pick up the peach in the napkin.

I watch her lift a single ten pound hand barbell from the floor. Seated to support the arm with elbow on the knee, she begins doing arm curls. I'm taking bites out of the peach until all that's left is the pit. Amy is looking at the muscles in her arm as it flexes and relaxes, and then she stares at the moving barbell with a determined look of concentration as she puts forth the effort for each repetition.

I hear foot steps on the basement stairs.

"You want to go to the lodge?" Max asks standing halfway down the stairwell.

"They want people to shovel snow."

"What time is it?"

"Almost seven."

Seven o'clock ... shovel snow? Schools tomorrow...

"Boyce wants people to do some driveways for some people. Yes, or no. He's on the phone."

I nod my head. "I'm going."

A cool August morning. Looking out the back window of the station wagon and it's dark outside as we drive away from the house though dawn's light is everywhere when Dad turns into Gates' driveway and we're rolling down to the garage doors of their house.

Soft clicks from the steering column as Dad shifts the transmission into PARK, and I have the hatchback window rolled all the way down.

"I'll go and get them," I say to Dad and Max, Steve Wozniack and Steven Jobs sitting up in the front seats.

Climbing out and stepping off the driveway I look at the miniature plaster figurines inside the azaleas, chrysanthemum, evergreens, and hemlocks along the sidewalk. I step to a mother goose and her chicks, and then look at the boy as he reads while lying prone upon the dark brown wood chips. His bare feet remain crossed and raised comfortably up in the air, and all of these plaster molds have still not been painted. The trousers and shirt, the book the boy is reading, all the feathers on the ducks remain a dirty, ice-white plaster color. I hear the front door opening.

"Hi Kurt."

"Top of the day, Mrs. Gates. They're not here?"

"They went to pick up some things at the 7-Eleven. They'll be right back."

"I have to say you look sharp in your Scout uniform."

My thoughts for a response are quickly interrupted. "Here they come now."

"Have fun."

The day is finally here. With Mr. Gates driving a second station wagon with sons Bill and Henry and passengers Anthony Baden-Powell and Paul McCartney, a two vehicle convoy from Boy Scout Troop 12 is on their way for a three day summer weekend at a campground near the battlefields of Gettysburg, Pennsylvania.

A Boy Scout is trustworthy, loyal, helpful, friendly, courteous, kind, obedient, cheerful, thrifty, brave, clean, and reverent. Basically most of the time, yes, I am all of these things.

An automobile traveling at a constant fifty, sixty miles an hour speeds create these subtle engine and transmission vibrations which permeate into the seat and door I lean upon. An almost hypnotic drone from rolling tires and I become so mentally and physically relaxed I fall asleep. I wake on the merge off an Interstate. An almost four hour drive brings us to the dirt road of the campgrounds and we'll drive until the plot of ground where Scoutmaster Boyce's van is seen. Scouts and their fathers are milling about outside a large open tent.

I walk with Dad and Mr. Gates to where Mr. Boyce and assistant scoutmasters Mr. Stewart and Mr. Willis are. After shaking hands and some small talk I follow everyone inside the tent.

I take myself to a picnic table where Ronnie Van Zant and other scouts are. Ron's house was a stone's throw from ours when we lived on Fenmore Drive.

Ron offers me the open end of a bag of corn chips.

"They got anything planned for today?" I ask.

"Don't know. Waiting for everyone to show up and get themselves set up, I guess."

I stand where a section of the canvas wall of the tent is brought up and splayed out onto the sloping roof. A light breeze of warm, humid air moves through the tent. Outside are two cooking grill, bags of charcoal, and Coleman food storage coolers arranged on top of half a dozen picnic tables.

I look all around the immediate area inside the tent. A Thermos water cooler and Dixie cups are on top of a picnic table, and I step over to get a cup of water. Ice cold water flows from the spigot.

"It's almost eleven o'clock," Ron says. "I heard Mr. Willis say food is gonna be served around six. I don't know what everyone is doing in the mean time," Ron has his arm pointing outside the tent towards a swimming pool a hundred some odd yards in the distance. "I'm going to the pool as soon as I can."

I look outside the tent. The hundred yards of rising ground in front of me becomes a mound of earth with a length of chain-link fence on top. People are running around and jumping off of a diving board.

"What's stopping 'ya?"

"Mr. Boyce wants everyone here for some reason."

I walk over to where Donnie Van Zant, Max, Paul, both Stevens, and Bill are yucking it up with Mr. Boyce, Dad, and Mr. Gates.

"Pitch two tents around the perimeter, anywhere near this tent," I hear Mr. Boyce say. "We'll start cooking around five, have everyone together around six and we'll take it from there."

I follow Dad to the back of Mr. Stewart's cargo van. Duffle bags containing four-man tents, poles, and stakes are inside or lying on the ground just outside the van.

"Grab some of the poles and stakes," Dad tells me.

I just want to get wet. I dive into the pool and swim a diagonal to the far side. Climbing out of the water and I'm not in a mood to exert myself too much. I walk towards the chain-link fence and sprawl myself out into one of the large wooden chairs.

The first thing that caught my eye is the bright red swimsuit. The bright red swimsuit dives into the pool, she moves underneath the ripples and waves of water for a fairly long moment, her head rising above water near the corner wall.

I watch two hands place themselves up upon the cement. She lunges up and out of the water to place that dripping, bright red swimsuit directly in front of me. Arms are straight along her sides, elbows locked and balancing herself and the lower, bottom part of that bright red swimsuit brings a leg up and in front of herself, her foot to place itself down flat upon the cement. Rising up and she turns away to walk and stand with her two friends.

Because I cannot make up my mind, a bright red or the dark, deep maroon color are my favorite color. Her swimsuit is the brightest red I have ever seen in a swimsuit. I simply must get up and introduce myself.

"Red is my favorite color. And that is the brightest red swimsuit I have ever seen."

She turns from her friends to look at me. Hazel eyes, the same color eyes as my own. Curly, shoulder length strands of wet black hair, and overall she's just a little bit chubby. She still hasn't lost all of her baby fat.

"You live around here?" I ask.

"From Baltimore."

Extending my hand, "My name is Kurt, Kurt Soldier."

She holds out her hand and I bring it up and then down once, letting her hand slip away from mine.

"Bonnie Sheppard." I look around her face and into her eyes.

"I'm with the Scout troop over there," I say pointing in the direction of where we've set up camp. "From New York. You know people around here?"

"Let's go," I hear one of her friends say.

I turn to Bonnie's friend and watch Bill, Paul, and Steve Jobs taking steps up to stand next to us.

"Bill, Paul," I say, "this is Bonnie and her friends. They're from Baltimore."

"Ivanka," Bonnie says towards Paul.

"I'm Joanne." Inflection of a British accent and I turn to look at Joanne standing on my right. I want to hear her speak again, to have her say anything with that accent, and I quickly say what I hope is something aristocratically sounding.

"From the other side of the pond?" brings only a smile and nod from her.

"My father's on a business trip at Harrisburg," Bonnie says to me. "We just came along."

"You're camping here?"

"That's our trailer over there, beside—in front of that row of trees."

"How long you staying?"

"Another day or two..., don't know yet."

"You've been to the battlefields?" I ask. Her eyes close and then open with a subtle turn of the head.

"No."

The notion is with me, to ask them if perhaps they'd want to accompany us and the troop to the battlefields tomorrow.

"Our troop probably isn't doing anything this afternoon. We're still waiting for everyone to show up."

I look over towards Bill, Paul, and Steve, and then to Ivanka and Joanne.

"Perhaps tonight we'll stop by your trailer, maybe go do something?"

"If you want," Bonnie says.

I step towards the edge of the pool and after a glance their way, I turn and dive into the water.

Drawing a short straw before dinner relegated me and two other scouts for cleanup detail.

Grilled hot dogs and hamburgers, baked potatoes and coleslaw with orange Kool-Aid served up to seven picnic tables of scouts and parents.

I place my plate of food down on the table.

"Let's walk over to their trailer after we're done eating," I say to Paul, Bill, and Steve. "Just the four of us, all right? No one else."

A passing moment and Steve says to me, "I'll take Andy's place."

"We'll take that other guys place," Bill says to Paul, and Paul agrees.

"His name is Andy, isn't it?"

Steve looks at the guy sitting at a nearby table. I look at him too, and I don't know what his name is.

After almost everyone finished and left their table, the four of us are tasked by Boyce and Stewart to wash the cooking grills and utensils, clean the table cloths and make sure all food stuffs were put back where they belong. Trash is bagged, tied, and then placed alongside the dirt road.

We put our green Scout shirts on and the four of us walk to the road. We find Bonnie, Ivanka, and Joanne on a picnic table in front of their trailer. All three have acoustic guitars in hand.

"Pretty neat," I say stepping up next to them.

"Play something," Bill says. "Play your best one."

Bonnie plucks a few strings and looks towards Ivanka and Joanne, and both nod in recognition. They begin to play and sing the lyrics of the John Denver song, *Leaving on a Jet Plane.*

Bonnie sings lead. Ivanka and Joanne bring up chorus, and I watch Joanne stop playing her guitar and place a frown on her face. She seems quite unhappy with herself, for making a mistake I suppose. Her frown disappears and she begins to strum the strings and merge back into the song again, joining Ivanka inside a chorus.

"*Oh babe, I hate to go.*"

Watching them relax with congratulatory nods and chuckles, Steve beat me to the question.

"You want to play for our troop, right?"

Bonnie answers without hesitation. "Sure."

I look at Steve, Paul, and Bill, and with our smiles of good fortune I'm wondering how to introduce them to the troop. I've thoughts of Mr. Boyce disapproving, and it's a fleeting image watching the three of them walk farther away from me.

"All they can do is say no," I say. "So, let's go ask."

Bonnie gets off the picnic table, steps inside the trailer, and a moment later I suppose it to be her father who stands with her at the open screen door. He looks at us, and nods his approval.

Stepping back towards our campsite and the man's voice is barely audible. "Don't stay out too late, Bonnie."

I think of Joanne's accent as we walk, and of Julie Andrews and the way the words were spoken and sung in the movie *Mary Poppins*. I'm curious and want to hear her say the place where she grew up. I'll reconnoiter my knowledge of British geography with the origin of her dialect.

"I want you to know that your accent reminds me of Julie Andrews, and Mary Poppins."

Joanne looks up from her pace of steps.

"Pleasant inflections, hearing you speak like that. Charming."

"Where in the United Kingdom you from?"

A moment for reflection eventually brings a self-conscious chuckle. "Despite a bit of Lancaster, Yorkshire, Kent … and Lyon in my roots, I am happy to be here."

Despite? An odd choice of word.

Stopping at one of the picnic tables outside the main tent, "I'll find Boyce and tell him what we want to do."

Bill and I step inside to find Mr. Gates with several scouts playing backgammon, chess, and Scrabble games on the picnic tables.

"Mr. Gates, some friends of ours want to put on a concert for us tonight."

He looks up from the game board and then out towards where the girls are.

"Where's Mr. Boyce?" I ask. Several scouts rise up and step away from their game boards on the tables.

"He's up at the pool. Go on up there. Find him. I think he'd like to know."

"There's isn't anything special planned or going on tonight, is there?"

Mr. Gates turns his head, "Nope, not till morning."

Stepping back outside, "It's probably all right," I say to the everyone.

"Our Scoutmaster is up at the pool. I'll go up there and find him and tell him what's going on."

"I guess just make yourselves comfortable," I say to Bonnie.

I take notice of the fact that the sun is setting down low along the horizon, and it's starting to get dark.

Walking along the chain link fence I see Dad standing at pool side and talking to someone in the water, and then to spot where Mr. Boyce stands with Mr. Willis. I walk through the entrance gate towards Dad.

"Where've you been? Were looking for 'ya."

"Dad, some girls we met want to sing for us down at the campsite."

Dad raises his eyebrows. "That so?"

"They're waiting. I wanted to see if Mr. Boyce had anything else planned though."

Dad shakes his head. "Not that I'm aware of. It's late. Gettin' dark, too."

I step over to where Mr. Boyce and Mr. Willis are standing.

"Mr. Boyce, I met some people who want to sing for the troop..., now, tonight."

Mr. Boyce turns to me.

"Some girls," I repeat. "We met 'em at the pool this afternoon."

"They're down there now?"

I nod. "Yup. Waiting, too."

Mr. Boyce says something to Mr. Willis and then motions for me to follow him the couple steps to where Dad is with Mr. Stewart.

"Another half hour and start sending everyone back," I hear Mr. Boyce say to Mr. Stewart.

Mr. Boyce pats my shoulder. "Let's go meet your friends, Kurt."

I hear the girls singing as Dad, Mr. Boyce, and I walk down the hill. We walk into a circle of picnic tables and scouts already sitting on the ground.

Amos Humiston is one-arm dragging a picnic table along the ground. Paul and Steve are walking with a picnic table in their hands. Scouts stand up and move so Amos, Paul, and Steve can arrange the tables near where the girls are. I help Amos adjust his picnic table and listen to the girls finish the Eagles song *Desperado*. The next song they sing is *Wasted Time*, another Eagles song. The way Bonnie sings reminds me of Linda Ronstadt.

The song is over and after a moment to compose themselves, Ivanka sings the Stephen Foster song *Way down upon the Swannee River*. I look around and notice three visitors have stopped to stand on the grass along the road in back of the picnic tables.

Bonnie, Ivanka, and Joanne finish the song and I step up in front of the picnic table.

"That's our scoutmaster, Mr. Boyce over there," I say pointing with my hand. "He's a good guy."

The three of them look at Mr. Boyce. Bonnie and Mr. Boyce bring up a hand wave of acknowledgment to each other. I walk over to the picnic table where Anthony, Paul, Bill, and Steve Jobs are.

Each of their songs end with requests from the scouts: *Blowing in the Wind, Sugar Magnolia, In-a-Gadda-Da-Vida, Hocus Pocus.* Bonnie nods to the request for

I Got You Babe, though she stops playing the song after the first two or three lines. I watch Bonnie turn to say something to Ivanka and then to Joanne, and the three sing Kris Kristofferson's *Me and Bobby McGhee.* When they finish I hear someone request the song, *I Am Woman.*

I hear Bill asking Anthony, "Who sent in the clowns?"

I watch the campers walking past our campsite. Several travelers stop and gather close to the picnic tables and listen.

Paul is behind me, saying, "Kurt, what'd'ya think?"

Bill turns to me. "They're cool, huh?"

"Yeah, sure," I say.

I turn around to look at Paul. An upbeat look to himself.

"This ain't Lake George and Roger's Rock at night."

A good sized crowd has gathered around. I hear the scout sitting in front of me request Procol Harem's *A Whiter Shade of Pale.* I hear another voice request something, though I couldn't hear what it was. With the chuckles I'm hearing the request must've been another goofball request for a song. I watch Bonnie lightly pluck and strum the guitar strings. Ivanka taps Bonnie's arm, and with a nod Bonnie will turn to us and say the name of the Simon and Garfunkel song, *The Sound of Silence.* Ivanka plucks the leading notes to the song, and then begins to sing the words.

Paul asks me, "Soldier, seriously, what d'ya think though?"

"What d'ya mean what do I think?"

"You know, once they're finished here, you may never see them again."

Paul obviously likes one of them.

"So what?" I say with an exaggerated enthusiasm, in jest.

Anthony leans close to me.

"So what? So what you lost a perfect opportunity?"

I chuckle to myself and at what they're saying and trying to do.

"Maybe you should go up there," I say to Anthony. "Right now go up and ask one of 'em if she wants to marry you. Which one you like?"

"Wow, Soldier," Bill returns with. "What's the matter with you?"

Anthony steps off the table and stands facing towards the girls. Lyrically and musically, *The Sound of Silence* is an eerie, somewhat melancholy song. I'd prefer to be listening to them sing than to be talking right about now.

"Seriously, there's something about them," Anthony says.

I have to believe they're smitten, to be talking silly as they are. I'm thinking to maybe get up and walk to somewhere else if they keep on talking.

I turn to Steve. "You hear these guys?"

He glances my way, leaning back with open hands on the table top. A nod to acknowledge what I said, and the smile on his face is on the verge of a laugh. Tapping his foot, he wants to keep his eyes forward and listen to the girls play. So do I.

I hear Paul behind me say, "Kurt, think about it. Suppose if when we come back tomorrow, supposing we went over to their trailer to find they'd gone and left? They never even got to say goodbye. You telling me you wouldn't care, or would you wish you did something now?"

"Something, what? What are you talking about? We just met them a couple hours ago. Wow."

For a moment I imagine myself a dolt. I'm missing something I should perhaps be more attentive to right about now?

Tomorrow night and they're not here? They didn't say goodbye?

To think of this as a reality of the situation, I imagine not minding or caring too much if they had to leave though, ... *I'm glad that they're here right now.*

They finish the Simon and Garfunkel song and a round of applause is in order.

"They sure do seem to know quite a few songs," I say to anyone.

I scan my eyes around and a quick guesstimate has me counting a half dozen groups of from three to five people gathered around our little concert area. I notice the man who was at the trailer door with Bonnie. He's standing towards the back of the circle of scouts and campers.

"There's that guy we met at the trailer."

Anthony climbs over the table and sits down next to me. I hear him sound out a quick, frustrating laugh.

"Yeah I saw him already," he says. "Bonnie's father. Hey, don't change the subject. This is important."

I'm incredulous, and shake my head, turning to look at him. With raised eyebrows he's trying to impress me with some exasperation.

I place the tip of my middle finger up against the tip of my thumb, and with the three fingers of my hand extending out like the horns from a threatening Triceratops, I slowly maneuver my hand up and over towards his face.

"Let me plunk your nose..., just once."

Anthony pushes off the table, steps back, folding his arms in front of himself. Facing towards the girls, he's paying me no mind.

I give myself a chuckle at this sudden, insistent display of adulation everyone is putting on.

They're like groupies..., and I recall standing at the pool with Bonnie, and the thoughts of having the three of them join us touring the battlegrounds.

"You know when we first met them at the pool? I thought of asking them to join us touring the battlefields tomorrow."

I watch Anthony step to sit back down next to me. I'm anticipating the reaction to what that giddy smile on his face is all about now.

"Hey man, what a brilliant idea...!"

"Hear! Hear!" Paul chimes. "I second that motion."

I turn to find Bill tapping my arm with open hand.

"A tactical genius," he says, and with a giddy chuckle I reach over to shake his hand. He pulls his hand away from mine, instead pressing the tip of his extended index finger onto his nose while making a short vocal utterance of error.

"Unbelievable," I hear Steve say.

All four of them..., they're pure nuts!

Paul is silent with these quick, subtle nods of his head, encouraging me to follow through with this idea.

"You guys having fun? Goofing on Elvis or something?"

"You should ask them." Bill says my way.

Me? Why me? The feeling creeps in. I'm realizing the fact that someone whom I know and care about a lot is, in actuality, sort of uncool at the moment.

"Yeah, yeah," I say. "Second thought and Boyce, Stewart, Willis—you know they'd never go for it. Who's kidding who?"

"We'll take care of—we should all talk to Boyce and those guys," Anthony suggests.

"Oh yeah, just ask and just like that they'll eventually go for it," I say. "I don't think some girls can just join in with us anytime anyone wants them to."

Steve is pronouncing each separate syllable in my direction.

"Hello? Dude. Think positive."

I look down and put my head into my hands.

Oh, wow...!

"All of us will go over and talk to Boyce, and whoever else needs talking to," I hear Bill say. "We'll say to them something like...? Like us guys...? That the troop should be doing something more. Maybe more than just say thanks for their performance tonight. 'Hey, thanks ladies, now goodbye,' or some other dumb token of appreciation."

I listen and feel as if I'm following a herd. I am an insignificant member of a pack, a flock. I pick my head up, look forward..., Steve steps in front of me. He's making faces with his fist swinging up, mimicking punches to the side of his head.

"Kurt, trust me. Anyone objects to letting 'em go along with us ... is doomed."

I step down in front of the picnic table and watch the girls play.

I hear Paul ask, "You do want them to go along ...?"

I turn around to see Paul is referring the question to me. "If they could, right?"

"Well, yeah sure," I say. "If they could it'd absolutely be cool."

Paul steps off the picnic table and I watch Steve and Bill follow him near the main tent. They stand and talk with Bill's father and Mr. Boyce.

Again, I'm thinking, *Just ask...*, to see if they can.

All Boyce and everyone can do is say no.

I hear the opening guitar riffs for the Jim Croce song, *Operator*.

"They know me better than anyone else in the troop," I say to Anthony. "It'll probably be best if I go over there and ask that guy over there, if they can, first."

I step away from the table, "Proper protocol and all, you know?"

Stepping over scouts and I work my way behind the tables and campers. The guy notices me as I take the last half dozen steps up next to him.

"Hi. My name's Kurt Soldier," I say with an extended hand. "You remember me, right?"

He nods his head in acknowledgment. A firm hand grips mine.

"Hi."

"Are you Bonnie's father?"

He nods yes.

Unlike thoughts of asking Mr. Boyce or Mr. Stewart or Mr. Willis if they could join us tomorrow, I have no hesitation whatsoever to simply ask Mr. Sheppard if they can come with us.

"Mr. Sheppard, our troop has a scheduled guided tour of the battlefields tomorrow. Some guys are now asking our scoutmaster if Bonnie and her friends could join us. You wouldn't mind if they accompanied us tomorrow morning, would you?"

He looks away from me and towards Bonnie and Ivanka and Joanne.

"They'll be all right."

He turns to look at me, and then rubs the palm of his hand against his forehead. The palm turns to rub into and around one eye socket for a moment. He folds his arms in front of himself and looks towards the girls.

"I'm sure they will be. If they want to, I have no problem with that."

"Thanks, Mr. Sheppard. I gotta go though. Glad to meet you."

Anthony is talking with Mr. Boyce as I walk up to everyone standing near the main tent. I look at Mr. Willis, and then at Bill and Paul.

"What'd he say?" Anthony asks me.

"Yes, good, no problem," I say.

"Mr. Boyce, what d'ya think? We should ask them to come along and tour the battlefields with us tomorrow. There shouldn't be a problem."

His eyes squint as if to study me and my face for a moment.

"You asked them already?"

"No, not outright, but I hinted—" *to myself,* "that they might be able to."

Anthony steps up to stand beside Mr. Gates.

"Mr. Boyce, come on, ... there's plenty of room in the vans for three other people."

I listen to Mr. Willis say, "Girls aren't allowed, guys."

"Oh come on," I hear Steve say. "Mr. Willis, geez. Rules are made to be broken."

"You should've asked one of us first," I hear Mr. Gates say.

"Where's it written that they can't? That they're not allowed?" Bill says to his father and Mr. Willis.

Anthony turns away from Mr. Boyce and speaks to Mr. Willis.

"It's not that they can't. It's whether they'll have permission to be like ...? How about they're our guests ... guests of Troop 12."

"That's one of their father's standing over there. The guy with the T-shirt on," I say to Mr. Boyce. "I just asked him a minute ago and he said they could, if they wanted to."

Mr. Boyce looks towards Mr. Sheppard. I look over towards Mr. Sheppard too, and take notice of the number of campers now gathered in the area. Quite a few people are standing around the three or four picnic tables. Mr. Boyce scans the crowd and then an exasperated look down to the ground.

"What's his name?"

"Her name's Bonnie Sheppard. I don't know his first name."

Mr. Boyce has a stern look in his eyes.

"I want to talk to him before this goes any farther. Don't get your hopes up just yet."

"You guys listen, and listen good. If they do happen to be with us tomorrow, everyone's on their best behavior."

Mr. Boyce turns to Anthony, and then to speak directly to Bill. "You're an Eagle Scout, and next year Anthony. Both of you make it clear to everyone there's no fooling around. Any shenanigans and I'll take it personally. Got it?"

Anthony and Bill nod to Mr. Boyce, and I totally concur too, nodding with enthusiasm.

"Definitely. We understand, Mr. Boyce."

I'm stepping out and away from Mr. Boyce and bring a suggestive nod towards Steve and Paul to also leave now too.

We're several steps of distance away and Paul steps up next to me.

"They're coming with us tomorrow."

"Yeah, maybe."

"Bonnie's father said all right?" Steve asks.

"He told me if they want to go, no problem."

I have the notion to thank Mr. Boyce for what he's doing, and I turn myself around to do so.

"And thanks, Mr. Boyce. Thanks a lot."

I'm watching Mr. Stewart stepping out from the tent. His arms wrap around Mr. Boyce and Mr. Gates shoulders, and with Mr. Willis all four have smiles on their faces. They're practically laughing. Mr. Boyce turns towards me, acknowledging me with a wave of the hand.

"Mr. Boyce, what time are we leaving for the museum?" I ask.

"We want to leave here early, Kurt," Mr. Gates says, taking steps to stand between Mr. Boyce and myself. "Around eight o'clock. We'll be at the museum before the tour guides arrive around ten."

Walking up close to where the girls are, I wait until they finish the Harry Chapin song, *Cat's in the Cradle,* and then step up to their picnic table.

"You guys wanna go with us to tour the battlefields tomorrow?"

"Great," I hear Ivanka say, and I give a quick look her way.

"Your father's over there Bonnie," motioning with a nod of my head. "He said and our Scoutmaster also said it's probably all right."

She laughs, surprised. "OK, with me."

Bonnie looks to Ivanka and Joanne.

I have not yet gauged Ivanka and her reason for slowly slurring that two syllabled word 'great' just a moment ago, and I turn to look at her.

A hint of a smile, and there's a sparkle in her eyes as if confirming an already expected …? Anticipation?

With quick nods of enthusiasm, "Have to be up and ready to go early," I say. Ivanka nods with me, miming the enthusiasm.

"Around eight we're leaving the campground. Spend some time at the museum. They said we'll rendezvous with the guides there around ten."

"Cool," I hear Joanne say.

"Definitely," I say back.

I turn to Ivanka. "It'll be fun."

I want to dispel whatever she may have been thinking. Ivanka nods to me with a bit more enthusiasm than before.

"Soldier," I hear someone say, "get out of the way. Quit hogging the show."

Stepping up, over and around the people sitting and laying on the ground and I see Max on a picnic table. I look around and don't see Paul or Steve so I step to stand close to where Max is.

I hear Joanne with the opening monologue to Donovan's *Atlantis.* Her English accent and the inflection of her words mimics Donovan's Gaelic dialect.

"And gods they were."

I listen to her oratory and carbonated bubbles travel up my spine. Loud chords strum from their three guitars. Joanne steps down from the picnic table and stands, strumming the guitar while leading up to the crescendo, *"Hail! Atlantis!"*

Chorus lines are tight and right on melody as they follow Joanne finger picking the notes on the guitar. Bonnie is oratorical with her background lyrics. Ivanka maintains a melodic choral background voice…, and Joanne cuts the song off because so many scouts are clapping and whistling!

I give several hand claps and a whistle, then reach inside my pants pocket for the butane lighter. I turn the gas flow regulator to maximum, spin the flint lock and raise the flame up over my head. Everyone standing and sitting are applauding and whistling, hootin' and hollering. Amusing to watch Bonnie and Ivanka laughing, offering congratulatory hand claps of applause over to Joanne. Joanne really hit it. Obviously she likes the song, and she must've practiced it a bit. Good song.

After thank yous to everyone in the audience, Joanne strums her guitar and begins to sing the John Lennon song, *Mind Games.*

Neil Young's *Heart of Gold* has Ivanka singing lead, and she brings to mind the peculiarly mellow voice of Stevie Nicks, at times injecting the commanding tone of a Grace Slick into passages of the song. The original recording of *Heart of Gold* ends with the interesting mix of backup vocals from Linda Ronstadt and Johnny Cash, and while Bonnie and Joanne sing the final chorus lines of *Heart of Gold,* I have the feeling the three of them also appreciate how that little contribution from Johnny and Linda enhanced Neil's song.

They're putting on a fantastic performance. Ivanka is taking lead to Thunderclap Newman's *Something in the Air.*

I'm impressed. The last four songs. The quality of song and the girl's enthusiasm as they play. They're great.

The scout sitting next to Max gets up from the table and walks away. I sit down next to him and point to where Mr. Sheppard stands.

"That guy's the father of the one with the black hair, Bonnie, in the middle. We asked Mr. Boyce and he's trying to arrange for the three of 'em to accompany us tomorrow."

"You're pulling my leg?" Max says.

"Nope. Boyce says don't get our hopes up just yet, he's checking it out, but if they are with us tomorrow he says no shenanigans, no fooling around. Anthony and Bill are gonna say something to everyone, to make sure everyone knows to be cool."

"They'll be going with us then."

"Maybe."

"You did it."

Max's words sound resigned. It's perfectly obvious how his inflection of the words stifled a sense of incredulity.

"We did it," I say, and turning to say the words directly at him, and to watch for his reaction.

"If we did it. Nothing's for sure, yet, but if we did it, it was Anthony and Bill, Paul and Steve and me that were talking to Boyce and everyone. Not just me."

A moment to imitate the comedians Carl Rowan and Dick Martin. "You bet your sweet bippy, we did it."

I hear Ivanka raise her voice. "What song is it you wanna hear?"

Two or three voices repeat the requests for the Lynyrd Skynyrd song, *Freebird.*

The girls smile though they look discouraged.

"Stairway to Heaven, Freebird, can't," Bonnie says, raising the acoustic guitar up from her lap, twirling it around once and then twice.

"Can't do justice to the songs. Won't even try."

"How 'bout *"Tuesday's Gone"*? Ivanka suggests to everyone. A sprinkling of whoops and hollers sound out. A surprised look on Bonnie and Joanne as the three of them huddle together for words. Ivanka closes her eyes and nods her head. A confidence is with her as she opens her eyes and turns to Joanne and Bonnie, plucking into the chords of *Tuesday's Gone.*

The attempt is sincere and touching but the acoustic guitar can't bring the notes to stand out and complement the dramatic sections of the song. A pleasing sentimental quality is brought to the lyrics.

"They obviously play electric guitars, too," I say to Max.

Anthony has climbed on the table behind Max and I.

"Soldier, Boyce talked to her father. They're going."

With a big smile I swat his hand in congratulations. "Where's Bill and Paul?"

I shrug my shoulders, and Anthony climbs off and walks away.

The Scouts are on a roll and the requests for songs keep on coming.

"Aerosmith, *Last Child, Sweet Emotion.*"

"Bruce Springsteen, *Candy's Room.*"

"Blue Sky, Allman Brothers."

"Chuck Mangione, *Feels So Good.*"

"ELO, *Livin' Thing.*"

"Enya, *Only Time.*"

"Led Zeppelin, *D'Yer Maker.*"

"More Than A Feeling, Boston."

"Neil Young, *Hey, Hey, My, My.*"

"Pink Floyd, *Wish You Were Here.*"

"Rod Stewart, *You Wear It Well.*"

"Time Has Come Today, Chambers Brothers."

"White Room, Brave Ulysses, Cream."

I watch Bonnie turn and speak to a pensive Ivanka plucking the strings of her guitar.

I Walk the Line, ... Layla, ... Rhiannon, ... Puff The Magic Dragon, ... American Woman, ... Turn! Turn! Turn! ... Wild Thing, ... Conquistador, ... Iron Man, ...

Communication Breakdown, ... Smoke on the Water, ... Suspicious Minds, ... The Weight, ... The Night They Drove Old Dixie Down ...

I've heard the saying, "Girls Can't Rock." I don't think this idea applies exactly at this moment though I'm unable to form cogent thought to understand how I feel when I listen to a female sing the lyrics to a song written to express the feelings, thoughts, and experiences of a guy. To now hear Bonnie sing the words to the Robbie Robertson song, *The Night They Drove Old Dixie Down,* these type of artistic expressions seem odd, and in a way I cannot put my finger on. I find nothing uplifting or aesthetic when I hear songs sung this way. Empathetically, they're sort of weird. Sort of.

At the end of that song a long round of applause is necessary..., and I watch Bonnie speak to Ivanka and Joanne, and the three begin the Pete Seeger and Lee Hays songs, *If I Had a Hammer,* and after this song, a once obscure but now popular rendition by Cat Stevens, the Christian hymn of Eleanor Farjeon, *Morning Has Broken.*

Perhaps the requests were becoming obnoxious and some of the scouts couldn't stop themselves once they found the humor for doing so. I look at my watch and it's almost ten o'clock. I notice fewer people gathered around and attending our concert.

Bonnie steps down from the picnic table. Ivanka and Joanne follow her away from the circle of picnic tables, and to stand beside Mr. Sheppard. I get up off the table and walk over to where they are.

"You guys were completely and absolutely the best!"

The girls have tired smiles. I glean some other unrelated matter of particular import is involved with the stare to the ground I see Bonnie doing. I turn to Ivanka and Joanne standing on the other side of Mr. Sheppard.

"The clowns..., though, you guys still want to come with us tomorrow, right?"

With definite and affirmative nods I hear Bonnie say, "Why not?"

"Exactly," is my response. "Great. Eight o'clock."

"We'll be waiting. Have to go though," Ivanka says, and with smiles and waves of the hand goodnight I watch them walk to the dirt road and back towards their trailer.

I hear Paul say to me, "Kurt, come on and look at this one over here."

Ivanka and I follow Paul through a corridor of the museum. We turn a corner, walk a little farther down another corridor and then step inside a vestibule where Joanne is looking at a collection of things inside a glass cabinet. Bonnie and Steve stand in front of paintings on the wall.

"This one," Paul says stepping up alongside a painting.

A dramatic scene captures the instance of time when the pressure of smoke and flames erupt from the barrel of a Napoleonic-style cannon. A single, powerful vortical of invisible shrapnel has traveled no more than fifteen, twenty feet before bursting into a group of three Confederate soldiers portrayed having run up directly in front of the blast.

The painting depicts a startled look of fear upon the face of one man..., I imagine he's probably startled from the initial feeling of pain from the impact of the blast, and, I suppose, realizing his life is about to become unalterably changed within the next moment or two. I look at the men who are running up alongside the three about-to-become-mortally-wounded soldiers. My eyes scan into the contingent of blue uniformed

Union soldiers that are kneeling and lying prostrate behind a not-stacked-tall-at-all stone wall. The Union soldiers create a long continuous line of rifle barrels pointing at all the men running closer.

There go I but for the grace of God.

A moment to decipher the author's signature on the painting: *M. Künstler*.

I step back. A reflective moment is upon me. My minds' eye conjures a picture image of the timeline strip to view. I turn to look at Ivanka. I watch her study the painting, … and I look inside myself, attentive I am to that place in the back of my eyes. For the next few moments I'll toy with this image in mind's eye, concentrating as I contemplate any thoughts that'll occur.

The timeline is nothing more than a curving line in contrast to a dark background. A line similar in appearance to what a flat, wide, continuous length of celluloid movie film strip would look like if cut from the reel and then if one end of the strip is held in hand while the other end uncoils farther out in front of me. Another time and perhaps the length of this timeline can appear similar to what a fairly straight and unkinked length of stiff electrical wire would look like after a length of it has been unraveled from its spool, then stretched out and cut away. My mind's eye at the moment pictures the flat film strip type of a timeline.

When it appears it's innocuous. To appear and disappear and perhaps animate itself in some particular way for a length of time. I'm usually but not always in a contemplative, pensive frame of mind whenever it appears.

For the next few moments I want to place myself from the perspective of that place totally in the back of my eyes. Kunstler's picture is vivid in my eyes but I'm not paying much attention to anything my eyes are showing me. I hear everyone moving about, talking.

Fleeting notions for States' rights versus Federal power. Whigs and Democrats in Congress talk secession. Agrarian, industrial, economic and moral entities of early middle nineteenth century America propelling and steering the forces to continue and to halt the practice of slavery within the United States. Once or twice realizing President Lincoln is definitely perturbed at certain times…, and I watch several adjacent square frames of the film strip duplicate and stack themselves one on top of the other.

The first four or five frames of the section of timeline appearing closest to me. Two at most three-seconds of thought has me observing stacks of duplicated squares elevate above the strip, squares sliding off stacks to adjacent stacks. I watch adjacent stacks rise up in piles, some stacks going down. Several square frames inside adjacent stacks quickly swap places, … and for a single moment it looks like a bubbling, dynamic histogram until all the stacks of square frames suddenly settle low, melting back into the one long, flat strip of single squares receding down and off into the distance of darkness.

Whenever I see it either as a flat filmstrip or as a thin tubular line, it always presents itself with the same curve and slant. Every timeline always curves ever so slightly to the right as it extends at a 315 degree, forward and downward direction until at a certain point it curves up in a parabolic sort of way just before blending into the distant darkness and out of sight.

"Kurt, the tour guides are here. I think everyone's heading outside."

I turn from the painting and look at Ivanka. Her hand curls the brim of the black cowboy hat down and along the side of her face. The way she spoke to me and I simply cannot help myself. I give her a smile.

"You know you look spiffy with that hat on? You know that right?"

She wears a white, snug-fitting short-sleeved athletic body shirt under a gold suede vest. An intriguing diamond stone pendant glitters above the body shirt. Denim boot-cut jeans slipping down over brown leather cowboy boots, and Ivanka is dressed for the outdoors. She's cosmopolitan though. Her speech at times makes me think private schools. She refused a stick of gum. An air of confidence is with her.

Wealth, bred lower-upper class, ... tempered Blueblood. These are my thoughts and first impressions of her.

I like her.

We walk from the vestibule and follow the last of the scouts in front of Mr. Willis and Mr. Stewart out through the doors of the museum. Stepping onto blacktop and then towards the vans I notice the ranger hats of our two tour guides moving above the crowd standing and talking with Mr. Boyce.

" Jim," I hear the one tour guide introduce himself to Mr. Stewart.

Before I climb inside the van I read the name tags of Jim Kerr and Shelli Sonestein. Mr. Kerr seats himself shotgun inside our van, and I watch Ms. Sonestein walking towards the other vans. Exiting the Visitor Center parking lot our van turns onto Taneytown Road.

Spontaneous timelines are not obtrusive. I don't think they've ever hindered any endeavor I've happened to have been involved with during the moment. I don't consider timelines inspirational or epiphanic in any sort of way. From as far back as I can remember they just appear when I think about things sometimes. As normal and as natural as an occasional sneeze or hiccup, I've never had a reason to refer to them in conversation with others, though, I suppose if for some reason I were to have ever been asked I could imagine a conversation leading me to acknowledge other people do, on occasion, have a similar appearance come to mind whenever they sometimes think upon things in a certain way. I did not deliberately construct this timeline image in my mind. I don't have a proper name for this line or strip with the darkness-in-the-background image-picture "thing," nor do I regularly think about it and cause it to do what it does whenever it appears.

I have given some but not a whole lot of psychoanalytic thought for what the elements of the picture image represent. I imagine the darkness-in-the-distance as a symbol marking some universal beginning point of time. The line or the strip that contrasts and extends out from the distant darkness represents a cumulative series of records for every past event that has occurred in the universe. A particular portion or segment of the line presents itself to stand out in some peculiar way, I suppose I'm projecting an inordinate interest into a historic epoch or event which I've recently been made aware of and concerned with. Epochal periods such as the Roman or Grecian empires, the last seven thousand years of recorded history pertaining to human civilization, or the three to seven million years for the evolution of the branch of primates that became Homo Sapiens.

I'll find myself reading a book, and come to a cleverly written set of passages. A timeline may appear and I'll watch a segment of the timeline breaking off, expanding in size to vanish from view, ... and I'll imagine a series of events, perhaps a gathering of gas and dust in the dark voids of outer space turning into a whirling nebula. I'll watch the swirling gas and dust collapsing upon itself. Physical matter condenses till it implodes initiating another system of nuclear fusion somewhere in the vastness of outer space. The image of the newborn star dissolves and the pages of the book I'm reading return to clarity, so I'll turn the page and begin to read the next chapter.

The timeline is interesting if for no other reason than because of its three dimensional representation of time, and the way in which it suddenly presents itself to me is cool too, I suppose. There are times I like to think I'm favored by the Creator and privileged to occasionally have this unique, novel timeline view of things. They're vapid impressions of mind though. There is little or no information of value to glean whenever they appear. They never appear to do anything more than present themselves to me at certain times, and then fade away.

I have been told I have an active imagination.

The van slows and then turns inside a tourist's parking area built along the shoulder of the road.

"Chambersburg Pike. This is where the opening salvos took place on the morning of July 1," I hear Mr. Kerr say. The vans stop, doors open, and we all bail out. With everyone together we walk across the two lanes of Route 30, following Mr. Kerr and Ms. Sonestein to stand near a memorial statue portraying what appears to be a Union officer holding a pair of binoculars at his waist. Everyone gathers around as Mr. Kerr begins to speak.

"I want to first welcome New York State Boy Scout Troop Twelve to Gettysburg National Park. I'm Jim." A couple quick whistle toots with a half-dozen disjointed handclaps.

"Call me, Shelli," and I watch Ms. Sonestein raise her hand to grasp and lift the dome of her brown ranger hat from her head.

"Jim and I will be your guides for today and tomorrow, and we'll try to convey the order of battle for the three days of July 1863. We want to hear your thoughts. Challenge us with your questions."

Shelli turns to Jim, and he speaks with a loud, clear voice.

"Decades of civil discourse during the first half of the nineteenth century have left intractable social and economic issues unresolved. Political and judicial mechanisms inside the capital of Washington have failed to implement practical solutions to address and bring resolve to these issues, instead the judicial and legislative members of Washington have allowed two competing systems of government to exist within the thirty-three States. The test of wills climax to the events of April 12, 1861, when Confederate forces began bombarding Fort Sumter. The Confederate States of America at Montgomery, Alabama and the federal government of Washington, D.C., are now at war, with the victor to determine who will write the future laws of the land."

Jim folds his arms across his chest.

"Many people at the time thought the war would find closure after only a month or two or three of conflict. Twenty-seven months of war have brought June 3, 1863, and seventy-five thousand men from General Lee's Army of Northern Virginia march north out of Fredericksburg, Virginia, into Maryland, and by the end of the month have spread themselves out into this lower central Pennsylvania region."

Jim extends his arm in a westerly direction.

"June 28 and twenty-two thousand Confederate soldiers of Lieutenant General A. P. Hill's Third Army Corps will camp for the night six, seven miles beyond those hills in the distance. Seventeen miles further west and General Robert E. Lee is ensconced with the First Army Corps twenty-two thousand soldiers under the command of Lieutenant General James Longstreet."

Jesse steps back and extends his arm to the northeast.

"Confederate General Richard S. Ewell has his three Divisions of the Second Army Corps twenty to twenty-five miles north of Gettysburg. Richard Ewell's twenty-thousand Confederate soldiers occupy the towns of Carlisle, York, and are menacing the capital at Harrisburg."

"On the night of the 28 a spy named Harrison brings information to General Longstreet that the Union Army of the Potomac is rapidly moving north. General Longstreet relays this information to General Lee who sends orders to all his Army Corps to consolidate around Cashtown, nine miles west of Gettysburg."

"The late morning hours of June 30 brings a vanguard of Federal cavalry under Brigadier General John Buford into Gettysburg. General Buford has orders to secure the town and to report any Confederate troop movements in the area. No sooner has John Buford's two brigades of cavalry enter Gettysburg when they were spotted by Confederate Brigadier General J. Johnston Pettigrew's infantry division marching along a road just outside town."

I hear someone in the group talking. Jesse nodding his head up and down, and I can't understand what is being said.

"The question is how many men are in a brigade, a division, a corps," Jesse says to everyone.

"Brigade and division troop strengths rise and fall ... depending on circumstances, though I'm going to say in theory approximately three hundred to a thousand men form a regiment. One to three thousand men to a brigade, and four to ten thousand will comprise a division. Corps consist of two or more divisions."

I watch Shelli stepping away from Mr. Kerr. She brings her arm up, her hand points someplace off in the distance.

"A division drawn into a line of battle would have two rows of men extending a little less than a mile in length. Two rows deep and shoulder to shoulder the line extends perhaps from the top of that wooded hill in the distance, the line continues through the field and down in the valley below, with the line ending somewhere near where we stand."

"Imagine if you will this mile long line of men separated into brigade strength," Shelli furthers, "and these brigades then commanded to move as five or six smaller battle lines."

"Perhaps after surveying the battle situation a commanding general decides the line of operation is to have two of his brigades, two to three thousand men move into and then through that stretch of wooded forest area off in the distance. While these men attempt to work their way through the woods and over towards the right side of where we are, where Colonel Gamble's sixteen hundred dismounted cavalry are, another two brigades are ordered to traverse the open field below us and up towards the top of this ridge. A fifth brigade will be stationed to maintain a defensive, reserve position inside the forest cover at the bottom, left side of this ridge. This fifth brigade will be positioned to prevent or at least to hinder soldiers stationed up along this ridge from moving down to the left and into a position to fire upon the right side of the line of soldiers moving through the field."

I watch Shelli bring her hand up to pinch the air near the side of her forehead. Her hand goes through a delicate motion of pulling something imaginary out and away from her head as she speaks, "This should give you a general idea of the strategy and tactics of battle."

Mr. Kerr removes his hat, combs his hair with an open hand before placing his hat back on.

"All commanders," Mr. Kerr continues, "are under orders from General Lee to break away from skirmishes that may escalate. Pettigrew's infantry division will retreat back from a confrontation with Buford's cavalry, arriving back in Cashtown during the late afternoon hours."

"The bulk of the ninety-thousand strong Union Army is fourteen miles south of Gettysburg, at Taneytown. The first infantry divisions will arrive in this area with a half days march. John Buford is certain the Confederates will return to Gettysburg in the morning, in force."

Mr. Kerr steps between us and raises his arm to the southeast.

"Two large armies are approaching each other and battle is imminent. John Buford surveys the area around Gettysburg and realizes the high ground of hills and a ridge south of town will be to the advantage of whoever is able to place a large contingent of troops there first. To keep this high ground from being occupied by the Confederate forces, and until infantry divisions from Major General John Reynolds' First Corps and Major General Oliver Howard's Eleventh Corps arrives, Buford employs an almost textbook perfect strategy of defense in depth."

"The theory behind a defense in depth is to have a number of predetermined positions for your troops to fall back to. Hold one position for as long as possible and then deliberately retreat to another established line of defense. Hold this line until conditions necessitate a retreat, and with each successive line of defense to prevent the larger force from a more rapid and steady forward advance."

"John Buford's first line are the squads of three to four soldiers, commonly referred to as vedettes in those days, placing these vedettes along the roads four to six miles north and west of Gettysburg. Rifle fire from these soldiers will give an early warning of the approaching Confederate columns as they advance along the roads."

"Let's begin walking in the direction where Colonel Gamble's First Brigade formed along Herr Ridge," Mr. Kerr says.

Occasional, subtle hints of vanilla. The fragrance is from the perfume Ivanka is wearing.

"Ivanka, what's Baltimore like?"

"It's great. I don't live there though. Joanne and I, our fathers are on business with Bonnie's father. We came along."

"Where do you live?"

"Different places. New York, most times."

"New York where?"

I watch her look down, subtle turns of the head from side to side, not wanting to answer the question.

"Manhattan."

"What do your fathers do?"

"Real estate, development projects."

We walk downhill, through the field and into the depression of ground I know to be Willoughby Run. I look towards the small rise of Herr Ridge where the soldiers began exchanging rifle fire. I think of myself standing or kneeling, and I'm firing and then reloading my musket twice every minute. I'm also always waiting for that one or two fifty caliber-sized chunk of hot metal to come slamming into me. Maybe it will be a cannon ball that slam rolls into me, or a mass of shrapnel from an explosion.

Mr. Kerr is in conversation with Mr. Boyce and a group of scouts. Ivanka and I step up to listen to Ms. Sonestein talking to a group of scouts.

"The fife's are fifing, drums are drumming, and then there are those bright red uniforms upon seven hundred British soldiers. Marching in two columns several hundred yards long. Making quite a spectacle out of themselves in the process they are. Making themselves an easy target as they march from Lexington and Concord back to Boston."

Ms. Sonestein removes her sunglasses. Wiping the lenses she looks at each one of us.

"All those soldiers walking along the dirt road probably kicks up a little bit of dust."

"So, imagine these British soldiers walking along the road. An arms length in front of one soldier is the back of the next soldier who, upon hearing the crack of distant musket fire inside a line of trees a hundred yards distant, the soldier in front falls forward and to the ground. A soldier may want to stop and help, and perhaps to realize there is nothing he can do to actually help the guy, and that a medic will eventually find him, he stands up, falls back into line and continues marching with the column."

She places her sunglasses on. The brim of her hat is brought down snug.

"The Minutemen follow the soldiers as they march back to Boston. Positioning themselves behind stonewalls, down inside gullies and behind the cover line of trees in the forests. They fire upon the contingent of seven hundred soldiers as they march along the road."

"Why? What stops the soldiers from breaking and going off after the Minutemen?"

I step closer to Ms. Sonestein.

"Why did they fight battles that way back then?"

I look around her to see Steve Tyler and Joe Perry. Both of them look attentive, as if waiting for her response. I assume it's Tyler and Perry asking these questions.

"Breaking from the order of the column and separating yourself from the larger body of soldiers wasn't considered a safe and the best military tactic at the time. It wasn't proper protocol."

"That's crazy to just keep walking or standing out in the open while you're being shot at," Steve opines.

Ms. Sonestein folds her arms in front of herself. Several steps and she brings a folded hand up to her chin, and a pensive pose.

"Perhaps to us at this time, nowadays it does."

She brings her arms to her side, to clasp her hands behind her back.

I don't know how this conversation began, but I think I know where it's headed. I don't think a few simple, politely spoken words can answer the question why hawks and doves exist in the world. Our Ms. Sonestein does seem to be searching for the better words in an attempt to do so, though.

"Many soldiers saw fellow soldiers fall that day," she continues. "There were only four British casualties alongside the twenty Minutemen that were killed or wounded at the battles of Concord and Lexington, though during the march back to Boston over two hundred British soldiers were killed or wounded."

I give a silent, perplexed glance to Ivanka, and she mimics my raised eyebrows. I stifle the urge to say something about this discourse.

"I'm sure the frustration was there. Perhaps Lieutenant Colonel Francis Smith, while on horseback and after listening to another volley of shots sound out from behind a hedge of trees, and again to watch another two, three of his soldiers fall to the ground, an act of desperation has him riding his horse down and across a ravine and into an open field. Stopping in ear shot of his soldiers, Colonel Smith shouts while shaking a fist over towards the forest.

"Come out and fight like men, you cowards!"

"The British regulars will continue to march along the road. Some will become heartened with this bravado from their commander, but the Minutemen are using guerrilla tactics the British are unable to counter against."

I look over towards Joe and Steve, and then to Ms. Sonestein, and the thought is, *A thought is more important than the life itself?*

Eventually to answer myself with, *I suppose, yes, some type of thoughts and beliefs can become more important than life itself.*

The Scouts have been minding their manners. A scout is spot on to hold a door open, to reach down and pick up something one may have dropped to the ground. I've heard no cute remarks directed towards the girls. Not once. Early this morning I heard Anthony say to several scouts, "Act as if they're part of family, and we're on vacation."

Sure, what else?

What I've noticed is that they'll deliberately separate from us, rather, from Ivanka and I. Paul and Steve and Bill, Bonnie and Joanne, they'll leave us together at certain times. It's odd. Scouts I don't know too well, they stare at me. I really don't want to think about it but something is going on I'm not privy to.

Ivanka and I take a sandwich bag and soda from the coolers at the back of the van, and walk to one of the picnic tables under the shade of an apple tree. Bill walks over to the table and settles himself down next to Ivanka. He takes the zip-locked plastic bagged sandwich out from the brown paper bag.

"Oh wow, what did they put on this sandwich? I'm not eating this," he says.

The sandwich is pushed back inside the plastic bag. Grabbing the paper bag and soda can he steps away from the table and towards the van.

"What grade you in?" Ivanka asks. I'm watching Bill rummage through a cooler inside the van.

"Starting eleventh this year."

"You like school, your classes?"

"Classes are all right. Can't really do much of anything yet, with anything you learn. What grade you in?"

"Tenth."

I take a bite out of the sandwich and then squeeze the middle of the sandwich. I'm looking for any condiment that may ooze out from between the slices of cheese, the lettuce and ham, and while I used to dip my French fries and things into mayonnaise, I try to refrain from eating the stuff anymore. I'm hoping they didn't spread the zit producing stuff on all the sandwiches, and as I pull one and then the other slice of bread up I'm glad to see the thin smear of yellow colored paste underneath. I now also have revealed the thick, oily strips of red pepper lying on top of the lettuce leafs.

I hold the slice of bread open for Ivanka to see.

"They put peppers inside."

"Grilled peppers," she says. "A hint of garlic in the olive oil."

"Kurt, what would you want to do if you learned enough to do whatever you want?"

With a pull to the tab of her soda can the rock around her neck sparks a flash of colors. The skin of her face is smooth, flawless. There are more than two or three red spots and pockmark scars from zits I know she sees on my face.

"I'd make myself millions of dollars."

"How?"

"Billions of years ago there were no life forms existing on earth. Then there was life, and, it grew to be what it is today."

I take a bite out of the sandwich and collect some of my thoughts.

"Some atoms on the early earth assembled into an array of molecules that became the basic components of the single-celled life forms. These molecules formed at the same time other similar atoms formed molecules that instead became part of another kind of rock on the earth, or they became some other kind of piece of dust floating in the air or something."

I watch Ivanka take hold of her cowboy hat and place it down on the table. The fingers of her hand curl a bang of blond hair behind her ear, and she lifts the sandwich up to take a bite. Again I watch her fold a lock of hair back behind her ear.

"One of the few remaining secrets of the universe is why and how some atoms went one way and towards life at the same time others did not."

I watch her take a sip of soda. Her words are spoken softly, as if a matter of fact.

"You're smart."

A silent nod of my head and shrug my shoulders to the complement.

I'm blessed.

"Into student government or activities?"

I shake my head no.

"Play any sports?"

"Not anymore."

"Why?"

Right now I don't want to start talking about why.

"Doesn't matter," I say with a hint of disgust. "You're taking classes to major in something?"

"Business management."

"Like it?"

"I'll be part of my father's real estate and development company."

The answer follows with a question.

"If you were President of the United States, what would you want to do?"

A question of magnitude, and I want to give it thought.

"Probably one thing I'd like to do as a President is to find out if an alien spacecraft did crash on some guys ranch in New Mexico back in 1947. I always like to think if a weather balloon and not a space ship had crashed it's odd that military personnel are first on the scene to recover what is reportedly an ordinary stray weather balloon instead of the local sheriff or town police responding and recovering some weather balloon from some guys property, ... and because military were involved right from jump street, these days even a President wouldn't be able to knock on the right doors or to find the right people to telephone and then to find the truth of the matter. Some things are classified *For Your Eyes Only,* and if a President isn't part of that clique, too bad."

I'm out of breath. I said those words and sentences fast. Adrenaline has my heart pounding hard inside my chest for some reason. I have to relax. Calm down.

I watch Ivanka sip on the straw from the soda can.

"Have you seen a UFO?" Ivanka asks.

Oh, wow. How humiliating to be asked. I look to see only a calm, inquisitive look on her face. A simple and genuine curiosity is all. My mouth is dry. I drink some of my soda.

A curt no is my response.

Does she really think I would say yes? I have seen UFO's?

I want to change the subject. Forget this line of thought.

"Advances in scientific research and technology should remain a priority."

I watch her lift and take a bite from the sandwich. The fingers of her hand turn the soda can on top of the table. I have a notion she's listening for any nuance in my voice. She's attentive to each word.

Every nerve in my body seems active, alive. I have to put forth a conscious effort to pace and slow the pronunciation of my words.

"People at NASA and the ESA are placing good marks for us in the history books of tomorrow."

I take a sip of soda and bring in a couple deep breaths of air. "One way or another though, five hundred years from now the world will be more Western, for a reason," I say.

She holds the soda can still, and looks up at me. Her eyes and face are inquisitive. Her tone of voice? I suppose it to be more of defiance, perhaps incredulity.

"How 'ya know?"

I think I know so because on average more people live better today then they did in the past. The quality of human life has improved over the last five thousand years. If kept on its present course there is a nature, a proclivity which will continue to improve the quality of human life for hundreds of thousands of years.

"As time goes on things just seem to get better."

I hear the side doors of the vans open and watch Scouts gathering around.

A spot of black lifts a flash of red and blue streaks from the rock around her neck.

"Let me look at that stone?"

She brings her hands underneath her ponytail. Her fingers clasp the two ends of the metal chain as the rock is brought to dangle in front of me. Four fingers of my hand hold the rock from motion.

The stone is the size of my pinky fingernail. From a distance it appeared square. Up close and I realize it's cut to six sides and oblong, octagonal. A light tinge of pink color pervades down inside clear cut facets. Two bars and four silver metal clasps hold the rock securely to the chain.

With the slightest movement the cuts of stone flash bright vibrant color. Facets near the center of the stone draw angles reflecting colors from deep down inside the stone.

"I saw it sparkle up black color, too."

Ivanka is happy, proud. "You like it?"

I nod, and the slightest movement of my hand cause facets of the rock to burst a rainbow of color. Facets draw instances of not always true black but deep, dark colors to shine up and out. I gotta smile.

"I'm no expert but whoever cut this stone, they made it so the colors burst out."

I take my hand away. "I'm impressed."

"Thanks."

"A friend?"

"My mother and father, sixteenth birthday."

I stand up and collect the paper bags and soda cans together.

"Colored diamonds are rare. Must've cost a small fortune."

I place the stuff into the trash receptacle and we walk towards the vans. I'm looking at her as we walk and eventually she turns to look over to me.

I'm feeling so many things I have no idea what to say, though I feel like saying something.

"My father knows a few people," she says. "I don't know how much it cost."

Middle of the afternoon and we drop the girls off at their trailer. It's a hurried exit from the van though it's agreed we'll see each other again somewhere, tonight perhaps, and we drive back to the campsite.

Dinner is still hours away and the first thing I and everyone else want to do is walk over to the pool and get in the water. My arms are red with sunburn. The skin around my neck and face feel hot.

I dive into the pool and turn myself on my back, floating motionless for the first few minutes. Waves of cool water crest up and over my chest and face.

I climb out from the water and walk along the side of the pool. Through the chain link fence I see the sun tarps shading the front of the Sheppard trailer have been removed. The pickup truck is parked to the trailer as if it's already hitched up and ready for travel.

"I think they got their trailer hooked up. They may be getting ready to leave," I say to Steve and Paul.

Bonnie is carrying a folding lawn chair inside the trailer as we walk up.

"Leaving already?"

"My Dad's finished," she says. "Ivanka and Joanne said they'd stop by your campsite. You didn't see them?"

I shake my head no.

"Nope. Went to the pool right after we got back."

I look over to Paul and Steve staring down at the ground.

"Kinda sorry to see you guys leave so soon."

Bonnie stands holding the lawn chair in her hands, and after a moment I realize its time to just simply leave.

"Glad we met you guys though. It was fun."

"Bye, Bonnie."

"Bye, guys," she says with a nod to each of us.

I watch her step through the trailer door, and then turn ourselves for the walk back to the pool.

It's where Moms rapped me on my head with the spoon a while back. I feel the presence of some pressure sort of in the back and top of my head. It's like someone has their thumb up there and they're pressing in on it.

Crouched down and aligning the rear wheel to the Deek, my DKW 125 Enduro motorcycle, I bring to mind something I'd read inside a *Reader's Digest* article. Maybe I'm recalling an article from the *Guideposts* magazine, though the story mentions how people who've had a limb amputated, later on in life these people will experience sensations of movement or pain where the limb once existed. I'm thinking perhaps this feeling of a thumb pressing in on the top of my head is there because my mind is still toying with this story somehow, in some way.

The chain remains taut while I snug the retaining nuts of the rear wheel tight onto the swing arm. I stand upright, and it's a phantom thumb-like presence pressing down on my head up there. I bring my hand up and rub my scalp with my fingers. Everything feels normal. I bring my hands down upon the leather seat. With my elbows locked back my wrists pivot and I rise up on my toes. I stiffen my fingers and knead them deep into the stiff foam rubber of the seat. I'm supporting myself playfully balanced upon the tail end of the Deek, and I bring to mind some things that happened several months ago.

I'm in my bedroom reading different kinds of Christian literature I'd had friends at school lend me or that I've had sent to me through the mail. Books and magazines and pamphlets are spread out on my bed. Most of it is Protestant stuff. I want to think and see how others talk about Christian things. I read it all to see what it says, and then maybe what I'll think about it after a while. I want to know.

It gets wild sometimes, all the views and opinions. So many things are thought to be important, prescribed, or practiced according to a denomination. I'm not memorizing or studying any of the stuff. I just read it and try to put it together and see what I come up with.

Right now I'm at the stage where it seems like either one single denomination is more right and all the other ones are off on a tangent and eventually wrong. Perhaps they're all a little bit right and I have to select within each denomination what may seem to be the right attitudes to consider as my own when relating with God, the Creator. I also think that if God personally wants someone to do something this type of person doesn't even need a religion. Because God has picked you, you really don't have any choice in the matter. Whether you like it or not you're "it."

Who knows.

Dad makes it seem simple. The universe and everything in it like electrons and protons and neutrons always was and always will be. There was never a beginning to time and so there will be no end to it either. The universe then never "began," and so it will never end. It just goes on and on and on...

When things have happened in the world that are difficult to explain, people picked up the mental crutch they called god and they used that to walk with and explain away what they can't rationally understand at the moment. God is just a figment of the imagination of people. God doesn't exist. Basically in a nutshell that's what Dad thinks I think.

Now, Dad makes sure we know you can't prove that God doesn't exist. In a court of law, let's say, bring the facts together and present a case that's conclusive. An ironclad irrefutable set of facts to state your case with any one who wants to listen and know, or may think contrary.

Nor with the scientific method of testing hypotheses has evidence ever been produced confirming the nonexistence of a supreme being, and proving the belief to a level of certainty so that someone else would not be allowed to use the word 'created' in a statement as you debate these type of things. No specious line of thought such as, *'In the beginning, when God created the heavens and the earth,'* can be brought in for consideration without first backing up and justifying all those suppositions in the statement.

Neither can anyone prove the other side of the coin that God exists. Not knowing and unconvinced with rational lines of thought giving credence one way or the other, I leave myself open to the possibility of either side being true. I found this an interestingly comfortable personal viewpoint to have. I'm careful using the word 'know' in any conversation, and I'm encouraged carrying on a conversation with someone else knowing that they also have this kind of respect for the word, especially when I find myself involved in discussions such as these.

There is a God, a Creator.

There is no God. There is no such "thing" as a creative, designer God.

One of those stated points of view is absolutely true. The other statement is by consequence totally false. No one knows though. There is only the belief in the one line and then train of thought or the other.

I tend to listen to another person's views on this subject with an open mind, or so I like to think. The bits and pieces I glean from some discussion have an initial vein of acceptance and tolerance as I ponder upon them, but I will not timidly agree and gullibly allow someone to present any old point of view. A herd of pink elephants did not create the universe. If you want and expect a little more respect for the notion of whether an extraterrestrial life form from another planet and solar system caused life to exist on the earth, you should think to put some facts on the table. I can tell the difference between the plausible and the absurd, and the space in-between, or so I like to think.

Given that the scientific method and the judicial process are the two best systems devised by civilized people to determine truth, and no one has yet proven false either of these views with either of these two systems of thought, the minds of the masses are still today and may forever be at odds with one another to answer the timeless questions of the sages: *How did all this get here? Why am I here? What is the meaning of life?*

If either belief that there is or there is not a God were to ever be proven true it would turn the social, political, and economic worlds upside down, so I'm told.

My readings have brought me into these crossroads and I realize I have to make some kind of declaration to myself. I can't keep reading things and ignore this anymore. I become antagonized realizing the perspectives inside certain Christian commentators who espouse literal views and interpretations of the bible. I imagine myself a member of an audience listening to a person on a stage who speaks the words I read: the entire physical universe was created in six days and nights. That the hand and fingers of God instantly scratched the Grand Canyon of Arizona upon the surface of the earth ten thousand years ago. Eve came from a rib bone of Adam? I think to myself that if Adam came first before Eve why do I, Kurt Soldier, have two nonfunctioning appendages of the female nipple on my chest? Did an omniscient God create Adam with nipples on his chest even before Eve was in existence?

I suppose it was a flash of critical reinterpretation to the comments of other people that allowed me to realize inside his letter to Titus, Paul will quote the sixth century B.C. Cretan poet Epimenides out of context. Paul already knew of the logical paradox implied by that statement. For Paul to misrepresent Epimenides to his intended audience by talking like this ...?

Inspired. I don't know exactly how I would want to define that word in a practical sense but some commentators use this word implying I should suspend or disregard my common sense and simply follow along and believe any train of thought they happen to be on, and I don't want to do that as I read and think about these type of things. As Bartleby the Scrivener would say, "I would prefer not to."

I've recently finished reading one book entitled, *The Life and Times of Jesus.* It mentioned how Jesus probably never tasted a tomato. My notions of Jesus' divinity and of his humanity brought together by that one sentence struck me funny and to a pensive frame of mind.

I like to read the different kinds of Christian literature I get. It makes me think. This particular day I've been sitting up on my bed and reading things, with the Bible, for half the morning and afternoon.

I'm lying on my bed and out of the corner of my eye I notice the bedroom door I'd left ajar move. I turn towards the door to see Charlie, our Siamese cat finish sliding himself through the narrow slot he created down by the floor. He's strolling over to the side of my bed, then jumps up on the bed and begins taking steps upon my lap. It's cool to feel each of his single blunt paws press down upon my T-shirt as he walks up on top of me, with the weight of his body firmly planting those two furry front paws of his up near my neck and collarbone.

Charlie lowers then swings his head up to hit my chin bone with the top of his head, and then slides the top of that soft, furry head of his to the back of my jaw. His four paws reposition themselves on top of me, ... sometimes Charlie swings that head of his up kinda fast, and with a little too much force, hitting my jaw bone kind of hard with that bone in his head, and a second time he'll slide the top of his head along the other side of my jaw. Again he repeats this procedure of tapping and then sliding the top of his head along one side of my jaw.

Charlie will often come up to me and say hello with these three separate taps and brushing motions of his head along the bottom of my chin. Coolest cat, Charlie is: dude material.

Charlie turns and begins stepping down and onto the bed, but I can't let him get away with what he just did. With one hand I reach over and grab him by a shoulder, dragging him back onto my lap. Rubbing my face all over the top of his back, neck, and head and then not too gently but not painfully brushing the fur of his body with my ten stiff fingers. I love Charlie.

I chose Charlie. I picked him up by the scruff of his neck, out and away from his brothers and sisters in the box. And till the end of that summer any chance I got to pick him up by the scruff of his neck to carry him somewhere, ... any chance I got to have a few words with him face to face while hanging by the scruff of his neck..., or just to smear and squeeze my hands all over its tiny little body, any reason I could think of to pet this brand new kitten for a while, I did. I played with Charlie every chance I got that summer. All this early attention I gave him paid off too 'cause now, to me, Charlie is absolutely the coolest cat in the world.

Early morning right after getting up I was getting something to eat out of the refrigerator and Moms tells me that Charlie had climbed one of the pine trees out in the front yard, and that he was crying up there last time she went outside, suggesting maybe later if I'd like to go out there and see if he's still up there in the tree. He usually always goes out of the house before we all go to bed at night, otherwise sometimes in the middle of the night he'll start meowing inside the house at the other animals he hears or maybe smells crawling around outside.

He woke me up once, a little after two o'clock in the morning it was, and I'm hearing this constant and eerie meowing from somewhere inside the house. I got up and out of bed to find him and let him out. With a full moon shining bright inside the house, and with his nonstop cries to guide me I find Charlie sitting up on his haunches on a back cushion of the sofa. For who knows how long he's been looking out from the second-floor living room window and down into the entire stretch of moonlight bright, open backyard space. He jumps from the cushions of the sofa to gallop around me and then waits at the foot of the door as I made my way through the foyer to let him out.

Some evenings I'll find Charlie sitting on his haunches by the front door, patiently waiting for I or someone else to stroll on by and then to open the door and let him out. When he does see one of us walking by and near the door he quickly rises up taking two or three steps forward and then freezing in a mid-stepped stride while waiting for I or whoever to manage to open the door.

Seeing him sitting near the door one evening and watching him go into this routine of one or two steps towards the door and then becoming stiff and motionless for the next second or two as I get myself closer to the door, this time I acted as if I was having trouble opening the door. There are actually two doors to our front porch entrance way here and both are a little bit thicker and heavier than regular doors anyway so sometimes the one door does get stuck a bit and needs a heftier tug to slide it away from the other door.

I'm looking down at Charlie now for the ten, fifteen seconds I'm making sounds for him by twisting the metal door handle mechanism around. I give a number of gentle tugs to the door handle too, and with just enough force to bring a portion of the wooden door to vibrate for a moment. A few more metallic clicks for Charlie to hear as I put the door handle mechanism through the turns, and Charlie remains motionless the entire time. His four legs remain locked into the position of their very last steps. His head and eyes are trained straight towards the bottom of that soon to be opened door. His tail has a curve to it. Slanted over at the broken tip but the entire length of tail from rump to tip, the entire column of tailbone didn't waver around or move an inch. A totally rigid, motionless body for the ten, fifteen-seconds I was at the door. If he blinked I didn't see it.

If anything I want to keep Charlie as tough as he can be so I definitely don't want to disturb or crack into that seriousness of the situation he's got going with him before he goes on out for the night, or to have him think of what I was doing a goof, so after the ten or fifteen-seconds I did open the door for him. Some evenings, seeing Charlie patiently sitting there by the door and then cautiously stepping himself out for the night? Charlie is definitely cool.

I hear the meowing cries as if he's in some kind of despair, and I walk to be underneath the tall pine he's climbed. He's sitting, sort of lying on one of the very top branches way up a good forty feet in the air. I haven't seen him look down towards me, so I don't think he knows I'm below as I watch and listen to him go through a series of long and drawn out meows. His cries are soft when they start but turn high pitched, like he's screaming and terrified of something at the end of each meow. It's quiet up there in the tree for a time.

He's locked himself into some kind of frame of mind about something, maybe a bigger animal chased him up there during the night. I'm thinking he'll probably know enough about how to climb down once he's hungry, but I thought of how Tarzan talked to certain animals to get them to do things, and I thought I'd try it.

Looking up in the tree I just thought of wanting to communicate a variety of slightly exaggerated emotions and feelings to Charlie. Speaking to him slowly, sometimes quickly, inflecting my words as if I'm an actor practicing my lines on stage.

"Charlie, what are you doing? What's the matter with you?"

"Aww man, get down from there."

I bellow up, "What! What? What's the matter with you?"

A few moments to think of some things to say, anything loud and with some gusto.

"Hey …! You know you're not happy up there, alone and all, correct?"

"And what about the neighbors, Charlie? They see you up there they're gonna start laughing at you. You definitely don't want that."

"Come on down..., will you please?"

I'm thinking of other things to say, and watch Charlie rise, lean back and stretch his front legs out in front of himself. He takes a couple backward steps to the trunk of the tree and then begins to claw his way down.

I'm astonished. I'm only sort of playing around with Charlie now.

Watching him extend any one, two, or three of his legs down lower upon the trunk of the tree, and I hear the soft, crisp crackle of sound as any set of claws slide and scrape themselves down a section of the tree. Charlie squirrels himself down alongside one branch, then another branch, until something happens and he stays still.

An odd twist and turn of his body. Charlie will push up with his legs and lift his body up higher, and then to twist any one of his four legs away from the tree. Charlie sometimes has trouble releasing a claw's prong stuck inside the bark of the tree. Sliding along various parts of the tree, a number of times he stays in one position for a moment, then lifts himself up to twist any one of his legs around. I imagine he's sinking them claw prongs deep into the bark sometimes, and I want to be a little bit more surprised than I actually am as I'm watching all this. Charlie is doing this for me.

I'm thinking he may stop climbing down while still half way up in the tree, and I start up with some more talking, vocalizing things to him until he's shinnied all the way down and jumps to the ground.

I really did not expect to have him start climbing down the tree just because of what I was saying to him. I realize he climbed down because of me, and for whatever thoughts and emotions I was putting into his head. Charlie is so cool.

I kneel down and pick him up and start rubbing him with my arms and hands. Soft and gentle at first then rougher and tougher, both my arms scrunching all of him into me until he can't take it any more. A burst of energy to squirm out from my embrace, jumping to take a couple of bouncing steps of distance away from me.

My leg fell asleep and I have to get up off the bed. Charlie jumps ‹to the floor and scampers out of the room. I step over to sit on the wicker chair near the window, and stretching my legs straight out in front of me. What I did next was only done to realize how the thought would progress, where it would go. Sitting comfortably in the chair I ask myself why the sun is yellow. Through my own volition I'll think the question through.

Because of the fusion process. The fusion process going on inside the sun, some of the radiated energy is in the visible spectrum producing all the wavelengths of white light.

OK, white light, but this wasn't the kind of answer I had in mind and wanted to hear, so I rephrased the question.

Why is the sun shining white instead of a blue or green or red color? Why is the sun not purple?

Again, as if I didn't already know, ... *the sun shines white light because the fusion process emits the entire range of light energy.* The sun is not burning a single type of element. If it were doing so the sun would then produce a single, unique color of light. The sun is burning many different elements all at once, hence many different colors of light are being emitted all at once.

I'm still in the frame of mind for thinking of the processes and systems that produce the color of the sunlight. The explanation I want is for why the results are the way they are instead of any other way that could be. I'll use a different tact. I seem to be coaching myself to the same answers.

What if when I see the color blue, another person will see green. So my red is possibly someone else's blue then now. Prove that what I see as a particular color—the red light on a traffic light, everyone else is also seeing that same red color of color that I do too.

I do quasi-prove it to myself. I imagine that the cones on the retinas of the human eyeball being stimulated by specific, can-be-precisely-measured-by-machine, quantifiable wavelengths of light radiation. The cones of the retina are just an area of body tissue where a condensed and specific set of chemical processes are taking place. All these chemical processes are occurring with a machine-like, clockwork order to them. These chemical processes and the order in which they occur producing our sense of sight are basically the same in every person.

Like a machine that turns on and starts running when the color of red is detected, these chemical cone areas of the eyeball will turn on and start running whenever a particular wavelength of light is effecting them. So when this specific machine-qualified wavelength of red light is running into the eye, onto the retina, through the optic nerve and into the brain, everyone has been taught early on to identify and label this particular frequency of radiation upon the retina with the specific word, red. My red is the same as everyone else's red, then.

Again these thoughts are only telling me how it's done. I want to know why it is the way it is besides any other way that could possibly be.

Fine. It's proved how. After all is said and done, after all the physics has run its course, instead of a yellow sun, why is the sun not radiating purple light?

I look out the window. Maybe just a moment or two while I focus on the trees, the green of the lawn grass and the blacktop of the driveway outside. In my mind I hear myself say the words, *... because I want it that way.*

Nonplussed, I pick myself up from the chair and look out the window.

Rain has been on and off since morning. I watch raindrops falling through the air, smashing down on the flat slabs of shale rock along the sidewalk. A wave of raindrops splash across the blacktop of the driveway.

I have thoughts of playing my guitar, and perhaps I will do so in a minute or two.

I watch a single raindrop splash against the window pane and then roll down the glass in front of me.

Jesus? If You're for real? Make the rain stop. Right now.

Recalling the New Testament verses chiding those who have done what I just did, I throw up a reluctant and smirking grin to myself and sit back down. Slouching forward I sit on the small of my back, throwing one leg up to rest an ankle on the knee.

I feel tired, and I am tired reading as much as I have been this afternoon. I'm sleepy in fact. For some reason it's easy for me to feel sleepy and tired whenever it's also raining.

Pulling myself up to sit more correct inside the chair, I begin the mental process to imagine that I am traveling inside my body. I'm searching for tense muscles. I usually begin to focus on the muscles of my face. Cheek muscles and the muscles around the nose and eyes always seem taut whenever I first put my attention there. A moment or two to find any group of taut muscles and once found I can begin the conscious process to release the tension they have. Smiles I may have will disappear. Every muscle in my face will eventually relax.

Recently it happens where the simple act of placing conscious attention to my face triggers a response where I'll feel all the tension inside my face quickly dissipate within a second or two. From the muscles in my face I'll focus traveling down through my neck, and then into my shoulder muscles. I'll stop in any different areas for a second or two to relax things. I'm inside an arm and then into my hand. Sensing no tense muscles I travel over into the other arm and hand. I feel my mind's eye travel out from the hand, moving out from the arm and then inside my chest. All the while I become oh so very relaxed. I'm refusing to acknowledge any other type of thoughts that may want to distract me from what I'm doing.

I focus on the muscles of my abdomen.

Light brightens the dark underneath my closed eyelids. I turn towards the window and open my eyes to see the rain has stopped. Sunlight broke through the clouds to outline a bright green patch of wet grass in front of the house. In quick time I watch the occasional rain drop fall from the metal brackets of the rain gutter above the window.

April showers bring May flowers. It's only a coincidence..., and I am really, kinda tired. I yawn, stretch my legs out, and set myself into a more comfortable sprawl inside the chair.

I'm conscious to keep myself from thinking anything. I could probably take a little nap if I was more inclined to do so, and the wind is throwing droplets of rain against the window. My eyes open to a gust of wind pelting the window with noisy raindrops. Bright sunbeams still course through the tall pines above the window sill.

I close my eyes to the sprinkles of rain, and again to try to think of nothing.

Wiping the smears of grease and oil off my hands with a rag, I ask myself in good humor, *Why is the sun shining white and not a purplish green color ...,*

I hear the sliding glass doors moving upstairs.

"Kurt, are you down there?"

"Ya-up."

"Your brothers didn't bring the cans to the road this morning."

A split second of thought to realize the garbage cans are the task that will take the least amount of time to do, so I don't even wait.

"All right."

"They'll be here soon."

"Yup, yup, yup."

I walk to the side of the house and grab a garbage can. I'll have to shake a leg and get a move on if I don't want to be late to the Valley this morning. I still have to oil the chain, and put a full tank of oil and gas, mix it up and pour it in. I want to check the throttle and brake cables, and tire pressures. Thinking about it again though, I'm not leaving till I decide everything on the Deek is ready. If I make it to the Valley before nine o'clock or not, that's just the way it goes.

The garbage cans would've gone up a little later if I'd've had only one or two other things left to accomplish to prepare the Deek. What now appears to be the quickest and simplest tasks to start and finish I'll begin first, leaving what seem to be the longer and more difficult tasks for later. The longer task at this moment is the list of all the things I think of to get her ready to ride for the day. The shortest and easiest task seems to go get myself to those garbage cans and bring 'em on up to the road.

I seem to have recently included this little snippet of code into my personal constitution. A self-conscious notion of awareness is upon me, knowing I've only recently included and then done this 'thing' to myself. This 'thing' of being aware of the want to follow heuristic thought to clarify and plan an order for how I want go about completing a given task. The notions of simplicity and expediency having recently been brought to my attention, and these notions do seem to form a system of priorities that I'm using to guide the decisions I make. Interesting.

The heavy metal garbage can swings with the motion of my leg as I walk up the driveway. I feel the force from one of the two metal handles wedging and then crushing into the soft underside of my left hand's middle and index finger knuckles. I stop and readjust the grip of my hand, tinkering with this notion of how and why I've set up this priority thing with myself. With the garbage can placed down on Val de Mar, again I glimpse inside myself with the want to become a lot more familiar with my mind and self. I wonder what I'll discover.

Having written the treatise last month I like to delve into and review the mechanics of my own thought processes. The last couple of weeks at any given moment my mind becomes a laboratory for introspection. I like to think I've distinguished phases or perspectives such as the objective and subjective sides of my self. I clearly recognize the Pain—Joy spectrum encompassing a more complete definition to my five senses, and I wonder if and how this Pain—Joy spectrum pertains to and can give definition to further clarify in any way any so called sixth intuitive sense.

The treatise is fascinating, and my imagination takes off. I try to picture the realm of extroversion being inclusive of every past, present, and future human introversive dimension, and then to realize the sense of the past and what will be the future times as a dynamic integral in motion to the notion for all the existant human, picture six and seven dimensions. From this vantage point I imagine myself as if viewing things from the perspective of the Creator of the human race, and to consider all things inside the universe and my intentions for causing all these human dimensions to exist as they do. Obviously one intention is for all these human life activities to be in some way a part of my own experience as the Creator. I have mixed feelings whenever I consider that as the Creator I caused all of humanity to exist, and then I will become preoccupied for long periods of time with things other than whatever us humans are about.

I play with the different aspects of the treatise. I focus on where it represents the entities of the mind and physical matter as polar opposites. One common denominator between thoughts of the mind and the mass / energy of fermions and bosons would be that the two consist of frequency waves, with the midpoint connecting mind and matter being the central nervous system. All the different frequency waves interacting to bring that thing in the back of the eyes into existence.

I don't know..., it's spooky to think I've identified that exact place where the particular entities inside the two introverted Pain – Joy | Evil quadrants exist. I know what's inside these two quadrants, too.

The thought that I discovered a mathematically based graphical representation for biological life is cool. Though I haven't talked too much to others about it, whenever I do remind myself of this accomplishment I think it's totally cool. Someday the theory of pain and joy regulating the metabolism of all biological life, and expounded upon *inside the pages of the treatise I wrote* will become common knowledge to one and all. Are those twelve concepts as I've defined them able to stand up to rigorous scrutiny, for all time? I can only suppose the basic ideas inside the treatise will survive. People will always be able to use the words and ideas I employed in the treatise to convey the ideas back to anyone who wants to understand.

Volition is an interesting thing now. A simple definition is that thing that I use preferring which fingers to first scratch an itch or to delay the urge and not to scratch an itch whenever I feel a want to do so. I'm really getting into it and I like playing around with everything the treatise is about when I haven't anything better to do.

The second garbage can is at the foot of the driveway and I now hear what I know to be the garbage truck accelerating past the curve at the top of the hill by the entrance to the power line truck trail. I hear the truck stop accelerating and it's idling, coasting down Carpenter Road. A quick pace of steps bring me down the driveway for the last two garbage cans.

I'm stepping up the driveway. Arms are locked straining with one can held in each hand. Powerful pressure bursts sound out from the big truck's muffler as it decelerates for the turn onto Val de Mar. Placing the garbage cans down alongside the other two cans, twenty yards away and they're in the process of emptying the garbage cans in front of the neighbor's driveways. How convenient within these few minutes my newfangled priorities and the timely, just in time arrival of the garbage truck have fallen together.

Six months ago if Mom or Dad or anyone had asked me in no particular order to do two or three things at once, I probably would have eventually done them all but I know not in any one particular order. Whatever task was mentioned first may have been the first task begun. Perhaps wherever I was and then in proximity to have me immediately involved with any one of the tasks would've been what was begun first. I don't really know. Why did I recently want to create an order and form a rule, or set up a priority for myself when I'm in these type of situations, and then use this priority to decide things with? Why didn't I just stay the way I was before, with no particular order or pattern to doing things? Why did I even care enough to want to change something so seemingly trivial?

Sometimes I think I should start writing things down into a notebook or a diary of some kind.

Stay Focused. Go Slow. Keep It Simple.

It seemed like the right thing to do at the time. To have Father Nicholas read my treatise and then I'd listen to whatever he thought about it. I want to hear what he has to say, anything at all.

I thought his reading should begin in a different context than if he were to jump right into biological subjects, so I wrote a preface for the treatise, telling Father at the rectory that it was a school paper I wrote a couple of years ago. Read it when he finds the time to and to get back to me whenever. Two days later I'm sitting on the bed in my room at the Hopewell Inn, tying up my boots and ready to leave for work when I hear the knock on the door.

"Hi, Father. Come on in." My room is small. A couple backward steps has my foot hit the bedpost and I sit back down on the bed. He places the folder with my treatise papers down upon the stool just inside the door.

"I can only discuss things with you in relation to the Church."

I sit there silent for a moment. His bluntness takes me by surprise. I'm expecting some conversation.

"What about you? Personally, don't you think it's kind of … interesting?"

His eyes dart around to different places inside my room, though no one particular place or thing holds his attention for long. I have the feeling he wants to be somewhere else, to be doing something else.

Father repeats himself. "I can only talk to you about things of the Church."

Rehearsed response…, and I realize how this conversation is going to end.

I stand up and step forward and look up into his eyes. I'm thinking Imprimatur and Nihil Obstat. I remind myself again, *ask how the Church qualifies and approves things like this, ... what formal procedures and processes with the Church ... would have to be gone through ...* and to have them recognize or acknowledge the thoughts I've outlined in the treatise.

Father steps back and looks away. His manner and an apparent lack of interest and I am not going to bother asking any other questions. I try to contain the rejection watching him stand at the door, silent.

"It's too liberal for me. Read some of the works of the early Church Fathers. Aquinas, Augustine," he says with nary a hint of emotion. A crush of disappointment wells up in me.

He doesn't even want to talk about it either.

His eyes turn to look down upon the door handle and I sound out a hurried, "Thanks, Father," and I watch an expressionless face retreat behind the door.

I'm surprised with my own lack of emotion. I pick the keys to the Mustang up off the dresser and look at myself in the mirror.

Repeating the words in thought, Thanks Father, ... I chuckle with a sense of disdain.

What would the world become if one of the major religions were to have one of their own discover the treatise? What if I were an ordained priest and in this capacity I had thought out and written the treatise over a period of time?

I make my way down the stairs and imagine I'd probably, eventually present my treatise to the Bishop of New York. Bishop Cooke would understand the implications for what it's all about and he would probably bring it to the attention of the Pope. After a personal reading by the Pope and his entourage I suppose a committee of the rank and file would be formed. With the best and the brightest minds brought together I am also included as one of many inside the group that begins the process of expounding upon the ideas and furthering the trains of thought that the treatise has only touched on. All details subtle and grand are worked through and smoothed out after months, years behind closed doors, until the day a public announcement to the world of its discovery.

Wow, because of my treatise ... the hordes of people who will now want to join and become a part of the Catholic Church...!

For the life of me I cannot understand why others don't immediately grasp the significance of what I'm saying inside the treatise. Doing so if only for the goof. Everyone is always so immediate and serious with their lack of interest.

Perhaps if I were to be more persistent and make the rounds to other dioceses across the United States. Surely one or two bishops would grasp what is being conveyed, and then to start the ball rolling ...

I think of my treatise as new wine. For some reason the Church won't give my treatise the status of a better wine that's saved and served at the end of a banquet. If I think through this allegory to its conclusion, then I'm attempting to pour the new wine I've found into the old wineskin of the Catholic Church. My wine will then burst the old wineskin, to put to waste all the wine and destroying the Church in the process. Jesus has set a stage blinding the Church at this day and age from appreciating the treatise ... at this point in time this is what is happening. Something like this is happening now ... anyway, maybe.

Perhaps whatever I'll say or do the Church hierarchy cannot, at the snap of their fingers just change course and steer The Boat in another direction. If I were one of them, and someone came out of nowhere to present me with the treatise, I suppose the best course of action would be to try to stall public awareness of the existence of that treatise. The next line of defense would be to trivialize the message and the messenger. With the messenger gone I'd flip it up upon some shelf down inside some cold, locked underground basement cellar room somewhere, and to have everyone else within the Church ignore its existence and simply continue on with business as usual. Generations will pass and with time a layer of dust settles upon my treatise and upon all the other quill penned quirks of freshly inspired thought mined from sages past. Virginal ideas that meld to no practical import, ... Galileo, da Vinci, the thoughts are buried, rendered stagnant. For centuries or longer the papers and ideas remain mute. One day for some reason someone walks down and rummages through the basement to find and then take hold of some nondescript folder. Shaking off the falling dust they open the folder and read the words on the first page they open up to:

A Treatise on the Nature of Life.

Tink..., tink.

Someone is throwing pebbles up from the parking lot to the second floor window of my room. I look down from the window and Ray stands with his Trident 750.

"I didn't know if you'd be here," Ray says to me. "Thought I'd stop by before work. Last day today, you know?"

He's reporting to boot camp this weekend. A four year sign up, and I won't be seeing him around for a while..., and maybe never again.

"Let's go inside. Get a beer or something," I say. "Hungry?"

"Nah. Yeah, all right. I'll get a sandwich or something."

We walk through the doors of the tavern and into the cool, musty, air-conditioned comfort.

Walking up to the bar, "Jenny, too early for a couple sandwiches?"

"Got some ham leftovers."

"You guys maybe want something to drink?"

"A Coca-Cola for me."

"Two of 'em Jenn-ski, please."

An inordinate amount of time with little talk of any importance between Ray and I. Even when the sandwiches arrive, after a few bites..., seems like we're both waiting for the not too distant future to greet us and take us into the next stage of life.

"When you reporting to Parris Island?" I ask. I already know it's sometime this weekend.

"Day after tomorrow night. Staying a day or two with cousins just outside Fayetteville, North Carolina, near Camp Lejeune, before showing up Monday morning."

I understand and nod.

"They ready for 'ya, or what?"

"Nah. Got up to five miles a day, three times a week for the last month and a half. Been doin' about..., gotten up to doing a regular hundred fifty sit-ups, three hundred push-ups, and hundred fifty chin-ups every other day. I guess I'm as ready for them big galoots as I'll ever be."

"They tell you what you're gonna do when you first get there?"

"Oh, never told you, did I?"

"My enlistment stipulates after basic training I'll train in fire fighting techniques. Learn fire science, get some first hand on-the-job fire fighting experience under my belt. I thought later I'll take more courses, get more training. Apply what I'll know towards designing industrial fire prevention devices. Become a consultant of some kind. Four, six years and I'll be in a better position to decide what's next, and what's best. To stay in the military, rise in rank, or it's time to get out."

"My compliments. Sounds good," I say.

"You know my cousin Ivan in East Fishkill? He came with us to play hockey at Lake Minnewaska. Moose."

"Yeah, yeah, Moose. I know who you're talking about."

"A volunteer firefighter with the rescue squad. He's with some ambulance group, taking Emergency Medical and more firefighting courses ... to stay on top of that job."

Something to do... Ray will become a firefighter and get involved in firefighting things.

Why? Only because he doesn't know what else to do with himself.

"Yeah, sounds good, Ray. Sure."

Whatever enthusiasm the treatise instilled within Ray after I showed it to him has worn off. I don't want to go into student loan debts if I don't have to so I decided to take some time off after my senior year and just be on my own for a while.

Two years out and each year I give thought for returning to school, doing so especially during the summer months before the fall semesters start. I imagine carrying a full load of courses for the following four to six years, and the years will go fast. Eventually I'll be participating in my own line of research to investigate the genesis of neural genotypes, and the Darwinian systems best describing the scenarios for how and why metazoan life mutated the more complex neurological systems into existence.

Nineteen years old and over the last two years I consider myself fortunate to have been working two steady jobs. I'm comfortably saving on average fifty dollars each week. Maintenance and insurance on the Mustang and rent at the Inn eats more than half the money I earn each month.

I do make time for regular trips to the library. I read a lot, even the TV Guide though rarely do I find anything inside the TV Guide worth the effort to make sure I'm in front of a television to watch. I listen to that inner voice of mine all the time, keenly, and I'm gathering ideas. I cannot just let the treatise go away 'cause I feel it's about something. Someday I will do something with it or the treatise will do something to me. It'll be a really, really big show.

"Did you get the taxi license yet?" Ray asks.

"Not yet. Should be here soon."

After I decided I'll work in New York, Ray and I drove down there to investigate the situation. A second weekend I went by myself to became more familiar to all the traffic and city things. I bought a Hagstrom map to bring back and memorize the street names and main arteries with, and to find where airports and points of interest are. I found the Jane West single-room-occupancy hotel in an advertisement inside the New York Post. I can check into the Jane West from day one. Anxious I am to get down there and get myself going..., and it should be anytime within the next week or two.

Ray turns his head from side to side. "I can't believe you're going to New York..., to live there. You just don't seem like—"

I raise my eyebrows and shrug my shoulders.

"Whatever." I could tell him why I'm going down there, but don't. It's something I have to do by myself.

The last year and a half I've worked part-time with the town of Hopewell Junction as a police cadet officer. Three sometimes four evenings a week I'll answer the phone, file papers, and do various custodial tasks at the Town Hall. From the Town Hall I drive to my other full-time job at Tuck Tape in the city of Beacon. For seven and a half hours I am responsible for a single machine which will wind a continuous five foot wide sheet of masking or duct tape onto a spool of cardboard. Some shifts and the machine is set up to have the sheet of plastic wind around two, three, or four different five foot long spools of spinning cardboard tubes.

I begin the graveyard shift at eleven. I'm usually taking over an already operational machine from someone else. So before I'll take over the machine I'll make sure there are enough of those five foot long cardboard tubes stocked in a nearby bin.

Sticky on one side, it's an approximate five foot wide, thin sheet of warm plastic material that's constantly exuding out from the machine and then falling down in front of me. Perhaps a two yard length of the material is brought out from this one section of the machine before it's long enough and I'm able to wrap it onto one of the cardboard tubes that are spinning down at the bottom of the machine. The plastic material wraps around the cardboard tube, the tube grows wider in diameter and after ten to twenty minutes a buzzer sound informs me a predetermined amount and length of tape has wrapped itself around the cardboard tube. I'll grab hold of the moving plastic sheet and with a boxcutter slice the plastic lengthwise to free it. Pulling the sheet away from the spinning tube I place the sheet around another spinning cardboard tube. A button on the machine stops the finished tube from turning and spinning, and I remove the five-foot long and perhaps six to ten inch wide tube off the machine and place it on a fiberglass pallet lying nearby. A number of people working similar machines place their finished tubes on this pallet too. A forklift arrives at regular intervals to transport the pallet of finished tubes to another section of the building. Each tube is eventually cut into individual rolls of tape. Four to six times an hour I make a cut across the sheet of tape. I do all this activity for seven and a half hours and wrap twenty-five to thirty-five tubes of tape a night.

I don't like the thoughts of me working a monotonous factory job for the rest of my life.

Saturday and then Monday mornings I'm in the habit to rise early for a drive into Poughkeepsie. I'm in the habit to read the local paper and magazines I'll buy at a newsstand near the Dunkin' Donuts I frequent, reading for the hour or two before the library opens for the day.

Hobbes, Hume, Kant, Locke, the readings of the Church Fathers, mathematical logicians Carnap, Russell, Tarski, Whitehead. Almost anyone and any subject I think may have some bearing in all this I'll become familiar with. I read a lot.

Assuming that it is a unique capacity of the human brain which enables us humans to perceive, acknowledge and ultimately to create all mathematical abstract concepts, and if I am correct to understand the discipline of physics as the application of mathematical concepts which help describe the reality of the physical world, how interesting it is to consider the different classes of numbers the mathematician has created, and how these numbers behave inside various contexts. I like to think it will have been a definite, personal accomplishment to someday bring a working, practical definition to the bridge spanning the realms of mathematical logic to the physical order and structure of the universe.

Some numbers represent distinct boundaries on a number line, and these type of numbers are useful for representing objects in the physical world, making them useful for common, everyday tasks such as distinguishing objects of a group by the count of one, two and three. These were the earliest type of numbers recognized and utilized by human beings and were created to determine proportions, ratios and relationships of size and dimension between two or more objects. Other numbers have no distinct boundaries and cannot be identified with a distinct, unique "size." 3.14192 or π is not an exact point or place upon a number line though it is a term useful when one wants to determine the circumference of a circle when the length of the radius is known.

My attempts to work through proofs in number theory is slow going, and difficult. A pleasant sense of accomplishment arises when I do tend to comprehend the gist of a particular proof. I know in the future I will not be able to simply glance at and then expect to comprehend the more complex mathematical equations presented in physics or chemistry or biology, doing so with any degree of proficiency if I do not have a grasp of what number theory courses will provide, so number theory is definitely on the roster of courses I'll be taking if I return to school.

So I like to think. Sometimes the thought for the importance of number theory is countered with the notion that number theory proofs are irrelevant and that zero and one, existence and nonexistence, these two numbers and the ideas they represent are all I need to further my understanding of the treatise.

When I find myself thinking through the step by step logic to a proof, and with a momentary pause of confusion or the extended stumbling block where my thoughts do not jell results and conclusions which further whatever I'm attempting to understand, at times like this I'll more often than not think thoughts that leave me content with what I already do and don't know about numbers, the result being that I simply give up, close the book for another day and go do something else.

Mathematical logic is an almost perfect descriptive tool to describe the behavior of particles of mass. To the agnostic and the atheist these symbols and logic systems employed within mathematical thought have been rendered only mere inventions of the human mind. I like to think the axioms of logic employed by mathematics were and are discoveries rather than inventions. If I follow my belief in the existence of a Creator God than the logic inherent in the behavior of particles of matter is prima facie evidence for a presently unknown structure or system that qualifies all the mass within the universe. A consistency to the order of the universe is realized and defined by application of the mathematical systems of logic. The common denominator connecting the laws of physics to chemistry to biology and then to genetics are the laws of mathematics. A consistent order to the universe seems neither capricious nor chaotic, rather a consistent order of the universe seems to be wrought for us humans to recognize only through mathematical constructs.

Where is that bridge, gap, and or point relationship causing the entities of mathematical logic to become the characteristics of interacting elementary particles?

The Big Bang is described as an event where a window was opened and then quickly closed, allowing a single force of pure, raw energy to eventually transform itself into a zillion subatomic particles. Within an instant of time total nonexistence became an existence of volume for three dimensional space to contain a profusion of quantum particles. Physicists employ the word fermion to represent these quantum, elementary particles of matter that exist only one or two steps away from the initial state of pure, raw energy that first entered the universe. These fermions interact with their respective force carrier particles called bosons to form the atomic particles called protons, neutrons, and electrons, and these atomic particles then form into the elements that form into the molecular compounds of all matter in the universe.

I give quick thought to this system of particles inside the universe. *Mexican jumping beans, …* that initial, amputated appendage of pure, raw energy is gloved inside the three dimensional space of our universe with characteristics for whatever the system of a zillion quantum particles is all about.

One characteristic this system of quantum and atomic particles is all about is that it does not behave in random, chaotic fashion. A modus operandi is that these particles behave in a pattern prescribed by mathematical laws. An order has been imparted to raw, chaotic energy. This order reflects the laws of probability, and the distributive, associative, commutative, and other laws of mathematics.

At the quantum level, what mechanism did God meld to the quark, lepton, and gauge boson which then allow the proton and electron to possess those fundamental electromagnetic interactive qualities of attraction, repulsion, and vibration?

The quantum weak and strong forces binding the fundamental fermion and boson particles don't appear to parlay an influence affecting the behavior of the larger, composite forms of atomic and molecular matter. The force of gravity has only a positional, orienting influence on the larger, composite forms of atomic and molecular matter. Quantum and gravitational forces play minor roles which turned the gears rendering the first electro-biochemical event causing life on earth [11,12]. Intuition has me focusing to the electromotive system of energy affecting the proton, neutron, and electron. Specifically here at the atomic realm is where it happened.

I'm a bit fascinated by any cleverly written article that focuses upon the interaction of matter at this atomic realm.

What is the nature of any force (boson particle) that causes the characteristic of the particle to interact with another particle in a repelling or attractive manner?

I imagine a single atomic particle vibrating in every direction left and right, up and down, forward and backward, and I can't help but wonder what is causing that to be. Whether I'm reading of coulombs of charge, or the electromagnetic properties of batteries or capacitors, or reading of quarks with color charges, I'm referred to the same redundant ideas of like charges repel, and opposites attract.

What is the nature of the positive and negative charge responsible for the repelling, attractive, and vibrational characteristics? Dittos with quantum color charges: what is the intrinsic cause for their observed behavior.

Until something comes along to persuade me to the contrary, I'll follow my belief there exists a mechanism causing the entities of mathematical logic to meld with the quantum particles of the universe. I may not become a rocket scientist but I like to think if I keep my thoughts along these lines perhaps someday I'll be allowed to discover and understand a metaphysical nature of these forces too.

A long time ago unknown conditions and circumstances on archean earth caused a collection of atoms to develop molecules that brought the very first primitive forms of life into existence. One moment there was no life on earth and the next moment there is life. One set of atoms became a form or component for life while identical atoms formed into the molecules that became hard rock, or dust. What caused the force to veer towards the direction of life?

I'm reading an interesting book on thermodynamic properties and entropy [13], allowing myself time to stop and think through any last set of paragraphs to better understand the ideas the authors are attempting to convey. The book uses college level words and ideas but keeps the mathematics to a minimum, and I'm able to follow a train of thought even though I did not fully understand what any related mathematical statement may have also conveyed. The authors expect the reader to be familiar with the many diverse examples they bring up for consideration. They also coin the phrase nonequilibrium thermodynamics (NET's) to define how the force of gravity with the second law of thermodynamics form gradients between the kinetic, potential, gravitational, magnetic, electrical, chemical and thermonuclear forms of energy found within different states of matter. With what I've read so far each chapter has been replete with examples and analogies and I'm confident I would be able to summarize at least sixty to seventy percent of the material I've read back to another person. The quantum, atomic and gravitational system of forces are definitely going through the wringer, and I'm glad to have found and begun to read this book.

The books and periodicals I like to read fall into three categories. One group of authors write their thoughts intending to convey the natural world wrought without a first cause. Some but not all authors in this group will attribute events and form conclusions concerning their subject matter by invoking phrases such as Mother Nature or evolution. These authors concede that apples and sunsets have their origins and causes but somehow the entities of Mother Nature and evolution and all the characteristics of force and energy inside the universe do not have origins or causes. The parameters of the universe that set Mother Nature to be as it is or evolution to do what it does are not recognized by these authors as having their own origin and cause. They're adamant a Creator does not exist.

A second category are the religiously biased type who seem to find difficulty speculating and reaching conclusions on topics without inferring religious dogma. A third group stay on track and present their thoughts with the facts. Whether I completely understand the message this third group intends to convey is less important than whether I feel confident whatever I glean are from a collection of filtered facts.

I don't know the mechanism that wrought into existence the 10^{79} electrons inside the universe and I don't know how the electron maintains its characteristics as it does inside the universe. Dittos with my curiosity as to the causes for how the eyeball and the flagellar mechanisms of bacteria came into existence. I like to think I'm pragmatic and I do intend to become industrious in my life, and so I prefer articles written from the latter group of authors who write to expound facts. I expect the more critical mind such as Carl Sagan or Richard Feynman to occasionally pepper their clever expositions with bias towards an unbelief in a Creator. I like to watch and read from those who have taken the time and put forth the effort to conduct their research and then to report their findings in keeping with the more critical and objective frame of mind. Because no one literally knows and is capable of proving if there is or if there is not a Creator.

I'm in my room one evening watching *The Tenth Level,* a CBS documentary reenacting the Yale University psychology professor Stanley Milgram's classic study of obedience to authority. William Shatner, Captain Kirk played the protagonist as one of Milgram's associates. The program finished and I went downstairs for a beer. I'm thinking of a pool game by myself or with anyone if so inclined. Sometimes a couple people are downstairs on weekday nights. Sometimes no one is down there. Boring, quiet time of the week. I'm thinking about that documentary as I take myself on downstairs.

I'm crouched down in front of the pool table and pulling balls out from the galley and then placing them by handfuls up inside the rack. I want to keep myself in that "look but don't touch" frame of mind as I take apart to make sense out of what I just finished watching on television.

Any of the factors and conditions I'll realize Milgram et al. had built into the experiment and that had wrought to cause those peculiar results from so many people I want to initially refrain from placing and categorizing any of these things as being somehow good or bad or right or wrong. I want my thoughts to stay as nonjudgmental to everything for as long as I am able to do so. I was not expecting a before prime time show this evening to be so gripping, and so compelling.

The volunteers chosen for the experiment were solicited from the local residents of the community surrounding the different universities where Milgram conducted his experiment. These volunteers were intended to be representative of average middle class folk.

"It is absolutely essential that you continue..."

"You have no other choice; you must go on."

I remember these to be the coercive mantras spoken by Milgram to many of the volunteers, and were sufficient to prod a majority of the volunteers to continue participating until the end of the experiment. The end of the experiment was to have each volunteer flick the last of thirty levers, and this last lever is supposedly discharging an electrical shock of four hundred and fifty volts to another person. Sixty-five percent of all those who volunteered for the experiment intentionally administered some thirty electric shocks to another person. The first shock being fifteen volts, each subsequent shock increasing at fifteen volt increments to the last and maximum shock of four hundred and fifty volts. At certain times during any experiment many of the volunteers would become agitated and reluctant to continue flicking levers and shock people. At these times Milgram or an associate, dressed in an authoritarian white lab coat would prod the volunteer with these predetermined verbal responses to encourage the person to continue on with the experiment.

"It is absolutely essential that you continue," Milgram would say calmly, politely, and I'm amazed recalling that the person would eventually succumb to these verbal requests and flick another switch!

A pathetic of human nature, I hear myself saying ...

Collect any group of people large or small, and three of the five people—A nation of fifty-million people have twenty-million people who know better given the same set of facts and circumstances than the majority of thirty-million.

Know better ...?

Someone is speaking to me as I stand at the pool table.

"How 'bout a game of eight-ball, ... for a beer?"

I turn to look at this guy standing behind me. He's pulling and rolling the cuff of his shirt sleeve up and around his forearm. I didn't see him or anyone walk through the front door. Looking around and I don't see anyone else inside the tavern.

"Sure. Good," I say, and start to collect all the balls on top of the table to set up another rack. I watch the guy pick off a pool stick from the rack on the wall and then roll it across the green felt of the table, checking for warp.

"Flip a coin, see who breaks?" I ask.

"You can break," he says softly, quickly. I'm pulling the tray up from the triangle of balls to hear him say, "Just passing through the area. Thought I'd get out and stretch a little. Wet the whistle."

I'm self-conscious and not concentrating to insure the tip of the pool stick strikes the bottom of the cue ball to have it spin back towards me after crashing into the rack. I swing the pool stick a few times and smack the cue ball, and scatter the rack..., and no balls drop.

"Visiting someone?" I ask.

The man is sharp, well dressed. In his late forties, fifty. The word dapper comes to mind as I watch him survey the balls on the table. Dark pants, light blue satin collared shirt. A gold-bronze colored tie hangs out from a black cloth vest. A single button holds the vest snug to his abdomen. A hint of cologne is in the air. Chalking the tip of his stick, scanning the arrangement of balls on the table, he responds to my question with a curt, "Business."

I wonder what brings someone on business and into this area. There are other places one would pass by after exiting off of Interstate 84 or the Taconic State Parkway before driving five, six miles out of the way over here.

"What type of work you do? If you don't mind my asking."

"Public relations." Pocket watch chain dangles from his vest. With a turn of his head, the side of his mouth scowls, as if any old answer would suffice.

He drops another two balls before missing.

"Albany. Washington. Different places," he furthers as I step near the corner where the cue ball is.

"Hamilton Fish, Jr., represents this area in the House," he goes on. "Mind if I ask your thoughts on a particular matter?"

I look up from above the cue stick. He's turned away and lights a cigarette, stepping to look through a window to the outside parking lot.

"Think the people who've told me of Soviet submarines sailing into the Hudson River are telling the truth?"

The evening hours are winding up and I'm still in a sense of fascination towards that movie with Milgram. I'm a little tired too. What he said doesn't ring of humor or alarm me, if that's what he's trying to do now.

I sink the ball I was aiming for.

"Be nice to knock those guys out without firing a shot."

I quit the position I was in at the table and straighten up. He takes a step towards me, attentively chalking the tip of the pool stick, not looking at me.

"Block off a jugular. Give those ghosts a little stroke. Keep that talk quiet in the third world for another thousand years or two."

He turns the pool stick in his hands, blowing off chalk dust. His eyes shifting as he speaks.

"Something not good, ... evil will happen the next ten, twenty years if things keep going the way they've been."

With a strained, contrived smile I turn to see he's been watching Jenny stepping towards us with a tray of food.

"Doesn't matter if other people can do it...," I hear him say.

Jenny places the tray down upon a table.

"I'll put this down, right here for you guys."

The guy continues talking to me. "If you yourself generated a couple million dollars in your lifetime, it'd say a lot. There'd be ammunition ... for a certain group of people in Washington to work with then."

"I made some roast beef sandwiches. There's potato salad. Corn chips...," with a mischievous smile Jen tips a beer bottle for me to see the St. Pauli label. "A tub of that red horseradish mustard too, Kurt."

I'm surprised by the gratuitous behavior.

Placing the pool stick back inside the rack on the wall, the guy pinches to lift corn chips from the bowl and then steps to the door. A moment to stand with his hand on the door handle, he turns to me, saying, "You totally on your own, or is God blessing America?"

Jen and I step to a table window and watch a smartly dressed chauffeur hold the passenger door to a black limousine open, and that guy walks to the open door and steps inside. The chauffeur closes the door, walks to the driver's side and after he opens his own door he takes his cap off, placing his arms up upon the roof of the limousine. His hands clasp his hat while he looks towards us. Looking to his left and right, apparently speaking to someone. I get the feeling he's speaking to others inside the limousine. I watch the chauffeur guy then duck down and out of view, and after a moment the long black limousine drives from the parking lot and accelerates onto Route 376.

"Who were those guys?"

I shake my head. Biting my lip.

"I have no idea, ... guy said he was just passing through."

I walk to the table and the sandwiches and stuff.

"He bought this?"

"Gave me a hundred dollar bill. Asked me to bring some sandwiches and things over to you."

Be nice to knock those guys out without firing a shot.

I hear Jenny say, "I thought he knew you."

Wow, ... federal, military? A National Security Agency.

I look at the plate of roast beef, half-sliced sandwiches. The bottles of St. Pauli beer.

"You're going to have to help me eat all this," I say.

The guy didn't bother to take his money off the tray. My fingers spread the bills out and I count up to and past eighty dollars before I grab hold of a half slice of sandwich and the tub of horseradish mustard.

Millions of dollars?

Jen steps over and I watch her count the money.

"Here, take half," she says to me, placing the money in my shirt pocket.

I reach up and place the two twenties in my pants pocket and then push the corner of the roast beef sandwich inside the tub of mustard. My fingers press the bread up inside the turning wall of the saucer and I bring a large purple and white dollop onto the tip of the bread.

I step up to and alongside the window table to pick up a box of wooden matches that lie on top. The matches were courtesy of the *Trump Tower, Fifty-sixth and Fifth, New York.*

—|—

I had the choice of twelve hours of daytime driving or driving around at night for twelve hours. Already accustomed to night hours I chose night shifts, and the thought being that I'd have less traffic regulations to contend with as I learn my way around the city.

No Left Turn: 3 - 6:30 PM.

No Right Turn: 8 - 10:00 AM, 2 - 4:00 PM.

Express Bus Lane Only: 4 - 8:00 PM.

Traffic signs telling me to do this and don't do that are all over the place. Most are positioned above ground level where all the important activity is taking place. On both sides of the street, on practically every block there is at least one explicit regulation of some kind posted upon a sign.

I have to negotiate the taxi with bicycles crawling between cars and around stationary trucks. I keep an eye out for the doors of any vehicles opening towards the street. Pedestrians moving around, a fare running towards me. All the while reading signs above me to understand whether I can or cannot turn through this intersection or into that street at any given moment. As the horns around me toot and honk I just gotta do it. That's the thought.

Many of these traffic regulations end after 8 P.M. My shift starts at 6 P.M. I'm thinking two hours of this every day is how I'll sort it all out.

Confined within the taxi at night the city becomes a mishmash hodgepodge of sights, light and dark, large and small shapes moving in and out of view. Shapes appear out of context to what I thought I saw just a moment ago.

The time I took a fare south on the FDR Drive and I watch buildings from sixty blocks away. Buildings in the Wall Street area grow from tiny to humongous. Especially the last few minutes beyond the Brooklyn Bridge I was quite impressed with that two, three minute view through the windshield.

I'm not yet accustomed to do things for long periods of time in the dark, at night. The pervasive presence of darkness to everything, upon everything I view through the windshield, is different.

Sometimes while driving I hear people yelling off to the side and I look at them wave to me as I pass on by. I don't know why I don't see them sooner though I must have had at least ten, maybe fifteen different incidents like this already, and I'm starting to wonder why. Very bright lights on spots of intense pitch black darkness, splayed upon the windshield, hour after hour as I drive. It's different.

I imagine my eyeballs get a good workout each night. Dilating, constricting pupil exercises that leave my eyes sometimes feeling tired. The muscles of my face around my eyes have become tense after the ten, twelve hours of night driving.

Stopped still in my cab, a big bright red traffic light sits above and in front of me against the darkening, unfocused blur of towering buildings rising into the night sky. For as far as the eye can see, the twenty or so traffic lights straight ahead stagger from the color green, to yellow, then to red. I've scratched three to four imaginary three dimensional lines across the windshield, these lines connecting the set of all these red dots now on top of the windshield. I'll use the lines to map the surface contours of the avenue immediately in front of me, amusing myself with an imperative sense of '*as if I need to know*' reason for doing so, waiting for the one red light to turn green again. It's kind of interesting watching the man-made order of ten, fifteen, twenty lights traveling up or down an avenue the first few times I began noticing it to do so.

My eyes scan left and right, focusing nearby or off in the distance to notice the next fare I'll want to scurry next to. I accelerate up to speed and the street lights above me cause the bubbles of light and then darkness to slip in through the windshield. Each expansion of light and dark that wanders around inside the cab is as if a pulsation. Each pulse withdraws itself from where I am only to draw in another, and then another and the steady rhythm of light bubbles is again flowing inside the cab…, unnoticed they are, then forgotten about while driving around until the presence of a single pulse slowly crawls itself back to my attention inside the cab, the pulse to eventually remain constant, and spotlight fixed, bearing down on me or some things on the seat as I slow the taxi to a standstill.

I tell myself there should be a name, a technical name to describe the phenomenon of city lights as they shine in and out of a moving vehicle at night. Doppler comes to mind first, but I'll use the syntax of the phrase "Brownian motion" to coin it "Soldierian motion" for now.

A hundred blocks of establishments on an avenue can pass by in a short amount of time. I travel up and then down the same two or three avenues a few times and I become a little more familiar with each one, correctly anticipating what I remember of things from the last time I was in the area. I haven't been here long enough to really distinguish one street or neighborhood from another in the dark, at night. Too much information, too fast for me to make quick, sure distinctions of one place from another.

Sunday morning, 7 a.m. My first full day off after my sixth consecutive twelve hour night shift. I take the subway back to my room, wash up, put my sneakers on, and I'm a little hungry so I'll get a good pile of breakfast in me before setting off. I want to have a good long look at this here New York City up close now, in the daylight.

I have to be careful how many eggs I eat at any one time. Any foods that I know have concentrations of Vitamin A in them, liverwurst and eggs and milk. I know I've eaten too much of something when for a few minutes I'll get these purple dots floating around in my eyes. Years ago for a couple of long minutes the retinol in five hard-boiled eggs once placed a single pulsating, fairly large purple dot dead center in front of both my eyes.

Lying on the couch, watching TV, and I thought I was going into a state of insanity. Within a two or three-second time period I felt this thing start moving forward from inside the center of my head and into my forehead, and for the next second or two I feel this thing in my forehead move down and I now start to see what I feel in my forehead as it moves to the top of my eyelids. It appears as a round purple dot, and it travels straight down, stopping dead center in front of both my eyes. Turning my head to the left and away from the television screen, I then look back at the TV screen, and this shiny, sort of pulsating purple dot will follow to remain directly in front of and blocking almost half the center view of everything. Lying on the couch and moment by moment I wait, expecting to see something else suddenly start to happen in my eyes.

I watch this shiny pulsating bright purple dot in my eyes grow smaller and than larger. If I'm scared in any way I don't recognize the feeling until the notion that this pulsating dot in my eyes is never, ever going to go away. I will have this purple dot-smear in my eyes to look at every waking moment of my life. This thought connects to and magnifies the sheer state of terror I'm now beginning to develop. Several moments go by as I suppress the feeling of terror. I feel my heart banging inside my chest. I'm thinking of getting up off the couch and to go find and tell the first person I see what's going on with me. The pulsation stops. The solid purple color begins breaking into smaller, string-like types of silver-purple fragments, and through a hole in the middle of the now dissolving purple dot I see the windowsill above and beyond the television set. The entire purple dot dissolves after a second or two. Everything was fine after that.

Moms said it was probably something I ate, so later I did some research and found humans have a two year supply of vitamin A stored in their livers, and I guess my body does not know what to do with a quick infusion of any more of it.

I haven't eaten any eggs for several days so it's two eggs sunnyside up this morning. Ham, potatoes, and a light spread of butter on toasted rye. I'll regularly ask for a tub of mustard to put on my food instead of the Vitamin A in the tomatoes of ketchup I was in the habit of using. I use to put ketchup on many things but not anymore. Whenever the want is for tomato juice I'll chose to drink orange juice instead. When they stop mandating that overdose of Vitamin A in milk and all milk byproducts I'll consider including more dairy food products as a regular part of my diet again. I have to be attentive to what I eat now days.

I exit the diner with a second cup of coffee in hand. Sipping coffee and tooth picking my teeth, I'm walking south on Hudson Street, and it's great. I'm great. Everything is great. The sun is up and there is a cool dampness in the air. I can tell it's going to be a wonderful day to be outside.

Walking south on Washington Street, I don't know why I told myself the area south of the Jane West and down towards the World Trade Center is for another time. I turn east onto Spring Street. At Varick Street I turn north.

The number of buildings I pass by after walking for half an hour is incredible. I put it in perspective with a little mathematics. Ten to fifteen buildings per block. There are two blocks on each side of me. I've walked thirty-five blocks. That's seven hundred to a thousand buildings I've glanced at so far. All of them being built over the course of a hundred or two years. I figure during my five or six hour walk I will have traveled by and taken at least a passing glance at some five thousand separate individual buildings.

I don't remember where I was when I saw this one particular building. Above Thirty-fourth and below Forty-second Streets I'm fairly sure. It's wedged in, squeezed up taller than the adjacent buildings. Marble surrounds the pedestrian entrance ways and all the way around the building at street level. Flat black metal strips define squares, squares that rise up the length of the four sides of the building. Metal strips of lattice work frame the windows inside each square, giving contrast to the corners and edges of each square block of window.

I'm thinking how majestic a building such as this would look if it were to stand alone and by itself. Where it is now situated and with a person preoccupied for the moment, or simply not inclined to take notice for whatever reason, someone could walk up to a building like this and not even realize how awesome it looks. It's sort of lost in the sauce where it stands now.

Someone should build a building like this in Hopewell Junction. It'd look cool, and be totally cool.

Rising from within the collection of one, two, at most three storied bland, mundane structures of Hopewell Junction, a building of this caliber standing twenty, thirty stories tall would be the cream of the crop. A definite hangout, for sure. To visit after school or on a Saturday morning, if for no other reason than just because it's there. I imagine so many others because of sheer boredom would walk, ride, or drive over to it simply for the act of doing so, for something to do. To see who's there and what may be happening there. It's existence is a retail advertisement and attraction all by itself, in its own right. I think for a few moments why no one has yet realized to build a structure like this in the little hamlet of Hopewell Junction.

One reason had to be cost. For the amount of money one would have to put up to construct such a building as this, a person would want to generate the largest amount of total square feet inside the building, and then to rent out all that square feet to get as much money back in the shortest amount of time. How much money would I get back every week, every month for the amount of money I spent to build it? Are there other projects or investments I may think of putting tens of millions of dollars into, and is this how I would want the tens of millions of dollars I control to work for me? A return on investment comes to mind and sums up everything I thought of.

Because no building like this exists in Hopewell Junction, I'll conclude that there were people who've thought like this before me, have already done the math, thought of more impressive and rewarding things to do with their money, which explains why no one has built a building like what I'm looking at in Hopewell Junction..., maybe.

I try to think of other reasons why tall buildings are not a part of small communities, and I can't think of any one other thing that prohibits a carefully designed building from being constructed. It seems only someone's personal pecuniary opinion prohibit it.

I'm walking towards Seventh Avenue and the tot strapped in and sitting up inside the approaching stroller has one of its pudgy arms raised up and across its face. He or she is about ten, fifteen months old and is straining towards one side of the stroller. I look down while the stroller passes and watch the gasping, out of breath convolutions of a sob, and tears run down the kid's face. Dad pushes the stroller past me, he's yucking it up with Moms. Both were smiling and wearing dark sunglasses.

Kids sometimes cry for no reason...

I'm trepidatious, at first. Several foot steps and a sense of empathy has me turning and walking back to the parents of that kid. The ball of sunlight shines high between the two towering walls of buildings on each side of the street. Walking up and pacing my steps alongside the guy, I'm looking down at the sidewalk and speak loud enough so I know both of them hear me.

"I believe your kid is upset because he or she does not have their own pair of cheap sunglasses!"

Satisfied, I turn towards Seventh Avenue.

With a steady pace of uphill steps and the realization for how gargantuan the city of New York is. New York is not a small size city like Poughkeepsie, Newburgh or Beacon. My idea, my definition of a large metropolitan urban environment, the word city is taking on a meaning that captures its definition more dramatically. From the distance, amount of time, and the number of buildings that I've walked past so far I'm forming a perspective to employ the adjectives small, medium and large towards the word city. New York is a very large city.

There are no gaps of empty space nor alleyways between each building I pass by now. The walls of the buildings are built right up to and against each other. Several times I stop to look as far back down the sidewalk and blacktop roadway of the avenue, and to confirm that I've always been for the most part stepping up a rising slope of ground.

I cross Forty-second Street and step up upon a large concrete pedestrian median. I recognize the view to the north as the merging crossroads of Times Square. The curve of Broadway rises up a hill. Twenty, thirty blocks of Seventh Avenue is a straight line of sight and I'm able to focus on the line of treetops along Central Park South.

I look around Times Square. The different billboards, theater marquees, restaurants, hotels and various gift shops. Quite a few people are walking around at ten-thirty in the morning, and I suppose during a Saturday afternoon the Times Square area is more crowded than now.

I want to keep moving. I have the option of veering off along Broadway or to continue north along Seventh Avenue, and I opt for the latter.

A storefront with pictures advertising *Medieval Time* jousting and revelry, food, and an afternoon of entertainment. A full suit of armor and sword is standing on a platform inside the store. Posters on the walls of the store depict a bus departing from New York and parked at Lyndhurst, New Jersey, and other pictures and posters capture the festivities of the event. Looks like fun, ... someday.

I continue an uphill walking pace. Cresting the hundred yards of rising sidewalk and a sweet, husky aroma of corned beef and pastrami stirs the senses. I look up and around the different storefronts, and then step over to the window of the Carnegie Deli.

"There's only room for take-out." I look at the guy seated on a stool next to a paper ticket machine. I nod my head in understanding and the guy hands me a paper ticket with a number stamped on it. I step over to stand with the other customers in front of the deli counter, and read the menu above, and I'll be buying a nine dollar and fifty cent sandwich? Uhm ...? Yikes!

"Pastrami on rye, extra pickles," I say to the guy behind the deli counter.

The guy places slices of meat cut from the flank on top of a saucer plate, the plate is then placed on top of the counter in front of me for sampling. Seems odd the meat is warm, not hot. The meat is tender with a delicious texture.

I take the quite heavy sandwich bag outside and walk up Seventh Avenue to find the first public area of metal tables and benches to sit down with. They stuffed five times the amount of pastrami between two slices of rye bread. With large packets of Gulden's mustard, a tub of coleslaw, the sour pickles, and I realize it will be a very satisfying meal.

Fifteen minutes later I'm stuffed. I am now fully prepared to venture further forward. Onward...!

I'm walking up to the crosswalk at Fifty-seventh Street and I just happen to catch out of the corner of my eye what seems to be a large pane of window glass swirling down from maybe twenty stories up. For two or three-seconds I watch the glare of light reflecting on and off the glass as it zigzags down in flight through the air, the flying pane of glass then shattering upon the sidewalk not fifty yards away. A female dressed in business skirt and jacket turns around and looks at the shards of glass lying on the ground a few yards away. She then looks up at the tall skeleton of steel beams and girders rising directly above her. I watch her turn around and continue walking west on Fifty-seventh Street.

I'm astonished. There are only a couple of people who must've also seen what I just saw, these people standing with the woman who almost got clobbered. They look up at the rising girders of steel beams, and then into the lower buildings construction area. I see no construction workers inside the construction area, and it seems only two or three other people have taken notice to what almost happened.

I cross the street and continue walking towards Central Park.

Three hundred years ago this same land was once thick forest, with the beavers, bears, and falcons roaming and ruling until Purpose forced a change.

I follow any of the foot paths bearing west and that eventually lead me out from Central Park.

Not some but most of the buildings are huge. Megatons of mortar, brick, steel, and glass. Towering, massive rectangles rising hundreds of feet into the air. Down below ground the subway trains momentarily shake the concrete of the sidewalk as they travel by. I hear the muted, doppplered roaring of the trains as they come and go. Warm tunnel air pushes up and rushes out through the steel ventilation grates embedded into the cement I walk upon.

The sandwich has made me thirsty. I stop inside another delicatessen for something to drink, and sit at a table inside the store. A steady walking pace I've been doing, and I want to keep doing for a couple more hours.

At Ninety-sixth Street I turn east and then walk north on Broadway to Columbia University. The blocks of buildings from Seventy-second to Ninety-sixth Streets I have just now traveled through were particular for something or other. Maybe it was because of all the trees along West End Avenue, and all the buildings were taller than the trees? I don't know. None of the buildings by themselves were anything spectacular in any sort of way. I don't know what it was but it was an impressive avenue I walked through for the twenty some odd blocks I was doing so..., for some reason or other it was.

At Columbia University I turn around, walk south on Broadway to Seventy-second Street and decide to cut through Central Park to the East side. I'm walking through Strawberry Fields and sense that familiar urge to collect my thoughts together and to think about something.

The last few weeks I've been in the habit of stepping out of myself, looking at the moments of any situation I happen to be involved with as if I'm some third person stranger to the situation. I like to think by doing this I'll bring a different perspective upon the machinations of thought, enabling me to derive other, novel psychological definitions of cognition..., the hope is to shake another lucent flash of brilliant ideas to mind.

How to go about investigating the things of the mind? It's tricky.

I reason that my thoughts and anyone's thoughts are real, just as real as a rock, something you could put in your hand to feel and see. The rock in your hand though can be hit against another rock, enabling definition of one of the two rocks as harder or softer than the other one, and in effect defining the rock further. If one chooses to do so other investigative acts can be performed allowing further definition of the two rocks.

I can't do even simple things like this with my thoughts and feelings. Thoughts and feelings aren't a "thing" that can be brought under some spotlight and then picked apart in the hope of finding a core or basic essence. I imagine having a laboratory with special tools that allow me to observe the flow of electrons through the system of neurons, and across the synapses of the axons and dendrites of some simple form of life, such as an arachnid. I imagine a system of flowing electrons within the arachnid ultimately intending the maintenance of homeostasis. How does a system of flowing electrons arrange themselves in a form to create a phenomena where the system of electrons is now actively creating the moments of cognition, or arrange themselves to create the quality of homeostasis inherent for life?

Supposing over the course of time my laboratory research has enabled me to propose several theories for how the system of electrons brings a preservative quality to a system or to cause a state of cognition. From these several theories I'm fond of one particular theory. As far as I'm concerned this theory of mine is simply word salad, and only by creating a practical, functional application from the information contained inside the theory will the theory have value. I have to bring or put some type of utility to verify and give legitimacy to the theory. I have to create a working, practical application of some kind ... someday.

I don't know.

Immanuel Kant is interesting. He defines the phenomena of human awareness to consist of three components: the first is the faculty of one's reason, or common sense. This faculty exists within the dual framework of ordinary space and time. The biological phenomenon of sentience and cognition involves an animal's mind developing awareness for three-dimensional space within the context of the always forward, entropic moment of time.

Kant thought the human ability to perceive and to recognize the phenomena of space and time is congenital. Recognition for space and time are not learned like the particular types of color which you learn about only because you have eyes. You learn about hot and cold only because you feel these things with your skin as you go through life. Sound you know about only because you have ears. Though a brain does not have an organ similar to the eye, skin, or ear to sense the existence of space and time. A brain doesn't learn but knows what space and time are because the capacity to know of these entities is hard wired into the brain at birth. I believe that a cerebral system of learning to coordinate hand movement with eye is what brings the necessity for creating and recognizing the four dimensions of space and time within the mind. There must be a section of the brain responsible for our perception of space and time, and it's the coordination of our five senses that causes the mind to create a system for being aware of space and time, and it's this system which ultimately creates every person's "thing in the back of the eyes." The infant on its back and swatting at the plastic butterflies hanging above the crib is bringing hand and eye coordination together and in the process creating those dimensions of space and time which will ultimately form into and be recognized as that thing in the back of its eyes.

Walking out of Central Park and south on Fifth Avenue, I recall the visual cliff experiment. Developmental psychologist Eleanor J. Gibson et al. observed crawling infants avoided and became distressed at the prospect of traveling across a large plate of glass placed across two tabletops. None of the infants had the time to learn through life experience that the distance from the plate of glass to the floor below is a situation to be avoided. The dimensions of space and time definitely seem to be present and dominate the perceptions guiding the behavior of these early human cognitions. Kant's idea of space and time being intrinsic to human cognition seems credible here.

The particulars to the conversation of a philosopher I'd read in a book come to mind. I forget who said what and when but the philosopher proposed a scenario where supposing someone was born without the faculties of the five senses. This person is born totally blind, completely deaf, without the capacity to smell the fragrance of a rose or taste the sweetness of honey, nor can this person feel the pain of the pin prick or the joy of the tickle. Having been born this way, this person is then fed, clothed, and basically cared for and kept alive by others for twenty years. The question the philosopher asked was, after this person has lived for twenty years with no stimulus from the outside world, would such a person have a thought in his head? If so, how did that thought get there?

I've put some thought to the question and I would tend to think such a twenty year old person has not yet had a single thought in his head. If the five senses of this person has not registered a single sensation into its brain, and thus this person does not have any fuel for recollections, then its difficult for me to imagine what the substance of the thought this person would be. This person has no fuel in its memory banks to start the fire for a single imaginative thought. The capacity to generate the sentient state exists within this person but this person's sentient state of mind has not yet had anything fed to it which can then be used to create an actual thought.

I like Kant for his recognition of the simple concepts of space and time and the role they play to form cognition. My thoughts seem to more easily expound upon the little bits of Kantian ideas I have managed to learn and understand.

I remind myself of the Koala bear and the Panda bear, and how they seem to be addicted to the eucalyptus leaf and bamboo stalk. With their low body metabolisms they're perfect creature candidates to verify the joyful stimulus and response statements I put forth within the treatise.

I think God wants me to be like this, and to be thinking along these lines. God, I sure do hope so.

Sometimes I think I should be doing something else. What that something else I think I should be doing is I don't know. Just another spurious insecurity that wants my attention for a while. A feeling of insecurity is what I am now instead of whatever else it is I should be doing. I probably should just accept it as the way it's going to be, and carry on, ... wayward son.

I don't know. I just don't know what to do some times with the treatise and everything.

I turn to read the block of letters protruding from reflections on polished bronze metal.

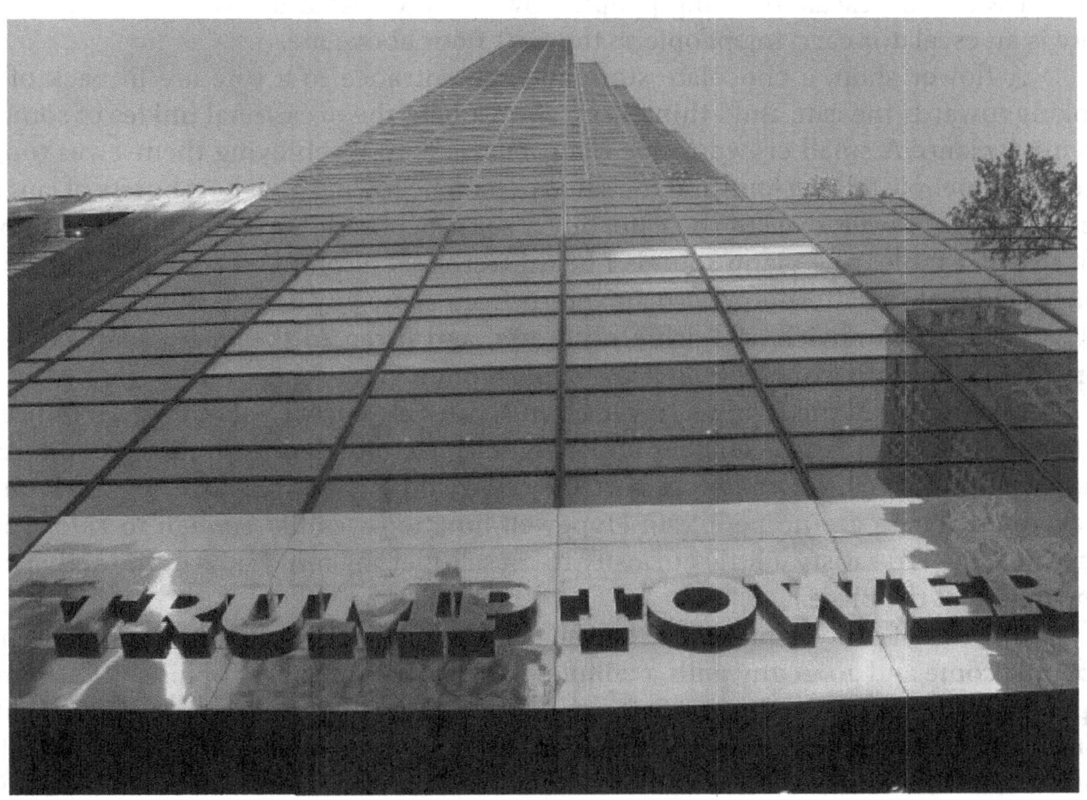

Well, ... howdy-do!

I step to the entrance and thinking a destination from one of my fares hadn't brought me to at least have passed by and then to have seen this place yet. I push the revolving door and amble on inside.

Wide open space. Polished pink and brown, white-veined marble rock covers the floor. The marble slabs rise from the floor and half way up the walls of the lobby. An incline of the floor brings me towards the middle of the lobby. A doorman stands at a podium and the doors to a passageway on my left. I step towards a display cabinet on the right side of the lobby.

The Donald has his own brand of quality shirts, ties, and handkerchiefs inside the cabinet. Watches and pen and pencil sets. His book, *The Art of the Deal*, is on a shelf inside the cabinet. I want to buy the book but right now I don't want something in my hands all the time as I'm walking around. I'm gonna buy the book, but not at this moment.

It's chilly in the lobby. They have the air conditioner turned way up, being a little warm outside I suppose.

Water falling down a wall of red marble at the end of the lobby. Standing along a glass railing in front of the waterfall and I count four levels of open floor rising up alongside the waterfall. High intensity lights recessed into the marble shine into the waves of water cascading down. Looking down from the railing the lower level is an open area containing twenty, thirty tables and chairs arranged in no particular order. A couple of people are unlocking sliding glass doors along the wall near the tables and chairs, and I imagine a restaurant situated down on the lower level.

I watch an escalator bring people down to the restaurant one floor below, and there is an escalator carrying people to the next floor above me.

A flower shop, a chocolate store and the entrance to a cafe are in back of me. Looking towards the cafe and I think I can almost hear the occasional tinkles of someone playing a piano. A small crowd inside the cafe seems to be enjoying themselves too, for sure. I hear people talking loud and the same person bellowing out short bursts of laughter every so often. I walk over to the cafe, buy a roast beef sandwich and take a cushioned sofa seat at a table. The piano sounds I heard were real. From the brochure lying on the table I read that the afternoon performance is from some guy named Billy Joel.

I eat the sandwich and drink my water, and listen to the Piano Man tickle the ivory. Before I get up from here I'd like a cup of coffee.

My interest in this Trump Tower extends not only because of that guy and that day at the Hopewell Inn. Fifth Avenue is upper-middle class, lower-upper class. People inside limousines are? Well, for the most part they're wealthy if nothing else is extraordinary about them. There are no people in Hopewell Junction wealthy enough to ride around in a limousine. To satisfy a little curiosity to myself I let my mind take in the activity and atmosphere of the place.

The cup of coffee is black with two sugars and I sit back down to watch the assembly of people come and go. A guy pulls a billfold from the breast pocket of his suit. A number of people wear sunglasses inside. Suit and ties for the men, and slacks or skirts, with a blouse under a type of dress jacket seems to be upon the female guests. The capitalist's uniforms, I think to myself. I imagine most people here must possess a considerable sum of money or they wouldn't be here. Just a plain, simple deduction.

The atmosphere of the well-to-do, together with a congeniality, an attentiveness amongst the folk here that isn't necessarily found in Hopewell Junction. The functionality of the place, an efficiency, I don't know ... something I couldn't have noticed or gleaned from a movie or television episode.

National Geographic would objectively portray the world of upper-middle, lower-upper class Westerners in an article, and in one sense portrayed in a scene as they're coming and going around me now ... I remember Moms once say, "*The best way to get people to do things is with money.*" I suppose it's true.

More people seem to use the lobby to get to where they're going, and not many people are using the escalators to the upper floors. I've finished my coffee and step over to the escalator for a ride up.

Stepping up the escalator steps and I see no people on the second floor. Standing along the plate glass railing on this floor and the water splashes sparkling water droplets through the air and down upon the plants on the restaurant floor. My hands rub the brass metal tube bannister topping the plates of glass. A family of two young girls and an older boy ride up the escalator. I'll have good views of the waterfall once I'm standing high up upon the top walkway.

I follow behind the couple and their children who immediately stepped off and then upon the next escalator. I think where I am now is not an egress for people who own residential units in the Trump Tower. Perhaps that doorman I first saw down in the lobby is where residents of the Trump Tower would enter or exit?

The family steps off and away from the escalator. I step off. The walkway is similar to the walkway one floor below. Dark glass windows and doors along the walkway. No other people up here and I step to the last escalator and ride while stepping my way up.

Paper has been rolled out on top of the marble floor along one roped off section of the walkway. Paint brushes and rollers, a ladder and paint cans lie on a cloth tarp. I step to locked glass doors leading to an outdoor patio. A sign on the patio says it's a Public Garden. Several chairs and tables outside are covered in plastic wrap as if recently shipped and uncrated.

A section of walkway extends across and directly in front of the waterfall. Five, six feet above the walkway and the water begins spilling over the top of the marble wall. People are moving about five stories straight down below from where I stand. The family has joined me to stand in front of the waterfall.

Stepping towards the ninety degree turn in the walkway and I hear people talking inside a vestibule. The sounds of children talking and laughing and their voices come from behind a row of doors inside the vestibule.

I step inside and in front of four gymnasium doors. Each door have waist level, long bar-rod handles to open the doors with. The voices I hear are on the other side of the doors and so I pull to unleash a portion of masking tape and paper, and then pull a small section of paper away from one door's rectangular pane of glass.

Good Lordy Lord ...

I'm looking at maybe a dozen or two little girls ... with leotards on. Grouped in three's or four's they're warming up, doing ports de bras, plies, and arabesques. Some girls sit on the floor together, chatting. From as many as I'm able to see through the small angle of paper I've folded up and away from the glass, the youngest girl is maybe five or six years old, the oldest maybe twelve or thirteen. I watch one group supporting each other for attitude exercises *a la barre,* minus a real bar.

Twenty, thirty-seconds of this and I'm beginning to feel a little ruddy about what I'm doing: hiding behind a door and peeking at some kids. They're cute though and it's fun to watch them. The way they're acting all by themselves. They're little girls that want to be...? Pretty. They want to be attractive and are doing what they're doing now wanting others to think of them so too.

It's difficult to find the want and the will to take myself away from behind the door until one of the kids walks towards me and turns to place her backside a foot or two from the door. She slowly declines, stretching and turning her legs out to each side as she brings herself down upon the mat. Positioned with her legs extended to her sides for a moment or two, she then brings herself to stand upright. I'm watching her go through the couple of seconds of finger motions that peel the fabric of her leotard out from between and then back around her little glutes, and to have me realize at this moment I am an uninvited guest to this private show going on. I think it's time for me to do a scad-doodle on out of here.

Wow, I think to myself somewhere as I step back down all the escalators and walk back inside the lobby.

I take notice of the restaurant on the lower level, and maybe I'll get another cup of coffee at the first deli I find outside.

"Taxi?" I shake my head with a wave of the hand. "No, thanks."

The flow of vehicles cascades in packs down Fifth Avenue. People, so many people in one place. Some walking alone. Others conversing with another as we all stroll along, sharing the sidewalk together.

Places to go, people to see, things to do. In one quick swoop I suppose that about sums up an aspect of New York.

Half a block's distance and for a second there I have to laugh with myself. I stop and turn around to look up at the Trump Tower. The smooth black zigzagged rectangular structure jutting up into the sky is totally cool. The waterfall and the shops, boutiques, the gilded ornaments, the opulent marble stone decorating to titillate the eye. Recalling those girls on the top walkway and I have to smile at it all. I wasn't prepared and expecting to see a room full of practicing ballerinas right at that moment is all. I'm sure it'll make the best part of the day.

Thanks, Jesus. That was cool, I consciously proclaim and turn to walk along the sidewalk. Quite exuberant I am now. He already knows how thrilled I am at the moment so I don't feel a need to extend the thought too much. If I feel it, he probably feels it too.

I believe my mind's thoughts and feelings have to always be known and are instantly recognized and uninterrupted to The Creator as they are happening. In 'real time,' as they say. I'm naturally and always in a constant state of communion with God. A steady, perpetually flowing state of prayer is my mind, and I suppose my thoughts to be a prayer that God occasionally and subtly dots on, too.

As I've come to know more about this relationship I have with God, by focusing my thoughts to a particular matter and to converse as if prayerfully speaking to The Creator about the matter, this seems tacky and quite unnecessary. I don't expect responses from my silent Partner even when on those occasions I do happen to have a few words of conversation with It. It's not a natural thing with me though, talking this way to God anymore.

It probably helped me in the past to do so. Focusing my thoughts upon a particular matter and carefully choosing my words of thought along whatever concerns me at the time, and knowing that the Creator is a member of the audience to these prayerful words. It was a habit of past but I don't often relate to the Creator in this manner now days, talking in my mind with so many words as if I was speaking to another person.

My intentions in mind at any given moment appear to be the mechanism where God has the governing influence over me. The presence of God isn't a dominant consideration during every trivial or important circumstance I find myself involved with during the course of the day, but when I do find myself acknowledging that an aspect of attention from the Creator is present, whether because I'm seeking Its presence or because I just happen to sense Its there and connected to whatever I find myself involved with at the moment, at these times I'll do a quick mental exercise using something intuitive as a tool to search for and encourage me to decide yes or no, right or wrong, to pause or go forward in the particular manner which I think God intends a circumstance to unfold as I'm actually involved with it.

For the most part prayer has evolved into an intuitive sense of searching my mind for notions about the details of any particular circumstance I happen to be involved with at the moment, without using clumsy, time consuming words as I'm relating to It. Not every moment of every circumstance do I intuitively seek some notion to ponder, or intuitively become aware of Its presence. Take me out of the ordinary though and I am never alone.

What the word prayer implies when used by others is not really an accurate description of my own personal repertoire with God these days. Packets of intuitive senses I suppose, rather than words are the forms of data and the type of communication that has developed between God and myself, I think.

I sometimes like to think this intuitive form of communication is a mode, a vehicle where after I have shaken off this mortal coil and all of my sense of and for this present world have been "put to sleep," I will awaken with this intuitive sense as an aspect of my spirit, and I'll use this intuitive sense to begin to recognize myself in the ether of heaven. The thoughts I have describing the beginning of my second and eternal life draws parallels from the passages retelling the incident of Jesus calling his friend Lazarus back to life after Lazarus lay dead in a tomb for four days.

Jesus performed the miracle upon Lazarus at a particular place on Earth, at one particular moment. I tend to think from all references of miracles performed by Jesus, the actual mechanism for causing a miracle to occur was through the mental thoughts and intentions of Jesus and not so much from any specific set of physical acts he performed or any particular set of vocal utterances he'd spoken. I think Jesus deliberately intended to leave no doubt in the minds of many of the witnesses to his miracles that he himself is responsible for causing what happens, so I imagine he would do any number of things to bring attention to himself before he would then cause the actual thoughts that were necessary to initiate a particular miracle to occur. The specific mechanism responsible for enabling Lazarus to rise and walk out of the tomb that day probably came from the intentions behind the mental thoughts of Jesus.

Eventually after my physical death Jesus intends to bring me to awaken from the sleep of death, and then in some way have me become conscious of myself again. I have to imagine whatever is after death is a more spiritual type of existence, without a physical body, so I cannot hear or see things. I cannot smell or feel the familiar sensations of pain or joy at any given moment. In some way or form or manner Jesus will wake me up a little bit, and being a spirit I imagine the first type of activities I will perform upon waking will be to bring a state of wonder upon myself. I can imagine asking and acknowledging myself with simple acts of thought, such as, *Hello?*

If I perform simple acts of thought I'll realize to myself I am thinking, and I will then recognize myself by acknowledging any type of thoughts I initiate.

During this early stage I imagine Jesus nurturing my embryonic spirit of thoughts by introducing familiar things I had known in the former life. I can only imagine that Jesus is doing something to egg me on and eventually have me wanting and desiring a more substantive and active form of existence than the ethereal dreamlike, spirit-state of existence God has deliberately, temporarily confined me to.

I have given thought to the notion of heaven as a place where Jesus has my palace already constructed. With a banquet table already prepared and with everything imaginable already in existence, heaven is a place to pick and choose and to come and go as one pleases. The only thing missing before my own big party begins is me. From my readings of the Bible the hand doesn't fit the glove by thinking like this.

I like to think of an embryonic, awakening spirit-state similar to a dream I once had while I was sleeping.

I'm maybe seven, eight years old and this dream opens with a view as I'm watching everything occur from behind the handlebars of my bike. I feel myself pumping my feet down on the pedals. My legs go round and around. Standing up or sitting down and the asphalt of Cady Lane is always rolling up and then under the handlebars in front of me. Single trees on each side of the road and the green grass of front yards pass by. I'll sometimes look to either side of the road, and I recognize a familiar house of the neighborhood and where I am with each new and different view of a neighbor's house or front yard I ride alongside of.

These views I have of single trees along the side of road, and the different driveways and front yards of any houses I'll look directly at or catch out of the corners of my eyes, this dream is a view of everything in front of me and to my sides moving eventually behind me as I continue to roll the bike down the road.

I like to ride my bike and this pleasant sense and state of mind is with me now. A comfortable sense of being where I am with the motion of me on the bike and the trees and houses moving along the side of the road to disappear behind me, it's fun.

I'm approaching the end of Cady Lane, noticing the thick forest of trees in the swamp along the far side of Kent Road. A notion I'll be turning onto Kent Road presents itself to me. Something that is a part of this dream is telling me to turn left, and that I am going to be turning left when I reach the end of Cady Lane. I feel myself moving my legs round and around as they pedal the bike forward, and I watch the asphalt of Cady Lane grow shorter and shorter in front of me. Something wants my attention now as I ready myself to turn left ...

I'm almost starting to watch myself begin the turn. I can almost feel and sense myself leaning into the turn—and several quick picture images of me pedaling up the steep hill that'll be coming up along Kent Road appear, and then a second set of picture image scenes of nearby Lake Oniad appear for me to view for a moment.

Starting to lean myself to the left and almost onto Kent Road I hear myself say to this something in the dream, *I don't want to go left. I want to turn right.* I feel the determination in my voice as I hear myself say the words a second time, *I don't want to turn left.*

I straighten up from the lean of the left-hand turn I was going into and watch my hands and arms turn the handlebars as I lean the bike up and over to my right, and with the view of passing shrubs along the far shoulder of the road there's also a moving line of trees and then the long line of Kent Road asphalt in the direction towards Lake Oniad appears in front of me.

A sense of surprise is with me as I finish the turn and bring the bike balanced upright. I feel self-conscious about what I'm doing and where I am. I stand up and feel my legs pushing each foot down hard on the pedals of the bike. I watch the asphalt of Kent Road quickly moving up in front of me.

I hear myself thinking, *I just turned right.*

I try to focus upon anything as far down the long length of Kent Road in front of me as I can, and while I'm peering down the road and attempting to focus on things I also feel like I just did something and then broke something. Something is not right. I want to stop the bike and I slow down to do so.

I stop the bike, get off and stand along the side of the road. My left hand holds the handlebars. My right hand has a grip to the back of the banana seat. A sense of something has happened and it's something not right. I'm looking forward at the scattering of brown leaves on the green grass of some guy's front lawn. I look straight up and into the tree tops and watch the dark colored leaves moving and waving around on the branches above. I look back down and over towards my left. A short distance away Fenmore Drive ends to join with Kent Road. I'm looking at the intersection of Fenmore and Kent and I hear myself say, *I'm in a dream.*

Those words I heard myself say made me more self-conscious or something because I'm now not in the back of my eyes looking towards the intersection of Fenmore and Kent, I'm now looking at myself from above and to the left, maybe from a ten foot distance I'm watching myself standing alongside my bike..., I'm standing there with my hands on the handlebars and the seat of my bike, and I'm looking at something over to my left.

I hear myself say, *I know I'm dreaming..., I know it.*

After saying and hearing those words, still watching myself standing with my bike, I hear myself say a third time the words, *I'm in a dream,* and I am now fully and totally conscious of myself behind my eyes. My attention is complete. I'm almost awake. I'm aware of myself while realizing anything happening each moment is happening inside of a dream. I realize I was the recent voice that I had just heard and that had just finished speaking the words, *I'm in a dream.* Each passing moment is another realization that I'm experiencing myself inside of a dream. I am so self-conscious of my self as I'm watching myself stand beside my bike...

A sense of wonder and curiosity come to me..., I want to know what I am as I watch myself standing over there. *What is this dream I am inside of ...* and that I'm watching myself with..., *what is this all about?*

I'm calm. I'm in wonder ... to have that view of the intersection of Fenmore and Kent appear in my eyes as before. I'm standing on my feet and looking over at the intersection to my left. I feel my fingers and hand as it grips around the handlebar. My other hand is touching down upon the seat of the bike, again. I am inside of a dream is the only and constant notion and realization as I look away from the intersection of Fenmore and Kent, turning myself with a footstep or two to look all the way down the long, tree-lined straight section of Kent Road leading towards Lake Oniad. I stand there holding the bike upright and all I want to do now is to experience each moment as it happens to me. I must have become too self-conscious sometime during the next part of the dream.

I look at and begin to stare at my hand holding the handlebars. I'm staring at my hand intently. I want to really feel the hand I'm looking at because I really can't feel that hand I'm looking at. I can't connect seeing it and feeling it at the same time.

I look up. Again to focus as far down the length of Kent Road as I can, and as I attempt to focus upon and then to distinguish any specific thing that may be all the way down there at the end of the road, I also now want to turn my attention inward. What is in back of this view of Kent Road I have in my eyes? I know in back of my eyes is where my mind is and where dreams happen. My attention is backing out and away from the view of Kent Road in my eyes, and my view turns dark as I'm trying to look inside myself as I'm looking at Kent Road. The thing in back of my eyes and my attention become one, and I feel myself open my eyes. I'm quickly making sense of the daylight on the dark lines of leafless tree branches outside my bedroom window. Beyond these tree branches the blurry, bright green lawn grass rises up with the steep hill of Lawlor's front yard. I pick my head up from the pillow and think, *that was the coolest dream...*

Never again have I performed a series of deliberate acts or thoughts while inside of a dream. All dreams either have me as a spectator or a participant to the events that occur and I have no control over the course of events. After that Cady Lane dream for a couple nights I would lay in bed and try to think of what I could do while I'm dreaming to do what I did within that Cady Lane dream. Trying as I did I never came up with even one idea. To this day the problem is once I'm asleep and a dream is unfolding I can't find a way to remember to try to do what I want to do before I fall asleep. Once I'm asleep the dream takes over and does what it wants.

My Cady Lane dream ended with me confined within a pensive, wondering frame of mind. Many New Testament verses have me believing Jesus will deliberately cause me to awaken, and then to become aware of myself, eventually to have me recognize his presence is somehow also involved with any of my thoughts at these moments too.

I may want to stay as I am now, to stay as an eternal spirit type of thought-existence, as if I were dreaming ... for all eternity. I may eventually begin to want to be and exist as something more, and I imagine my want for a more perfect physical body similar to what Jesus had given me before I died would not be too preposterous a proposition. I wouldn't be surprised to find myself wanting and then creating a familiar environment similar to what Jesus had me living within while I was on earth. When Jesus and I have finished creating and perfecting these first wants and desires for myself, I do have a few other things I'll want to do next.

"Jesus, what was the purpose of the dinosaurs for millions of years?" I'll have to ask. What was happening when it was decided that the nipples were to go on men, too?

I can imagine Jesus having his own wants and desires. He enjoys creating juicy, tangy-tasting red tomatoes he then carries inside a pouch as He walks along a favorite street or path which leads him to a beautiful palace beside a lake or ocean shoreline. Alone or with company Jesus likes to lay on the beach sand, eating tomatoes while watching another wonderful sunrise and sunset occur.

I like to think one reward of a Christian will be the possession of this power of the will to create whatever one could possibly imagine, and being able to do so for all eternity. All Christians are capable of creating their own little worlds, their own large or small dwelling places in heaven.

My treatise implies universal answers as opposed to anyone's particular answers for the questions of why good is good, and why evil is evil. One purpose for my own Christian life seems towards realizing and appreciating the Creator's sense of good and evil that It has defined to this world. My experiences on earth will undoubtedly temper the future thoughts I'll have and the judgments I'll make whenever I wish for something later on. I imagine Christians will give a variety of eternal companionships to the otherwise lonely but powerful Creator God in this way too.

I really cannot think of other more important or thrilling things for me to do for an eternity. I'm sure while I'm in heaven I will be in the habit of thanking God, having anything I could imagine.

I am unorthodox. I read nothing from any Christian denomination that talks like this. Actions like bowing my head, genuflecting, making the sign of the cross, when I think of the magnitude, the omniscience of God, such behavior serves no purpose other than for a personal, perhaps serving as a publicly acknowledged gesture of respect, and I want to think The Creator couldn't possibly care whether I do or don't do such things. If I'm on my knees or resting on a chair I can relate to Its Presence any time I want, and one posture is not noticed or respected more than another in the eyes and mind of God.

I would tend to think religious rituals have to be good for some people's spiritual life, for them to know and become intimate with the Creator, especially if that is what It wants for some people. Though if I have no desire to become part of religious rituals, at this point of time in my life I have to think God wants it to be that way with me. Later on, things may change in this regard. They may not change, too.

Jesus is my buddy Pal, my true Companion, my lifelong Friend, and by knowing of Jesus as I think I do my relationship to God has been built less on fear than on a desire to make It happy and honored to have chosen me for whatever purpose It has on Its Mind. I'll believe God and Jesus want me to watch real ballerinas during my first week in New York.

I walk off Fourth Avenue, stepping onto the meridian of Astor Place, and then continue south along Lafayette Street.

Gotta be. Why else did I see those kids up there like that then for?

I ponder the question..., and I can't come up with a reason why I saw them up there like that..., and maybe I'll never know because it doesn't matter if I know or not.

If Jesus is employing me to do something in the world, and if I am on a mission of some kind then he knows my future concerning whatever these events will be. I do accept the notion of him nudging me back and forth, into and out of some event before I get involved within the moment. Ultimately he caused and set up the circumstances that put me up there on those floors inside the Trump Tower to see what I did.

At East Houston Street I climb aboard a westbound M21 bus and make myself comfortable. As the bus rolls along I look out the window … and I think I've realized a simple reason for why I saw all those kids up there like I did. Because Jesus wants me to quickly start out in New York with a favorable light towards it, as favorable as can be gleaned from the act of watching a troupe of ballerina's practice by themselves.

I like driving a taxi. Six months of working and living in New York and I wake up each day glad to be here. I love be-bopping all around the five boroughs.

It's a thrill to be handed ten, fifteen dollars after driving someone for twenty minutes, half an hour to La Guardia Airport. A Manhattan fare will hand me thirty, thirty-five dollars at the end of a ride to Kennedy Airport. Two or three times a day if someone does this and I feel great. A late night, early morning fare will want to travel twenty some odd miles outside the city into New Jersey or Connecticut and this is another fare to pocket thirty-five, forty dollars with. At two, three o'clock in the morning traffic is light on all the major arteries into and out of the city, and I make for excellent time going to and coming back from these out-of-town destinations. Being paid so much for doing so little amazes me. I'm not used to it.

Twelve hour shifts seem like a long time to drive a taxi, six days a week, but I'm in a habit to show up early at the dispatcher's office hoping to get a cab maybe to take out half an hour early. Some times I can do this and sometimes I can't. Perhaps a time will come when all this enthusiasm I have will wear off. Right now though the city is invigorating and chock full of interesting things to see and do.

During these last few months I went to see Jerry Jeff Walker at the Lone Star Café. Jerry drinks from a whiskey bottle while playing an acoustic guitar on stage, and doing so until he can't or doesn't want to play anymore. After sitting on a stool for an hour and a half and while starting into another song Jerry stopped strumming the guitar. He stood up and then waved to us in the audience as he took himself offstage. No encore.

I went to a vocal presentation of an opera entitled *Andromeda Liberata* in the *Winter Gardens* at the World Trade Center. The opera was intended as a teaser for the full, live performance at Lincoln Center, and they advertised the opera as a recently discovered work of Antonio Vivaldi.

I make my way inside the pavilion to the *Winter Gardens* and to the rows of folding metal chairs at the front of the stage. I take a seat and psyche myself out a little bit, anticipating what I'm about to hear. I imagine I'll be listening to the vocal acrobatics of men and women who will sometimes sing as if screaming at each other in French or Italian. Reading the pamphlet and I find the opera is based on Greek myth. It is a *serenata* scored for five voices and an orchestra of trumpets, horns, oboes, strings, and continuo.

I'll be judging this performance, and I'll be using the criterion of the five basic sections to the generic Rock band to do so: the vocal, bass, rhythm, lead, and percussion sections. I don't believe one can appreciate quality rock music if such a person cannot distinguish and then understand who is responsible for the sound from these five components of a rock band they happen to be listening to.

It was a toss up with Joan Jett, and I choose to wear my Black Sabbath concert T-shirt tonight.

The players of *Andromeda Liberata* walk onto the stage to sporadic applause. They set their instruments up and after being introduced the orchestra begins to play the first aria. With no amplification I realize the acoustics of the pavilion are responsible for the surprisingly loud musical sounds I'm hearing. Vocals for the most part are mellow and low keyed. Certain times vocals are briefly bouncing, flipping, and prancing about within that acrobatic style I expect from an operatic performance. Melodic inflections to syllables are pleasing to the ear. The female voice within a few of the compositions sound almost natural, as if it were the normal, natural vocalized sound of the female voice in speech…, and then Katerina Beranova began to sing the aria *Con Dolce Mormorio*, and the thought is clear. A pleasing set of sounds is created.

Katerina finishes the aria and I'm thinking how great it would be if God were to have created the human female to naturally, always talk and speak in conversation the way Katerina spoke and sung the words in that aria.

I imagine hearing the words put to melody as if Katerina had just sung them.

"Kurt, could you take out the garbage?"

"Kurt, go mow the lawn."

"Kurt, I think I love you."

Antonio Vivaldi and his friends composed a set of musical notes to bring out the best of the female voice with that *Con Dolce Mormorio* aria. For that one single aria alone I plunk down money for the double disc CD as I exit the place.

I splurged and bought myself a brunch of lobster and linguine in Little Italy one Tuesday afternoon. Perhaps I'm used to or wanted a larger meal and to have felt satiated after I left the place. I was still hungry, wanting a lot more juicy lobster meat and linguine to fill the belly with.

I went to CBGB's and saw a couple Grunge Gothic rock bands play. Four females made up the first band. Two females playing bass and lead guitar, the third and fourth females play percussion and electric keyboard. Introduced as *Svelte Sex Creatures*, they back up another four piece, all dude band called *Fusion Engine*.

One stanza of lyrics from the *Svelte Sex Creatures* stood out all night:

I felt his hand on top of mine / Put some meat on them bones, girl / Put some meat on them bones...

An amazing stage show! I never saw anything like those females. All four are at least six feet tall and thin in stature. Make-up has brought their faces to appear gaunt. It is one obviously very long flexible tube that will fluoresce different colors and intensities along different sections of its length as it travels through the four pairs of denim jeans, coiling around four suspender straps and then up into and out from all four long-sleeved, halfway buttoned-down flannel shirts of each *Svelte Sex Creature*. It's the same tube of light that connects to something behind each of the three guitar bodies. The tube connects to the bassist in the middle of the stage which then extends back behind her to connect with the drummer.

Vibrant colors of red and blue pulse from an arm and a leg of one *Svelte Sex Creature* at the same time another *Svelte Sex Creature's* shirt and pants glow a constant glossy reddish-pink color. Segment lengths of the tube can change colors rapidly while other lengths will stay with one or two colors for a time. One's legs are green while another's are red. A right arm is solid blue while the left arm pulsates a kaleidoscope of colors as the arm slashes through the chords of the guitar or beats a rhythm to the drum. Colors glowing soft or shining bright weave in and out of their clothing as they move around on stage. Whoever is running their stage show is attempting to synchronize the pulsing colors to the beat of the song they're playing at the moment. Their stage show is awesome, and totally cool! Totally loved it.

The drummer of the *Svelte Sex Creatures* especially caught my eye. The tube creates a circle of light around her neck and another circle crowns her head. Light balls of different colors spin in circles at different speeds round and around the circumference of her neck and skull. Cool to be watching her getting into some songs. Her arms flailing and bobbing her head around while she played those drums. A fantastic light show from the *Svelte Sex Creatures...*! Absolutely.

I stopped going out and doing stuff like this. Something just doesn't feel right entertaining myself..., as much and as often as I do, which isn't often but it's often enough. I've told myself at some later time, for sure I'll do things like this. Maybe really hit the town big time after I've done what I want to do. Once I'm set up better I'll reward myself to all the city has to offer. I just don't feel like sitting in some establishment and listening or eating, ... and I don't have to watch the movie a third time that day..., knowing what I'm going to do now.

Seated in the middle of the theater as the big screen in front of me portrays the electrical machinations from a Model 101, T-800 series cognitive computer imprinting data across it's cyborg eyes.

Good Lord..., and wow. Epiphanic, and for the rest of the day and as I drive around that night I am enthralled with thoughts of this movie.

This can be a reality in my lifetime..., and to think the treatise can play an important role causing the existence of the first of future cyborgs? The mathematical framework outlined inside my treatise is a perfect template to begin designing a computer system mimicking the human cognitive processes. I must try to make this a reality.

Thoughts of collaborating with others on this and I realize there already are a certain number of us already in possession of what my treatise is about. There always have been people who took my treatise seriously.

For several days I have to think. I must come to terms with where I've led my life up to at this point. The treatise has gone where and to whom? A reevaluation of recent world events is needed, and to wonder why things have turned out the way they did.

The Soviet Union has recently installed a former KGB chief, Yuri Andropov as General Secretary, which doesn't bode too well if one is hoping for a more liberal, younger group of officials to rise to power in the future Soviet Union. Pope John Paul II has been encouraging a grass root level type of dissent in Poland. There's a bishop Romero in Central America making headlines every so often. What dialog goes on behind closed doors between us and them?

I grew up and went to school having George Washington, Thomas Jefferson, Alexander Hamilton and James Madison, John Paul Jones, Alexander Graham Bell, and Thomas Alva Edison to read about and tell me more or less how this area of the world I live in came to be what it is, and how it developed over time, and to envision what this nation should and can become in the future.

I imagine myself a citizen in the Soviet Union and taught early on in my life the significant people and epochs that shaped the fifteen hundred year history of the very large area I live in, and of course it's only a matter of time before I form and develop my own personal, critical impressions of the world, of other people, and of my national character as I learn more of the details to those people and epochs.

It's probably not that Ronald Reagan and Margaret Thatcher and their crews can't talk to these guys in the Soviet Union. It's the pessimism, the cynical heart and mind that allows them to believe that they know better and that history has done all the talking that needs to be done and now is the time to stop learning and start doing.

One system of government, their political order will identify and prevent any future social conditions to crop up causing the calamities of the past. One government to exist providing basic economic marketing and law enforcement entities which function to structure and give definition to the order of civil life. Do I know? I think so. If people keep talking eventually ten, twenty-thousand nuclear tipped ballistic missiles do not have to be offensively directed towards each other.

Either Jesus did do miracles and he circumvented the laws of Nature by walking on water, raising Lazarus from the dead and resurrecting himself after crucifixion, or he didn't cause these things to happen. Presenting a case for the validity of all the worlds religions in such a black and white fashion has impressed no one but me.

If Jesus did not do miracles then the New Testament was probably just a fabrication by a group of disgruntled Jews who most likely weren't getting their way or weren't being recognized maybe as much as they thought and felt they should be by the populous, and to get some attention to themselves they concocted a story on par with a William Shakespeare. Throughout recorded history and within every culture there have always been good people brought into the public spotlight, and if Jesus is just another one of these type of people than we all should add Jesus and his words to the list that includes all the other good people of the world who've come around preaching benevolence to their fellow man.

Though if Jesus had caused the forces of Nature to become subservient to his volition then Jesus is the Big Guy, the Dude. If Jesus actually did indeed repeatedly perform those type of acts that were written in that book? Then absolutely and without a doubt Jesus is a special type of model to humankind from the creative force I refer to as God. God can do anything and so if some people do not realize Jesus being It, at that moment God deliberately does not want them to realize Jesus being It and then this line of thought should not be of too much concern to me. As far as I am concerned towards another's beliefs, if Jesus did those miracles, personally I could not care what any other religion says or believes important towards the true definition and understanding of what the Mind and Intentions of the Creator God are. If Jesus did in reality actually do miracles then all the other religions practiced on the earth today and in the past are..., were...?

What would they be then?

I cannot recall exactly when I first realized I was privileged to have been born and to live the first quarter of my life in the northeastern region of the United States of America, and to have done so within the last half of the twentieth century. A sense of privilege with me probably came as the result of afterthought, realizing that I have never encountered a single destructive earthquake while I grew up. Neither tsunamis, tornado, hurricane or typhoon, a major destructive flood or mudslide came near me either. I do not wake up every day in some dry, hot desolate corner of the earth or on the top of some freezing cold piece of ice as I venture my way through life. So far so good. Thanks.

The books I'd read, the television or radio programs I'd watch and listen to in the past were the best vehicles to so many different places and situations and to sources of information. I would have had less enthusiasm or the opportunity to access and then to engage my mind with if I happened to live in another time and or another place in the world. I never recall in the past ever once seriously wishing that I was someone else, or to wish I could've been born within another part of the world and to take me out of this one I'm presently living in. I know for various reasons other people do wish and long for such things. My world was a great platform to live my life within. Again I must give a hearty and sincere, "Thank you very much."

After discovering the things of the treatise I've changed. I rarely watch television or listen to records or read a fiction book for pleasure anymore. I only skim the sections of any newspaper or magazine I happen to have in my possession at any time. I used to read at least a little bit of everything inside a magazine or newspaper I'd pick up, though now days I don't bother reading into the details of most news stories. I have little desire to read or watch TV or listen to music for two or three hours at a time anymore. No one talks about anything I'm really interested in either. I listen to the morning and evening news maybe once or two, three times a week, ...

I don't know. I liken any book's fictional story as if I'm floating on the back of a bumblebee through a patch of daisies, and I start to but don't ever seem to finish reading any of the books of fiction I have happened to pick up over the last few months. I sense moments of time passing as I read the words of a page, an author contriving to induce me into some state of mind about something and I simply don't care after a while what the words of the book are trying to do to me.

Those times of reading the Bible and then reflecting upon an interesting set of passages, or pondering upon some idea I may have just come up with, the enthusiasm I once had to do this is now gone. I'll see the Bible lying under the bed and feel obligated in some way to read it, if only for a while, but eventually I end up feeling and telling myself what more can I do or derive from reading the Bible than I've already done? I'll pick up and read the Bible now infrequently, for recreation maybe on a Sunday if I see it there and if I'm so inclined to do so. Every now and then I do go in there to clarify something that may stay on my mind for a length of time.

The truth is there are still times and moments where I'll end up in thought to feel that the idea of Jesus doing miracles a long time ago is like I'm reading of someone floating on the back of a bumblebee through a patch of daisies, with a whole lot of interesting, didactic la-la-la, la-te-da's spicing up the passages to the story too. I know these type of thoughts about Jesus are not of my own volition, and I entertain them only till I've begun to sense that I've lost that attitude..., that attitude and that sense that I know.

So many questions and attitudes about my life have answers and purposeful meaning if a Creator exists as first cause for everything. Over the years I've put together a fairly simple system of thought in an attempt to prove the existence of the Creative God. I return to it every now and then and review it, especially when certain types of news reports are made public and illuminate the subject.

I am totally impressed with our National Aeronautic and Space Administration and the European Space Agency. The recent Cosmic Background Exploration satellite that confirmed and detailed the cosmic background radiation of the universe first detected and discovered in 1964 by Arno Penzias and Robert Wilson of Bell Laboratories. What a wonderful and beautiful machine the Hubble Space Telescope is! I never owned a telescope though I'm stunned and awed while looking at all those beautiful, fascinating pictures. The organization of people that brought the Hubble Space Telescope into existence is a Western treasure, an absolute gold mine. I am totally proud to be a citizen of a nation that thinks and taxes its citizenry in pursuit of the want to do stuff like this.

These and other science projects have confirmed an accelerating expansion to the universe and give credence to the Big Bang theory for an origin and beginning to the universe. More information such as what the COBE satellite and the Hubble Space Telescope have produced needs to be forthcoming in the future though as I've come to the conclusion that the existence of a Creative Force cannot be determined given our present understanding of the nature of space and time. I gave it my best shot though.

My attempt to prove the existence of a Creator God went along the following lines:

Things either exist or they do not, I thought to myself one day. *Something that does not exist cannot cause some other thing to exist. Only things that exist can cause other things to exist.*

Furthering this train of thought to myself, ... *some "thing" had to have caused the universe to exist. Some "thing" had to have done so because something that does not exist could not have done so. Things either exist or they do not exist. If the one thing isn't responsible than the other thing must be.*

With these simple inferences to form a hypothetical I began my own quest to think through and define an informal proof for a definition of the existence of a Creator.

Interesting ideas developed as I began to clarify key words.

Existant is not a word in the dictionary. I find I'm using the term whenever I'm in thought and implying something from either or both realms of Introvertive mind or Extrovertive physical reality. Existant brings the suffix-ant implying the agency of existence without explicitly referring which of the two realms the subject originates or exists from. The statement *All thoughts in her mind are existant* implies the thoughts to be the subject and are distinct objects of reality. The statement *All thoughts in her mind are in existence* doesn't bring the clear sense of distinction I want to the word *thoughts* because existence commonly refers to tangible, physical objects. Once I thought of and continued to use the word existant regarding both the physical and cerebral entities, it stuck.

Whether something is intangible and derives its substance for existence from within the thoughts of someone's mind, or the substance of the object is tangible and comprises mass and occupies three dimensional space, every thing in the universe can be labeled into a first category of 'Things That Exist,' and or into a second category of 'Things That Do Not Exist.'

The thought within someone's mind, such as a rock, is something that exists. The thought exists in a different manner than an actual physical rock but in the total sphere of things someone's visual thought of a rock, and the actual rock are existant as 'things.' Someone's thought of pink elephants exists only in the mind of the person thinking of such a thing; there does not exist generic pink elephants outside of mind's realm.

To differentiate the two categories of introversion and extroversion, physicists conduct experiments to understand the properties of light, and observe light behaving as both a wave and as a particle. The introvertive mind cannot comprehend and finds it difficult to form a mental picture describing the reality of light existing with both properties of wave and particle. The (extrovertive) reality of the situation from a double slit experiment challenges the introvertive mind to conjure practical models for explanation. Albert Einstein also found it difficult to accept explanations of quantum phenomena that were not represented with mental pictures, though his objections were baseless given the probabilistic nature of quantum phenomenon.

I realize four sets or subcategories of existant things or entities from this line of thinking. Describing these four categories taxes my command of the English language.

A first category is for things which exist within both realms of introvertive mind and extrovertive reality. An example would be a declaration of truth that confirms entities from one's mind coincides with a particular set of events from physical reality. A second category is of things which exist in the realm of the mind but are not to be found existant in extrovertive reality. Little green men, mermaids, unicorns, and ideas such as *money doesn't grow on trees* are examples found in this second category. A third category are of things that exist in reality but are impossible for the mind to comprehend and to conceive a picture of. Quantum phenomena are examples that pertain to this category. I make mention to a fourth category of things that exist in neither introvertive mind nor extrovertive physical reality and as such are represented as the logical complement to a picture six or seven but incomprehensible for my mind to conceive the nature of.

The logical complement of a picture six? What is that?

With these four categories I have nothing else to consider alongside 'Things that exist' and 'Things that do not exist.' That is, when I conclude this train of thought by posing the question whether something that exists or something that does not exist is capable of causing something else to exist, someone could not propose another third category for consideration what may be responsible for causing things to exist.

The apples came from an apple tree, yes this is true. All things came from something else. Explaining the methods and systems which cause any one thing to come from another is not necessary. I only want the recognition and acceptance for the fact that whatever is causing the transformation of matter from one appearance to another requires there be an initial mass in which to perform transformation with. For any one thing to exist something else within the universe has to exist and transform its appearance to the other. Though I've heard reports to the contrary, the cause and effect maxim rings true: things do not pop out of thin air.

Whether inside the realms of introversion and or extroversion I propose the statement all things either exist or they do not exist, and I cannot recognize another third category to consider placing alongside these two categories of existence and nonexistence. I've exhausted this train of thought. Nothing of substance to further clarify these ideas seems to come to mind.

I began drawing simple Venn diagrams. I represent the Introvertive realm with a small circle and place this set of all Introverted things inside a larger circle as the subset of the Extrovertive realm. I look at this particular Venn diagram and with Introversion as a subset of Extroversion, a state of Truth exists when the particulars of thought from introversion correlates to corroborate relevant extroverted existence or activity. I also realize a hurried, plausible-sounding definition which describes what everyone commonly refers to as common sense now, too. I don't know enough to bring a rigorous mathematical method or procedure to verify these correlations and definitions within Introversion and Extroversion, and so they remain a future task at some later time.

The bridge spanning mind and matter, Introversion and Extroversion. The logical laws of mathematics and the observed order of particles of matter in the universe. There is a common denominator and I like to think Venn diagrams will someday bring unique perspective to the many discussions arising from the duality of mind and matter. I have not thought of anything, as of yet.

I place ideas within Venn diagrams and there are times I have the sense I'm looking through a portal and into another dimension. Simple relationships such as union, intersection, and complement describe a world of raw logic, relationships uncluttered with extraneous, superfluous things to consider relevant when thought of within the everyday, worldly context. I've rendered a number of simple and somewhat interesting relations with introversion and extroversion and the entities of pain, joy, love, hate, good and evil. Interesting to consider true the statement all human beings are capable of enjoying hateful, evil states of mind, or tolerating the painful but loving states of mind.

I drew Venn diagrams that resembled the clouds of electron orbitals of hydrogen and helium, but their appearance represented nothing mathematically. I'm loathe to disfigure or trivialize the intrinsic mathematical beauty of these Cartesian graphs. When I know more mathematics I'll be able to tinker with these graphs with confidence.

I think of how a Soldierian of Jesus would be represented as. His volitive intentions direct energy which temporarily circumvent and supersede a natural, physical order of events for particles of matter at any given moment. I imagine Jesus reaching up and touching the bleeding head of Malchus. Jesus creates a mental picture of an ear in his mind while his hand touches the lacerated skin. Within a second or two of time the blood stops running down the neck of Malchus ... skin forms into the shape of an ear..., and Malchus' rejuvenated ear functions like the ear that had been cut off...

Certain arrangements are interesting to look at and to ponder upon, and I was optimistic when I first began drawing them though Venn diagrams brought more a sense of entertainment than a practical system or model I would've liked to have seen emerge as time went on. I don't maintain an empirical basis to non-simple relations and too many inconsistencies develop. I didn't bring working trains of thought concluding to and unlocking the doors down hallways ... to reveal other secrets of the universe.

I move on. *Keep it simple* is the idea. I want to give more precise definitions to these concepts of existence and nonexistence, and thought to have all things inside categories of existence and nonexistence also labeled with cardinal numeral zero to represent the state or quality of nonexistence, and the cardinal numerals one, two, three and on to infinity representative of individual, unique states and qualities of existant things.

Infinity. I like to define the mathematical term infinity as a system or method that is repeatedly adding one to another term. Only when I considered a mathematical term *k* involved within a continuous process of simple addition to itself was I to realize the necessity for containing large and small numbers inside limits when a point or value to a sequence, sum, or function was desired. To think of a term undergoing a dynamic process of addition brings a complete definition to the idea of a large quantity increasing still larger.

The thought of employing zero and one to define existence and nonexistence seemed cool though when I began to think of worldly examples to qualify total, absolute and perfect nonexistence, I am soon to realize there is no one thing or place in the universe where absolutely nothing exists. There is always something contained inside every part of the universe, whether it be the stray hydrogen or helium atom crawling through the most distant voids of space and time, or the simple coordinate plots of height, width, and length which pinpoint any distinct volume within three dimensional space. In reality there is something contained inside every piece of real estate in the universe. No voids of absolutely nothing exist inside the space of this universe I am inside of. An absolute, ideal definition of zero has no corresponding counterpart in the physical world to map itself to. This was an odd realization to bring to mind and conclude with.

The cognitive process of thought to define some type of thing that doesn't exist defeats the ability to ideally define it. My thoughts give a form of existence to the idea of nonexistence I attempt to define. I don't know what steps to take to resolve the absurdity to this predicament.

I came across the same conundrum attempting to find practical examples for the ideal definition of the numeral one. The proton is considered the most stable particle of matter inside the universe. All the other elementary particles of the universe are known to degrade into some other type of thing. With a mass and charge of force that varies little over trillions of years time, protons are considered the most stable forms of matter. Because of its stability it is difficult to determine and know whether the proton may or may not ever decay into other states of matter. I would tend to believe the proton is only one of the most stable forms of matter known to science, and that it is not inherently stable and completely resistant to the forces of entropy. For me to think otherwise I would have to consider a number of objects as stable as the proton seems to be, and then within these particular half-dozen or so very stable family of objects determine the quality that exists within all these objects bestowing the characteristic of total, absolute stability. I would then in confidence state that there exists one thing in the universe that always was and always will be. I could then employ a numeral one and have an ideal definition of existence for an object inside the universe.

If there were ever to be found inside the universe an absolute one thing that always was and always will be, I would be inclined to think of this thing as one step away from a *first cause* to the universe.

A first cause for the existence of the universe...

The total energy inside the universe is a constant. No mechanical system can create to add or to destroy and subtract from this finite amount of energy inside this universe of ours. The total amount of energy in the universe always was and always will be a constant amount…, and so a force is the first cause which caused the universe to exist.

The Big Bang theory postulates the early universe as an infinitely small, dense point of mass. Thirteen billions years after the Big Bang the initial energy released transformed itself into all the forms of mass inside the universe. Every time I think this through I'm brought to a specific area of thought. I want to better understand the essence of the negative and positive electromotive forces carried by the electron and proton causing the observed attracting, repelling, and vibrating characteristics of the elementary particles. How and why do they do that? Even were I to bring an answer to myself with *'because God wants it that way,'* I still want to know the specifics for how It causes this to be the reality of the situation.

Both definitions of existence and nonexistence appear similar to the graphical representations of complex numbers used in mathematics. Setting an x axis to represent a range of qualities within the pain / joy realm. An y axis connotes qualities within a Preservation / Debilitation to Love / Hate realm, and the z axis will pertain to the dichotomy between nature's dual realms of mind and matter. These three axes create a framework to record the sentient state of biological cognition. A fourth parameter of time creates a dimension where individual x, y, z frameworks are portrayed in succession, as if frames to a cinematic movie. Each of these Soldierian snapshot pictures are a four dimensional reality of the situation. Each Soldierian immediately relegated to the past and rendered to memory while another framework is constructed.

Practical applications of the quadratic equation within a Soldierian graphic would be a beautiful thing.

I've devised fairly elaborate if incomplete definitions for the concepts of existence and nonexistence, and I'll use these definitions to contemplate upon whatever type of environment is outside this universe of ours. I can speculate and state with a little bit of certainty that,

Some force that exists either outside or inside this universe caused this universe of ours to exist. Employ whatever word one wants though the word force is sufficient to describe and recognize a specific thing to focus upon, and to state that some force or "thing" caused the universe to exist because I know that any thing that does not exist cannot have caused some other thing, such as the universe, to exist. Things either exist or they do not.

How can it be otherwise if there are only two categories of things to answer what could have caused the universe to exist?

Someday evidence will present itself giving more credence to show cause. Maybe evidence will never be forthcoming. Without a smoking gun I gave it my best shot.

Right now I want to design a cognitive computer. Designed from and using my treatise as a template of sorts. I enter the Queens Midtown Tunnel with a passenger to La Guardia airport, and as I do so I stew on the thought of putting the next ten, twenty, thirty years of my time and money pursuing this one goal.

How does this sit with me as I'm rolling through the tunnel?

Such thinking suits me just fine.

Thanks, Jesus. The Best! … for sure.

If I don't get a good seven, eight hours sleep and if I miss a couple hours of sleep three or four days in a row, driving can be a problem. I also have to watch the foods I eat. Otherwise I'll get tired, sleepy-eyed behind the wheel. Sometimes my eyelids are forcing themselves down when I'm driving, and I have to really fight the urge and keep them open as I'm barreling down some street or avenue.

I've pulled over at these times thinking I just need a nap for ten or twenty minutes. Parking the taxi on some side street and trying for a little sleep I'm never that tired to fall asleep. Maybe it's a lack of exercise too, I thought. I'm always just sitting for hours at a stretch. Any food in me, in combination with the vibrations of the car, hour after hour, maybe this makes me feel tired though not tired enough to fall asleep. I think that my brain sometimes just needs a more vital blood supply to refresh itself with, and I should bring some type of physical exertion to these situation.

I'll get out of the cab and take the time to walk or run around the block. Get the heart pumping into those tiny capillaries and really flush out those stale pockets of blood. It doesn't work. I don't know what it is but it's more of a nuisance than a hazard. I just want to slowly close my eyes sometimes as I'm sitting there driving. Lower and lower, the eyes seem so heavy. I think about maybe seeing a doctor if it continues, see what they say about such things.

I'm up and out the doors of the Jane West before noon and a hot tuna fish sandwich with a couple sour pickles is lunch on a park bench at Abingdon Square.

The IBM PC Junior seems like a basic computer to get my feet wet with. I know practically nothing about computers, and the magazines I bought at bookstores only confirm how little I do know about them. I'm told in one magazine that a particular computer has 'large hard disk capacity' to store information with. Another computer has three expansion slots for accessories. The PC Junior I've decided to buy has no expansion slots. None of these details relates any information which help me to decide what is a better computer system to buy for what I want to do. I've concluded though my twelve hundred dollar purchase of IBM's least expensive computer model will be the equivalent to six months tuition money spent at *The School of Self-taught.*

I walk to the IBM building at the southwest corner of Madison Avenue and Fifty-seventh Street. Soon I'll have a computer in my possession. I imagine being inside my room a couple hours from now, and I'm taking things out from their boxes, setting everything up and then turning on the computer. Then what? How am I going to go about doing this?

Her name is Meghan. Her very red hair is tied back into a pony tail, and I found my speech particularly awkward, talking in generalities, and to be picking at her for bits of information. I simply could not find the right words to ask the kind of questions I needed to answer the thoughts I was thinking for the entire time I was talking to her…

"So machine language is the lowest level the computer understands or uses," I clarify to myself, and let her continue.

Meghan nods her head yes.

"Yes, you wouldn't want to program in a machine language, in zeroes and ones, though. It's tedious. The next level up is assembly. In assembly language you can address the registers of the CPU, or to access any of the various chips inside the computer. You can directly alter specific memory locations in these chips, access any ports and extensions and peripheral devices you have inside or outside of the computer ..., to do whatever you want."

This does sort of sound like what I want to do. Whatever is in the computer to make it tick and tock as it does, this is what I probably will want to do. I want to be able to manipulate it at the core if need be. To get it to do whatever I decide it should do, whatever that may be in the future.

"Are there other languages like assembly?" I ask.

Meghan, listen. I'm buying a computer today because I saw 'The Terminator' movie and I want to begin designing a computer that mimics the human cognitive process. What do you think is a good language to start learning how to do this?

Thinking of telling her that a movie is why I'm buying a computer, and then explaining what I want to do with it once I've bought it..., for the second or two I imagine doing so...? It's too humiliating.

Meghan raises her eyebrows. "Depends on what you want to do." Meghan and I stare at each other. The realization is beginning to dawn on me that at this point in time I really can't say with any specificity exactly what it is I want to do in a practical sense, and I can't find the words to say to myself much less to her where and what I want to explore more of with this computer I'm going to buy today.

I am personally proud of the fact, thank you, knowing that I do, most times, possess an excellent command of the English language to express myself with. Having this loss for words is disturbing.

"I just want to learn about computers. Maybe the things that...? What they can and can't do."

"A higher-level language like Pascal, Cobol, or FORTRAN is used for work in the sciences. Crunching numbers quickly, making equations," Meghan tells me.

"Like finding pi to the hundred and fiftieth decimal place," I say nodding my head up and down, hoping the response sounds encouraging.

Meghan's lips and her cheeks tense, and I can tell she stifled a smirk. A smirk of curiosity.

"What do you want to use a computer for?"

A moment to collect and to listen to any thoughts I may have.

"Nothing specific. I just want to get a little more familiar about them, with them. What they can and can't do."

"Basic. It's an easy to learn, general purpose language," she suggests. "A good first language to learn if only to get a feel for what a programming language is all about."

I try to picture a single basic operation of a computer, and realize if I press a key on the keyboard a letter appears on the display screen. If I were to then press other specific key combinations and then hit the return key, the computer will put an array of letters I have typed to the screen into any number of storage devices on the computer. What exactly have I done inside the computer in each of those simple events?

I challenge myself. Someday soon produce a list of steps describing to myself in detail all the operations that happen inside the PC Junior when a key on the keyboard is pressed, this action displaying a letter upon the monitor's screen, and then exactly what happens causing those letters to be recorded onto any storage devices. Six months from now I want to know all the things happening inside the PC Junior with any of these seemingly plain Jane actions that are performed. This is what I want to learn about first for the next several months.

"Put the Basic and the assembly language software in with the PC Junior. It probably sounds like what I want to get into."

"Check or credit card?"

"American Express, ... and thanks Meghan."

There's rarely a moment now I'm not somehow occupied with the computer. After work it's back to my room and if I feel like doing so I'll get some sleep first. Early afternoon and I'll go out for a hamburger or couple slices of pizza, and if I'm not planning a trip to the library or the bookstore I'm back inside my room.

It was just a matter of days before I realized I needed a system, a structured method to learn all this stuff with. I'm convinced that a classroom lab environment, after work, and if I had the time and didn't have to sleep, this would be the ideal substitute for what I am doing and trying to accomplish. Too many interesting things are competing for my attention all at once as I learn about any one thing. My curiosity flips from one thing to another too often to be able to stay on any one thing, to then understand any one thing to any great extent. Though I'm quite excited with thoughts for what all this could possibly turn into for my life.

I know if I were to involve myself in a curriculum of college level courses quickly exposing me to more of the subjects and topics in the computer science field I would then have a broader, more general insight into all the current thoughts and technologies that computers are being built from. I'd be in a better position to realize what I specifically should focus on and then devote my energies to. I'd be realizing the specific important things I want to know about a little bit quicker than the way I'm presently going to go about it. I thought this right away, after the first couple days of playing around with Junior.

A little project I thought up and undertook confirmed the world of computers is eventually going to take me into a slew of academic disciplines.

I thought of an ordinary, everyday door knob mechanism. When the knob is put through a quarter turn twist either to the left or right the door knob mechanism slides a metal bolt inside the door out from the frame holding the door to the wall, this allowing one side of the door to be swung away from the frame. The mechanism of twisting the door handle to the left or right will be the method of inputting two states into the computer and a combination which will cause the computer to lock or unlock the door.

Turning the door handle twice to the left, then once to the right, then two more twists to the left and voila! There's a combination. Any combination of twists left and right to the door handle will be programmed as a key to a preset order I initially gave to the computer. The computer then causes activation or deactivation of a locking mechanism for the door. The simplicity to the whole idea was just what I needed to learn the stuff while also doing something practical with Junior.

Writing in the Basic programming language, using the computer's keyboard in lieu of what will be door knob twists later on, I wrote code to realize the action of pressing the letter k down on the keyboard simulating a left turn of the door handle, and pressing the letter j simulates a right twist of the door knob. If the correct sequence of k and j key presses were AND true to an array of numbers I initially programmed into the computer, I envisioned a peripheral RS-232 cable activating a stepper motor which would draw a metal bolt inside the door away from the frame, allowing it to be opened.

I had an outline to the functional aspects involved with a lock in my head, and I'd begun writing the first lines of code. It was cool. The code toggled a switch inside Junior enabling a connection between two pins of the attached RS-232 cable. The correct combination of j's and k's sent a pulse to activate the switch positive and into an enabled state if the switch was already in a disabled state, or the pulse disabled the connection to the switch if it was already enabled.

I then edited the code where pressing only the j and k keys would flip the relay switch back and forth inside Junior's white plastic computer case. A quick series of keystrokes produces a clicking sound reminding me of hearing a newborn baby urping on the towel over Moms shoulder while she pats its backside.

I needed a block of code where if I made a mistake while I'm inputting k's and j's, if I keep the capital letter M pressed for five-seconds, the cache is flushed and I can start to sequence a series of letters from the keyboard again.

I bought a joystick and attached it to the door. A thin length of metal rod connecting the door knob to the joystick brought a complete left to right twist of the door knob to sweep through an entire axial range of input upon the joystick handle. Rewriting the code to now replace the k and j letters from the keyboard for the inputs from a joystick didn't take a long time, but using the joystick presented its own set of conditions causing me to put more thought into how the code I was writing was working the data I was bringing to the computer.

I wrote the code mapping a full left twist of the door handle to a third of the axial range of movement on the joystick handle, and I delineated this movement to the range of numbers between zero and thirty-nine. The resting state of the door handle I let register to the joystick the numbers between forty and fifty-nine, and a right twist started registering to the joystick the numbers between sixty to ninety-nine. The initial code I wrote, without the joystick employed, involved just two states, the two keys of k and j simulating a left and right door handle position. Now that I have attached the joystick to the door handle I found there is another third state I could possibly employ into any combination I may think up. The resting state of the door handle turned neither to the left or right and the range of numbers between forty and fifty-nine can be implemented as a third state of code with the left and right twists. Working this idea for a third state brought my very first bugs into the code. Yahoo! ... and it's cool.

If I thought of using a combination involving two right twists of the door knob registering back-to-back in sequence, or if I wanted a combination of a right and then a left twist to register in sequence one after the other, with either of these two situations I always have to turn the doorknob into or through that middle range of forty to fifty-nine, and by consequence the code now always registers and includes that middle state into any combination I'm trying to input into the computer.

The way the system has come together so far, anytime I twist the door handle to the left or right to sequence through a combination brings that middle state automatically registering itself into every other step in any sequence, and this I do not want. I want two right twists of the door knob to register in sequence, not right-middle-right states registering in sequence. An interesting programming challenge I have now. I have to think up and then devise a number of different routines of code to exclude that middle state, and or to include the middle state only when I want to include it in a combination. I have the beta software to my lock. The prototype with bugs. I have to perfect the product..., and this is getting to be interesting. I like challenges like this.

I tried adding time periods between door handle twists of left, right and the rest state. One second of time to turn the handle and two seconds to hold between any twist of the door handle. This was difficult to estimate the time for three different states of door handle positions, and quickly rejected this method as unreliable. I also tried code to allow for anytime the door handle is in the middle, left, or right for at least five but not more than ten-seconds this would enable a step in the code to register and I could turn the door knob again. Again, totally unreliable code that did not function.

For several weeks I'm reading books and trying different arrangements of code, putting different lines of code together to find the code isn't performing they way I want. I'm guessing and trying so many different lines of code simply to run it and to watch what happens, hoping one time the program eventually does what I want it to do. There's a knot tightening up in my stomach some days, realizing I don't know what I'm doing. Writing and trying different arrangements of code becomes frustrating because I'm employing a hit and miss approach, instead of knowing how and simply build the code.

Eventually I'll think to pull that middle state out as an active state, and revert to a two state mode. I'll use the middle resting state of the door handle as a stepping stone for combining the other two left or right states. Anytime I enter into that middle resting state the computer is coded to expect the very next twist of either left or right to be registered as the next state in the sequence for the combination. Any sequence of left and right turns were now registering into the computer without error. Two right hand turns in series now functions inside a combination.

I rewrote the code to shrink both left and right ranges from forty delineations to twenty, this allowing the middle resting state of the door handle to encompass a larger range of sixty delineations. I now twist through any number of fifteen, twenty door knob states rapidly and with a more natural manner of hand movement.

The week, ten days of trying to write different types of code to work that middle, third state into any sequence, I had a feeling of relief come to me soon after I reverted to the two state mode. Feeling better for no other reason than to have all of my lines of software code functioning again, and functioning in the simple and uncomplicated manner which I was not expecting it to turn into as I was writing and testing the lines of code with three states.

Most of the time the code wasn't functioning the way I wanted, or performing erratic and inconsistent when each series of door knob twists I put to the computer. The experience made me realize there are logical systems of thought that can be brought to bear upon a situation, and these systems of thought can bring me to realize what specific arrangements of computer code I need to have the computer always performing the way I expect and want it to within any given situation.

Eventually I have the code for the two-state combination functioning flawlessly every time I run it through, and I'm thinking of as many real world situations this lock may find itself in, like inadvertent bumps to the door handle that may unintentionally register a state into the sequence. Blocks of code were inserted for the condition that after five minutes of inactivity everything resets itself. Also, if someone turns and holds the door handle for ten-seconds at its full rightmost position, this will reset everything too.

I'll be paying a visit to a company in Long Island City who sell stepper motors and the circuit boards needed to run them. I found their company name in the Thomas Register catalogs at the library.

It's cool realizing the Basic programming language supplied the tools enabling me to bring the idea I had for a lock into an actual and functioning gadget. A computer programming language allowed me to write functions and routines to accomplish what I set out to do. I am impressed with what a computer programming language is, and it's interesting to imagine what the potential could be for this large programming toolbox called Basic. I look inside the reference book to familiarize myself with everything the Basic programming language is about, and to realize I have all these other programming tools which I have no idea how to use yet, but I know someone put them in there with the thought to do some specific set of programming tasks.

A month of time and the assembly language notebook I've only skimmed through a couple of times. I've pushed onto then popped off of the stack the letters, TO BE OR NOT TO BE, and placing these letters onto the display screen with assembly code, but there is so much basic stuff to learn first, so many things to understand before I even think of attempting to put together any type of real, serious program with the assembly language. It's all pretty cool so far, I suppose.

I stay in my room for hours. Without an antenna the channel reception on the television is poor. I rarely have it on. Half the time the radio is tuned to one of the Rock stations. The other half the radio plays classical music on WQXR. To have the voice of another person singing lyrics in the room is, somehow, distracting me. I don't want to hear someone speaking to me, even lyrically in a song I've heard many times before while I'm concentrating on something. Classical music allows me to remain inattentive to the sounds of the music if I want. Classical music inside my room is a pleasant background environment.

My visits to the library to research the subject of artificial intelligence has left me unimpressed. A spider or parrot have a form of intelligence Alan Turing ignores. I'm going to adopt a bottom-up instead of a top down strategy while I go about understanding how any of the lower forms of biological life implement the capacity of intelligence into the pain-joy, preservation-debilitation, and construction-destruction spectrums.

I contemplate devising neurological systems and models mimicking the lower forms of biological life such as nematodes and jellyfish, and eventually I'll bring myself to focus upon the more complex, class three systems of arthropodic cognition. An arthropod's cognition will someday be my expertise, and I suppose this middle ground being where the more fascinating systems of computer sentience and cognition will be invented.

I imagine future models and systems I'll promote commercially. Packaging of the product or an advertising phrase proclaims, "Mimicking Biological Sentience." Depending on the class of cognition I'll use phrases such as, *Mimicking Class One Cognition, Mimics a Class Two Cognition, Computer System Mimics Sentience.* I'm categorizing classes of biological cognition? Wow.

There is a confidence of sorts to hear myself tell myself, ... *there's no turning back.* My heart and mind has to be fully committed if I expect to accomplish something of importance. No lackadaisical attitude and to think to only try to create something as time goes on. Resigning myself to a *maybe I will and maybe I won't* attitude will not accomplish things. I have to believe I will accomplish something with my efforts.

It's cool to think and believe I'll someday bring a very high-scaled integrated chip into existence. At the press conference I claim this chip mimics the neurobiological cognition of an arthropod, and I will definitely make known that I used the treatise as my guide in doing so. Unless I find something better to do with myself and with the treatise I will be staying with this idea of designing a cognitive computer. It's definitely cool.

I have at times imagined myself displaying to some stranger a working part, a functional circuit board component which brings some aspect of cognition to Junior..., how totally cool it will be if someday I've devised a working, functional system or component of computer cognition which causes others to rally around and perfect. Someday someone pays me tens of millions of dollars for a license to a system I devised ..., and how cool is that?

I will leave no stone unturned, no idle time spent while in pursuit of this one goal. A magnificent goal when I reach it too, especially if I'm the first one to put something together. Good God almighty. People will be reading my name in the history books of five hundred years from now. This is so cool.

Will Jesus be proud of me and what I intend to accomplish? My quest for computer systems mimicking biological cognition are the intentions of the Creator.

After looking at the types of locks sold at the neighborhood hardware stores, for the time being I've given a thumbs down to a commercial application for my computer lock. If someone wanted to put a lock on a door for ten dollars or so, a mechanical device could be bought. A simple and inexpensive ten dollar metal mechanism that's reliable every time you lock and unlock whatever it's attached to. Over time and as the years go by the mechanical locking device remains in a durable, reliable condition, ready to be used again for another locking or unlocking episode. I didn't see the same durability and reliability at a reasonable price coming out of an electrical lock.

Batteries go dead. The environment can do unexpected things to an electrical system. The idea of having so many components to a complete electrical locking system, designed and built in such a manner to make the lock reliable in real, everyday usage, all this was not encouraging enough for me to take this idea to the next step. I saw too many things that could go wrong in my scaled down version of an electric lock, and the buying public just wouldn't trust its reliability. I wouldn't trust it anyway.

I'm sure someone could build a reliable electric lock like what I've got. Someone probably already has been selling them..., for a thousand dollars a unit. To compete commercially with the mechanical locks crowd, for me to manufacture something someone will then put on a door, and that they could buy at a hardware store for twenty or thirty dollars, and to seriously think of using my own money to start up a business with, I don't think it's feasible right now.

The electric lock idea went up on a shelf, to collect a little dust for a while. I know where it is, so I can always go get it, take it down anytime I want. I imagine it's not going to be anytime soon though.

The first winter has come and gone, and warmer weather appears more often during my nights.

I'm convinced that a full load of college type computer science courses would be helpful to get myself in second gear, and to get things moving a bit faster. An exposure to the latest ideas that other people are playing with as I tackle the neonatal field of 'computer systems that mimic biological cognitive processes.' It's intriguing to realize that this specific topic subject I'm pursuing is so new it's not mentioned within any serious articles or literature in the library. The idea of robots acting with human characteristics is science fiction.

Pavlov's salivating dog experiment is interesting. I can imagine designing a system or systems which are predisposed to conclude interpretations of various environmental conditions with specific behaviors, like instincts are and do. I recall another psychology experiment, these guys placing metal rods in areas of a cat's brain and then applying an electric current to stimulate a specific area of the brain. Depending on where the electrodes were placed within the brain, sometimes the cat would have these long aggressive moments where it's ripping up everything in its cage. Other times the cat will be completely docile and passive for long periods of time, remaining so even if live mice are placed inside the cage with the cat. Each of these passive-aggressive behaviors observed were dependent upon where the electrode stimulated the cat's brain.

I want to schedule more of my free time to learn the mechanicals of neurobiological processes. To become knowledgeable in the fundamental physical structures and systems involved in nervous systems of lower life forms. I'm particularly fond of the unique way I've phrased those words together, 'Computer systems mimicking the biological cognitive process.' Whether that phrase is with the word cognition or sentience I haven't decided. I'll have the phrase in mind when I think of registering trademarks.

I'm learning things, but I'd learn things faster and more in depth if I was within a structured learning environment. In such an environment I know someone more knowledgeable of the entire subject field has already sifted through and picked out the important ideas for me, and then step by step each day's presentation of things eventually presents all that information back to me. In the shortest amount of time a large body of the specific type of subject material I want to know about has been brought to my attention. Right now this is exactly what I could use.

Just being able to follow along with all the esoteric jargon I come across would be a big step up. Following a discussion involving higher mathematical ideas in any of the heavy duty books or magazines I come across is, for the most part, not to be. Day before yesterday I was at the library spending a better part of the day browsing through some of the specific subjects found under the heading of information technology. One area called case-based reasoning. Most of the information within the computer science books I've gone through are written for someone to apply towards a business or commercial application, such as databases and financial, accounting tasks, and these books expect the reader to already have some years of college under the cap to understand its train of thought.

From the material I've read and that I'm able to make sense of, I do realize two paths opening up in pursuit for practical working prototype systems of cognition and sentience. From what I can tell so far I'll have to travel upon both of these paths at the same time if I am going to be the one to design and create something.

One of these two paths involves having me to acquire a working knowledge of the components of the basic integrated circuit. Registers, busses, ports, clock cycles, the different modules and controllers. As I envision things, the system of cognition will eventually live within the Very High Scaled Integrated Chip, and so I should have an understanding of the workings to any generic integrated chip. I should be able to look at a schematic of any computer chip and understand everything that is happening.

Tempering my thoughts to 'Keep It Simple,' and focusing on one aspect of a biological life form, such as the optical system of a fly or of a reptile employed into a system of cognition, I realize military aircraft seem to already have optical components and electronic systems to do whatever I could imagine necessary as far as gathering forms of information about an environment, and then to store the information into a form of data I can manipulate. Since military systems and their components are already being designed, built, and perfected by others as time goes on, I will always try to stay abreast of the latest in research and technologies along these lines.

What exactly is a system of cognition that it will sense light phenomena, interpret the light radiation and then act on this data in some way, shape or form? A cognitive computer system is more than just a light made active by relay that turns the headlights or windshield wipers of on an automobile on or off if it's night or day or raining. The system is more than a switch on the stove that turns the heat off after forty-five minutes because a human programmed a timing mechanism to that setting. If a system possessed all the similar human optical, auditory, thermal and tactile capacities, and possessed a capacity to collect and interpret chemical compositions of objects in the environment like our human senses of taste and smell, how should I then design the system to act cognizant to all the information it's now receiving?

I definitely should begin my designs intending to mimic the characteristics of the lower forms of life, the arachnid, the praying mantis, ant, or cockroach, because it's too much an intellectual leap to think of understanding human cognition, and to then begin mimicking it in any practical sense. I want to someday invent a functioning system, and not just have theories on paper when I'm seventy or eighty years old. Thinking like this leads me onto that second path, and it is on this path here that I think I will find the fame and fortune in whatever endeavors I happen to pursue in the future. It is from this second path where I'll make practical systems from any of the theories I wring out of my holy grail.

The sentient state of the lower forms and the state of cognition in the higher forms of life is caused within the biological system of neurons. The first scientific paper that outlines what causes that unitary aspect of perception and awareness of mind, outlining the functional, mechanical details causing that thing in the back of the eyes, this person or group of individuals will have opened the doors for those who will in the future invent and perfect the computer systems mimicking biological cognition.

These researchers will forever be with the titans of Science: Aristotle, Newton, Einstein, ... Soldier. I'm blessed, and it's cool to think of myself in league with these guys.

Investigating how a biological nervous system functions, and processes information. When wealth allows me all the time in the world to do so, this is the subject matter I'll circle my wagons around and organize my research efforts towards. Mathematical number theory, groups, rings and sets, too. I can't seem to shake this idea that mathematics is somehow integral to that unitary aspect of cognition. A better understanding of mathematical concepts together with a better understanding of the different forms of nervous systems found in biological life. These two subjects I'll concentrate on in the future.

I have to keep in mind that whatever I may someday think up as theories for what is going on in the nervous system of an arachnid, only by turning these thoughts into some practical, functional and working model or system of cognition will the theory have any worth. I want to have the sense for an immediate hands on practicality to any theory, and to think of immediately applying the theory to a working, functional prototype system of awareness. A thrill it is to think I will travel this road and someday stumble upon a commercial product that then places me into multimillionaire status.

I realize it's a daunting task I'm taking on. An ultimate challenge I've created for myself, and I accept the challenge, thank you. Totally committed and resolved to someday seeing this to some kind of conclusion. Rather, I just cannot see myself doing something else more important with the treatise. What else of importance would I do with myself?

If I need help with something I won't hesitate to ask. I have to be careful though. Loose lips sink ships and it'll be my ship I'll be sinking. At the moment things don't appear unmanageable to continue alone. Sometimes things happen though, like the guy I saw the other day walking down the street with a ferret on a leash. I immediately turned thinking someone's with me, and I thought I could share the surprise I felt at seeing the thing. I realized instead that I was in fact quite all by myself. I thought it a bit funny that I was alone among all the people that were also on the street at the time. An odd feeling there for a moment.

I walk alone. I'll keep as much of the pie for myself as I can. It's best way to accomplish what I want to do.

I hear the back door open. The cab rocks as the passenger climbs into the back seat.

"Mickey Mantel's on Central Park South, driver." I hear the door close with a solid catch of the second latch.

It'll take me ten minutes to get over to that part of town. At the first traffic light I write the information down on my trips sheet. It's seven twenty-seven post meridian. I picked this guy up on the Avenue of the America's and nineteenth street, just one passenger, and the letters CPS are penned into the rectangular area for the fare's destination. Just before turning onto Central Park South I'm informed we will be picking up other passengers and then continuing to another destination.

I'm moving the taxi at idle speed along Central Park South, squirming away from the line of standing double parked town cars. It's usually not this congested around here. Something out of the ordinary has to be going on.

"There they are. Those two," the fare says, then sticks his head halfway out the window, his arm waving up.

"Rhiannon! Chihiro!"

Several car lengths of distance from these two people but I can't go any farther towards them until some of the traffic around me starts moving a little bit. Chihiro and Rhiannon do eventually see or hear this guy as he waves from the open window, and I watch the two of them start up a brisk pace of steps along the sidewalk, squirreling themselves between and then out from two parked limousines in front of me.

I hear intelligible broken English spoken into the back of the cab.

"Michael, please. Elizabeth Ann and Allen are here. Come up ... say hello. They'll be leaving tomorrow."

A pause then before hearing, "Esra'a, Kawthar, and Judy are with them."

"I'll get out here, driver."

I hear the door open. The taxi rocks while he climbs out, and he hands me money through the passenger window across the seat.

"Keep the change."

Traffic is all backed up on the three east bound lanes I'm inside of. Sandwiched in as I am now within all this crawling traffic, I inch my way towards the intersection of Fifth Avenue. For the next hundred yards or so and for the next ten, fifteen minutes I'll be only crawling forward I realize no one will want to get inside my taxi while I'm stuck within all these other cars around me. I force the taxi to the middle of the six lanes of Central Park South and at the first opportunity to do so I do a U-turn into much lighter westbound traffic. Immediately I see someone waving for me.

"Are you free?" the guy asks me through the passenger side window.

An affirmative nod of my head.

"Your light is still on," the fare informs me.

For the two or three minutes after I'd dropped off the last fare I've forgotten to turn the meter off and so the lights on the roof of the taxi weren't on to signal to other street fares that I was unoccupied.

"There's two others that'll be going with us," this guy says after he gets himself inside. "They'll be here in a minute."

The meter is turned off and then back on as I steer the taxi closer to the curb and wait for these two doodle-brains to show up and get inside.

I now finish logging the info for that last fare into my trips sheet and start writing in this new fare.

7:51 for the time. The initial of CPS for where I've picked up these people, and 3 is for the number of passengers. I put the clipboard on the seat next to me, look in my rear view mirror, still don't see where these two passengers we're waiting for are, and while waiting for them to climb aboard I start toying with this idea of me being an author of some kind; a screenwriter or choreographer.

I watched a performance of the Paul Taylor Dance Company at the Winter Garden in the World Trade Center. One forty minute performance was enough for me to realize the possible artistic potential of the treatise somehow being rendered to dance. A dynamically presented treatise, the particular facts of it interpreted through body motions ... doing so without using words. It's an interesting and attractive idea to think of. I've been quite upbeat as I drive around, thinking about it as I have the last few days.

I hear a door being opened and then slammed shut, and I'm waiting for someone to say something.

"Lincoln Center please."

Three o'clock in the morning and parked off Hudson near Jane streets. I have a small, mostly salad and tuna fish meal on my lap. I've been toying with the commercial aspect of my latest project all night now, and I've effectively shut down the research and development operations part of me, as far as computer systems of cognition is concerned, until I figure out what I want to do with this new idea I've got cooking...

Can I write a screenplay, an opera, maybe a dance routine for some company to perform to? For me to write a performance that goes to Broadway or the big screen, employing the treatise in some way? Wow, this I just have to think through the possibilities of.

I like to keep thinking of any story I'll be telling as having Unidentified Flying Objects included as part of the plot. Instead of discovery I have the entire graphical representation of picture things inside the treatise imparted to me somehow from extraterrestrials, and I use the treatise to save the world from a nuclear catastrophe or something. Having the treatise originating from an alien life form makes it an important object and causing the audience to focus upon it. I like this kind of theme a lot. Of course the story will have to bring out the fact that these aliens somehow, in some way acknowledge the same Creator God we know of on Earth. Perhaps the aliens discovered the treatise the same way I did.

To think of a complete story will take some time. To think of my story somehow placing dancers and singers together is not exactly up my alley, but it's cool.

I've transferred these first of two songs onto floppy disk. I sometimes feel quite thrilled at the prospect of what I'm doing now.

The song *Slow chasin* tentatively reads as such.

You're a little kitten rubbin' under my chin
I'm gonna get you, gonna get you
Like a butterfly in the wind
Gonna catch you, gonna catch you.
Oh I know I'm kinda slow when it comes to gettin' you.
But a foot then two steppin' closer to you is how I get next to you. Yes, that's how I get next to you.

You're a fish just learnin' to swim
I'm gonna catch you, gonna catch you.
Like a tadpole without a fin
Gonna get you, gonna get you.
Oh I know I'm kinda slow when it comes to gettin' you.
But a foot then two steppin' closer to you

Slow chasin' after you, I'm a slow chasin' after you.

A brass instrument solo. Repeat first stanza with last verse of second stanza for last half verse of first stanza, with brass instrument solo to fade.

At the beginning of my story I'm singing these songs to a girl during a picnic out in the boondocks somewhere, maybe at night. We're having a telescope party or something. I don't know what we're doing exactly but the two of us then watch these miniature spaceships arrive. The fleet of half a dozen spaceships are silver, golf ball sized with a disc protruding from the middle of the sphere. The disc spins flashing lights round and around.

After singing songs for a while and just as I'm getting set up to give her a kiss, a number of these spaceships begin to hover around us like dragon flies, and directly in front of our faces. Of course we're startled as we lie on a blanket with an open picnic basket of olives, prosciuto, cheese, and wine spread out on the blanket.

I'll use these thoughts to create a general outline to the story … and for now write things just to see where this line of thought leads to.

The second song, *If You Were A Tomato?* I wrote in my room about an hour after writing *Slow chasin.* I have to slow the tempo to sound out each syllable of a girls name after every *friend, dear friend* line. I don't know, I'm sure if I kept at it I'd probably devise a way to maintain tempo, but for the time being a name with one, at most two syllables of sound is easier to pronounce.

Sally,
If you were a tomato? I'd pick you.
If you were some peaches? I'd have two.
A handful of lettuce on my sandwich are you.
If you were a coconut? I'd…? still … love you.

Sally,
If you were a penguin? I'd waddle to you.
If you were a duckling? I'd quack for you.
Even for a silly ol' canary I'd sing along too.
Why I'd never stop flying south for you.

Sally, dear Sally, don't you see what you do?
Every time I see you I fall in love with you.
I know you think I'm crazy but what can you do?
Every time I see you I fall in love with you.

Sally,
If I was a bumblebee? I'd be making honey for you.
(I know, I know, bumblebees don't make honey.)
A spider in a barn spinning webs around you.
What? Insects aren't romantic? Really? They're not?
Well, maybe, that's true. I'd still be a fly just buzzing for you.

Sally, I got it, listen...,
I'm a big tall giraffe that's looking for you.
A snake in the grass that wants to slide around you.
A screeching hairy monkey making noises at you.
I'd even go to the zoo if...? If you were in there, too.

Sally, dear Sally, don't you see what you do?
Every time I see you I fall in love with you.
When you turn the corner and pass on out of view?
My mind thinks instead of...?
Of food, and birds, and bugs, and you.

Sally,
If I was some bread? You'd be fondue.
If I was a banana? I'd give it to you.
I'm getting hungry now let's make some beef stew.
You be the dumplings and I'll be the spoon.

Sally,
If you were my pillow? I'd hug you at noon.
If you were my socks I'd buy up the looms!
I want to be though your underwear—I mean your tutu, too.
Promise you won't color me in...?
Pink, black or blue...? and polka dots too?!

Sally, dear Sally, I've had enough of this tune
Enough of this talk! I'm not foolin' with you.
You'll be my guitar and I'm a...? Bassoon.
Come on, we'll make some tunes under the moon.

—|—

My UFO story is casting a tone to the human race that I don't like. The human people appear inferior and the extraterrestrials are portrayed as technologically superior, and thus better than we are. I don't like the idea of some Martians from another planet being better than those of us who live on present day Earth. I'll rewrite things and think further on how I want this story to take shape and unfold.

My free time is spent fifty-fifty between research of cognition and writing the manuscript. All my time is devoted to seeing these two projects to completion, and I'm excited waking up in the morning to begin another day.

I absolutely love New York.

Farewell, But Not Goodbye

The fare was near the entrance to Trump Tower on Fifth Avenue as I pull over, and she climbs aboard.

"Metropolitan Museum of Art, please."

A left turn onto Fifty-sixth Street, one block east and I turn left at the light. I coast up to the waiting red light on Madison Avenue.

"Driver, stop at the next phone booth, on the left, please. I'll only be a moment."

I bring the taxi to the curb, and the clipboard to my lap. Scanning the trips sheet I find no missing boxes of information. All correct time, pick up and destination locations, and the amount each fare paid are written in. The clipboard is brought to the seat and I bring out the wad of bills under my thigh and start counting.

I find it's almost impossible for me to think into the details and to engage myself inside of a good, uninterrupted train of thought while driving the taxi. Perhaps if I were a trucker on an Interstate and all I have to do while driving for eight, ten hours is to keep the gas pedal depressed a little bit, and with the occasional adjustment to the steering wheel, turning at most half of the way around once or twice an hour, if this were all the effort and concentration my driving time entailed perhaps I could delve into some detailed trains of thought. With no obstacles or distractions I imagine one could maintain a train of thought for long periods of time. This is definitely not the situation as I drive the taxi in the city.

The traffic light two blocks in front of me is turning green as I hear the back door open, the taxi rocking, and I hear the door slam shut.

"The Metropolitan, please."

I take the taxi from the curb and up to speed. Traffic lights change from red to green in front of me, and I'm at the tail end of a wave of cars traveling with staggered lights as they flow nonstop up Madison Avenue. At eighty-first street I'll turn left off Madison to travel one block further west and I'll have this fare across the street from the entrance to the museum. This is a quick, five minute ride.

I came across the term Quantum Consciousness in the library. I don't yet know what to do with the idea of biological cognition and that unitary aspect of self lodged in back of the eyes, this being a product of a subatomic quantum phenomena occurring within the neuron. Quantum physics is spooky. To think of focusing research into this area? Indubitably, an expensive endeavor should I have to follow this path with expectation for discovering something significant. I'll have to generate more than a couple million dollars to myself over time if I expect to invent and accomplish something.

Having set volition as the ideal and the ultimate goal for any computer system mimicking biological sentience and cognition, my thoughts are always humbled at the majesty of this project. I'm imitating God in a way, and maybe I will accomplish things greater than Jesus.

I remember Dad say that fifty to sixty percent of the information one learns at university is never used in any applicable way during the twenty or so years they're at work and doing whatever they do while on the job. I suppose this to be true.

Maybe later I'll care but right now I don't care if I matriculate for a degree or not. I just need courses that will bring my math skills up to par, and courses to better understand neurological subjects. If I do attend college I'll think about talking to an admissions officer or someone at the school who is keen to what I specifically want to do, and then together we'll pick only those courses that are relevant towards understanding what this computer system will be like.

Through the windshield I notice several tail lights shining bright towards the left side of the avenue. Cars are slowing down a couple blocks ahead. Those having stopped are inching towards the middle of the avenue. I keep a steady speed to the taxi as I veer to the right and away from the approaching crowd of traffic, and once around the bottleneck I scan my immediate surroundings to have three cars in front and two cars in back of me.

The manuscript is taking shape. I have an electric lock up on a shelf, too. All I need now is a couple more of these brain storms to contend with and to concentrate on and I'll really have my hands full. I feel anxious at times knowing that soon I'll want to make a move with one or two of these ideas. Spend some real money to enroll in a number of college courses or maybe just devote all my free time to writing the manuscript. I'll have to take a chance on whatever I choose to do will be…? Will turn successful? Yes, exactly that.

If I could wake up every day and then do whatever I want, instead of thirteen, fourteen hours of commuting and driving a taxi six nights a week…, wow, what a great thought that is.

I bought a book on self-incorporation. The ideas from the book are too fresh in my mind to know what I want to do with any of them.

I was just thinking the name again, *Kurt M. Soldier, Inc.*, hearing it sound out and what I thought about it. I turn to see the headlights approaching the side of the taxi.

Those headlights slam into the two right side doors of the taxi with a swift, short sound of crunching, crushed metal. The metal trip meter fixed to the dashboard punches my chest. My forehead smashes into the rear view mirror on the windshield. Tires screech as the skidding taxi swirls onto the sidewalk of Madison Avenue and into a collection of waste basket and corner newspaper boxes.

Everything becomes still, quiet, and calm. I turn around and look at my passenger.

Her arm is up against the door and her hand supports her chin. She looks as if nothing happened. I think of her seated on that right side as the taxi was hit, and lucky. That right side had a mighty good wallop of momentum into it if it spun over and hit her seated on the left side.

"You all right?" I say.

She looks over and stares at me for a moment, then blinks her eyes.

Nodding her head up and down. "I'm all right, but you're not."

I don't like how she just said that because I'm fine, I can tell. That punch she might've took has her irritated.

I lean over and open the glove compartment for the registration and I'm thinking concussion, then shock, and I'll have to watch her until city's Emergency Medical Service team arrives. I get up to open the door and go find the clowns in the other car, to see if they're OK.

I open and lean outside the door and watch the drops of blood falling from my face to the sidewalk.

"You're bleeding," I hear her say as I step outside.

I feel the blood oozing down my nose, falling in drops from my eyebrow and lip. I bring my fingers to touch my face. The skin is numb around my forehead and the left side of my face. I dab my forehead with the T-shirt and then press the cloth to my face. Pulling the cloth away and I see a good amount of blood has already splattered on it.

I walk to the other car stranded in the middle of the intersection and note the license plate number. Traffic slowly crawls around my left and right sides, and I watch a female passenger in the back seat of the car step from the car and walk to stand close to me. The two male occupants of the car walk up to stand behind her.

"You shouldn't run red lights," she says to me.

I ignore her and with my license in hand I turn to the guy who was driving. He stands with his arms folded in front of himself.

"You wanna to show me your license?"

"I was driving the car," the female says to me, showing me a wallet with a flick of her hand.

I turn back to face this guy and he turns to walk away from the four of us. He folds his arms up in front of himself and takes a sitting posture on the hood of the car. Cross traffic crawls around us. A yawn, gazing up and around at nothing in particular. He's looking up into several of the dark angles of skyscrapers congregating above us, then placing his foot up on the bumper of their car, to stay.

"Fine," I say and with a nod turn to walk back to the taxi on the sidewalk.

Before I get back inside the cab I take a look through the back window at my passenger. She apparently seems calm and alert sitting back there. I get inside and write the license number of their car onto the back of my trips sheet.

"You didn't see who was the driver of that car, did you?"

She doesn't answer right away and I turn to look at her. Staring out the window she shakes her head a few times, implying she didn't. I'll stay in the taxi and wait for the police to arrive and to make out a report.

Later through depositions that both parties gave of contrary versions for who and what was responsible, and because of no-fault insurance coverage, that was the end of the matter.

A couple of days after the accident I noticed how that collision could have caused me serious injury had the sequence of events been different. The angle and force of the crash had brought me and my forehead snapping the rear view mirror off the windshield. If I had been wearing a seat belt my body and head would not have gone above the square metal taxi meter, instead I would have slipped away from the shoulder strap and throwing my forehead into the left corner point edge of the steel framed taxi meter. Days later I will sit in the driver's seat of a taxi and with the seat belt strapped on I'll lean forward and towards the right and realize how my head and face could've hit that metal taxi meter in a nasty kind of way. I began to wonder if others are aware how close that metal box attached to the dashboard is to the driver. I have to take notice of a fact like this, cause I know "they" are out there...

It was on my tenth night of driving the taxi in New York. On behalf of me, myself, and I, and the band, I had hoped I had passed the audition. Obviously not.

I'm writing things into the trips sheet at the departures terminal at La Guardia airport. The passenger is somewhere outside the Checker Cab I'm driving tonight. I look up and into the rear view mirror to see the trunk lid raised up, and obviously this fare is taking his time taking his one piece of luggage out from the trunk. I turn to see that the passenger door is still open, and then the thump from the trunk lid closing down. I watch the fare now wheeling his suitcase away from the taxi and towards the terminal doors.

He forgot to close the door.

I put the clipboard down on the seat. My hand is upon the door handle when the back of the taxi tilts, a single rocking up and then down motion and this bounce tells me someone has gotten inside the back of the taxi.

Terse syllables bring Fordham University to my attention. I'll get myself familiar with the immediate area just outside the taxi and a moment later I'm turning the taxi from the curb.

If this guy hadn't gotten inside the taxi I probably would have driven to the taxi stand at the arrivals section of La Guardia. The last couple of times at both La Guardia and Kennedy airports had me waiting at arrivals over an hour with maybe thirty, forty, fifty other yellow taxi cabs. All of us unproductively standing around idle while waiting for the next planeload of passengers to arrive at the airport. I'm glad to have gotten this fare right out of the departures terminal like I did. Driving down the ramps of the terminal I wonder whether I broke any taxi regulations by picking this fare up where I did. I look into my rear view mirror to see that my fare is a Catholic priest.

"I'm new to driving the roads around here," I say to Father. "If you have a preferred route it'd help. Otherwise I'll have to stop for a moment and look at a map to know how to get there."

There's only one traffic light between the road out of the airport and the Brooklyn-Queens Expressway. Once on the Expressway there will be no time or opportunity for me to look down at the map on the seat and find a best route to Fordham.

"Do you know how to get to the White Stone Bridge from here?" Father asks me.

"North on the Van Wyck."

"I'll give you directions the rest of the way after the bridge," he says.

The Hagstrom map is indispensable. If some fare of mine wants to travel from inside Manhattan to anywhere in the outer boroughs, usually before I've left any of the streets and avenues of the island of Manhattan I'll have found the destination street on the Hagstrom map. Stopped in traffic or at a traffic light I'll glance down at the map to reconsider how to get further along if need be.

Traffic is light to medium on the expressway and becomes congested approaching the Whitestone Bridge Expressway. An elevated ramp quickly raises traffic up from ground level. A warm evening. Light remains though the sun has just gone down over the horizon.

A steady thirty, thirty-five miles an hour with the taxi. A fifteen, twenty degree upward incline and the roadway is banked to the left at an unusually steep fifteen, twenty-degree angle. The taxi loses traction and spins counterclockwise. I have time to react to the slide and turn into the direction of the spin, but it does nothing. The taxi twirls, dropping Father and I down inside the slow moving left lanes on the ramp. All traffic comes to a stand still.

I am surprised I didn't collide with another car! Spun two hundred seventy degrees and the taxi faces perpendicular to all the standing traffic around me.

I restart the engine and look to my left. The driver of one car has his head out the window and looking back over his shoulder towards me. Traffic begins to move forward and I look towards the line of cars on my right. Through their windshields I see a number of drivers are also looking at me, so I get the taxi back up to speed and into the flow of traffic again.

Through the rear view mirror Father is looking out the passenger window, seemingly unperturbed at what just happened. I'm thinking probably oil drops maybe made the surface of the roadway a little slick.

Not a full minute of time passes before the taxi is now rolling downhill towards the tollbooths two, three hundred yards away. The traffic around me has spread out, expanding from four lanes into a dozen separate toll booth lanes for every car and truck to jockey into. I'm idling downhill at thirty miles an hour and grasping the forty, fifty dollars in small bills I have wedged underneath my thigh. Ready for these tollbooths coming up and with one hand on the steering wheel I'm ready to go into another episode.

I'm quick to realize the front end of an adjacent car on my immediate right—this is preventing me from turning into that lane as I fast approach a line of stopped yellow taxis some thirty odd yards in front of me. The back ends of three taxis spread out in a line and blocking each lane directly in front and to the left. A fourth taxi is spaced an open traffic lane of distance from the furthest three taxis on the left. I made brief notice for this open lane of traffic between the third and fourth, knowing I have the tires of the taxi locked up tight and I'm not slowing down. The taxi silently slides forward and I release the brake to steer towards that lane of open space on the left.

The taxi hurtles forward. It's doable though I have to bring the taxi to travel a full two car widths of distance to the left with the short distance in front of me. I put a continuous and smooth rotation to the steering wheel until I sense I'll lose traction and stability up in the front end of the taxi. The front tires are on the verge of losing traction as I aim the front of the taxi to the back end of that fourth taxi. I hold the steering wheel until I know I absolutely have to turn the other way and correct for the angle and the momentum of the turn I've put the taxi into. I bring the taxi traveling from left to right and with all four tires almost breaking traction. The yellow side of the fourth taxi quickly slides up to my door and then disappears. Silence as I travel out from between the taxis, and to realize I hit nothing.

Rolling forward the hundred yards ahead of me and I see no cars around. There are no vehicles nearby except those way up ahead near the tollbooths and the four stopped taxis I see receding behind me.

A couple deep breaths and a chuckle..., and as I drive to the university a number of times I'll look at Father in the rear view mirror. He appears pensive, and so composed, as if nothing had happened, or, it matters not whatever happens.

What should he look like sitting back there, and for me to think one way or the other about what is going on? I don't have an answer for that.

That night I had taken Father to Fordham, I'm driving the taxi back to the garage near the end of my shift. Five-thirty in the morning and I'm waiting at a traffic light just a few blocks from the garage, and someone slams into the back of my taxi. Stepping out to see what happened and the driver accelerates around the Checker Cab, and then stopping a couple dozen yards up the road.

Brake lights flashing on and off as the back end of the car jerks a series of rocking up and down motions.

He wants you to go and chase him. Don't.

The engine accelerates with a roar. Rubber tires spin, screeching across the blacktop and the car swerves sideways, quickly traveling up between the steel I-beams and girders supporting the empty roadway of the Queensborough Bridge. I step inside the taxi and listen to the spurts of acceleration and the moments of silence as the car navigates between other cars on the bridge towards Manhattan.

I don't find fault so much with the attitudes of these crippled mentalities who advocate socialist policies. Jesus put me here in the United States and not somewhere in Asia or Europe or South America as I go about whatever I have to do each day. Though it appears my personal agenda has put me in contention with these kind of folks. Interesting this is so.

Hey, the next evening I'm back in the saddle, again.

I want to get up early this afternoon, walk around, and think about things.

How am I going to do this?

When I concentrate I see the words in my minds eye. I'm trying to bring the words logistic and strategic into some plan I can work with.

—|—

References

Copyrights to the *Treatise on the Nature of Life* were registered June 11, 1984. There were no references cited in the copyrighted version. During six years of composing, editing, and polishing the *My Quest For Computer Cognition* manuscript, I found these scholarly papers relevant to further expound upon the ideas within the *Treatise on the Nature of Life*.

1. **Alberto J. L. Macario and Everly Conway de Macario** (1999). The Archaeal Molecular Chaperone Machine: Peculiarities and Paradoxes, *Genetics Society of America; Genetics* 152: 1277-1283.
2. **Alberto J. L. Macario, Marianne Lange, Birgitte K. Ahringand, Everly Conway de Macario** (1999). Stress Genes and Proteins in the Archaea, *Microbiology and Molecular Biology Reviews,* Vol. 63, No. 4: 923-967.
3. **B. C. Mazzag, I. B. Zhulin, and A. Mogilner** (2003). Model of Bacterial Band Formation in Aerotaxis, *Biophysical Journal,* 85, 3558-3574.
4. **Dietmar Kültz** (2003). Evolution of the cellular stress proteome: from monophyletic origin to ubiquitous function, *The Journal of Experimental Biology,* 206, 3119-3124; doi:10.1242/jeb.00549.
5. **Robert M. Hazen, Patrick L. Griffin, James M. Carothers, and Jack W. Szostak** (2007). Functional information and the emergence of biocomplexity, *Proceedings of the National Academy of Sciences of the United States of America,* 104, 8574-8581; doi:10.1073/pnas.0701744104.
6. **Woese, Carl R.** (1998). The universal ancestor, *Proceedings of the National Academy of Sciences of the United States of America,* Vol. 95, 6854-6859; doi:10.1073/pnas.95.12.6854.

7. **Woese, Carl R.** (2004). A New Biology for a New Century, *Microbiology and Molecular Biology Reviews,* Vol. 68, No.2: 173-186; doi: 10.1128/mmbr.68.2.173–186.2004.
8. **R. B. Laughlin, David Pines, Joerg Schmalian, Branko P. Stojkovi, and Peter Wolynes** (2000). The middle way, *Proceedings of the National Academy of Sciences of the United States of America,* Vol. 97, Issue 1, 32-37.
9. **Roger P. Hangarter & Howard Gest** (2004). Pictorial demonstrations of photosynthesis, *Photosynthesis Research,* 80, 421–425.

A comprehensive book on the geology of New York State:

10. **Isachsen, Y.W., E. Landing, J.M. Lauber, L.V. Rickard, and W.B. Rogers, Editors** (2000). Geology of New York: A Simplified Account, Second Edition, *Educational Leaflet No. 28.* ISBN: 155557162X ISSN: 0735-4401.

At the present time I focus my attention upon the electro-biochemical realm to understand the first instance(s) of Archean and Cambrian forms of life on earth.

11. **R.B. Laughlin, David Pines, Joerg Schmalian, Branko P. Stojkovic, and Peter Wolynes**. (1999) *The middle way,* PNAS 97:1, 32-37.
12. **R.B. Laughlin, David Pines** (1999) *The Theory of Everything,* PNAS 97:1, 28-31.

The book and their Web site at www.intothecool.net is a challenge.

13. **Schneider, Eric D. and Dorion Sagan** *Into the Cool: Energy Flow, Thermodynamics* (2005). The University of Chicago Press, ISBN: 978-0-226-73936-6 (ISBN-10: 0-226-73936-8).

—|—

—|—